"May McGoldrick w_____an
excellent essence of_____n

Praise for the novels of May McGoldrick

Borrowed Dreams

"A definite keeper. A Perfect 10."
—*Romance Reviews Today*

"Well-paced and convincing." —*The Romance Reader*

"[An] engaging Georgian romance. . . . Readers will strike gold with this deep tale."
—*Midwest Book Review*

"A beautifully written romance. . . . Millicent is an ugly duckling with a heart of gold. Watching her blossom into a swan, loving a man who can physically do nothing for himself, but whose pride hardly allows anyone to help him, was such a treat. . . . It's always more enjoyable to watch a hero and heroine struggle through realistic conflicts and overcome them in the name of love."
—TheWordonRomance.com

The Promise

"Filled with warmth and emotion . . . *The Promise* is a wonderful book for any lover of historical fiction . . . Cuddle up in a chair and simply enjoy. . . . Don't miss it."
—*New York Times* bestselling author Heather Graham

"This vibrant Georgian historical is perfect for readers who like a nice mix of history and passion." —*Booklist*

"If you like passionate stories about people you can care deeply about, that take you on an emotional ride, that tell of battles between good and evil, I promise you will love *The Promise*." —*Romance Reviews Today*

"Readers will strike gold with this fabulous historical romance." —*BookBrowser*

continued . . .

and other novels

"Love triumphs in this richly romantic tale."
—Nora Roberts

"Wonderful! Just the right blend of historical detail, romance, and intrigue." —Jill Marie Landis

"May McGoldrick brings history alive, painting passion and intrigue across a broad, colorful canvas."
—Patricia Gaffney

"Impressive . . . A splendid Scottish tale, filled with humor and suspense." —Arnette Lamb

"Brilliant . . . A fast-paced, action-packed historical romance brimming with insight into the 16th century Scottish-English conflict —*Affaire de Coeur*

Previous books by May McGoldrick

Dreams of Destiny

May McGoldrick

A SIGNET BOOK

SIGNET
Published by New American Library, a division of
Penguin Group (USA) Inc., 375 Hudson Street,
New York, New York 10014, U.S.A.
Penguin Books Ltd, 80 Strand,
London WC2R 0RL, England
Penguin Books Australia Ltd, 250 Camberwell Road,
Camberwell, Victoria 3124, Australia
Penguin Books Canada Ltd, 10 Alcorn Avenue,
Toronto, Ontario, Canada M4V 3B2
Penguin Books (N.Z.) Ltd, Cnr Rosedale and Airborne Roads,
Albany, Auckland 1310, New Zealand

Penguin Books Ltd, Registered Offices:
80 Strand, London WC2R 0RL, England

First published by Signet, an imprint of New American Library,
a division of Penguin Group (USA) Inc.

First Printing, May 2004
10 9 8 7 6 5 4 3 2 1

 REGISTERED TRADEMARK—MARCA REGISTRADA

Printed in the United States of America

PUBLISHER'S NOTE
This is a work of fiction. Names, characters, places, and incidents either are
the product of the author's imagination or are used fictitiously, and any resemblance to actual persons, living or dead, business establishments, events, or
locales is entirely coincidental.

BOOKS ARE AVAILABLE AT QUANTITY DISCOUNTS WHEN USED TO PROMOTE PROD-
UCTS OR SERVICES. FOR INFORMATION PLEASE WRITE TO PREMIUM MARKETING DI-
VISION, PENGUIN GROUP (USA) INC., 375 HUDSON STREET, NEW YORK, NEW YORK
10014.

False friends are common. Yes, but where
True nature links a friendly pair,
The blessing is as rich as rare . . .

—Anon. 2nd century B.C.

To Shirley Hailstock

Our dear friend . . . a talented writer.

You give so much to so many.

Chapter 1

Baronsford, Scotland
August 1771

The cold breezes of the spring morning brushed across his naked shoulder where the blanket had slipped down. Still more asleep than awake, he snuggled closer to the warm back that had fit itself to the contours of his abdomen.

He was not entirely conscious of the leg that was lying between his own, nor of his own arms that had encircled her body. Her head lay on his arm, and her back was pressed against his chest. The shirt that she wore had ridden up, and the skin of her legs lay warmly against his own.

The Highlander's hand was lying on her breast, and when he moved, she responded to his tightening embrace by pushing her body even tighter against his.

As she did, his hand brushed lightly across the sensitive—

"Gwyneth Douglas!"

At the sound of the deep voice, Gwyneth started, the tip of her Keswick pencil breaking and skidding across the paper. In her rush to shut the note-book, two letters inside slipped out and fluttered a moment in the air before sailing toward the ledge. She jumped to her feet from the stone bench beside the cliff walk and shoved her writings under one arm, grabbing in panic for the letters before they glided off the bluff and out over the river Tweed below. The first one proved an easy mark, and she quickly stuffed it deep in the pocket of her skirt. She whirled around and dove for the second, but as she did, Gwyneth was mortified to see the black boot descend upon it. She looked up at the officer's uniform, and her heart leapt.

"David!" she cried and then tried to control her excitement. "I mean, Captain Pennington . . . so you are back in Scotland."

"Could I miss my mother's bloody birthday celebration? But why this formality between two old friends?"

Gwyneth gasped as the tall officer swept her into his embrace and lifted her off the ground, whirling her around. She closed her eyes, her arms wrapping uncontrollably around his neck. For those few seconds, she imagined the gesture was more than just the friendly affection toward a neighbor that he had not seen in over a year. Her head was spinning slightly when he finally put her back down.

"I cannot believe it. You have grown so since I saw you last."

Gwyneth realized she was still holding on to him, her body pressed against his tall and powerful frame. He must have realized the same thing, and her face caught fire when David took her hands from around his neck. He held them, though, as he stepped back to look at her at arm's length.

"Definitely taller. And your hair is more fiery red

than I remember. But I'm happy to say those freckles on the bridge of your nose have not disappeared."

Gwyneth freed her hands and took a step back, frowning up into the deep blue eyes that were so dear to her. She had fallen in love with David Pennington the summer she had turned nine years old, the same summer that she had been left an orphan. She'd been sent to the Borders to live with the family of her uncle, Lord Cavers, in his country house at Greenbrae Hall. David was the youngest son of the nearest neighbors to the east, at Baronsford. Gwyneth had grown up trailing after her cousin Emma and David, riding and running through the hills and forests between the two estates.

"I would suggest you keep all your comments to yourself, Captain, if you cannot think of anything *nice* to say."

"You are even thinner than I remember, too," he continued in the same tone. "Do they feed you nothing at Greenbrae Hall?"

"I am well fed, I assure you." She spotted her notebook lying open at her feet and quickly snatched it up. David picked up the letter he still had trapped beneath his boot. Gwyneth could see it had been ground into the dirt. She extended her hand toward him. "That is mine, I believe."

He gave it a cursory glance. "This had better not be a love letter from some secret admirer."

" 'Tis no such thing!" She snatched it out of his hand and shoved it into her pocket with the other letter. With her secret safely tucked away again, she felt a bit of confidence return. "But on the slim chance that 'twas a note from some gentleman, I cannot see why you should object, Captain Pennington."

"I believe I have every right to object to a child's receiving that kind of attention from some rogue."

"*Child,* did you say?" she cried, trying to sound indignant, but fighting back her smile. "I'll have you know I am seventeen . . . on the verge of turning eighteen. And just because you no longer come around to Baronsford or Greenbrae Hall, that doesn't mean that life has ceased to move ahead. People do age, Captain . . . and mature . . . and make their own lives."

The sun was sinking steadily in the western sky, and Baronsford—its majestic walls and towers a picture of gleaming gold and shadow—sat high on the hill behind him. David looked like a hero from one of her stories. He stood tall and straight. His jacket of crimson was brilliant in the setting sun, the color set off by the gold trim, the white breeches, and the black boots. He had a face more handsome than any she could ever invent or describe. His hair was so dark it was nearly black, tied back in a long queue with a black ribbon. He studied her closely, and Gwyneth felt her blush return, scorching her skin.

"I can see that a few things have indeed changed." He sat down on the stone bench overlooking the river and pulled her down beside him. "So tell me, my fiery-headed nymph. Who is the scoundrel?"

She laughed and shook her head. "There is no one."

"You cannot fool me." He tugged not so gently on a wayward curl, making her yelp.

"David . . ." she scolded.

"There are over a hundred guests milling about Baronsford. At least a dozen lasses your age are gliding arm in arm through the gardens, acting as if they're promenading along the Grand Walk at Vauxhall. Still, you leave that excitement and come all the way down here to the river. And why? To read some villain's letter."

All Gwyneth could do was to shake her head. Their shoulders bumped together, and he leaned over to look at her. Gwyneth's breath caught in her chest as his blue eyes stared into hers.

"Not just reading . . . you were answering him, were you not?" he whispered.

A delicious tingle ran down her spine. Gwyneth wrapped her arms around the notebook, hugging it tightly against her chest. "I was only writing in my journal."

"Oh, of course. That fascinating chronicle of pirates and Highlanders and bloody battles you used to read to me." He looped an arm around Gwyneth's shoulders and smiled into her face. "I'm glad to know you are still writing your tales. I always thought you had a gift for storytelling."

Hidden in her pocket, the two letters that had nearly fallen down the cliff reaffirmed whatever gift she had, Gwyneth thought. At least, in the opinion of Mr. Thomas Ruddiman of High Street, Edinburgh. One of the letters had been accompanied by twelve pounds. The second, received two months later, had contained fifteen pounds. A momentary lapse made her almost blurt out her news that Mr. Ruddiman planned to print and distribute her long tales in serial form. Gwyneth contained herself, however. She didn't think it would be wise to share any of that with David now—considering the fact that these tales were scandalous enough that the publisher intended to print them anonymously.

"Would you read me what you were writing?"

She bit her lip and shook her head, looking away. In spite of the excitement of seeing him, that would be too embarrassing. She had been writing a tender scene between two people in love. The woman's emotions were a mirror of how Gwyneth herself felt about the hero, who in her imagination was none other than the officer standing before her.

He took hold of her chin and drew her face back to his. "What have you done with my talkative and spirited Gwyneth? The young lass who could not wait to tell me everything she'd dreamed, or read, or written in her notebooks? What is the reason for this sudden shyness?"

Instead of searching for an excuse, she found herself studying every feature of David's face. His eyes were a shade of blue that she'd never been able to describe in her stories. His lashes were dark and long, curling slightly at the tips. He had changed much this past year, too. There was a weariness about him, creases at the corners of the eyes and a furrow in his brow that Gwyneth had not seen when he had stopped at Greenbrae Hall for just a single afternoon thirteen months ago. David was no longer the tireless and carefree young man who rode between the two estates with Emma beside him.

The thought made her shiver and tear her gaze away from his face. Her cousin was the one David had always loved. Emma was the reason he was here.

Gwyneth knew the blade had cut deep when her cousin married David's oldest brother two summers ago to become the Countess of Aytoun. That was when he'd begun to stay away from Baronsford for long stretches of time—just like a tragic hero in her stories.

"Well, 'tis all the same to me," he said breaking

into her thoughts. He ran a hand affectionately down her arm and gathered Gwyneth closer to his side. "We can just sit here and enjoy the—"

"So this is where you have been hiding!"

Gwyneth's chin sank at the sound of Emma's voice. David's hand dropped away, and she carefully hid the notebook beneath her skirt on the bench. When David stood to greet the other woman, Gwyneth turned slightly to look at her.

The world around them suddenly paled with the appearance of Emma. The sun spread only its most radiant light on her. The breeze seemed to sweep the grasses clean for Emma's feet. Her golden curls, stylishly arranged, shone in the afternoon sun. Her white and gold brocade dress fit her slim body to perfection, and the low neckline was perfect for drawing a man's attention. Her skin was flawless. Her lips were red and turned up in corners. She looked as regal as a young queen, more beautiful than the moon and stars . . . and she knew it.

And now, Emma's blue eyes were on David.

And his face . . .

Gwyneth's heart ached as she noted the pain in his expression. He watched Emma's every step. His gaze paid homage to her, from the tips of her silk slippers up to the feathers adorning her hair. Gwyneth watched, though, as one large hand fisted once and opened. He did not walk toward Emma, but stood waiting for her. Always waiting.

One did not have to be an expert in knowing people to recognize that he still loved her, and how tormented he was by her. Gwyneth turned her gaze back to the cliffs and the river below, unable to bear witness to his pain.

"I am very disappointed with you, David Pennington. I had to hear that you'd arrived from Mrs. MacAlister . . . the old dragon. Why did you not come looking for me?"

Gwyneth guessed her cousin was only a dozen paces from the bench. She grabbed her notebook and rose to her feet, intending to walk quietly away, giving them the privacy they sought. David's hand on her arm made her look up, surprised. He wanted her to stay.

"I thought I would come see this one first. I cannot believe she's had another birthday while I was gone."

Gwyneth had no option but to remain where she was, and Emma's gaze never wavered from David. She swept up against him, pressing a kiss to his cheek. Her fingers lingered on the front of his jacket before reluctantly falling to her sides. Gwyneth noticed that he did not return the kiss, but instead quickly backed away a step. The obvious reserve in him brought a tint of red to Emma's cheeks. Her eyes became hard when they turned toward Gwyneth.

"Oh, indeed. Our little heiress. Always buried in her books and never having time to pay attention to how she looks or to the displays she makes of herself. And never a thought about the fortune she has coming to her. Mother keeps telling her that in another year, every wolf from London to Edinburgh will be knocking at the gate at Greenbrae Hall, hoping to steal her away." As was her habit, Emma then shifted her attention to another topic without taking a breath. "But didn't Augusta tell you that there would be many distinguished guests here at Baronsford for my party? I hope you are not planning to dine in that dress."

"I am not staying for dinner," Gwyneth replied quietly. "Nor staying for the party."

"Oh, nonsense. Your endless scribbling can wait," Emma scolded. With a pretty shake of her head, she cast aside her annoyance. "I have gone to a great deal of difficulty making the arrangements for this party, and I shall not allow you to miss a moment of it. You might surprise yourself and actually have fun."

Emma looped an arm through Gwyneth's, and the other through David's, turning them back up toward the house.

"Come, you two. I cannot allow you to hide yourselves away down here. I shall have Truscott arrange to have Augusta's carriage take Gwyneth over to Greenbrae Hall and wait until you change into something appropriate. Wear that green gown I helped you pick in London last month, the one with the satin sash. The color matches your eyes. Also, bring back the yellow dress for tomorrow."

"I really do not think—"

"Do not argue," Emma ordered as they continued on across the fields toward Baronsford. "But if you must have a reason to come, then think of it as doing me a favor. I know that if you are not here, Augusta is going to fret over you in addition to her usual threats to leave every time she loses a hand at whist."

At the age of fifteen, Gwyneth had lost another person she cared for, her Uncle Charles. Since the death of Lord Cavers, she had been under the direct control of his wife, Augusta. At the time, Emma had just married Lyon Pennington, and Lady Cavers had been quite amenable that Gwyneth should remain as her companion until she married and came into her inheritance.

Having Emma marry well—which meant finding a husband with a fine income and a title besides—had been a priority in Augusta's life. She saw it as a reflection on herself, and she made it known to them both on many occasions. Gwyneth always sensed, though, that there were storm clouds ahead, for in her own mind she believed that Emma was destined for David, and Augusta would never allow her daughter to marry any third son, no matter what his income might be.

When Emma had married Lyon instead, and had become Lady Aytoun, Augusta had fairly crowed at her success, and Gwyneth had won a couple of years reprieve. This year, however, the subject of marriage was becoming a continuous source of contention between her and her aunt. Augusta wanted to place her on a marital auction block and take offers from potential suitors before the young woman had even experienced her first Season in London. Gwyneth rebelled at the mere idea of it.

She was happy with her life as it was. She was not fond of the burdens polite society imposed on someone of her age and gender. She enjoyed the solitude of the country. She needed no entertainment and was happiest when she was left on her own to spend endless hours on her writing. Without anyone knowing, she was even beginning to draw a modest income from it. She had no need for a husband in her life. Like the heroines in the stories she was writing, there was only one man in Gwyneth's life—one love. She peeked at David, who was not looking entirely happy, but was staring straight ahead.

Emma released her arm, but Gwyneth noticed how her cousin's arm remained linked with David's. The three of them continued to walk up the long hill toward the house. Emma was telling some story about arriving at their townhouse on Hanover Square in London last month, only to be told that her husband had left that same morning, even though he had been informed that she would be arriving. She was complaining of Lyon.

Gwyneth took a step away from them, not wishing to hear any of this. Complaining about her marriage to anyone who would listen had become a favorite game for Emma. They were coming up to the formal terrace gardens, where numerous guests were enjoying the late afternoon sun.

David broke in on Emma's story. "You know very well that one quality . . . or flaw . . . that Lyon and Pierce and I all share is our fondness for routines."

As Gwyneth began to veer off toward the gardens, David came around and took her by the arm, keeping her with them.

"After two years of marriage, Emma, you should be an expert at knowing how long my brother likes to stay in London or at Baronsford, and when he likes to travel."

"Indeed I do know, all too well, about his precious routines and schedules. But what I am finding out is that he is even changing those to avoid me." Emma lowered her voice. "This might sound ridiculous, but 'tis the truth. I need to make an appointment through his manservant Gibbs to have even a single private moment with him."

"I am certain if you really needed to see Lyon, he would be available. You are making too much of a single incident."

"I am not. That was one of the dozen incidents that I've kept to myself. He avoids me. Treats me like a stranger," she said dramatically. "But when we are together, 'tis even worse. I haven't told you about his outbursts of temper."

"Lyon's temper has always been foul, but we all know how to handle him. He shows a lot of teeth, but he rarely bites."

"That was the brother you once knew. But you have been away so much." She took David's other arm, leaning against him as they walked. "Lyon has changed. There is not a month that goes by that I do not hear of some duel he's fought with some unsuspecting victim. He cannot control his temper. He overreacts to any innuendo or gossip, with no regard to how false it might be. He listens to no reasonable explanations—especially if they come from me. I am starting to fear for his safety, David . . . and for my own."

Gwyneth wanted to shut her ears. She didn't want to hear this drivel. Several times in the past two years, she'd been forced to overhear arguments between Lyon and Emma. Each time, she'd heard the provocation—generally the rumor of some indiscretion . . . or worse . . . that Emma had committed. She'd heard her cousin lie openly, too, all the while pushing Lyon as far as she could. No matter how explosive their arguments had been, though, Lyon had stormed off each time. Gwyneth had never thought to fear for Emma's safety.

"I do not know what is happening to us—to our marriage," Emma continued in a whisper. "More than ever before, I need your support now. I need you to intervene on my behalf and make Lyon realize the error of his ways before 'tis too late."

"I cannot," David said, his voice thick. "This is *your* marriage. This is something between the two of you, Emma."

"Not anymore. I cannot go on alone . . . feeling so helpless." She slowed down. "With you away, I have taken only a few of my troubles to Pierce. But he already wearies of it all. He is tired of fighting with Lyon. You are my last hope, David. If you will not help me, I do not know where I can turn. I am desperate."

Gwyneth pulled her arm free and stepped back. David turned to her. Emma stopped, too. Responses to her cousin's words bubbled up within her, threatening to spill out, but she forced them back.

"I shall go and find Walter Truscott." Gwyneth turned and fled toward the stables before David could say another word. She could not listen to one more lie.

She and Emma were almost six years apart. Coming to Greenbrae Hall as a child, Gwyneth had doted on Emma. She had followed her cousin, admired her beauty, her spirit, tried to imitate the older girl as much as her age had permitted. The fact that they both carried a torch for the same young man could not even diminish how much she idolized her cousin. Emma was the heroine in every romantic story Gwyneth read. Emma was the model for the early tales she weaved in her imagination. There was more to her than physical beauty. She was outrageous, daring, exciting. No walls could contain her. No man could resist her allure.

At the stables, Gwyneth asked a groom for a horse. One was brought to her, and in a few moments she was racing toward Greenbrae Hall. Even the feel of the wind in her face and hair could not cool her anger, cool the fever burning inside of her.

The first blow to Gwyneth's adoration had come when Emma had openly shifted her attentions to David's eldest brother. Lyon had recently inherited his

title after the death of the elder Lord Aytoun. The
new earl had returned to Baronsford after his years
of military service. It did not matter to Emma that
ten years separated them—that for all the years of
growing up, David was the one she had been closest
to. Once she made up her mind to marry Lyon, the
eldest brother had no chance. They were wed that
same summer.

The temple of devotion Gwyneth had built around
her cousin began to crumble rapidly after that. And
her growing disillusionment had nothing to do with
the wrong that Emma had done to David. It was in
London, not even a year after her marriage to Lyon
that the walls came crashing down.

Emma's mother always spent the spring in London,
and Gwyneth was required to go. It was there that
she realized the dangerous extent of the games Emma
was playing with her marriage. The constant arguments with Lyon that started immediately following
their union were a very small part of it. A side of
Emma she'd never really seen emerged. Vanity,
selfishness, cruelty. Emma lied to get her way. She
accused others unjustly, and was unkind to many. But
what was most shocking, Emma had affairs.

Gwyneth had been stunned when she'd walked in
on her cousin and a strange man in Lady Cavers's
town house in London. She had left behind her notebook after writing a letter that morning in the library.
It was early in the afternoon when Gwyneth returned
to fetch it. She'd hurried into the room, hardly sus-
pecting that anyone would be inside. She could still
see them so vividly . . . Emma straddling the man as
he sat on a sofa. His breeches were down around his
ankles, and her skirts were up around her hips. His

mouth was suckling one exposed breast, and she was writhing on his lap and making noises Gwyneth had never before heard. Neither of them had even noticed her presence, and she'd fled.

Later, Gwyneth had confronted her cousin about it. Emma had just laughed, at first. Then, she had threatened her to keep the secret. Gwyneth had little choice. To whom could she go? How could she stop her cousin from such brazen infidelity? Augusta, still elated over her daughter's advantageous marriage, would hardly be receptive to such a report . . . if she believed Gwyneth at all.

She skirted the wooded deer park along the river. Golden rays from the descending sun looked like streaks of fire across the sky overhead. It was so much easier to live one's life within the pages of a book. To read or to create lives in which passion was shared between a man and a woman who were truly in love . . . where the union of two souls was forever. Gwyneth was not ashamed of the intimacy she wove into her tales. Her characters were true to each other. They were honest. They loved each other. Lies and deceit belonged to villains, and they were punished in the end. Goodness and love always triumphed . . . at least in fiction.

Gwyneth's admiration had vanished, and Emma knew it. But they remained outwardly civil. They even managed to display moments of friendliness for the sake of Augusta and others. Gwyneth decided finally that it was not her place to make a judgment about her cousin's life, although there was more and more evidence of other affairs. There were moments, even in Baronsford and Greenbrae Hall, when Gwyneth felt she'd arrived in the midst of something, obviously spoiling a rendezvous. Still, she held her tongue. As David said, this was between Lyon and Emma.

Still though, she could not stomach seeing her cousin play the two younger Pennington brothers against Lyon. Emma was tearing their family apart. But they were at fault, too, Gwyneth realized. At first, it had been just Pierce who'd allowed himself to be blind when it came to Emma and her lies, but now David was doing the same thing. As far as they each were concerned, she had no flaws. They trusted her now as they had trusted the young child they all had adored.

She rode up the hill to the stables behind Greenbrae Hall and swung down easily from the panting steed. A groom took the reins from her and she started up the path toward the house. The sound of another rider caused her to look back. It was David. His irritation was obvious in the way he dismounted and strode toward her.

"You ride like a madwoman. Did you not hear me calling you?"

She shook her head. "What are you doing here?"

"You left so abruptly, without taking a carriage. I wanted to be sure you were not unwell."

"I am quite well, thank you," she said, unable to mask the sarcasm in her tone. "And you?"

"Quite well. Why shouldn't I be?" His words were clipped. Whatever cheerfulness he'd displayed when she saw him first by the cliffs at Baronsford had disappeared. There was a fierceness in his face now.

She tucked her notebook under her arm and started up the path.

He fell in step with her. "Why are you acting like this?"

"I don't know what you mean. I was eager to get

back to Greenbrae Hall." She was too angry to look at him. He'd been used. He'd been manipulated and formed into the shape Emma wished him to be. "So how did your talk go with Emma?"

"You were there for most of it. She is very glad I am back. She has problems, and she needs help. Lyon is being very difficult. 'Tis nothing new. I promised her that I would talk to him when he arrives." He let out a deep breath. "She has gone through all this work—planning this affair for the dowager. Two hundred guests, half of them already arrived, and he decides to wait until the last moment to make his entrance. I do not understand why he is treating her so badly. She does not deserve this, to my thinking."

Gwyneth hurried up the path. His foolishness brought tears to her eyes. She needed to get away from him. David grabbed her arm, though, and he forced her to stop. She stood looking at the ground, her arms clutching her notebook to her chest.

"What is going on?"

"Nothing! Nothing is going on with me." She looked up.

"You are crying."

"I am not." She stabbed at the runaway tears. "The wind blew something into my eye as I rode."

He didn't appear happy with her answer. "What are you running away from?"

"I am not running away. I just do not care to be at Baronsford right now. That should not be too difficult for you to understand."

"As a matter of fact, I don't understand your behavior at all. But 'tis obvious something is bothering you." His tone became confidential. "Are you in any kind of trouble?"

"No!"

"You can be honest with me."

"I *am* being honest with you."

"Gwyneth . . ." Her name was spoken like a reprimand.

She stared at him, trying to keep her composure. She failed.

"What is it that you'd like me to tell you?" she asked curtly. "I am in no trouble. And no, I was not rushing back here for a secret rendezvous with my lover. And no, I am not carrying anyone's child. Nor am I afraid that time is running out on me and unless I do something drastic, one more secret will be exposed and I will be truly ruined."

"You are speaking nonsense."

"Am I?" she challenged before turning up the path again.

His grip on her arm was hard when he turned her around. "What is this all about? Why these bloody riddles, Gwyneth? You were behaving normally one moment and then, as soon as Emma arrived, you turned into this enigmatic brat. What has she done to you?"

"Nothing." She tried to wrench her arm free. "Let me go."

"Who is having secret rendezvous? Who is carrying a child?"

"Why not ask Emma?" she snapped angrily. "Open your eyes, David. Why do you think she wants all these people around her? Why, suddenly, does she need so many protectors? And do you *really* think this whole affair has been arranged for your mother? The dowager is not fooled by that. Why are you?" She gentled her tone. "Try to see your brother's side, as well. He is your own flesh and blood. For once, try to understand his suffering."

David stared at her, obviously shocked by her outburst. But Gwyneth knew it would be no use. He was under Emma's spell. He always had been. His large hands clamped onto her shoulders when she tried to turn away.

"I know, Gwyneth, that you must be going through a difficult time. Lady Cavers has never been much of a mother. Not to Emma, and I'm certain she must be doing even less for you. I'm sure it must be hard to watch Emma get so much attention." He leaned down and looked into her face, speaking to her as if she were a child. "But this does not mean you should be so openly hostile to the one person who's been like a sister to you. 'Tis understandable that you would be jealous, but I have never known you to be so disparaging of her. Emma truly cares for you. She does not deserve to be treated like this. Not by you and not by Lyon."

Tears rushed into Gwyneth's eyes. He was blind to it. He didn't want to see the truth.

"I shall wait for you to change your dress, and then we'll go back to Baronsford. Emma never need to know the things you have told me. She—"

"No." She shook her head and stepped back. "I am not going back. Tell them what you wish, but I am not going back."

Gwyneth turned and ran up the path as fast as her legs would take her. The tears turned to sobs, but as she entered the house, she couldn't decide for whom she was shedding them.

Perhaps for herself. She'd been made to sound like a jealous and foolish child for speaking the truth.

Perhaps for Lyon. His wife had churned up his life, making it a bloody mess, turning his own family against him.

Or perhaps she was crying for David, so blinded by love that he was incapable of seeing or hearing the truth.

Perhaps, Gwyneth thought, her tears might even be for Emma. She was a woman who didn't know how to be happy, didn't know what was enough. But how could she shed tears for someone who didn't even know the misery her schemes were causing those who cared for her? For Lyon. For Pierce. And most important, for David.

No, Gwyneth realized, she could not cry for Emma. Not for the woman she hated.

Not long after sunset, the storm rolled in from the west, and a fierce rain pelted her windows through the night. Gwyneth tossed and turned every time the thunder rolled across the valley, every time the wind buffeted the walls of Greenbrae. A feeling of doom infused her dreams, lying like a shroud over her, suffocating her. She imagined hearing voices coming up the stairs, but she could not tell the reality from the dream. She thought she could hear arguments, but her mind excused it as the sound of the storm outside.

She wished she had gone back to Baronsford. She felt alone. She was horrified by the visions her imagination invoked on nights like this.

Dawn brought an end to the storm, but a light rain continued to fall and the skies remained low and gray and heavy. Gwyneth found no relief in the soft whirr of activity that she could hear as the servants readied themselves for the day. It was mid-morning when she finally forced herself to dress and leave her bedchamber. Coming down the steps, she heard shouts and the sound of horses clattering up to the front door.

At the top of the landing, Gwyneth clutched the banister as the door was thrown open and the steward rushed back in. He looked up at her.

" 'Tis horrible, miss," he cried, wringing his hat in his hands.

"Emma," she whispered, sitting down on the steps.

"Aye, miss. She's . . . she's *dead*! They say Lord Aytoun threw her from the cliffs with his own hands . . . and then went over himself!"

Emma's hair caught and reflected the sun like curls of spun gold. Wherever she went, men and women stopped to stare and admire. She was like a fairy creature from a verse of a poem or the page of an ancient story. Many afternoons, he found himself standing by the ledge, looking down at the river as she and David raced along the bank and waded or swam in the pools where the Tweed turned one way or the other.

She would climb the wet rocks to the cliff walk with her dirty hands and bare feet with surprising speed, and he tried to be waiting there for her at the top, stretching a hand down to her when she triumphantly reached the ledge as David climbed steadily beneath them.

Emma always had a special smile for him at moments like this. A wee thing, her face conquered all with the brightness of that smile and the shining and restless blue eyes. But the woman was emerging in her. He shouldn't have noticed, but at his age a boy's gaze couldn't miss the curves of her growing breasts, especially when she'd been swimming and her thin dress was wet and clinging. There was no way he could ig-

nore her affection for him either, when she looped her arms around his neck and pressed herself against him when she reached the top. She would pretend she was afraid and was going to fall off the cliffs.

He was young but he knew the truth. The last thing Emma was afraid of were those cliffs.

Chapter 2

He'd had enough. It was time for a change.

The decision had been one he'd been thinking about for months. Then, when the orders had come through, transferring him from his regiment in Ireland to a special assignment in Massachusetts, Captain David Pennington finally made what his superiors believed was an imprudent choice. He simply decided not to go, resigning his commission instead.

No one outside of the regiment had yet been told about it. Admiral Middleton, to whom David was to report in Boston, had been sent a letter written by the regimental commander that perhaps there was still a chance that the young officer might change his mind. David had not given them any specific reason for his resignation, nor had he mentioned to anyone what he planned to do now that he was giving up the army life.

This last question, however, had become the topic for dozens of toasts from the group of officers who had gathered in the Rose Tavern near St. James's

Square. The drinking had started hours ago, however, and the more articulate comments were now only a foggy memory.

"Nonsense! I hear David is leaving us to pur . . . pursue his love of singing and learn to play the harpsichord."

Though few could understand the slurred enunciation of the final word, a loud cheer went up and everyone drained their glasses. In an instant, the serving lasses—some sitting on the laps of revelers, some fighting off wandering hands—had filled the glasses again.

Another officer, jacketless and missing a shoe, staggered to his feet. "I heard that our good fellow here plans to work with those Scotch country lasses on perfecting his technique of . . . er, his dance steps. A gennelman cannot work too hard on such things."

"Aye," another pitched in. "And *hard* is the right word, lads. 'Twould never do for our David to *fall* in the middle of a dance."

Lewd comments and laughter followed. More glasses were raised. David had lost count of the number of toasts an hour ago. But he decided he must be more sober than the rest of the men, for he could still count eight of them sitting around the table. A buxom serving wench, a bottle of wine in her hand, continued to lean against his shoulder, her large bouncing breasts spilling out of her dress as she laughed at the toasts. The heavy curtain that separated his party from the rest of the tavern had long ago been drawn back, and David peered through the smoke at the ever watchful proprietor, standing on the tilting floor at the far end of the room. Happily, the man still had only one head.

As he watched, a woman wearing a hooded cloak

entered the tavern and took the proprietor aside. David vaguely recalled there were rooms upstairs for travelers who were arriving or departing London.

One of the older officers stood, gathered himself, and bowed gravely to the party. "I propose a toast to David's aspiration of mastering his skill with the feminine coiffure. In his new profession as a hairdresser here in this fine city, one only hopes that instead of simply demolishing these spectacular structures when he services the ladies, he may apply his talents of erection—"

The loud cheers and laughter of the men drowned out whatever was to follow. The other patrons of the tavern were beginning to join the cheering and the toasts. Ignoring them all, David stared at the woman speaking with the proprietor. Locks of fiery red hair had escaped the hood of the cloak.

"Gentlemen! Gentlemen!" The same officer waved his cup in the air, sloshing half of it on David's arm. "Allow me to finish, gentlemen."

The din lessened momentarily.

"What I intended to say was this . . . may David's creations be filled with entire gardens of shrubs . . . and rose gardens . . . and clumps of peonies . . . and of course every other bit of nonsense that fashion dictates." He raised his cup higher. "And may our good fellow have ample opportunity to drive his erections . . . of ladies' hairstyles . . . to new heights."

Laughter and calls of "Hear, hear!" went round the table, and everyone drank heartily to that. As the glasses were again filled, two men across the table started arguing over who was to give the next toast.

David's gaze was drawn to the woman again. Her hood had inched backward on her head. The red curls framing her face caught the light. He had a brief glimpse of an upturned nose, pale skin. He leaned forward, tried to focus, but she turned her back to him and headed for the steps. He immediately rose to his feet, nearly upending the wench hanging on his shoulder. The room whirled around him, and he had to sit down. But planting his hands on the table, he pushed himself up again.

The officer to his right stood, too, draping an arm around David's shoulders to keep his balance. "Gentlemen, may I have the . . . the divine honor of introducing a man we all know, Captain David Whatshisname . . . late of His Majesty's 46th Regiment."

Cries of "Speech!" and "A toast!" rang out, quickly giving way to shouts of laughter as the officer tried to sit down again, but missed the chair and went sprawling. Paying no further attention to their fallen comrade, they all waited for David to say something, their glasses raised.

"Considering the gravity of the moment," David started, "I shall need a few moments to weigh the merits of your thought-provoking career suggestions. Enjoy yourselves, gentlemen. I raise this glass to you all, and I shall return . . . perhaps."

Ignoring the loud cheers and protests, he made his way unsteadily across the room toward the tavern keeper. The floor was rolling like the deck of a ship on the Irish Sea. What should have been a straight path to the man was a blurry hazard of moving tables, chairs, faces, and serving wenches. David couldn't recall the last time that he'd been this far gone.

Not that there was any fault in that. He'd worked bloody hard for too many years, and he was now at . . . well, at a changing station on his life's road. He needed a fresh team of horses and a new direction, by the devil. He could do as he wished. He had ample income. His father had provided both the younger brothers with enough to live in luxury for the rest of their lives. Still though, he was not accustomed to idleness. He needed to make choices about what team of horses to pick . . . which clubs to spend his evenings in . . . which direction to go. True, he had no immediate plans, but he found no fault in that, either. He would remedy that soon enough. For tonight, he was too drunk to care about such things. Tomorrow would come soon enough to deal with the future.

The tavern keeper's bagwig had to be older than the wine he served, but David knew the heavyset man did all he could to please his patrons. Everyone in the place, including the proprietor, knew he was the guest of honor in the party of officers. The bewigged head bobbed when David asked about the woman who had just come in.

"Aye, sir, I know who ye mean. She's a pretty little thing, and well dressed. Quite young, I should think. Gave the name of Mrs. Adams when she came by earlier to take a room. I had one of the lads take her trunk up, and not a moment or two later, she went off to make her final arrangements for a carriage, she told me. She just come back, Captain, but she's off tomorrow, she is."

"Is the lass traveling alone?"

The tavern keeper glanced toward the stairs where she had disappeared. Winking his eye, he leaned toward David confidentially. "She wishes to make it look that way. But the carriage she was asking about has taken more than a few of these young folk to Gretna Green. I'd put my money on some scoundrel tricking her into meeting him along the way."

David wished he'd gotten a better look at the woman's face. Since the Marriage Act, an underage woman could no longer be married in England without the banns being read or her parents' consent. An eloping couple needed to go to Gretna Green now, just across the Scottish border.

The red hair and pale profile looked the same as Gwyneth's. She was about the same height and nicely built, just as he remembered the nymph looking last year. He was too drunk to recall where Augusta took her niece at this time of the year. But what would she be doing alone at this tavern? And where the devil did the name "Mrs. Adams" come from?

"What room is she staying in?"

"Begging your pardon, Captain," the man said apologetically after a slight pause. He pointed at the table of revelers across the taproom. "But all my serving wenches here are of the eager sort, if 'tis companionship ye seek. I'd wager you might have your pick of any of them. If 'tis the red hair ye fancy, I'm sure we can find—"

"Which room, man?"

"Begging yer pardon, sir, but I'm thinking that the young miss upstairs might not be so willing to have a strange gentleman calling on her tonight."

David reached in his pocket and took out few guineas. His vision was too blurred to count them, so he dropped them all on the counter. "Well done, man. You've done your duty. This is a place of honor and discretion, to be sure. Which room?"

"I can't take yer money, sir." He shook his head apologetically. "She might be telling the truth, and her husband might be waiting for her in Scotland. In your condition, Captain, I cannot be sending ye up there—"

"I don't want to bed the blasted creature," David

said irritably. "She looked like a family relation . . . and if she is who I think she might be, then she has no right to take a room alone or use a fictitious name or go meet some bloody fortune hunter in Scotland. If she is the person I think she is, her kin knows nothing of her doing all of this."

The energy to say that much with any coherence— at least David thought he sounded coherent—took a great deal out of him. Still, he drew himself erect and looked down at the tavern keeper, who was clearly thinking hard.

"Well, man?" David roared. "Will you tell me or must I find the bloody chit myself?"

Quickly, the man swept the coins off the counter and pocketed them. Hurrying around David, he gestured for him to follow.

"In that case sir, I'll take ye up to her room myself."

Though he knew he was not thinking too clearly, David knew it was better this way, in case he had the wrong woman. He was also glad the tavern keeper hadn't just given him directions. In his condition, he might arrive at the door of St. James's Palace as easily as the right door.

The stairs heaved and shifted as he tried to follow the proprietor. He needed to stop a couple of times along their way and lean heavily against the walls. They seemed to be moving in and out on him. The older man chatted away the whole time they were moving up the steep steps, but David didn't hear most of it. He should have drunk more . . . or dipped his head in a bucket of cold water before coming up.

Upstairs, the hallway was dark. It was hot and airless in the narrow passageway. Doors lined both walls.

One swung open when he swayed a little, banging it with his shoulder. David found himself staring in at a good-sized bed. The window was open and—though it was August—he could smell smoke from a bonfire on the street below. The sudden urge to lie down and sleep almost overwhelmed him.

"This one's not let for the night. Ye can have it no charge, Captain. A nice comfortable bed, that one is, sir."

He tore his gaze away from the temptation and turned to the man at his shoulder. "The woman . . . take me to this Mrs. . . . Mrs. . . . what was her bloody name?"

"Mrs. Adams." The man pointed. "This way, sir. Her room is the last one there on the left."

Curiously, it appeared that his legs had turned to stone. By the time David got his feet moving again down the hallway, the other man was already knocking on the door. A muffled response came from inside.

"I've a gentleman here, Mrs. Adams," the tavern keeper called out. "He says he's some relation to ye, ma'am."

David thought it was stupid to warn the woman that she'd been found out. Talking took too much effort, though, and the narrow space was starting to feel like a crypt. Pushing the proprietor out of the way, he leaned heavily against the woman's door, waiting. She was taking her bloody time. He thought to ask if there were a window she might climb from. His mouth was too dry, though, to say anything, and he decided to rest a little where he was.

"He must be mistaken," she answered from the other side of the door. "I have no kin in London . . . and my husband would not be happy if I were to open this door at this time of the night to—"

"Gwyneth," David managed to say. "Is that you?"

There was another pause. Then a latch lifted hurriedly on the other side. The surface he was leaning on suddenly gave way, and David went tumbling into the room.

The young woman tried to get out of the way, but David reached for her, and both of them ended up landing on the hard floor . . . her on top of him.

"David? Are you hurt?" She slid off to his side, her hands touching his chest, his face, running over his hair. There was worry in her voice.

He somehow got hold of her wrist. He wanted to make sure she didn't run away.

"I guess the captain was right in saying he knew ye, ma'am," the tavern keeper said with a chuckle, backing out of the room and closing the door.

She worked her wrist free and leaned over him again. "What are you doing here?" She caressed his face. "The last I heard, you were in Ireland."

David blinked to clear his vision. She wore no fashionably tall headdress. She didn't need such ridiculous ornamentation. Her curls were the color of fire in the flickering candlelight. He reached up and touched her hair. It was so soft. The way it used to be. His finger looped around one curl and he tugged once, the way he always did. She didn't cry or complain though. Instead her fingers gently freed her hair. His gaze caressed her face, focused on her lips. This was not the girl he remembered, though. She had become a woman.

"You are not helping me. Sit up, David."

She stretched her arm under his shoulders and tried to lift him. He stared at the pulse fluttering beneath the ivory column of her throat. The skin looked soft. Her eyes were huge and as green as the hills of Eildon.

She smelled of lavender and a freshness not found in London. He did help her. He raised himself onto one elbow, facing her.

"Who is this bloody Adams?"

"Never mind that." She leaned over him, trying to get him to sit up. "You seem to have too much wine in you. I should like to get you out of here and downstairs. We can find you a carriage or a sedan chair. I do not think your family even knows you're back from Ireland. And why are you not wearing your uniform?"

He reached over and cupped the back of her head, drawing her face close. "Who . . . is . . . Adams?" he asked again.

"You are in no condition now for any explanations. I should like to get you to your brother's house."

Her mouth fascinated him. He kissed her. If she was surprised, there was no struggle. David pressed his tongue into her mouth, and his hunger surged as he heard her make a small surprised noise in the back of her throat. Her taste was sweet, her breath warm. He took a fistful of her hair and her mouth opened. In an instant, he was devouring her, mindless of why he had come up here. All he knew was that her mouth was like some luscious flower, and he was drawing the nectar.

Suddenly she came alive, her tongue answering his call to play. When he finally drew his head back a little, her mouth followed. David lay back, pulling her body on top of his. Her soft curves fit in all the right places, and he felt his body growing hard. His hand slid downward over her bottom, and he kneaded the sweet, firm flesh.

"David." She lifted her head, breaking off the kiss. Her skin was flushed. She was breathless. "We shouldn't."

"Why is that?"

He rolled them on the floor, cradling her head as he moved on top of her. He fit himself against her and saw the pulse in her throat now beating wildly. He put his mouth on it.

"I love the taste of you here." He trailed his mouth down to the neckline of her dress. "And here, too."

His hand gently squeezed her perfect breast, and a small gasp escaped her lips as she arched her back into his touch. Lowering his head, he nipped at one breast through the layer of clothing.

"I would like very much to strip this garment off of you so I can taste you here, too." His hand moved downward beyond her belly. "And here."

Her body grew still, and then she took hold of his face in both hands. She drew his head up until he was looking into her face again.

"I fear you are too far gone with wine to know whose body is lying beneath yours," she said quietly. "Look at me, David."

His body throbbed. The woman was beautiful, and he knew she was willing. He tried to focus on her face, though. Green eyes. That dusting of freckles on her nose. He wanted to make love to her. He pressed his hip into the juncture of her legs.

"David!" she pleaded. "I want you to see me. 'Tis Gwyneth."

He tried to focus again and this time reality sank in. Gwyneth! He closed his eyes for a moment to gather his sanity. He opened them and looked at her again. Her eyes had grown misty.

"Bloody hell! I am so sorry, I—"

She pressed her fingers against his lips and shook her head. "Do not apologize. I understand."

He couldn't roll off of her fast enough. He pushed

himself unsteadily to his feet. As he stretched down a hand to help her up as well, the room tilted, lurched once, and began to spin wildly. He staggered back, hitting the door with his back.

"I think I am going to be si—"

The window was open. But there was no breeze, no relief from the heat burning Gwyneth's face and body.

The sounds of the taproom below had finally quieted. Outside, the noise of the street was dwindling, too. Dawn was only a few hours away, though, and soon the early coaches leaving London would rattle through the town, the harnesses of their teams jingling and the drivers' gruff shouts breaking the silence. Then the calls of the early morning vendors would begin to be heard.

Gwyneth walked away from the window and came to touch David's brow for the hundredth time. He was not feverish, but his sleep was restless and fitful. She'd helped him out of his jacket when she'd laid him down. Still though, she thought he must be far too warm in his waistcoat and shirt, but she didn't dare touch any of his clothing.

He had been so sick, but he wouldn't let her help him. The only thing he'd asked of her was to go downstairs for a clean pitcher of water. She'd done that, and afterward neither of them had said much before he'd fallen asleep on the narrow bed in her room. She had little experience in dealing with effects of drinking too much wine. She assumed sleeping, though, would be his best medicine.

She quickly snatched her hand away from David's face when he rolled toward her in his sleep. She moved to the window again and sat on the rickety bench. The moon was still high, though she could see thickening clouds covering much of the starry sky. They would be setting off in the rain, she decided. His jacket and his sword lay beside her and she ran her fingers over the fine new cloth of his coat and the ornate metalwork of the weapon, which gleamed in the moonlight. She looked across the room, watching him as he slept.

Her body still tingled from the way he'd touched her. No one had ever touched her like that. No one had ever kissed her the way he'd kissed her. She touched her lips, which still felt slightly swollen. She remembered how shocked she'd been to hear his voice outside the door. Actually, how thrilled she'd been.

Of all the times that she might have run into him here in London, though, it had to be the hand of fate that had arranged their meeting tonight.

She was eloping in the morning. She was leaving an hour after dawn in a carriage she'd hired. North of London, in Hampstead Village, Sir Allan Ardmore would join her, and from there they would travel north and marry at Gretna Green, just over the border in Scotland. It was not love, of course. She looked at David, who stirred slightly at that moment. No, it was not love nor passion nor even affection that was driving her to elope. It was just business.

Gwyneth didn't want to think about any of that now, however. Instead, she stared at David's muscular arm draped over the side of the bed, the knuckles of his large hand brushing the floor. She groaned inwardly. She'd been so tempted to let him have his way with her. Ardmore had hinted that after the ceremony he expected their marriage to be consummated. During those few wild moments, lying beneath David, feeling his hands touching her, she'd considered how much more meaningful it would have been to give her innocence to the one man she had always loved—as the heroines in her stories might have done. At least she would have been left with a precious memory to carry with her for a lifetime.

She rested her head against the window frame. Dawn would arrive soon enough. It would not be safe for her to leave the room now, for the dark streets still belonged to the ruffians and the footpads. And there was the complication of carrying her trunk, too.

She would wait. David was sure to sleep for hours, and she would be gone when he awoke. Perhaps he wouldn't even remember seeing her.

Gwyneth's eyes drifted shut, and she soon found herself dreaming of lying in that bed with David as his hands and mouth did wicked and wonderful things to her.

The tap on the door was light, but David heard it in his sleep. He scrambled out of bed and dashed to open the door at the same time that Gwyneth up-ended a bench in her rush to beat him to it. Reaching for the latch first, he glanced into her sleepy eyes. Her curls were tangled prettily and some of them fell across her face. Her dress was wrinkled. She looked soft and beautiful and young, and the thought that some rake was planning to steal her away made him suddenly mad as a bull.

He yanked the door open.

A boy of eleven or twelve stood in the dark hall. He immediately snatched his hat from his head, taking an unconscious step back in the face of David's obvious fury.

"Beggin' yer pardon, sir, but I was sent to fetch a trunk fer a lady."

Gwyneth shouldered her way past David and smiled at the boy. "You've come to the right place. Thank you. 'Tis there in the corner."

She actually had the nerve to put her shoulder to his chest and push him out of the way, showing the boy where the trunk sat. David's head, which he'd left in the bed, finally caught up with his body. It felt like a smith's anvil, in both weight and ill usage, for there was suddenly a pounding and a ringing that nearly blinded him. He forced his eyes to stay open, but the taste of bile was in his throat. He leaned a shoulder against the doorjamb for a couple of seconds as he tried to find his legs. He was sure they must be there, for he knew he was standing, but he was damned if he could feel them and he didn't trust his balance to look down.

He turned miserably to the room, where Gwyneth was chatting amiably with the nervous boy as he fetched her trunk. She draped her cloak around her shoulders and started for the door.

"You should go back to bed and try to get some more rest. And I really think you should let your family know that you are back in England. They have been terribly eager to hear some news of you."

He rubbed a hand wearily over his face to clear his vision. The woman had lost her mind. She was talking to him like she was on her way to some Sunday service. She smiled and patted him once on his shoulder and disappeared behind the boy into the hall.

David staggered toward the bench, somehow managed to pick up his coat and sword without tumbling out the open window, and started after her. They were on the stairs when she noticed he was following. She waited and took his elbow as he groped his way down the steps. She was helping him as if he were a bloody invalid.

"You do not look very well. Probably I should have the proprietor secure a carriage or a sedan chair to carry you to Hanover Square."

The pounding in his head was getting worse, and he could barely hear her with the dozen or so hornets buzzing in his ears. It would take too much effort to let her know what he thought of her idea.

Outside, he had to close his eyes for a moment to avoid being blinded by the gray light of day. A drizzling mist felt good on his face, though. He was dreadfully thirsty. Cracking his eyelids slightly, he peered at the boy and the trunk a few feet away. Gwyneth was exchanging a few words with a swarthy fellow across the alley. She handed him a coin, and the man went off.

"You can wait right here," she said, coming back across to David. "They shall bring a carriage for you from a stable just around the corner."

He leaned against the building, and she gave his arm a friendly squeeze.

"Good-bye, David."

The closed carriage she'd hired rumbled to a stop in the lane. There was a driver and a groom handling the team of four, and David saw her walk toward it as her trunk was loaded into the boot. He started after her, but a hand on his arm stopped him. He turned to a stableboy behind him.

"Brought a carriage fer yer lordship. This way, sir." He pointed in the opposite direction.

"I need no carriage."

"But 'er ladyship said—"

"Bugger off!" David's bark sent the boy scrambling.

The ringing in his head was becoming nearly intolerable now, and his throat was as dry as a parson's scalp. His stomach continued to be quite disagreeable, but as he focused on the back of her cloak disappearing into the carriage, he forced himself to lengthen his strides. He reached it just as the driver raised his whip to start off. David jerked the door open, fully expecting the scoundrel she was running away with to be inside. Gwyneth was alone, and her face showed her surprise.

"David, you are not coming with me." She shook her head and reached out for the door.

Without any ceremony, he pushed her back into her seat and climbed inside, slamming the door. Signaling for the driver to start, he plunked himself down wearily beside her. As the carriage lurched into motion, she immediately moved to the seat across from him.

"I am going to Scotland. There is another carriage in front of the tavern that will take you to your brother's house in Hanover Square."

"What is the name of the filthy vermin?"

It took a few seconds for his question to register, but then her green eyes widened with alarm. Hiding it quickly, she made a show of removing her cloak and folding it deliberately before placing it on the seat next to her. "We'll deliver you to Hanover Square first. It should not be too far out of our way."

She leaned toward the window to call up to the driver, but David pulled her back.

"I am going to kill the bloody fox." She stared at him as if he'd grown two heads. David wished he did have two heads so he could cut off the one that was pounding unmercifully right now.

"I don't know what you are talking about."

"You are eloping with some villain to Gretna Green. I am coming along. I am warning you, though, when I meet him, I shall kill him." He closed his eyes as a blinding pain shot through his head. He was being far too chatty.

"You're still drunk."

"I wish I were."

"I do not appreciate your attitude, nor your temper . . . nor your interference. Your entire behavior is frightful."

"Your appreciation is the least of my concerns right now." He stretched out his long legs, crowding her into one corner.

"I am delivering you to Hanover Square." She leaned toward the window again, but he grabbed her wrist and pulled her onto the seat beside him.

"Not until a certain cowardly dog lies dead," he growled under his breath.

Gwyneth scrambled to the seat across again. "You *must* still be drunk. David, civilized people do not go around killing each other."

"I shall be sober by the time we get there, and— civilized or not—I intend to enjoy watching him die."

The carriage rattled through the narrow streets. The calls of the street vendors indicated a city coming to life, though there was still not the traffic that would soon clog these same thoroughfares in an hour or so.

"You have lost your mind," she said incredulously. "I could forgive you for barging into my room the way you did last night, since you were drunk. This morning, however, is an entirely different matter."

He leaned his head back against the seat and closed his eyes. "I need to rest before we get there."

"David . . ." She touched him on the knee, but he pretended to ignore her. "You are not a family relation. None of this is any business of yours."

He heard the pitch of her voice rise, and he crossed his arms and shifted to get more comfortable.

"I cannot believe this. You are not coming with me. Do you hear me? I shall not allow you to come with me to Scotland."

He knew she was leaning toward the window again, and he grabbed her wrist once more. This time, he moved across, placing himself next to her and effectively trapping her with his shoulder and the side of the carriage.

"You have become so arrogant!" She punched him hard on the shoulder. "I shall not tolerate such treatment . . ."

All of her whining and even the colorful cursing that followed would have been much more amusing if it were not for the punishment he had inflicted on himself in drinking too much last night. Still, despite the thundering ache in his head and the nausea he was fighting to subdue, his attention was drawn to her intoxicating scent. There was something familiar and exciting in pressing up against her.

He had only a vague recollection of what had happened last night, other than following the tavern keeper down the dark hallway and then finding himself tangled on the floor with Gwyneth. This was where his memory became clouded with a fog that continued to hang over him. Still though, he remembered kissing her, becoming lost in that scent. Almost in spite of himself, he felt a stirring in his loins.

"David. Captain Pennington. Please."

He was fully aware of her change in tactics. Her

body went soft against him. Her voice had become a whisper. He kept his eyes shut.

"Will you at least look at me?"

He would have ignored her if she had not trailed her finger across his cheek. Her touch had a sudden and disconcerting effect on his body. He moved in the seat and turned to look at her through partially opened eyes.

"You are confused. I am, too, of course. I never expected to find you at my door last night. You have been away so long, and we've had no news of each other." A lock of hair had escaped and she tucked the reddish gold curl behind her ear. The gesture distracted him momentarily, and he stared at the delicate curve of her ear and the soft skin beneath. He remembered kissing that very same spot. "But one thing we need to remember is that we are both rational people. And we've always respected each other. And I think all of our confusion this morning has something to do with lack of adequate sleep."

He yawned and closed his eyes.

"I am not finished yet." She shook him hard.

He reluctantly pried open his eyes and looked at her again.

"I think . . . I believe . . . once we gather ourselves together, explanations can be made and we can each go on our separate way."

"Are you planning to elope today?"

She blushed. She stammered. She tried to lie, but it was obvious she couldn't.

"So . . . so what if I were?"

"Very simply, the dog will die," he growled, turning slightly and leaning back onto her shoulder again as he closed his eyes.

"You are *not* my protector. Do you hear me?" she yelled into his ear, shaking him hard. Her temper was back. "You cannot bully your way into my life. I shall not let you. I have made plans, and I intend to carry them through."

Her voice was becoming too shrill for his weakened condition. He wearily straightened in the seat. "And I intend to alter those plans."

"But why?"

He turned toward her until their faces were inches apart. "Because eloping indicates scandalous behavior. Because only a ruined or desperate young woman of your station in life would consider something so rash. Because I care about you and do not wish to think of you in such a situation. And because if the mangy cur who has lured you away is such a coward that he cannot approach your guardian and seek her approval properly, then, by Jove, he shall face me and pay the penalty."

She appeared to have a few things to say, but wisely crossed her arms over her chest and sat back in silence, staring out the window.

"Now, Gwyneth, I need to sleep," he said, stretching out against her again. "And I don't want to hear another word until we get to your appointed place of rendezvous."

"Take me to Lady Cavers."

He didn't answer.

"Listen, you have found me out," she said in a thick voice. "I want you to take me back to my aunt's house right now. I am resigned to your interference in my plans, and you may hand me over to her. She can decide what punishment she sees fit for me."

She sounded to be on the verge of tears, and this

tugged at David's heartstrings. What was the point of making her suffer any further? He'd stopped her from eloping. If the fortune hunter who had arranged to run away with her was thwarted, then who was he to pursue the villain?

"I do not want the blood of anyone on my hands. Please take me back to my aunt," she said, sniffing back the tears.

He was in no mood to deal with hysterics. Drawing a deep breath, he called to the driver and directed him to Lady Cavers's town house.

She had her wits about her, and he didn't.

Gwyneth knew that David still felt ill from his party last night . . . and she fully intended to take advantage of that. As the carriage pulled up at her aunt's house, she climbed out before he could move. Pretending to adjust the cloak around her, she secretly gestured to the driver to wait. She was relieved that the astute man decided not to ask any questions. David took his time climbing out after her, and she watched him raise his face to the misting rain and simply stand there for a few moments. Though he was a little pale, and his temperament resembled that of an angry boar, he did not look like a man who was suffering much from the effects of his revelry. He was as handsome as ever. She shook off such thoughts.

"Will you at least allow me to try to explain my situation to my aunt first . . . alone?" she pleaded, holding on to his arm as they climbed the steps to the front door. "I promise to speak the truth to her."

He nodded. "But I am not leaving until I see her," he warned.

Gwyneth smiled weakly. "I would not expect you

to. At the same time I would be quite embarrassed to have you witness Augusta chastising me for my . . . my indiscretion." When they arrived at the door, she dropped her chin onto her chest and—as an added effect—wiped away a nonexistent tear. "After she is finished with me, she certainly would want to speak to you."

He nodded curtly, and she was relieved to see that tears still had a strong effect on him.

Before David could knock, the door opened.

Gwyneth greeted the doorman, giving him no chance to express his surprise at seeing her. As far as the household knew, she had gone off to Scotland yesterday, to stay in Edinburgh before traveling to Greenbrae Hall. Taking David's arm, Gwyneth glided through the entryway and hurried him up the wide stairway that encircled the high open foyer. When they reached the top of the stairs, she turned to the trailing servant.

"Could you please escort Captain Pennington to the library?" she asked, releasing her hold on him. David's face showed his suspicion. "I shall go speak to her immediately. It should only be a few minutes before she receives you."

She continued up the next flight of stairs as he disappeared into the library. Gwyneth didn't bother to remove her cloak. Saying nothing to two upstairs maids who looked at her with surprise, she headed directly to the servants' stairs at the back of the house.

If anyone deserved repercussions for this elopement, it was Gwyneth herself. It had been her carelessness that had led to the troubles that she now found herself in. She was the one who had gone to

Sir Allan Ardmore in the first place. The marriage of convenience had simply been his suggestion for resolving the problem. How unjust it would be for the baronet to suffer for trying to help her!

David was in no condition, however, to hear any of her explanation . . . not that she could make it sound believable if he were to give her a chance anyway. Even if he were capable of understanding, though, she was determined that no one but Sir Allan would be acquainted with her secret until after she was married. Near the bottom of the back steps, she ran into one of the kitchen servants coming up.

"Why, Miss Gwyneth! I'm sure we weren't expecting you."

Gwyneth turned her back down the stairs. "Please take some breakfast to Captain Pennington in the library," she told the young woman. "And if he asks about my aunt, tell her she should be down in an hour."

"But Miss, Lady Cavers left for Bristol the day before last."

"You know that and I know it, too. But we have to keep Captain Pennington from learning the truth for a couple of hours. Would you please help me with this?"

"Aye, Miss."

"Hurry." The young woman gave a quick nod and ran down in front of her.

Gwyneth waved to a number of the other servants as she ran through the servants' hall and dashed out through a kitchen door onto the walkway that ran next to the house. Hurrying out to the street, she saw the carriage. The driver was in his seat and the attending groom was standing by the door. She was relieved that they had understood her silent plea and had not unloaded her trunk. So different than she'd planned, her elopement was ending up to be quite dramatic. She had a momentary vision of exchanging vows with Ardmore as David tried to break down the door of the blacksmith shop at Gretna Green.

"Sorry about the little side excursion," she told the man as he opened the door of the carriage for her. "You can continue on now as originally planned."

Gwyneth was halfway inside the carriage before she saw him.

His muscular legs were stretched out, his boots up on the seat opposite. His arms were crossed, and his chin was resting on his chest. He looked as if he were sleeping.

The door clicked shut behind her, and the carriage lurched forward, tumbling her into the seat beside him.

"I expected you sooner," David said, never opening his eyes.

For so many years, the building had been a ruined tower house, abandoned long before the Pennington family built Baronsford. No more than a remnant of the time when the Borders had been a constant battle-ground, the place had stood empty for longer than anyone knew. Fire had consumed it, and then wind and rain had battered the structure until all that was left was a skeleton of stone walls with holes that were once windows and portions of a shattered roof.

He liked to come out here at odd times. He enjoyed standing on what remained of the rough wooden floor-ing of the Great Hall and imagining what the place had once been. As he grew a little older, he enjoyed the feeling of accomplishment in rolling up his sleeves and climbing high on the walls to try to repair the roof to keep out the rain.

This was a forgotten house. He was a forgotten boy. He'd pretended it was his place now, his castle. On warm summer afternoons, he liked to sit on the ramparts of the tower and dream of a future for this place—of a future for himself. And he continued to work at the place, reclaiming it piece by piece.

But he kept it to himself. All of it—his work, the gradual changes, his dreams. The old ruined tower had become his sanctuary. He wanted no help. If it took days or months or years to make the place live again, then that was as it had to be.

She found him, though. He didn't know how. But one day he came down the spiraling stone stairwell, and Emma was standing there.

Chapter 3

"Barefoot, starving, and ragged she was. Feverish, too. A blind man could see the lass was sick, as well as being with child. Still, they just left the poor thing at our door during the night."

The old cotter's wife stood with Walter Truscott just outside the open door of the cottage. The sky above was gray, and the air was warm and thick with the threat of rain. The cottage was the farthest one on the land that belonged to Baronsford.

"I dunna know if the sorry lass will survive with her bairn and all, but something about her made my Angus send the lad to ye. He wanted ye to come if ye were able."

Walter ducked his head as she led him through the door. The single room of the cottage was hot and smoky from the cooking fire, in spite of the open door. Leather hides covered the two small windows, and there seemed to be no fresh air getting in at all. He could barely breathe inside.

"She hasn't stirred since we laid her down. I tried to get her to drink something, but 'twas a waste as it just trickled down the side of her mouth."

He could see the ancient quilt and tattered blanket

that had been spread over the woman in spite of the lack of air in the cottage.

And then he saw her, and Walter felt a sharp twist in his gut. His breath caught in his chest. The blond curls. The pale face. The small nose. The woman's eyes opened for a few seconds, and she stared without focus in his direction. Even their eyes were the same color. She closed them again. He stood stock-still for a moment, confused, feeling as if he were looking at a ghost. It couldn't be. He'd seen her dead. He had been the one who had carried Emma's cold body up from the river. He let out his breath. A chill washed down his spine.

"She must have been traveling with the folk coming in from the west and the north," the old woman conjectured. "Every day, we've been seeing more than a few of them that have lost their farms come passing through."

Her face was much thinner. Walter tried to focus and see through the thick fog of guilt. As he approached the bed, all the similarity disappeared.

"What they were thinking, I've nae idea. One of her kin could at least have knocked on our door to tell us they were leaving her. The poor creature was near drowned with the rain. We dunna know her name, sir, nor where she come from, nor where she was going. The rags I peeled off her had once been a fine dress, though. Lord knows, but she might even have been gentry."

This close, there was a look of angelic innocence in the face. Her features were more delicate. Long eyelashes lay peacefully against cheeks that were deadly pale beneath the dirt. She shivered, and Walter pressed the back of his hand against her ashen cheek. Despite the suffocating heat of the room, her skin was cold.

"The bairn could come at any time, sir," the cotter's wife said over Walter's shoulder. "I dunna think 'twould be wise to go and move her. The midwife from the village should be by soon, too."

He couldn't tear his gaze from her face. Her chin quivered a little as he watched, her lips opened to say something but closed again. She looked to be caught in the middle of some nightmare. One hand pushed restlessly at the blankets and then lay still on the bedding. Walter saw the calluses on her long slender fingers. These were working hands, not the hands of gentry. He stared at her swollen belly showing prominently beneath the blankets.

"I can send for the doctor from Melrose to come and check on her, but perhaps you and your husband could manage if she were to stay here a few days?"

"Aye. We managed last night. A few more nights will hardly kill us." The cotter's wife went around and tucked the blanket under the sleeping woman's chin. "Angus was talking about sweeping out the shed and laying some bedding in there for her, but we just dunna know if the lassie will survive the day."

Walter glanced at her again and saw a tear trickle from her eye even as she slept. It ran across the dirty face and disappeared into the blond hairs at her temple. He reached down and wiped the trail with his thumb.

"Perhaps the midwife can do something for her. Still, I shall bring the doctor back myself. I can also arrange for some things to be brought out from Baronsford for you. I know his lordship would not want to reward your kindness with any more of a burden on you both than is necessary."

The old woman led Walter out of the cottage, her comments making him believe that she was happy with the arrangement.

Moments later, Walter was riding hard for Melrose, wondering at his own sense of urgency. He certainly couldn't understand the emotions that were surging through him. Hundreds of tenants were being pushed out of their farms all over Scotland. The land clearing was forcing people to pile their belongings on the backs of carts and donkeys, and go off looking for work or passage to the colonies. So many had been coming through the villages around Baronsford. So many poor and hungry folk. So many heavy with child and desperate . . . as Josephine's mother had been this past spring.

When Millicent, Lord Aytoun's new wife, had found her, the frightened lass had been barely surviving, living like a dog on scraps of bread and hiding beneath a vagrant's cart in the muck by the river's edge.

No kin. No husband. No home. Still, the woman called Jo had been too afraid to accept Millicent's offer and leave the squalid encampment. The next day she went into labor. The doctor Lady Aytoun had sent to Melrose for had come too late. Jo had died with her tiny rag-swaddled daughter in one arm while her other hand had clutched Millicent's.

Jo had left her daughter to the safekeeping of Lady Aytoun. Millicent and Lyon had in turn named the child Josephine. They would raise her as their own. Not all the bairns of Scotland would be as well cared for, though.

Responsible for managing Baronsford and all of its farms, Truscott tried to be a compassionate man. He helped wherever he could, but his time and responsibilities never allowed him to get too closely involved. And he preferred it this way, for these people were vagrants, passing through. They had no connection to

Baronsford, and he had no control over what was to become of them once they left. So why had this one made such an impression that he was spurring his horse on toward Melrose beneath a gray and threatening sky?

He knew the reason. He didn't want to admit it, but he knew it as certainly as he knew every bend and turn of the Tweed, every play of sunlight and shadow on the Eildon Hills.

For a few brief seconds, when he had entered that one-room cottage and had looked across at the young woman with her blond hair strewn around her, she had been Emma.

Emma.

The moment had passed. She wasn't Emma. She was just a sick and homeless young woman, unwanted by anyone, it seemed. An uncomfortable feeling lingered within him, though, goading him, driving him on. Perhaps this was a second chance though to do right where he'd gone wrong before. Perhaps this was an opportunity to redeem himself.

Large drops of rain began to fall, stinging his face and blinding him momentarily. Still, Walter pushed his steed even harder.

The rain had come down relentlessly for what felt like weeks. The family was away. Boredom had just about crushed his body and soul. When the clouds finally showed a rare glimpse of blue in the sky, he was like a bird who'd suddenly grown new wings. He left Baronsford with only one destination in mind. He didn't mind his boots sinking ankle-deep in the mud. He ignored the showers from the heavy leaves on the trees soaking him as he ran through the deer park. He was going to the ruins, though he no longer thought of it as that. His determination and hard work was gradually reshaping the place. He had even mentioned it to the family and had been told the old tower house was his to do with as he wished.

His own.

The ominous clouds had once again closed in overhead as he arrived at the tower. A sudden crack of thunder exploded behind him. He ran up the wooden stairs and went inside just as the sky once again opened its floodgates and the rain fell again with no mercy.

Sheltered in the stone entryway, he turned to watch the storm sweep across the valley. That was when he saw her. Emma running from the woods and straight toward the building.

His heart leapt with joy at seeing her. Her absence of nine months felt like nine years. He noticed that despite being covered with mud, she was wearing shoes. And her hair, although soaked, was gathered on top of her head. Her dress was made of fine cloth, but it was now ruined, to be sure. She had grown during these past months—in womanly ways. She was now fourteen.

She smiled as she ran toward him, and he saw the old Emma in her sparkling eyes.

"I knew I'd find you here," she said, laughing as she came up the stairway and collapsed into his arms. When he said nothing, she looked up at him. "My God, you have changed."

He knew he had grown, too. The top of her head only reached to his chin. He now had a man's body. But the changes in her were of more interest to him. He admired the droplets of rain making their way down her flushed cheeks. Smiling, she took his hand and drew him inside the tower house.

"Tell me what you have been doing while I was gone. No, first show me what changes you have made in this place since I went away."

They'd spent so many hours here together. Since that first summer, when she'd showed up one day at this door, a special bond had been forged between them. This was the place where, while he worked, they talked and shared their deepest secrets.

It was strange, though, the connection between them. He was the same person wherever he went. But she was different when she stepped beyond these walls. He didn't like that other Emma, for she was distant and aloof to him, as if denying their friendship—innocent as it was. He never asked anything of her before the others. He never pressed for more. Still though, he could not deny her anything when she came back to him here at the tower house.

He wanted to show her everything he'd done, but soon after he started talking, she slipped her arms around his waist and just held him.

"I've missed you." She pressed her face against his heart.

He stood there awkwardly, trying to draw back, incapable of returning her affection. His body's reaction to her embarrassed him. She was soaking wet. The budded tips of her breasts showed clearly through the wet dress. Her scent clouded his mind and conjured images in his mind that terrified him. He reminded himself who she was, of how young she was, and tried to separate himself from her.

"Let me show you what I have done."

"Later. You are the reason I came here." She held on to him. A smile broke out on her lips when she looked down his body. *"You have changed."*

Embarrassment burned his face to the tips of his ears.

He froze when she looped her arms around his neck. Her blue eyes looked up into his.

"Kiss me."

He stared at her wet lips. He wanted to. His need burned in his hardened body. He shook his head and tried to back away. This was Emma.

"David will be back any day now," he said weakly.

"I want you to be the first man who kisses me."

His back came in contact with the wall behind him. She pressed her breasts against him, and her hands drew his face down to hers.

The moment their lips touched, he was lost. She tasted just as sweet as he'd always dreamed. Their mouths greedily fed on the other's as if they'd both been starved for this moment. He was the one who forced them apart, though. He understood the need for control, and he knew that he was on the brink of losing it.

"I want you."

His knees almost buckled at the look he saw in her face.

"We cannot," he said hoarsely, pushing her away and stepping toward the door. "This is a mistake."

"You and I are alike. I want this."

A peal of thunder cut the air nearby, crackling and booming. The rain poured down in buckets, but he didn't care. He ran from the tower house and did not stop until he was standing on the cliffs, panting and looking down at the rushing brown waters of the Tweed.

Chapter 4

⌒

No arguments. No explanations. Once assured that she was trapped securely on the seat next to him, the beastly man had simply appeared to go to sleep.

Gwyneth let the wound from his intrusion fester during the first hour or so of their journey. As the carriage made its way northward out of the busy streets of London and into the open countryside, the names she intended to call him to his face arranged themselves in her mind like lines of lancers on a broad battlefield. The injuries she planned to inflict on him were horrid. She jabbed her elbow into his side at every turn and bump on the road. She managed to push his boots off the seat and tried to unsettle him every time he managed to get comfortable. He was somehow able to sleep through it all.

The passing time, though, and the sight of the little cluster of houses at Pond Street to the north of London brought home again the reality of her situation. Almost too soon, the carriage started making the long climb up Red Lion Hill. No matter how severe she might reprimand David for his heavy-handed interference, she didn't think she could stop him from facing Sir Allan Ardmore. And a fight or duel between them would surely prove to be no contest whatsoever. Sir Allan might outduel him in a battle of words, but with swords or pistols or whatever other barbaric weapon David would force him to use, the baronet was sure to be beaten. And Gwyneth did not want anyone's blood on her conscience.

Pushing the door open and leaping from the slow-moving carriage was out of the question. The couple of times that she'd tried to move to the seat across, David's heavy hand had clamped on her arm, forcing her to stay. He appeared to be sleeping, but she now knew he wasn't.

Gwyneth considered their exact arrangements. Sir Allan was to join her near Spaniard's Tavern in Hampstead Village, at the top of the long, winding hill the team of horses was now laboring to climb. But was she to wait for him, or would he be waiting? She couldn't even ask the driver to forgo the stop and continue northward without arousing David's suspicions. Hampstead Village was a customary stop for changing horses.

She shoved her elbow into David's side and, hearing a grunt, felt slightly better.

The carriage finally topped the long hill, and she could see they were entering the village proper. She leaned over the sleeping beast next to her for a view of the shops on his side of the street. Soon they would be stopping at the tavern, and a feeling of dread washed through her.

"I am quite hungry," he growled under his breath. His eyes slowly opened.

Gwyneth fought back the quiver of excitement that flashed through her when she found him staring at her mouth. In her effort to look out, she was resting an elbow on his chest, her body practically draped across his. She tried to pull back but the sudden lurch of the carriage as it came to a full stop flattened her against him. Gwyneth tried to scramble off of him, but his powerful arm shot around her, holding her where she was.

"And are *you* hungry, Gwyneth?"

Their faces were so close. His blue eyes, heavy-lidded with sleep, stared into hers. The day's growth of beard on his face was strangely appealing, and for a brief moment the memory of their kiss last night made her heart pound.

Sanity returned in a rush with the thought of Sir Allan opening the carriage door to welcome her. She yanked free of David's embrace and moved to where she could push him toward the door.

"Of course I'm hungry," she said, throwing open the door in the face of the surprised groom. "Starving, in fact."

She managed to push him out ahead of her. The rain had stopped, and patches of sun were peeking through the layers of clouds. Climbing out behind him, she immediately spotted the baronet standing by the doorway of the whitewashed brick tavern a few yards up the hill from where the carriage stopped. He saw her, too, and she was relieved to see him pause as David stretched to his full height and yawned. Gwyneth shook her head at Sir Allan, pointing to David's back and shaking her head again. Two merchants who had just stepped out of the tavern glanced at her oddly, but she ignored them.

As far as she knew, David and Sir Allan had never met, so another fear sprang up in her. What if the baronet, thinking David was just a stranger who had somehow forced his company on Gwyneth, decided to come to her aid? What if he even decided to challenge David? No, she reasoned. He would not be so foolhardy.

"The food at the Spaniard's Tavern is good enough," David said, pointing to the door Ardmore was standing beside. In front of the tavern, a coach from London was having a fresh team of horses harnessed to it.

She shook her head firmly and turned her back to it. "I do not like the looks of it. There must be another tavern."

Shaking his head, he took Gwyneth by the hand and pulled her behind him up the hill. She was horrified to see that the baronet was still standing there, watching them approach.

One man had an elegant, almost feminine look about him; the other had features sharply hewn by war and weather. Sir Allan was dressed impeccably in a style that was the height of fashion. David's clothes, though they fit him well, looked like he'd slept in them, as indeed he had. Their physical difference was the most upsetting thing, however, for they were as different as a willow and an oak. No weapons would be needed. David's bare hands would be enough to break Sir Allan in half.

As they drew near the tavern entrance, she shook her head at the baronet, covering the movement by straightening the hood of her cloak when David glanced at her suspiciously.

"Captain Pennington," she said in a loud voice. "If we must travel together, you cannot expect me to have no say in where we eat."

David said nothing, but Gwyneth didn't mind when

she saw Ardmore turn on his heel and walk away from the door. She was relieved that he had recognized the name.

There were no private dining rooms available. Looking about the tavern, she saw there were a number of ladies seated with other parties. Only half of the tables inside were occupied. She didn't care which one David chose. She also made no complaint when he ordered breakfast for both of them.

"I assume you plan to come to Gretna Green with me," she began when the serving woman went off to fetch their food. "But we must travel five days to arrive there, and you've brought no change of clothes with you. And frankly, David, you look absolutely horrid after your riotous carousing last night. You should really think of some way to amend that."

He was paying no attention to her. Instead, she realized he was studying every person in the tavern, searching for his prey. A uniformed cavalry officer, sitting alone by a window, immediately drew his attention. The man had been watching them from the moment they stepped inside. He nodded curtly at David and then turned back to his meal.

"He is already here, isn't he?" David asked in a low voice.

"No, he is not," she whispered.

"You were planning to meet him here," he asserted. " 'Twill not take five days to settle this. 'Twill take only five minutes, I should think." He rose to his feet.

Gwyneth grabbed his arm. "David, where are you going?"

"I am going to introduce myself to someone . . . unless you have something to tell me."

She shook her head. "David, I . . ."

He pulled away, moving toward the unsuspecting cavalry officer.

At that moment, the thought occurred to her that if she did not care for the thickheaded man, she might have walked out of the tavern at that very moment and escaped with Sir Allan Ardmore, who was certainly waiting in the vicinity. Instead, Gwyneth found herself dashing after David. She caught up to her self-appointed protector just as he arrived at the other man's table. The officer immediately stood. The stranger was nearly David's size. She glanced at the man's fisted hands. They appeared to be as big as hams.

"My apologies, sir," she interrupted quickly, grabbing David's arm. "My husband here has mistaken you for . . . for a brother he lost during the Seven Years War." She successfully shoved herself between them. "And yesterday, he suffered a fall from a horse, striking his head. Why, I only found him this morning. And as you can tell from his appearance, he is still somewhat confused."

"I beg your pardon?"

"Indeed, I fear he will try to fight you . . . as he enjoyed an occasional bout with his late sibling. So I am begging you to ignore whatever nonsense he says and kindly allow me to take him back to his seat."

As she turned to try to steer David away from the stranger, she realized that the officer was looking at her as if *she* were the one who had fallen on her head. She glanced up at David and found him looking at her oddly, as well.

"Captain Pennington." The man extended a hand past her to David. "I wasn't sure that was you. Seeing you out of uniform threw me, sir."

"Lieutenant Chadwick."

She felt about as intelligent as yesterday's porridge. As the two brutes chatted over her head, Gwyneth tried to edge away. But David draped an arm over her shoulder, forcing her to remain where she was. And what in heaven's name was she thinking in trying to save him? He was ruining her plans, complicating her life. She should have walked away when she'd had the chance. She should have run.

". . . Miss Gwyneth Douglas."

She realized David was finally getting around to introducing her. She looked up in embarrassment into the officer's smiling face. "I must apologize for the theatrics, Lieutenant. But my two ambitions in life are to perform on stage and to inflict severe pain on your friend, Captain Pennington. Now, if you would be kind enough to forget we ever met, I shall just slink off to our table."

Ignoring Chadwick's laughter, Gwyneth shrugged off David's arm and left the two men. Sir Allan had not returned to the tavern. She considered attempting an escape even now, but decided against it. She couldn't bear the thought of another embarrassment, as David would undoubtedly chase her around the tables if she attempted to leave without him.

The food was brought to the table, and she immediately began to eat. Her self-appointed warden didn't deserve any courtesy from her. He was quick to appear though.

"Well, is he here?" he asked, digging in to the food, as well.

Gwyneth looked around the room, hoping to find some beastly and dangerous-looking man to push him toward. Instead, she nearly choked when Sir Allan entered the tavern and sat at the next table. David's chair backed up to the baronet's.

"No," she managed to get out, wondering what she had done to deserve being surrounded by such dull-witted men. The baronet knew about Emma and her marriage to the eldest Pennington brother. He was also well aware that Greenbrae Hall was the nearest neighboring estate to Baronsford, the Pennington family seat.

" 'Twas certainly a surprise to find you in that tavern this morning, Captain Pennington," she said loudly, knowing that Sir Allan was now listening to every word.

"You mean last night. We cannot forget about last night."

She blushed despite herself and glared at him. "I would think you might forget about that, since you were hardly in full use of your senses when you arrived at my door. I believe even someone as ungentlemanly as you would not wish it known that you ended up sleeping in my bed, while I was forced to sit uncomfortably in a chair for the entire night."

"As you know, you were more than welcome to join me there." His gaze caressed her face and moved admiringly down the front of her dress. "I could have been easily persuaded to make room for you."

At any other time in her life, she actually might have been thrilled with his flirtatious manner. After all, this was David Pennington, the same man she had followed around for years like an adoring pup. The same one who had never shown any romantic interest in her, always treating her like a child . . . until now.

"I wish you would put an end to such foolishness." She leaned toward him, lowering her voice. "Your teasing could be interpreted as improper by anyone overhearing this conversation."

He leaned forward, too. "I am surprised to hear that you give a tinker's damn about propriety, considering what you were planning to do."

"You mean what I *still* plan to do," she retorted angrily.

"Of course, which brings us back to why I am here. To escort you to Gretna Green and your rendezvous, but not before I find your lover and wring the vile rascal's neck."

"You shall do no such thing."

"Indeed I shall. In fact, I am very much looking forward to meeting this lying and cheating scoundrel who hasn't the decency to ask for your hand properly, this coward who hopes to make his fortune by compromising you in such a way that you have no option but to meet his every demand. This false-hearted, two-faced . . ."

Gwyneth planted her elbows on the table and hid her face in her hands as Ardmore rose to his feet. David continued to rant, and she knew the baronet was certain to die the moment he turned to their table. He would call David out, they would fight, and Sir Allan's blood would be on her hands as surely as if she herself had run him through or put a bullet in his heart.

Her own foolishness in trying to go through with her plans after she'd been found out by David added to her guilt. She should have stayed in London. A few days would not have mattered much. The latest blackmail letter she'd received had given her a month to respond. She and Sir Allan could have rearranged their elopement for a later time.

David continued to assail her future husband's character, but Gwyneth heard no tables or chairs upended, no angry retort from Sir Allan. She peeked through her hands and found Ardmore had gone out without so much as a word.

He couldn't have.

She dropped her hands and looked around her. He really was gone. Only out of the tavern though, she quickly assured herself. Sir Allan wouldn't walk out of her life over something as insignificant as a threat. He had simply been too much of a gentleman to embarrass her here in public. Sitting back in her chair, she realized that Ardmore must have reached the same conclusion as she did herself—that they would try to rendezvous later. She looked back at the boor before her.

"I was able to tolerate your interfering much better when you were doing it silently." Despite his tirade, he'd somehow managed to finish his platter of food as well as what was left on hers. "I am ready to go."

She grabbed her cloak and tried to rise to her feet, but his large paw clamped around her wrist, forcing her back into her chair.

"You will wait until I have settled our bill with the proprietor," he said.

The rain was finished when they left the Spaniard's Tavern, and the sun shone brightly overhead. The number of people in the streets of the bustling little village had grown. She searched the faces, looking up and down the street. There was no sign of the baronet.

"I wish to return to London," she announced as they walked back to the carriage.

"Is that so? Well, we are not returning to London."

"You cannot force me to go to Gretna Green!" she

replied, her temper flaring. "I said I wish to return to my aunt. I have already realized the error of my ways. I no longer wish to elope."

A few passersby actually stopped at a discreet distance and stared at them. Gwyneth realized that those watching could only assume that he was forcing her to go through an improper marriage. This had real possibilities.

"I beg of you, Captain," she wailed louder. "Please! I cannot bear to be away from them. They'll shun me. Please return me to my family."

"No."

"But you know I am under age. I cannot marry without my family's consent. Do not force me. Please take me back to them."

"Not while you're unwed and with child, my dear." With a roguish grin, he pulled her into his arms in front of everyone. She hadn't time to recover from his outrageous lie when he kissed her hard on the lips. "Despite your ruined reputation and the fact that you are carrying some other man's child, I am gentleman enough to do the right thing."

"Why, you—"

Before she could say another word, she found herself lifted bodily and literally tossed into the carriage.

She was nothing like the saucer-eyed lassie he had once known. Outrageous, stubborn, peculiar, Gwyneth was much more of a challenge than he could have ever imagined. Despite it all, though, he was not about to back down from his threat.

During the few minutes he had spent in Lady Cavers's town house in London, David had learned that Gwyneth's aunt had left for Bristol two days earlier.

But as was characteristic of the older woman, her plans were vague. The servants did not know . . . or would not say . . . where she was staying or for how long. They only told him that, depending on the weather and the crowd in Bristol, she would consider forgoing the spa town and instead go on to the estate of one of her friends in the countryside. The only thing that had been certain about her ladyship's plans was that she would eventually be returning to Greenbrae Hall in Scotland, where Gwyneth was supposed to be awaiting her.

That was where David intended to take Gwyneth, where he would drop her in Augusta's lap.

Taking a direct route there or adding a day and a half to their travels to pass through Gretna Green was another matter entirely. In spite of his threats, he didn't care so much to hunt down the villain whom she'd planned to elope with. Not that he wasn't willing to engage the cad in a fight if they were to meet on the road. Still, it was Gwyneth's attitude in deciding against going to Gretna Green that had made the decision for David. Her fate was sealed. Just to spite her, they were going to Gretna Green and he was going to enjoy every minute added to their travels.

David watched her, sitting in the opposite corner of the carriage, her notebook open on her lap, her pencil scratching madly across the page in spite of the occasional bouncing and lurching of the carriage. Her gaze occasionally drifted off the page to the passing countryside, and a moment later returned purposefully back to the notebook.

She was quite a sight. Her red curls were in total disarray. An impish smile occasionally appeared on the corner of her sensual lips. The sprinkling of freckles on her upturned nose was more attractive than ever. One thing he'd failed to admit before now was that he was not immune to her newly blossomed beauty. There was even something quite charming in her hardheaded, forthright manner.

"You haven't given up your writing," he commented. His earlier headache was nearly gone, and his full stomach put him in much better mood. "Is it a journal you are working on or one of your old tales?"

Her green eyes met his. " 'Tis a true story, a narrative of my own life. I was just about to draw and quarter you." She went back to scratching away in her notebook.

David was tempted to reach over and steal her book and read for himself what she was writing about, but as if she were reading his mind, she quickly closed it and held it against her chest. She looked out the window. They were on the outskirts of a city.

"I see we are arriving at St. Albans," she announced, looking at him expectantly.

He glanced at the houses and shops they were passing. "I told the driver that, except for changing horses, we would make no more stops until we reached Northampton."

"I wasn't asking for anything," she replied. "I was only making the announcement for your own good. You know . . . St. Albans? Hertfordshire? Melbury Hall?"

He continued to stare at her.

She slid along the seat until she was directly across from him. "You do know about your brother Lyon's marriage, do you not?"

"Of course," he said curtly. He had received a letter from their mother about it, followed by a letter from

Lyon, himself. Lyon was recovering from his injuries after the fall from the cliffs. He appeared happy in his second marriage, which had been arranged by their mother, the dowager.

It had been a marriage of convenience for the benefit of both parties. The union had been intended to bring financial relief to Millicent Wentworth, a widow who was trying to dig her way out of the financial ruin her late husband had left her in. Lyon would gain someone to look after his injuries, and Melbury Hall, her estate just north of London, would offer him a place to live away from Baronsford.

The letters clearly led David to believe that both of them had gotten a great deal more than they had bargained for. The descriptions portrayed a state of marital bliss.

David had sent a very brief congratulatory note and had then successfully put Lyon's situation out of his mind. He had just come to prefer avoiding certain memories of his life. The death of Emma was one of them.

She had fallen from the cliffs overlooking the River Tweed at Baronsford. Lyon's badly injured body was lying next to hers when Pierce found them. He and their cousin, Walter Truscott, had been the ones who brought them up. Some called it an accident. Many thought it was murder. Lyon had been terribly injured in the fall, and the doctors had warned that the earl would most likely be crippled for life . . . however long that should be. Due to the care of his new wife, though, Lyon had ultimately recovered.

And apparently, the rumors never stopped.

Lord Aytoun had not been charged with Emma's murder, but the court of public opinion had found him guilty. And for his part, David didn't know if he would ever think of his brother without thinking of Emma's death.

Gwyneth interrupted his thoughts. "You must also know that Lord Aytoun and his new wife spend a large part of the year at Millicent's estate at Melbury Hall."

"So what are you looking for? An invitation?" he responded shortly. "I told you that we are not stopping for anything but a change of horses until we reach Northampton."

"Of all the impertinent . . . David, you are the most stubborn man that I know. I already told you that I mentioned it for *your* benefit." She shot him a narrow glare. "You are back in England, but you say nothing to anyone. Believe it or not, they all care for you so much. I attended Pierce's wedding earlier this month. Your entire family was there, but their happiness would have been so complete if you were there. Now, why could you not have come?"

"You seem to forget that I have been dutifully serving king and country in Ireland." David looked out the window again. The news of his second brother's marriage was partly responsible for the decision he'd made regarding the resignation of his commission.

When he had received his orders to report to the Massachusetts Colony, he had sensed that something was not right. There, he was to report to Admiral Middleton, a man rumored to work at the shadowy edges of military activity. David had heard other things, too, about what was happening in Boston and the other cities in the colonies. He had already heard that his brother's business transactions in Boston were being questioned. Efforts were already under way to link Pierce to the infamous Captain MacHeath, a man with a bounty on his head, who was smuggling arms by sea and selling them to the rebellious Sons of Liberty. Knowing Pierce, David suspected that his brother and MacHeath were one and the same, but that was not a thought he cared to dwell on. There was no doubt in David's mind that Admiral Middleton, who had a reputation for shrewdness, was moving him to Boston to help trap his own brother.

Despite their lack of correspondence, David was troubled by that. It was true that his duty lay with the Crown. As an officer, he had sworn to protect the interests of the British government. While in Ireland, though, he had struggled with British policies that were clearly unjust. Now, he simply would not allow himself to be used as a pawn against his own family.

While he was still considering his course of action, he had learned that the woman Pierce was marrying was a granddaughter of Admiral Middleton—a newly acknowledged granddaughter, he corrected. This put the Admiral too close to the door of MacHeath. If David were in Massachusetts and under Middleton's command, he would be expected to provide the key. Rumor and complication were piling on top of each other until it was all starting to take on the look of a tavern brawl in Belfast—no clear sides and no possibility of any bystander or participant coming out unscathed. No, it was time to step away from the fray. It was time to take his life in a new direction. David looked across the carriage at his new direction.

"When do you need to return to Ireland?" she asked.

"I am not going back. I have sold my commission."

Gwyneth made a face and slid back into the corner.

"Too bad," she said quietly, going back to her writing. "I liked you far, far better when you were not around."

Standing by their horses behind the grove of scrub oak, the three riders gazed intently at the wayside stable and the small blacksmith shop attached to it. Several small cottages and a mill clustered around the shop, and that was just about all there was to the sleepy little village.

"Are you certain this is the right one?" one of the watchers asked, motioning toward the carriage that had reined up at the stables not an hour earlier. The horses had been changed for the next leg of the journey, and the driver and the groom had finished with their pints of ale. The two stood by the carriage, inspecting the new team and talking with the burly smith and his soot-covered apprentice.

"The ruddy carriage is here when it should be," the leader replied. "And the wench fits the description." He continued to keep his eye on the young red-haired woman now standing before the open door of the carriage and talking to someone inside.

"Considerin' what we're to make on the job," the first man grumbled, "I don't see why we can't jist snuff the chit here and go get paid."

"The take is what 'tis, ye scurvy dolt," the third man said hoarsely, " 'cause they want us to put a musket ball in 'er 'ead after she's done with 'er business at Gretna Green. We do it right, and this job'll pay better'n holding up the St. Albans coach a dozen times."

"Hold there! Who're ye callin' a scurvy dolt?"

"Enough of that." The leader of the three kept his

eyes on their prey. "Biding our time, following them north, keeping enough distance to raise no suspicion, and doing the killing right is the trick."

The men moved their horses back a little as the passenger inside the carriage stepped out and stretched. He was a giant of a man, and all of them took notice that he was armed with a sword. He probably had pistols in the carriage, as well. Few traveled without a brace of loaded weapons these days. He exchanged a few words with the driver and the groom before turning to the woman.

"The bloody bull looks to be a bit much to handle, I'm thinkin'," the third man said wearily. 'Tis all to the good we were told to leave 'im be."

"He could still be real trouble, though, when we go for the chit."

"I was told nof to worry about him, lads," the leader assured them. "He should cause us no trouble."

She was a habit that—no matter how hard he tried—he could not break. Sitting in the fields by Greenbrae Hall, watching from a distance, hoping for a glimpse of her. Always trying to be where he knew she was. Still though, he kept away from the tower house for what was left of the spring—for fear of her showing up. For fear of lacking the shred of control he'd displayed the first time.

True to her way, Emma ignored him in public. She never spoke to him in the company of the others except in the most casual way. But in those few instances when they passed each other and there was no one else around, there was not even a trace of cordiality in her. When the warm, drier days of summer arrived in Baronsford, he started going back to his tower house.

She never came again. Her indifference made him begin to believe that perhaps their first kiss had been only in his imagination. He felt foolish for placing so much weight on something that obviously mattered so little to her. What he witnessed one afternoon while walking back through the deer park to Baronsford, though, changed his mind.

There were playful voices ahead. As he approached, he recognized them as belonging to Emma and David. In a clearing past the line of trees, he espied the two beside the small loch that tumbled down through a glen into the Tweed. David was lying on his back on a flat rock, gazing up at the sky. Emma was crouched beside him and laughing at something he was saying. It was an innocent scene. It was a moment like so many he'd seen the two share.

Emma's gaze riveted on him when he moved at the edge of the clearing. David said something he could not hear, but her laughter stopped. Suddenly, she sat down on the rock, her arm resting on her companion's chest, but her eyes remained focused on him.

When he saw her lower her head and kiss David's lips, he turned and ran until he could run no further.

Chapter 5

Whatever foolish, immature infatuation might have still been lingering within her toward this tall, handsome barbarian, it was gone now for sure, dissipated into thin air like a summer mist. Just who did he think he was to treat her so foully? She was no criminal. He had no right to lock her up like some wandering miscreant. She was not even *related* to him. And none of what he was doing looked in the least like protection, no matter what he said.

He was being a tyrant, pure and simple.

She continued to pace the six feet of space at the foot of the bed. She was too upset to sit, never mind sleep. The tray of food they had left on her trunk by the bed had long ago been thrown out the second story window. The horrible man did not even want to eat with her. He'd asked for her trunk to be sent up to the tiny cell that they called a room, ordered that her food be brought up to her, and then walked out, turning a massive key in an ancient lock.

She didn't know what in heaven's name she'd done to deserve this. She certainly could not understand what it was about him that had *ever* appealed to her.

Gwyneth went to the window and looked down at the narrow alleyway that ran beside the tavern. A foul smelling ditch lay beyond it, and then a muddy looking pasture. She could just see the open door of the stable behind the inn. A few buildings lay beyond that. She glanced once more up and down the alley. She could not understand why no one had answered her cries of help.

And why wasn't Sir Allan following them? She'd hoped he would leave a message with the driver suggesting a time and place to rendezvous. He could easily have come to her window now. This was the time when she needed him.

It was a very sad situation when the men who populated her stories were far more heroic than anyone she knew in real life.

Gwyneth turned away from the window and stared at the cramped and run-down condition of the room. David could not even pick a respectable tavern in which he could lock her away. They appeared to be the only travelers staying in this isolated inn on the outskirts of Northampton. When they arrived, she saw only a half-dozen drunken farmers gathered about a smoky hearth in the taproom and a portly woman who appeared to be in charge of things. From the condition of the place—including this room—she guessed that nothing had been cleaned in months. Perhaps longer.

The idea came to her almost out of desperation. Running away would be complicated. She would have no trunk. She would need to find their carriage tonight or hire another. She would need to pass through the dark streets of an unknown market town to accomplish it. But even if she were not successful, Gwyneth thought, it would be worthwhile to at least give David a scare. She might even just take another room and let him panic when he couldn't find her in the morning.

She looked again out the window at the alley below.

The narrow way was littered with stacks of wood and old ale barrels in a variety of conditions, piled up and lying on their sides, as well. What looked like a pile of straw—most likely there for the stables—was sitting near the corner of the building. There was another window next to hers and another one beyond that. She might be able to hang from the sills, work her way along, and then drop onto the straw. Even without it, though, the fall should not be too bad . . . except for the barrels.

She looked one last time for anyone passing through. No one. No one had come or gone for the couple of hours she'd been locked in there. They had no reason to. David had intentionally chosen a room that overlooked nothing.

Gwyneth tucked her notebook into her dress pocket, tied her purse around her wrist, and then, with just a quick glance behind her, started to climb out through the window.

Because of the warm summer night, the doors of the stables had been left open. The young stableboy working there had disappeared some time ago. With the exception of the occasional racket from the ill-tempered creature upstairs, the night had been still. David almost enjoyed the solitude of sitting on an upturned barrel just inside the stable door, his back against a post, waiting for what he believed was inevitable and thinking of his family.

Taking Gwyneth to Greenbrae Hall meant that he was going back to Baronsford. That too was unavoidable. His brother Pierce had told him in his letter that he and Portia intended to stay there for a few months after the wedding before making the journey back to the colonies. Since it was August, David assumed Lyon would be there, too.

Since Emma's death, his brothers had clearly moved on successfully with their lives. David considered this for a moment. He was ready to move on, as well. In fact, he had already set the wheels of change in motion. Marriage, family, the responsibilities that went along with such things had a certain appeal. None of that frightened him; he knew in order to keep the past successfully buried, he needed to cultivate the ground for a harmonious future. This meant finding a wife, of course. Even that posed no particular problem. Tasting different wines to find the one he liked, though, had never been his way of doing things. He was certainly not willing to endure the boredom of another Season in London just to see who was on the marriage market. Indeed, he had specific tastes, and that was why it was easy for him to narrow his search.

His wife would be someone that he knew. Perhaps someone who had carried a torch for him for most of her life. Someone with a reasonable income and from roughly the same station in life. Attractiveness was an asset, of course, and so was a sense of humor. A calm, patient temperament was a must, naturally, and a . . .

David jumped to his feet when he saw Gwyneth's feet emerge from her window. So he wasn't going to get everything he searched for in a wife, but he was close.

He stepped out of the stables and watched her slither out, her legs and then her shapely bottom, followed by her back and shoulders. Suddenly, she was hanging by the tips of her fingers from the window and looking around somewhat desperately.

Good, he thought, watching her with mild surprise as she reached out and successfully grasped the next windowsill. As her body swung over, though, she didn't have the strength to get a firm hold with her other hand. She was obviously going no farther. He quietly moved across the stable yard to the alleyway.

"Need help?" he called up to her.

She gasped in shock, twisted around slightly, and her fingers lost their remaining grip. He took a step forward just as she fell into his arms.

She didn't stay there for more than a second, squirming and pushing at him. And her immediate squawk of protest was loud enough to awaken every person in Northampton. He put her down but held her tightly.

"You . . . vile . . . suffocating . . . beast of a . . ."

She turned in his arms and punched him repeatedly in the chest. When she aimed her fists at his face, he managed to get hold of her wrists.

"You locked me in that room . . . without food or water." She kicked him in the shin, though the blow was largely ineffective against his boot. She tore one wrist free. "And you call yourself a friend? I am going to kill you."

Her next blow caught him on the ear. In an act of self-preservation, he tumbled both of them onto the pile of straw next to the building. After receiving a sharp knee to the vicinity of his groin, he somehow trapped what had to be her dozen limbs under his body.

"Let me go, you beast. You're crushing me. What kind of gentleman are you? I am going to murder you with an ax. I am going to strike you between the eyes and fell you like a decrepit old bull."

David couldn't stop the laughter from bursting forth. Yanking her hands above her head and holding them there, he looked down at her flushed face. "You know how to use an ax?"

"Just give me one, and I'll show you," she said threateningly, twisting under him and churning up the straw and sinking them both deeper into it.

"I shouldn't do that, if I were you," he whispered, holding both of her hands with one of his and reaching down to remove some of the straw out of her hair. The silken ringlets curled caressingly around his fingers.

"Give me one reason why I shouldn't murder you." She moved again, stretching, trying to free herself. "I don't even need an ax. A knife will do, too. Even a fork. I am not picky. I'll be very creative. I could cut out your stony heart with a spoon. But I shall make certain that you feel every bit of the pain."

"No doubt." He stared at her mouth, and his thumb gently traced her bottom lip. "Now I remember. I remember last night."

"And such a grand memory, to be sure. You and a group of your fellow rogues being so loud and obnoxious that the Lord Mayor of London himself was probably ready to send in his men." She moved her head, trying to rid herself of his touch. "If I were you, I would be trying to forget it."

"I remember what happened in your room after the innkeeper left us."

She went completely still. David touched her fevered cheeks with the backs of his fingers. She was so soft, so beautiful. He looked into her eyes. Even in the darkness of the alley, her gaze was bright and alert.

"I kissed you . . . and you kissed me back."

It seemed he couldn't stop touching her. The tips of his fingers lightly caressed her furrowed brow, the ridge of her nose. He touched her lips again. She didn't appear to be breathing. A good sign.

She finally shook off his touch, turning her face

away for a moment. "You had too much to drink last night. You mistook me for someone else."

He smiled down at her. "I'm sober now."

He brushed her lips with his own for a taste. She didn't fight him. His hold on her hands loosened, and he bent his head and kissed her again, this time delving a little deeper. A soft moan escaped her throat, and her lips opened up beneath his.

David took what she offered. He kissed her deeply, and she responded hesitantly at first. Then gradually she became bolder as he encouraged her with his lips and tongue. Her arms encircled his neck. Her breasts pressed softly against his chest. That small noise she made in the back of her throat was the most erotic sound, and his body became hard. He threaded his fingers into her hair and pulled back.

Both of them were breathless. David willed himself to think of something else—anything but the perfect fit of his body between her legs, anything but how exquisitely her breast would fit in the palm of his hand, anything but how much he wanted to tear away the clothes that separated them.

He wanted to make love to her.

He had to ask the question, though, that had been hovering in his mind. "But what of the villain you were running away with? Are you carrying his child?"

Her body immediately stiffened. She tried to push him away, but he kept her where she was.

"Indeed I am," she said fiercely, looking away again. "The bairn is due within the month."

"Do not do this to me, Gwyneth," David said more harshly than he'd intended. He turned her face until he was looking into her eyes. He gentled his tone. "Please, 'tis important for me to know."

"And would you believe anything I tell you now?"

He gently pushed a lock of hair off her brow. He rolled to his side, releasing her in case she wanted to go.

"About something as important as this," he said quietly, "of course I would believe you."

She immediately sat up. Without looking at him, she pulled angrily at the bits of straw covering her sleeves and skirt. She batted at the creases on her skirt and pushed herself to her feet.

"The answer is no," she said over her shoulder. "I am carrying no one's child."

The candles had been snuffed out. The window had been left wide open. The only light in the room was the reflected glow of the moon coloring the floor beside the bed.

Gwyneth was back to the same room she'd been trying to escape from before. She was lying on the narrow, musty bed, and fighting a very different feeling than the one she'd been struggling with before she'd gone out the window.

David was here, too. From her place, she could see him lying on the thin blanket he'd spread by the door. He'd discarded his jacket. His shirt was unbuttoned, exposing his tanned skin and curls of chest hair. One hand was tucked under his head, and his gaze was focused on a ceiling beam.

He confused her badly. She wanted to hate him. He gave her so many reasons. She could not stand his meddling, for one. But the way he'd kissed her tonight! This was no mistake caused by excessive drinking. He knew who lay under him. He knew who it was that he was kissing. The fact that he was physically attracted to her made Gwyneth burn with excitement, in spite of herself. Those few moments of lying tangled with him on the bed of straw was perhaps the most exciting thing that had ever happened to her. This was David, after all.

His question, though, had brought her tumbling back to reality. She could have lied about carrying another man's child. In fact, if she'd only been able to go through with the deceit, he might have escorted her to Gretna Green and then remained to make certain Sir Allan married her. But she couldn't.

Gwyneth understood David. She understood his family. She knew what they had gone through and how they had suffered. She could not lie to him, just as she could never bring another scandal to their door. They'd had enough to last any family a lifetime. Emma had seen to that.

David rolled to his side, and he found her awake. "You cannot sleep, either?"

She shook her head.

"Why?"

"You have been snoring too loudly."

He smiled. "I have a perfect remedy for passing the time."

An enticing warmth ignited in her belly and moved with tingling speed to the juncture of her legs. She drew her knees onto her chest and pulled the sheet more tightly around her shoulders.

"I think not, thank you." She pretended a yawn. "I can manage just fine by myself."

He chuckled as she closed her eyes. A few minutes later, she heard him roll again onto his back. She opened her eyes. He was staring at the ceiling again.

He would need only a trace of encouragement. And how much she would love it if he . . .

No, she told herself, rolling over and trying to ignore the unsettling ache within her. It was desire, she knew it, and it seemed to be growing stronger with each passing hour . . . with each passing minute.

This feeling was one that she tried to capture in certain scenes in her stories. She never imagined it to be so enticing in real life. She never thought it could be so strong.

Over the years, there were many people in London who had become acquainted with Augusta Douglas, the Countess of Cavers. A woman with pleasing looks and extravagant tastes, she attended many social gatherings but also had many friends to accompany her to functions that she might otherwise have not attended. Augusta's place within the *ton* was such that upon the death of her daughter Emma last year, she bragged to have received over five hundred letters of sympathy.

The one thing that Augusta was quite proud of, but never boasted openly about, was her awareness of everything that was happening in society. There was not a secret anywhere from London to Bath that she did not get wind of. And she took great satisfaction in the fact that she had trained her servants well to keep their ears open and to come to her immediately. People talked, gossip spread, and the rarest kinds of news were sure to reach her. She even heard that Lady North, the wife of the prime minister, had once told a friend that if Lady Cavers were in league with the French, fat old Louis would never have lost Quebec. A very satisfactory report, indeed.

Despite Augusta's penchant for being in the know, the news that arrived this morning was both surprising and distressing. She and Lady Lennox were taking breakfast in the morning room of the country house her friend kept in the hills near Bristol. Augusta's personal maid entered and quietly relayed the information that Gwyneth was back in London only a day after she'd left. The more upsetting part of this news was that Gwyneth had been accompanied by David Pennington and that they had departed inexplicably in a coach together.

"I haven't the slightest idea what that young man is doing back in England, but I do not like it," she complained to her friend, pushing her chocolate away. Unable to quell the rush of heat her temper had brought on, she snapped open her fan and waved it in agitation before her face. "The last I heard, he was with his regiment in Ireland. He has no business in calling on Gwyneth. I cannot imagine how the two of them could have possibly connected in London. Gwyneth was not planning on attending any parties or receiving any visitors. She told me herself that she was leaving directly for Edinburgh the day after I left. She was going to remain there until I arrived and from there we would travel together to Greenbrae Hall. So what, I'd like to know, is she doing back to London . . . and with someone like him as the escort?"

Still fanning herself, she rose to her feet and walked to the window for some air.

"I see no reason to worry so much, my dear," Lady Lennox said soothingly. "There could be hundreds of explanations for why Gwyneth returned to your town house when she did—and I assure you all of them understandable. As you have told me yourself many times, she is a very responsible young woman. And to my way of thinking, if there are any gentlemen who might be escorting her about town, who would be better suited than Captain Pennington? I have only had occasion to see him once or twice over the past several years, but he is quite a catch if—"

"The man is a Pennington." Augusta spat out the name as she turned away from the window. She touched her forehead and found beads of perspiration. She was so upset that she was becoming feverish. Or maybe this was more of those incomprehensible flashes of heat that she'd been afflicted with more and more lately. No, she decided it must be due to the upset that Gwyneth was causing her. "I for one have had enough of that family. I would not care if he were to become the ward of King George himself. I tell you the way the whole lot of them have been treating me has been simply horrid. They ignore me completely. And the way they neglect the memory of my daughter . . . 'tis simply unconscionable. Well, no Pennington will ever get his paws on Gwyneth's fortune, let me tell you. And between us, I believe that is exactly what they are all about. That old Methuselah, Beatrice, is surely behind this whole thing . . . scheming to take control of Greenbrae Hall and add it to the Pennington holdings. Since my poor Emma didn't inherit the estate, I always knew 'twas just a matter of time before she'd send another of those young rogues after it."

Lady Lennox sipped her chocolate and sent a doubtful glance in Augusta's direction over the edge of her cup. "Greenbrae Hall and everything that goes with it is a pittance in comparison to what that family is worth. With all of their wealth, my dear, do you really think they'd even bother—"

"Wealth?" she snapped at her hostess. "What value does wealth provide to a family so riddled with depravity? That family is the embodiment of scandal. Just because Lyon Pennington has a title and ten thousand a year, does that excuse him from murdering my daughter?"

"Really, my dear. Those . . . those were only rumors. No one saw him do it. And think of the way he was injured himself."

"I've seen better staged injuries at Drury Lane," she scoffed. "How else could he be back on his feet and walking less than a year later? And married again, too. Why, they didn't even wait a respectable period of mourning after Emma's death. Imagine, giving the title that belonged to my daughter to a plain-faced, slave-loving, impoverished woman. Why, he and his wife are already expecting a child, and my poor Emma is not even cold in her grave!"

Augusta took out a handkerchief and dabbed at the tears that spilled on her cheeks. She was relieved when Lady Lennox rushed to console her.

"You are still grieving, my dear. Time is the healer of all wounds. You should not torment yourself with such thoughts. You must let go of the past. You must try to forget."

"How can I when another Pennington is obviously forcing himself back into my life?" She turned to the window again, shedding more tears. "I wanted to be rid of Greenbrae Hall last year after Emma's death, sell it off, be done with the memory of it . . . but Gwyneth would not let me. 'Tis hers, you know. My late husband was so worried about his precious niece's future that he totally neglected to look after his own wife."

Her friend sat her down on the settee near the window. "You are distraught. You mustn't give in to these feelings. You told me yourself that you were left well provided for, my dear. You live the same lifestyle that you did before Lord Douglas passed away. You have not suffered in that way, nor should you."

"That is only because Gwyneth is not married, yet. I am forced to rely on her charity, her servants, her cast-off clothing . . ." She impatiently waved away the rest of what she was going to say. "Charles left her at least three times what he left me. Tell me what is fair about that?"

Lady Lennox, about ten years older and a widow herself, sat down beside her and gave Augusta's hand a gentle pat. "I am lost myself at how men's minds work. But you are allowing too much to depress you, and I believe you should stop worrying about what was done. Remember that Gwyneth cares for you and respects you like a mother. Whatever she has is yours . . . though I know you have your own income. Still, Gwyneth is not one to deprive you of anything now or ever." She gentled her tone. "I would have gladly forfeited everything . . . well, nearly everything . . . if I had someone as loving as that young woman to look up to me as a mother. Look at all you have, my friend. You are not alone. You never will be."

"You are right about her, of course." Augusta wiped her tears and nodded. "She is a good-hearted girl. But that is why I am so worried about her. She is too trusting, especially when it comes to those vile Penningtons."

"You do not know what the circumstances were that brought Gwyneth and Captain Pennington together like that," Lady Lennox said soothingly. "The two of them could have already gone their separate ways. You might be fretting over nothing."

"I might be," Augusta said reflectively. She rose to

her feet and looked sadly at the breakfast she had no desire to eat. "But the worry will not allow me to remain here. I fear I must desert you and journey north in pursuit of her. My mind absolutely will not rest until I know what is happening to my innocent niece."

"You are in no condition to travel without a companion."

"I have my servants."

"No, my dear. You need a friend." Lady Lennox took Augusta's hand. "We shall travel together to London, as Gwyneth might still be there. But if we do not find her there, then we shall find another friend who can escort you to Scotland."

"You are too, too kind, my good friend." Augusta dabbed at more tears before tucking the handkerchief in her pocket. "But I am causing you too much trouble."

The older lady patted Augusta's hand gently. "My dear, this is what friends are for."

Throughout the rest of the summer, his infatuation turned to hurt and then anger. Jealousy battered away at him. He could not escape it. He could not escape Emma. She was everywhere, even haunting his dreams.

There were other times when he again found Emma and David kissing each other. In the stables. In the deer park. On the bluffs overlooking the Tweed. Their swims in the loch or in the river no longer appeared to him to be so innocent. She made certain that he knew where she had been, and with whom she'd been alone.

He was not rising to her bait, though. She was playing a game—trying to punish him for pushing her away. He knew she expected him to take out his frustra-

tion on David, to challenge him and fight him. But he wouldn't. He knew David had as little to do with all of this as he did himself. No, this was Emma's doing.

Besides, he was happy where he was. He had a home. He had been given a second family. He even had the possibility of a good future. He had much more now than his own family had ever given him. And he was not about to give it up. Not for Emma. Not for anyone.

With his mother gone, his father, Sir William, had long ago given up caring for his two sons. Deep in debt after decades of drinking and gambling and womanizing, Sir William was seen occasionally in London. At sixteen, Walter's elder brother had boarded a ship for the American colonies. The younger boy's salvation had been his father's half sister, Beatrice Archibald Pennington, the Countess of Aytoun.

No, indeed. Walter Truscott was not about to ruin the chance he'd been given by this family years ago. He was determined to not become a pawn in Emma's hand.

Chapter 6

⌒

"The doctor ye sent from Melrose arrived before suppertime, Mr. Truscott," the cotter's wife explained as Walter dismounted from his horse. It had rained most of the night, and his boots were covered with mud from his morning's travels. He scraped what he could from them. "The old gentleman looked in on her and said the bairn was coming . . . as if I couldn't have said so myself. He said it looked to be far too early, though. Either that or the bairn would just be a wee thing. The midwife came before dark, and we stayed with the poor lass through the night. 'Twas to nae avail, sir."

"What happened?" he asked impatiently, fearing the answer.

As the woman shook her head, he walked quickly to the open doorway of the cottage. The place where she had lain was empty. The cotter's wife had cleaned out all traces of the visitor.

"The wee lassie was stillborn," she said, standing at his side.

He leaned a hand against the doorjamb. Giving birth was risky business. Many healthy and well-to-do women died in childbirth every day. He should have known someone like her would have little chance of surviving. What he couldn't understand was how she had cast a spell on him so quickly. Last night, in his rooms at Baronsford, he hadn't been able to stop thinking of her. All morning, as he went about his business around the estate, he'd found himself continuing to worry about her.

And it had all been for nothing.

"We asked the poor lass about a husband or other kin, but she'd say naething of them to us. So my Jamie dug her a wee grave right outside the kirkyard of the auld ruined kirk. Buried the bairn in unconsecrated ground, we did. It would've been much better for the young mither, though, if she'd have stayed away. In her condition—"

Truscott turned away from the door. "The woman is still alive?"

"Aye, sir. For now, at least."

"Where is she?"

The cotter's wife pointed along the path. "She went up to the kirkyard . . . just o'er the brae. I warned her about the fever and the need for her to be staying put, but she'd have none of it. The lass got up and took herself off to the bairn's grave. There was nae holding her, sir. I went up there myself before noon to look on her and to take her some water." The woman's voice cracked. " 'Twould break yer heart, to be sure, to see her just lying there keening and moaning o'er the wee pile of dirt, rocking herself like she had the bairn in her arms and weeping all the while."

Walter started for the hill.

"I have bedding laid for her in the shed if ye can bring her back, sir," the old woman called after him. "Yer doctor from Melrose said she should stay put.

The lass has eaten naething and drunk less since the bairn came."

It took only a few minutes to reach the base of the hill. This young woman—whatever her name was and wherever she came from—was still alive. Suddenly, he felt like a man who had been given a second chance. He didn't know for what purpose, but the feeling was real and strong within him.

Walter's shadow lay on the hill ahead of him as he climbed through patches of heather and long grass. Beyond the rock-studded crest he could see the top of the ancient gray stone of the deserted kirk's squat tower. Past the tower, heavy clouds of even darker gray were rolling toward them.

It was a desolate place, that kirkyard on the hill. A low stone wall separated the consecrated ground from the vast moors of the Border highlands. A stunted, twisted pine stood alone against the rising wind, and a chill went through him. It was a cold wind for this time of year, and Walter knew the rain would be cold, as well.

He had no difficulty spotting the grave, a small mound outside the wall near the pine tree. The ragged bundle of a woman lay over the black dirt, obscuring much of it. Part of the blanket she had wrapped around her had fallen away, and the gray cloth flapped in the wind, keeping a strange rhythm with the pine boughs above.

There were no sounds coming from her, no movement as Walter approached. Anxiety again gripped him, for she lay there over the freshly packed grave as unmoving as the dead. He stopped a few feet away from her.

"The air smells of the rain," he said for the sake of something to say. He took another step closer. Her cheek was pressed against the dirt. Her eyes were open, and he saw the tears that were streaming down and soaking into the dark soil. She was looking directly at him, but Walter didn't think she saw anything.

"You cannot stay here all day and night, lass," he said softly, crouching down beside her. He took the end of the blanket and tucked it gently around her shoulder. "The cotter's wife tells me she has a place ready for you down there. You can come back here again tomorrow morning."

She didn't respond. Her blue eyes, brimming with tears, stared vacantly into space. Hesitantly, Walter reached out and touched her cheek. She immediately recoiled from his touch. The gesture brought as much relief to him as distress. At least she'd moved, he reasoned. She'd responded to something besides the grief that was gripping her.

"I'll not hurt you," he said quietly. "The same goes for the old cotters down the hill. We only want to help you."

The blankness in her gaze returned. Walter looked around at the countryside again, at the wild rolling hills. The heather was in bloom, its subdued purple lending color to the pale green of the summer grass. The same scenery that would be breathtaking on any other day looked barren now. He couldn't leave her here. At the same time he would not force her to desert her newly buried bairn. The woman needed to work through her grief. He knew about that.

He sat down on the hard ground and leaned his back against the low wall. With his legs stretched before him, he picked up a fistful of the freshly turned dirt.

" 'Tis good to cry, lass. 'Tis important to let your

suffering out when 'tis crushing your soul. In fact, I'm thinking that the way you are dealing with your loss is far better than I might be doing," he said thoughtfully, letting the dirt sift through his fingers. "You do not know me, but in my lifetime I've lost more people than I care to count. Still, never have I been able to face my loss when it happens. I've always buried my pain, thinking that's the manly way, only to have it come back and haunt me later. That's the way of it for me—just let it sit inside me, festering . . . ugly and painful . . . like an ancient sore."

Walter took another fistful of dirt and let the cold dampness of it penetrate through his skin. "Then I end up doing foolish things. Things I regret later. But it feels like a chain that I've wound around me, growing heavier all the time."

The end of the blanket had loosened and was again flapping in the breeze. Walter reached over and tucked it around her shoulder. She had not moved. The tears still glistened on her mud-streaked face. He noticed her blue gaze was now focused on his face.

"I am Walter Truscott," he said quietly. "I should like to know your name."

She gave no answer, did not move, gave no indication that she even understood what he'd said.

"I do not know who your kin are, or where they might be. But the people that we think left you at the cotter's door two nights ago must be far away by now. Still, you should not worry about what is going to become of you. Those good people down the brae have offered you a place to stay for as long as it takes you to heal. And after that, if you are willing to work, I can find you a decent job if you want it."

Walter didn't know why he'd said that. He didn't

even know if anything he'd said made any sense to her. He doubted she cared right now what would become of her. He doubted that she cared whether she lived to see another sunrise or sunset.

"I know you're listening to me. As I said, you are teaching me a good lesson about how to grieve. But I want you to pay attention to what I say now, for I could teach you a thing or two about the importance of holding on to life."

Despite her earlier reaction, he reached out and pushed a few strands of the dirty blond curls off of her brow. His fingers fleetingly brushed against her cold skin. This time she did not recoil.

"You might not think it now—as I could not imagine it when I was feeling wretched myself—but there are people out there who need us. People who count on us. People who are waiting to meet us someday . . . waiting for us to make a difference in their lives." He raised a knee and rested his elbow on it. "I'm a believer that we each have a purpose in this life. We are born to do some good. But life is never easy. Our roads are never too clear. Most of the time, we just stumble though the darkness, we fall into the ditches. We feel deeply the cuts and blows of man and nature. We make wrong decisions. We sometimes find ourselves on the wrong road entirely. But we have to somehow work our way through, find our way back. We have to believe that the final reward is worth it. We have to work through the challenges and find our destiny."

The first droplets of rain fell on them. The wind was picking up, beginning to whistle through the pine boughs. The dark clouds now sealed off the sky. Walter leaned toward her and placed a gentle hand on her shoulder, waiting for her reaction. She again did not flinch.

"Did I mention the blows of nature?" he asked. "Those storm clouds promise to soak us to our bones. Now, I am not about to leave you up here alone. If you stay, I am staying. You may already have a fever, lass, but I want you to understand something. If I end up spending the night out here with you, I am sure to catch the same thing, which will cause a number of good folk a great deal of trouble. So why don't you come down with me. You can come back up again tomorrow. And the day after, as well. As many days as you wish."

She said nothing, but her gaze remained on his face.

"I do not want to put too much pressure on you, but think for a moment how troubling 'twould be for those two old folk down there . . . and for me . . . to have you lying out here in the cold and rain. I already told you I am staying. But knowing Rita, she's sure to be fussing over you and me and bringing us food. Now, old Angus is not about to stay down there alone, and he'll be climbing up the brae, too. In the end, they'll both be wet and probably catch their death. If you persist in staying here, lass, you'll be putting those two old cotters' lives in danger."

Either she'd heard what he was saying or she was sick of listening to him talk. No matter what it was that spurred her, Walter's heart rose when she very slowly pushed herself into a sitting position. The rain and wind began to whip at them. He immediately moved next to her, not wanting to scare her but ready to help her if she let him.

She sat there for a while, staring at the small mound where her bairn lay. Walter stayed there beside her, allowing her to gather her thoughts and her strength. Some time passed before she raised her face to him, and Walter realized that this was the first time she was really looking at him—perhaps even seeing him.

She looked even younger now than he had thought—and much more vulnerable. She was clearly ill, and he wondered for the first time if she would survive the difficult birth.

"Let me help you," he asked her gently, extending a hand.

She looked at it, but then, on her own, she started pushing herself to her knees. He stood up. The wind swept the blanket off her shoulder. He reached down to grab it as she sank back down onto the dirt.

Kneeling beside her again, Walter was relieved to find her conscious, but she was obviously exhausted. The rain was falling hard now. Tucking the blanket over her, he scooped her into his arms.

Her eyes were open, and she watched everything he did. If she intended to complain, she was too weak to voice it. Carrying her in his arms, he started down the hill. She was a small thing, a rain-soaked bundle of rags. Still though, she had the most unusual effect on him. He felt with each passing moment some invisible threads drawing them closer together. Perplexing as it was, he welcomed the sensation.

"You would not think it, after all I've been saying, but I am thought of as a quiet sort of man. A man of very few words, they tell me. But of course, I have never had such a pleasant audience. By that I mean, someone who is so agreeable to everything I say."

She closed her eyes. She was not ready for humor. Walter could understand that. She needed to get well. He lifted her higher in his arms, gathering her closer against his chest, and almost smiled as she laid her head against his shoulder.

There was a growing crispness in the air with each successive morning. Summer was sliding inevitably into autumn. Having been caught in heavy fall rains the preceding year as they traveled south, the Douglas family had decided to leave Greenbrae Hall early this year. The servants were ready to close most of the manor house. When they were gone, only a caretaker and a few servants would remain behind.

Carriages and carts were stuffed with trunks and servants and Lady Cavers was just being handed into her new chaise, when someone noticed that Emma was missing. A groom was sent out to Baronsford, but she was not there, to everyone's surprise.

Neither David nor Pierce had seen her for at least two days. Lyon had been absent since the spring with his regiment. When Walter heard she was missing, he slipped away. He knew where she was.

He found her there at the tower house. All of the reprimands and hard words he'd planned to berate her with withered away when he saw her. Emma's eyes were swollen practically shut. Streaks of dirt covered her face. Her hair and dress were a mess. She was sitting alone, hugging her knees in a corner of the cold fireplace in the Great Hall, looking as if she'd done without food or water for some time. Upon seeing him, she simply turned her face to the stone and continued to cry.

"What happened to you? What is wrong?" He did the only thing he was capable of doing. He went to her and sat beside her, and she immediately moved into his arms.

"I hate them. I hate all of them. 'Tis unbearable to live with them. No one understands me. No one cares for me. No one wants me. I am a burden to them all."

"A burden to whom?" he asked, already guessing this had to do with the sometimes open animosity that existed between Lord and Lady Cavers. Emma had spoken of it often over the past few years. It was because of them that she preferred to be at Baronsford. She had told him many times how she envied the harmony that existed in the Pennington family.

"My parents," she explained. "My father was going to Edinburgh, and my mother to London. And I overheard them. I've known for a long while, but I never heard his lordship say it openly before."

"Say what, Emma?"

She hesitated, and then looked up at Walter. "He cares not where I go, for he does not believe I am his."

"In the heat of an argument, many things are said that are not truly meant," he replied gently. "He does not mean it."

"He does," she said tearfully. "They did not know I could overhear them. I heard his lordship accuse my mother. She denied nothing, even when he said I was just the wild product of one of Augusta's affairs. He accused her of the vilest things, and she laughed in his face."

He could think of no proper answer.

"Walter, he will disinherit me," she wept, pressing her head against his shoulder. "Then what is to become of me?"

Chapter 7

With any luck, they would reach Stoke-on-Trent soon. She'd asked David about it and had received the answer when a particularly bad stretch of road had forced her to put aside her writing. That had been the extent that Gwyneth trusted herself to converse with him.

She could admit—at least to herself—that he was making her nervous. The nearness placed upon them by the close confines of the carriage was getting to her. The memory of last night's kiss, so vividly alive in her imagination, was not helping either. Whatever the reason, she was struggling against her inner chaos, and she was having great difficulty pretending to be indifferent to his presence.

Casual conversation was out of the question. When David was awake, she pretended sleep. When he dozed, she forced herself to stare out at the passing countryside, fighting all the while her desire to watch him. When they both were awake and she could no longer pretend sleep, she kept her notebook open, writing intently. Of course, she did not think for a moment that anything she was writing would make any sense. Still, it made her look busy and discouraged communication. She knew it was her fault that even the stop they made for a noon meal had been marked by a strained silence. She couldn't help it.

David was not making things any easier for her, either. Today, he had not once ordered her about. And during the long stretches of silence, while she was trying to immerse herself in the tale she was writing, she found him watching her . . . as he was doing now. This made embers grow hot in Gwyneth's stomach while her body tingled in unmentionable places.

"Do you think they might possibly have a tub at the inn in Stoke-on-Trent?" he asked.

The image was too provoking. Gwyneth decided not even to acknowledge the question.

"Maybe they'll have one made of bloody china."

She stole a quick glance at him but didn't respond. She seriously doubted that Mr. Wedgwood's pottery works made tubs for bathing.

"If they haven't one, I may just go for a swim at the Trent to wash off this dust. Perhaps you'd care to accompany me."

His long legs were stretched out on an angle across the space between the seats. He'd discarded his jacket sometime early in the warm afternoon and rolled up his sleeves, displaying muscular arms marked with evidence of his former profession. He had not shaved for the two days they'd been traveling.

She wondered if he planned to take a room for himself tonight. He *must,* Gwyneth quickly answered herself. She could feel the heat rise in her face, though. To hide it, she turned her gaze out the window at the passing scenery. She assumed they were very close to Stoke-on-Trent.

"How do you think your beau would feel about you and me sharing a single room?"

Involuntarily, Gwyneth shot a look at him. He had

a roguish expression on his face, if ever she had seen one. She looked down at the notebook on her lap.

"How he feels about you, I should not care to say. But as to his feelings about me, once I explain the circumstances of last night, I am certain he will understand the situation I was forced to endure . . . and my inability to change any of it."

"But what about tonight, and tomorrow night? How are you planning to explain sharing a bedchamber with me for the entire trip?"

Her brain was insisting on arguing the impropriety of his suggestion, but her body was rebelling against it. Reason versus passion. Lord, she thought, she'd become a philosophical argument on two legs. Luckily, she was still able to fight down her body's impulses . . . so far.

"And furthermore, last night I found the floor too bloody hard to sleep on."

"David, you must make separate arrangements. It is totally unseemly for us . . . for you and me . . . we cannot travel in such a manner."

"You had no thought for decorum when you were planning the elopement."

"That was then. This is now."

He shook his head. "After what you tried to pull last night—trying to escape through your window—you have left me no choice but to keep a constant eye on you."

"You are *not* my keeper, David."

With a smug look, he crossed his arms over his chest. "Say what you will, I cannot leave you to yourself and allow you to wreck your future, Gwyneth. You are the one who has forced this need for vigilance on my part."

For the sake of maintaining her sanity, she wanted

to argue his point. Arrogant. Stubborn. High-handed. Belligerent. All of these words were rattling about in her head. At the same time, though, she knew there was no purpose in it. David had the look of a man resolved to do what he saw as his duty. Where this sense of duty sprang from, however, she had no idea.

"And you still haven't told me how you are planning to explain this to your beau."

"No explanation will be required. I have been given no choice in any of this, have I?" She closed her notebook and held it tightly against her chest. "Considering the unfortunate circumstances I find myself in, he will certainly understand."

"He is a very understanding fellow, of course. Cowards always are."

She told herself she wasn't going to be baited.

"And obviously naive, too, to think *nothing* could happen between us after so many days together."

"*Nothing* has," she said with alarm. "And *nothing* will."

David's blue eyes focused on her mouth and Gwyneth felt herself growing flustered all over again. If she could only quell these remnants of her childhood infatuation and see him as the bully he was trying to be now.

"Deny it all you will. We may yet prove that wrong."

"A gentleman would know from my refusal that I despise your attentions."

He moved one knee just enough to brush it against hers. "If the way you kissed me back last night . . . and the night before . . . are any indication of your aversion, then you have done an excellent job of fooling me."

She could create pages of stories each day, but she

could not think of a proper lie now when her sanity most depended on it. There did not seem to be a flippant return in her repertoire of jaunty retorts. Her body, her face, her heart, and now her tongue were all traitors. Gwyneth pulled from him, pressing her knees against the door of the carriage. She opened her notebook and focused on the words she'd written today.

Considering all she was going through, it was fairly good. Excellent material to lose herself in, too, she thought. All blood and gore. Not a sensitive word or a passionate passage.

The vengeance of heaven shall surely overtake the wicked! The blood of—

Gwyneth yelped in protest when David snatched the notebook out of her hands. She dove after it across the seat, but he managed to sweep her to the side, staying her with one arm as he held the open notebook with the other hand.

"Give it back to me this instant, you blackguard." She tried to reach around him. "You have no right to read my private writing."

"I have given you more than enough opportunity to share your work with me."

"But I don't care to."

"But you did at one time in our lives."

"Because I liked you then. But I do not anymore. In fact, I am growing to hate you. Now give that back to me." Gwyneth struggled to reach around him again, but she froze when David's lips pressed against her neck. The unexpectedness of it made the fight drain out of her. The breath caught in her chest, and she felt suspended in midair when his lips moved down to the neckline of the dress. A moment later, he was nibbling on her earlobe.

"You taste quite good."

She moved her face slightly toward him, and David's mouth was there.

The kiss was hot and consuming, and Gwyneth's body caught fire when David lifted her onto his lap. Her arms closed around his neck, and his mouth was relentless. There was no holding back. She couldn't. She poured all her frustration and temper into the fervor of the kiss, trying to punish him for what he was doing to her. But she ended up punishing herself, as her body strained for more. She couldn't explain it, didn't try to understand it, but she ached to be closer. She wanted to touch and be touched. David's hands were all over her back, her sides, pressing her against him. She was suddenly aware of the bulge of his hardening manhood beneath her.

She couldn't deny it. There was no ignoring how his touch made her feel. Gwyneth's mouth feasted on him ravenously, and she let out a soft cry of satisfaction when his hand cupped and gently squeezed her breast. The reality was so much sweeter than her imagination. The insatiable excitement rushing through her surpassed anything she could have dreamed.

"After today, you can never say there is *nothing* between us," he growled, tearing his mouth away. His teeth scraped against the sensitive skin of her neck. "And I promise the pleasure you'll feel when I make love to you will make you forget any fumbling attempts you have had to endure from that cowardly dolt of yours."

His words were like a bucket of ice water over

flames. Gwyneth froze when he reached for the hem of her skirt. He captured her mouth under his lips, but she pulled her face away, crying out softly as she felt his palm touch the bare skin of her leg and move upward.

Breathless, she knew that she had to stop him. At the same time she was lost for words. His hand was on the inside of her leg, her skirts were pushed up, her skin burned from the excitement . . . but her mind was racing.

"David!" she gasped.

He thought she was experienced in these things. He assumed that she had already had a relationship with the man she was eloping with.

"You are as soft as silk." His lips were again on her neck, his palm moving ever slowly upward.

"David . . . no," she whispered. "I never have . . ."

His hand reached the juncture of her thighs, and she would have leapt from his lap if his other arm were not looped tightly around her. She grabbed for his wrist, forcing reason to pierce the haze of passion fogging her mind.

"Please, do *not*!" Gwyneth managed to get out. His fingers stilled. She forced herself to look into his eyes. "Despite . . . what you assume . . . about me, I have never done this. No one has ever touched me. I've never gone down this path before."

His hand withdrew, gently pulling the skirts down her legs again. Her face was burning. She moved off his lap, but he didn't let her get too far away. Holding on to her wrist, he kept her beside him. Gwyneth thought she would die of embarrassment, but she had to speak her mind.

"What is happening between us . . . I cannot deny

my attraction to you. I cannot deny how I have felt toward you for most of my life. But this physical . . . whatever 'tis . . . is happening too fast. I am confused by it, terrified by it, and I do not think 'tis wise for us to encourage it . . . or to let it control us."

A knot rose in her throat, choking off her words. She looked away, unable to withstand the intensity of his gaze. The contradiction between how she was behaving and what she was saying now was mystifying and confusing. She didn't want to think how deceitful he must imagine her to be. She wondered if he thought she was lying now.

"Explain to me why you were eloping with this man."

She hadn't expected the question. Still flustered over what had almost happened between them, she looked away. There were no coherent thoughts in her head. She could not chance explaining everything to him, not at a moment like this when chaos ruled her.

"You are not with child. He has not taken any liberties with you. What hold does he have over you?" he asked impatiently. His face suddenly changed. "Is it possible that you were running away because you love him?"

Gwyneth stared at his large hand still encircling her wrist. "Could we please not talk about this now?"

"Then when can we talk about it?"

Never, she thought. Or at least not until the deed was done and she was married to Sir Allan Ardmore.

"I am not going to let this go, Gwyneth. If you really believe eloping with a potential fortune hunter is the right course, then why not explain it to me? You cannot tell me you love him."

It was impossible to ignore the temper still icing his

tone. "I shall explain it to you . . . but not now. Not after what . . . what we almost did. I need time to think, to shape the reasons in my mind so that you can understand them. 'Tis much easier just to do things than to try to explain them."

"Explain later if you must. But I need one word for an answer. Do you love him?"

She wished she could lie. "No."

David stared at her for several moments, then released her wrist. They rode along quietly for a while, each gathering their thoughts. Gwyneth did not look at him, but she could feel his gaze on her.

After a while the silence became vexing, and she found herself searching for a way to distract David. She did not want to talk about Ardmore. At the same time, she knew how quickly the spark between them ignited. They were sitting too close to each other. She glanced around and saw her notebook lying facedown on the seat opposite them.

"You said that I have not read you what I am writing. Would you like me to read some of it to you now?"

She waited anxiously and tried to not wither beneath his glare. He took his time. He made sure she suffered as long as possible. Finally, he reached over and picked up the notebook. "Can I take this as meaning that you've decided to like me again?"

Gwyneth almost let out a sigh of relief. Looking up into his face, she was relieved to see him piecing together a smile. "I believe you already know the answer to that."

She took her book and quickly opened it to the last page, to what she'd been working on today.

"I shall only read you this page, which opens in the

middle of a story about a missing ship and crew. Here, the old father of the missing captain arrives at a tavern and meets an ancient mariner who may have some information." Gwyneth tried to look over the page quickly to make sure it was proper to read. The havoc inside her was slowly receding. They had come so close.

David snatched the notebook out of her hand again. "You've explained it enough. I should like to read it myself."

She reached for her work, careful not to lean over him for fear of getting back to where they'd started. "But 'twould be much better if I—"

"I think 'tis in your best interest for me to keep my hands occupied right now."

He was right. Gwyneth quickly withdrew and edged away from him as David focused on the written page.

"I have not had a chance to read it over," she said as a way of excusing any fault he found with her work.

"Then I shall read it aloud." His gaze dropped from her face to the page.

" 'The vengeance of heaven shall surely overtake the wicked! The blood of the murdered will rise in judgment against the murderer.' "

The old sailor took the visitor by the hand and led him to the window. He pointed to the ship lying in the harbor directly opposite the house and continued in a low whisper.

" 'See ye that old, black, hell-smoked hulk? Well, there has been a deed done aboard that cursed vessel, during this last voyage, that was enough to have sunk her to the lowest depths of perdition. 'Tis a marvel beyond all comprehension that, since the sea has not engulfed us, the ground has not opened up and swallowed us since we come ashore!' " His voice sank even lower. " 'Oh, 'twas a foul deed! We did it with hatchets. We struck them down, one after the other, like bullocks. We clove their skulls, bespattering our bulwarks with their brains, and drenching our decks with their—' "

David looked up at her. "With their . . . ?"

"With their blood." She looked up at him mischievously. "I shall tell you another secret. Do you know who they were that we butchered with our hatchets?"

David nodded. "Tell me."

" 'Twas . . ." She leaned toward him in the seat, squinting one eye like an old seadog. " 'Twas Captain Pennington. The same Captain Pennington of Baronsford. The very man who has been a thorn in my side from the moment I ran into him in London." She took the notebook out of his hand and closed it with a snap. "I had no choice. I had to teach him a lesson."

His laughter filled the small space of the carriage.

David's reaction to her work pleased Gwyneth greatly. She had already established a growing audience for her work out there—according to a very happy publisher—but she had no personal connection with the people who were reading her tales. No one that she could hear laugh at the humorous moments. No one whom she could see lean forward expectantly . . . as someone reading aloud paused to draw a breath.

She received no letters from admiring readers. No one knew the identity of the anonymous writer of the tales printed by Mr. Ruddiman.

One person knew, Gwyneth quickly reminded herself. She moved across the seat again. The blackmail notes had started arriving at Greenbrae Hall this past spring. She'd received three of them so far. The villain knew her identity, knew where she lived, knew who was her guardian, knew how much she was worth, and—worst of all—seemed to know the damage the truth would mean to her life.

The blackguard's demand for keeping quiet was a fortune, and he was asking for money that she did not have. But even if she had already come into her inheritance and could part with such a large sum, she would not do it. She knew that tomorrow there could be some other rogue making the same claim on her . . . and another the day after that.

The only answer to her problems lay in becoming invulnerable to such charges. That kind of protection came only with marriage to a man who was unaffected by scandal. She needed someone who would benefit by their union as much as Gwyneth. Someone financially in need—but with few expectations otherwise from a wife. She needed a man who would be satisfied to think of their union as a business arrangement in which he would be allowed to pursue his own interests and she hers.

These were some of the reasons why Sir Allan was perfect for her. By the provisions of her uncle's will, once she was married Gwyneth would inherit what was coming to her. At the same time, the will stipulated that she could lose her entire fortune if any scandal touched her while she was still unmarried. To be sure, Charles Douglas, the Earl of Cavers, had his own reasons to be doing things—including making her an heiress—but Gwyneth had wondered more than once what lay behind his decisions. Nonetheless, that was the situation in which she now found herself.

"When you were younger, your cleverness in weaving together stories and in making these characters seem so real always impressed me." David smiled at her. " 'Tis almost impossible to imagine, but you have become even better at it over the years." He extended his hand toward her. "More! You *must* allow me to read more."

Gwyneth drew the book protectively to one side. "Very sorry . . . but you, sir, are dead. I killed you in my story. You have no need to know any more."

A look of challenge lit up his eyes, and she feared he would force the notebook out of her hand.

"Honestly, there is no more," she explained quickly. "That is as much of the story as I can show you. The rest of what I wrote today consists merely of scribbled notes to myself."

"What about the pages leading up to this?"

"They are not ready to be seen. But I promise to let you finish reading it once I am done."

His arms crossed over his chest. After a moment of consideration, he nodded, apparently satisfied, but his handsome blue eyes remained focused on her face. Gwyneth felt every inch of her skin tingle from the brush of his gaze. She pretended to not be affected by it and turned her attention out the window of the carriage.

"You have other tales in that portfolio, too, if I am not mistaken."

She couldn't read them to him . . . not any of them straight through, anyway. She gave a halfhearted nod in answer.

"And you have other books and many more tales written in them, is that not true?"

Gwyneth looked back at David. For few seconds her heart racéd in her chest. With the prospect of telling him the truth, a thrill swept through her. To share with someone—with David—the story of her success would be a dream come true. In slightly over a year, she had sold eight of her tales. And due to popularity of them, Mr. Ruddiman was eager to buy more. She just had to write them.

"I have known other women who were fond of keeping diaries and such things, and letter writing is an art to some, of course. You, however, weave volumes of tall tales." He shook his head. "That is quite different."

As she was growing up, Gwyneth had never thought of her writing as having anything to do with conformity. It had nothing to do with anyone else. Even though she had been teased somewhat for her love of making up tales, stopping was never a consideration.

"You know that this is something I have always done. Writing down the stories that form in my mind is part of who I am."

"I understood that when you were young and parentless. Even then, I recall thinking that you sometimes had a fantasy world that you escaped to—a secret garden. I knew it must have been difficult to come and live with an aunt and an uncle that you did not know." He stretched his legs before him, but his eyes were fixed intently on her face. "I thought 'twas wonderful that in your mind you could substitute the kindness of a fairy for the touch of a mother and conjure a heroic king for the father whom you had lost. I remember, even then, thinking that making up stories was a good thing for you."

"But you no longer think that?" Gwyneth said a bit defensively.

David shrugged. "It all depends."

"On what?"

"On what you allow to go undone now during those hours—no, days—that you lose yourself to the fantasies you are creating."

"I have no commitments that are left unfulfilled. Augusta happens to be my only relative living, and she rarely needs or desires my company. If I do not busy myself with socializing, no one is harmed by that. Besides, I have never been very good at sitting around gossiping with other women about people or about the latest fashions. So, whatever time I spend pursuing this thing I enjoy deprives no one of my company."

"I disagree. You are now an adult, Gwyneth. Rather than balking at society, you should consider embracing it. You need friends, female companions, and even *I* know that not all the young women out there are as shallow as you make them out to be. By the way, did you involve yourself at all in what London had to offer this Season?"

She rolled her eyes and looked out the carriage window.

"Did you?"

"Of course . . . once or twice. I went to the theater several times. I saw Garrick in *King Lear*. I went to the opera once and to a reception at . . . well, it doesn't matter."

"The men must have been falling over each other to dance with you."

"If you must know, the young men of the *ton* are worse than the young women."

"So in the months you were in London, you really allowed yourself very little opportunity to meet others. Which means that you spent too little time outside of your shell. You didn't give anyone a chance to get close . . . except one fortune-hunting fraud."

David reached out and tugged on one of her curls, drawing her gaze back to him. The gesture reminded her of the way he used to treat her—like a younger sister or an innocent young friend, someone to whom he could give brotherly advice. She resented it.

"Gwyneth, you are a very attractive young woman, in addition to being an heiress with a good name. 'Tis time you moved beyond this whimsical world of yours. Instead of the nonsense you spend your time on, you should be thinking of the hard and fast realities of your future."

Bristling at his words, she made no attempt to mask her anger. "And what makes you believe that I do not think of such things?"

"Eloping, for one." He leaned forward, planting his elbows on his knees. His expression showed his irritation, as well. "If you were paying attention to the present instead of wandering around lost in the romantic, adventurous worlds of your Highlanders and pirates and such, then you might have a chance of behaving like any other sensible young woman. You certainly wouldn't let some penniless rogue fool you. Do you not see the scandal you will be subjecting yourself to? And what 'twill cost you?"

"I know what I am doing. And there will be no scandal," Gwyneth said in defense of her actions. "We shall be married and that will put an end of any talk . . . if there is any. And for your information, I am not some flighty dreamer. I happen to know the details of the conditions of my inheritance better than anyone. My uncle's lawyers cannot deprive me of what is coming to me if I am married."

"So *this* is why you are doing it," David snapped angrily. "You are marrying to get your hands on your inheritance?"

"No!" she answered, hearing the frustration in her own voice. "We were arguing about my writing, not about the man I am to marry. I am not desperate for my inheritance. In fact, I care little about it."

"More proof that you are lost in dream world and do not see what is happening in your life."

"Why? What now?" Gwyneth leaned forward, meeting David's fierce glare. "Pray tell me, since you know everything, what have I said wrong now?"

"You *should* care about what is coming to you. Your uncle thought you were intelligent enough to leave a fortune to. 'Tis your responsibility to know how to take care of it rather than simply allowing some weasel of a husband to steal it away."

"I do not inherit until I wed, which tells you even my adoring uncle believed that I, as a young woman, am incapable of caring for my own affairs. So my husband can do as he pleases," she said out of spite. "He is not stealing it. In fact, if he wants to gamble and lose my inheritance, he is welcome to do so. I am not concerned about it, I cannot see why you should be."

"You are just being a brat and you know it. You have known no hardship in your life, never gone hungry a day, but you have no means of supporting yourself other than this inheritance. Do you have any written contract to protect you? No. Has your dog of a future husband agreed to any settlement that will provide for you? No. One day soon, you *will* care what the scoundrel will do with your money, but by then 'twill be too late."

"I think not," she said, forcing herself to be calm.

"In the event of such dire circumstances as you imagine, I shall have no difficulty supporting myself."

He gave her an incredulous look. "By what means?"

"By publishing my tales."

His bark of laughter lacked any hint of mirth. "And that would be a scandal of some note."

She should not have been hurt. She had known this would be his reaction. Still though, it took a great deal of effort to hide her feelings. Gwyneth shrugged and forced herself to smile, lifting her chin bravely.

"I do not care what the world thinks. If you are correct, and my inheritance is stolen and lost, my life shall not be ruined. I shall have a husband who will not mind at all if I can bring more money into our marriage. And I *shall* provide another source of income. In doing so, I shall be free to spend all of my time in the wonderful worlds that my imagination creates. I shall live my life doing what I love . . . writing."

"You call that wonderful?"

"I call it heaven."

"I call it hell," David grumbled as the carriage rolled to a stop before the inn at Stoke-on-Trent.

He didn't see her for nine long months, but when she returned, Truscott saw much had returned of the young Emma whom he had befriended long ago.

He could tell she cherished his trust and friendship. She stole away many afternoons during the summer to be with him at the tower house. He was relieved that Emma stopped trying to tempt him. No kissing or testing his body's ability to withstand her charms. She understood his concern, his fear of intimacy with her, and she did not press him.

True to her old ways, though, Emma's behavior when they were with others remained the same. Beyond the old tower's walls, Walter did not exist as far as she was concerned. She chased after David for every minute that he was back at Baronsford. And later that summer, another distraction appeared, stealing time that she could have spent with Walter. A parentless cousin of hers—a lass of only nine years old—was brought to Greenbrae Hall to live with them.

Walter felt for the young child. He saw in her the same caution and confusion that he had faced himself not so many years back. He understood her loneliness and her tendency to follow Emma everywhere, despite the older cousin's protests. Gwyneth Douglas was doing the same thing to Emma that Walter had done to David, Pierce, and Lyon.

Then, one gray afternoon when Emma had been able to get away by herself and come to him, her bitterness came through.

"I know why Gwyneth was brought here," she told him, glaring off in the direction of Greenbrae Hall. "She is to be the instrument of his lordship's punishment of me and my mother. She has been taken in to inherit what was to be mine. I am on my own, Walter. From this point on, I shall need to find my own way in the world."

Chapter 8

An assortment of stones arranged neatly on the dirt outlined the infant's grave. At the head of the spot, a rude cross made from a couple of broken branches cast a shadow over the dark earth. Around the stony border of grave, writing in the dirt was visible, and Walter Truscott got down from his horse to take a closer look.

He had seen the young woman scratching words into the dirt twice when he'd come up here to visit with her over the past two days. Each time, she'd stopped immediately and said nothing as she brushed the markings away. It was clear to Walter that she didn't wish for him to press her about what she was doing, so he hadn't pursued it. Finding the grave site unattended now, though, he took the opportunity to kneel down and peer at the words.

She was a curious woman, but certainly a resilient one. Her fever was gone. Physically, she appeared to have recovered from the difficult childbirth. Her melancholy and her reticence continued, however. They still had no name for her. She would say nothing to Walter and had said almost nothing to Rita, the cotter's wife. She had been quick to offer her help with the chores about the cottage, though, but had done so with only a word here or there. The cotter's wife told Walter that the young woman didn't use the tongue of the Highlanders. Oddly, her accent—at least what Rita could make of it—sounded like that of an English woman.

The mystery of who she was and where she'd come from only intrigued Walter more. Though she never said a word, he knew that she welcomed his visits. Even so, while riding his horse there each day, he feared that he would arrive to find her gone. Every time the thought occurred to him, he told himself that he shouldn't care if that were to happen. Strangely, though, it did.

He stared at the writing. They appeared to be names, written in a circle—a chain of words and names around the grave. They were written in English, but some of the letters were too small or indistinct for him to read. Several of the names were repeated.

Holmes. Vi. Violet. Mary. Truscott focused on those he could read. *Page. Kneb . . . Kneb . . .* He carefully lifted a twig from the word. *Amina. Ohe . . . Ohe . . .* His brow furrowed. *Moses. Ami . . .* One of the names caught his attention. *Millicent.* He moved around the small grave and discovered the name was repeated three times. Walter looked back at the letters *Kneb* and tried to imagine if the rest spelled *Knebworth.*

He didn't know whether to hope it did or didn't. Walter knew Knebworth was a village near Melbury Hall, Millicent's estate just north of St. Albans. She and Lyon still spent large stretches of time there. In fact, the earl's manservant Gibbs had stayed there permanently as the new steward. Could it be that this young woman had come all the way from the South of England? Ohenewaa, the black former slave who had become a close companion to the dowager countess, was staying at Baronsford now. The two women had traveled north from Melbury Hall for the wedding between Pierce and Portia and were planning to stay at least until Millicent had her baby. Truscott moved around the grave, tried to see if he would see any other mention of Ohenewaa. The first letters were the only thing left. But what else could they be?

He pushed up to his feet and looked off in the direction of the cottage. What was she doing here, if she had come from Melbury Hall? One thing he knew, she was not here to do any harm.

Taking his horse's bridle, he started over the hill toward the cottage. Rita's husband, Angus, was working on a ditch at the bottom, and he straightened up stiffly as Truscott approached.

The older couple had been very hospitable in taking the stranger in, and Walter could see that both of them had taken a liking to the wan traveler. After exchanging greetings, the old cotter leaned on his wooden shovel.

"Ye can stop sending me those lads to lend a hand with the work here. I'm so set with everything that I'm fixing things that need nae fixing." He gestured to the ditch. "And my Rita says nae more baskets of food, neither. The lass is hardly a burden to us. And she eats less than a bird, and we're more than happy to share what we have with her."

Truscott tied his horse to a branch of a gnarled apple tree that huddled with several others by the ditch. "I stopped first by the grave of the bairn. Has she said anything about all that writing she's been doing in the dirt around the thing?"

Angus shook his head and looked up the hill that

Truscott had just descended. "She says naething to me, sir, and I just let her be. I do see her up there, though. I've seen it. The missus thinks 'tis some charm to keep the wee thing safe."

Places and people that are somehow connected to the woman and child, Truscott thought. Surrounding the lone dead child with a sense of family.

"Where is she now?"

"Inside." The cotter motioned with his head. "Not an hour ago, Rita was out here, bragging to me about how good an eye the lass has with a needle. Manor house skills, she's thinking. She'd given the lass some simple mending to do, and then ran out to show me the fancy stitches she'd done . . . as if I'd know one from another."

Walter chatted a few more minutes with the cotter about the weather and the man's ailing knee and such. He stopped hearing whatever Angus was telling him, though, the moment the young woman stepped out of the cottage. She was wearing no cloak and the tangle of curls gathered on top of her head caught the golden rays from the sky.

The first thing running through Truscott's mind in that moment was that even in her disheveled condition, she was prettier than sunshine. As she always did, whenever she saw him, she immediately stopped and her blue eyes looked his way.

This was it. No smiles. No words. No other gesture of greeting. But Walter was still satisfied since she now appeared to notice him at least.

And this was enough. For now, at least.

The two women and their entourage arrived at the Lady Cavers's town house in London to find out that there was no news of Gwyneth awaiting them. The servants who'd seen her last simply assumed that their mistress was on her way to Scotland with Captain Pennington. To ease Augusta's upset, Lady Lennox assured her friend that none of this was conclusive of anything. Any one of a hundred reasons could be thought of why Gwyneth had arrived with the youngest Pennington brother. In fact, she argued, it was more than likely that they had separated shortly after leaving the house. Despite Lady Cavers's immediate reaction, however, Lady Lennox refused to allow her friend to depart for Scotland right away without an escort. Meanwhile, listening to Augusta's steady stream of complaints, she prayed for guidance.

Relief arrived that afternoon when a longtime friend of Lady Cavers, apparently having heard of her unexpected arrival back in London, showed up at the door.

Lady Lennox had never had the good fortune of meeting the gentleman whom she'd heard so much about, but she remembered her friend describing Sir Allan Ardmore as a kind and refined gentleman who was unfortunate enough to inherit a title but little else from his dissolute father.

The man's youthful features, along with his average size and gentle manners, made him appear to be younger than Lady Lennox had imagined. But after only a few moments of being introduced, the older woman could understand completely why Augusta held the baronet in such high esteem. Sir Allan Ardmore was not only observant of Augusta's distress, but quite attentive of Lady Lennox, as well. And he was obviously an old and dear friend.

"I am truly sorry that you were forced to undergo

such worry," the baronet exclaimed as soon as he'd heard about the root of Augusta's concerns and why she was back in London. "And I cannot help but feel that my lack of judgment has caused much of this trouble."

"I appreciate your sympathy, my dear. But you can take no blame in any of this," Lady Cavers said.

Augusta had taken up a position at the window of the second floor library. Lady Lennox imagined her friend still half-expected Gwyneth to arrive at the town house at any moment.

"If there is anyone who should be at fault over this, 'tis I," Augusta lamented. "Too much independence. I have been too trusting. I assumed in error that my ward was more mature than to engage in such irresponsible actions."

Sir Allan stood awkwardly by the unlit hearth, looking embarrassed and uncomfortable. "I am afraid, milady, that I possess some information that you do not. I saw Miss Gwyneth at Hampstead Village the very afternoon that she must have stopped here."

Augusta turned abruptly. "Did you? Was she alone? Did she tell you what this change of plans was all about?"

The baronet's thin fingers brushed a speck of dust from his sleeve. Lady Lennox noticed the redness that had crept up the young man's neck, disappearing at the edge of his fashionable powdered wig.

"Well, milady . . . she was in the company of a gentleman and obviously did not wish to address me, so I did not approach her."

"Another man?" Augusta replied shrilly, taking a step toward him. "Who was this man? Pray, do not tell me they were traveling together?"

"Indeed, milady. I fear your suspicions are correct," Sir Allan said. "I was close enough to overhear some of their conversation. And my understanding was that the man traveling with your niece is the youngest brother of the Earl of Aytoun. And from the looks of things, they are indeed sharing a carriage and traveling north together."

Augusta sank down on the nearest sofa, looking forlorn. She patted away the beads of perspiration on her upper lip and forehead. "Were any of my servants with her?"

"None," he replied with a shake of his head. "Just the two of them . . . unescorted."

"The horror of it! The scandal! Gwyneth shall never be able to make a proper match after this. I dread to think of the repercussions."

"The Douglases have been neighbors to the Penningtons for years." Lady Lennox joined her friend on the sofa. "Your own daughter was a member of that family. No one would think of this arrangement as odd unless you spread such ideas yourself. With all the thieves and highwaymen on the roads these days, her mere safety could have convinced your niece to seek this travel arrangement. Truly, Augusta, this is not as bad as you are making it out to be."

"The girl could have taken half a dozen grooms and servants with her for protection. This is not the first time she is traveling that route." She shook her head unhappily. "I must go to Scotland at once. My mind will not rest unless I know she has arrived safely either in Edinburgh or at Greenbrae Hall."

"You cannot travel alone. We need to arrange for an escort," Lady Lennox said emphatically.

"If you would allow me to go with you, Lady Cavers," the baronet offered, stepping forward, "I would be greatly honored."

"I certainly cannot impose on you, Sir Allan."

"If you please, I would like the opportunity to redeem the wrong I have done. I was so stunned to see Miss Douglas there with this brute of a man that I failed in my duty as a friend to approach and demand at least an introduction of him. I did not even try to speak to Miss Gwyneth to ask after her health. You must allow me to accompany you on this trip."

Augusta looked at Lady Lennox for her advice.

"I believe 'tis a fine idea." The older woman turned to the baronet. "When can you be ready to travel, sir?"

"I shall be ready at first light tomorrow morning."

Lady Lennox patted Augusta's hand, silencing any complaints. Both women remained in the library after the baronet bowed and left to prepare for the journey north. She was relieved to see her friend's color much improved. Her mood was definitely brightening.

"All your past praises of him were so justified. He is a delightful young man."

"Indeed, but what a fool I was not to grant Gwyneth the permission she sought before this entire muddle occurred." Augusta sat down and leaned back tiredly against a pair of silk pillows.

"What did she want?" Lennox asked.

"Our young baronet here has expressed a certain tenderness for my niece, and she is partial toward him, as well."

"Has he asked for her hand in marriage?"

"Heaven forbid! He wouldn't, for he is too proud and thinks he has nothing to offer in a match such as theirs. I believe he would not ask for fear of jeopardizing his friendship with me if I were to reject his proposal." Augusta shook her head. "But Gwyneth came to me this past week, hinting at her desire for my approval . . . should Sir Allan express his interest."

"And I take it your response was negative."

"Of course! With no mincing of words I told her there would be no marriage between her and Sir Allan, though I hold the man in high personal regard. I reminded her of the baronet's financial difficulties and how, to any onlooker, 'twould only appear that he was marrying her for her inheritance. Also, I brought up their difference in age, not to mention that as a recluse she would only be looking at disaster in marrying someone with his active social proclivities." Augusta let out a heavy breath. "Chastise me if you will, my friend, but at the time I thought them very ill suited for each other."

"But have you now changed your mind?"

Augusta shrugged. "I want her to be safe. And if she is doing all of this to gain my attention, then she has succeeded. But if Sir Allan will still have her, I plan to give them my blessing."

Early in life, Walter had learned the necessity of hiding his frustrations. He was a master at keeping his temper in check. He didn't complain. He accepted life and its trials as the road that was laid for him.

More and more, though, his discipline was being cast to the wind. He was angry and unhappy and he was finding it increasingly difficult to keep his anger subdued. As the summer had progressed, he'd found himself in a few skirmishes already with David. He was chafing under the restraints of his duties and under the constant tutelage that the Earl of Aytoun had started

*him on regarding the management of these lands. Wal-
ter found himself questioning everything, everyone, and
he was never happy with the answers. As a result, he
spent endless hours at his refuge in the tower house.*

*He knew what it was all about. His growing frustra-
tion and restlessness. He was no fool. It was about
Emma.*

*When she came to him that last time before they all
left him to his misery for the lonely winter months, he
finally decided he needed to confront her.*

*"He follows you around like a devoted hound. For
him, no other woman exists but you. He cares for no
one but you. Is he the one, Emma?" Walter asked her.
"Is David the one you've chosen?"*

*A smile unlike any he'd ever seen before broke
across her lips. He realized at that moment that she'd
truly begun to comprehend her power. She was only
fifteen, but she already understood the magic she could
wield with her woman's charm.*

*"After you, David is the closest in age to me. And I
suppose if I were forced to decide on him, he would
do." She shrugged. "But Pierce is devoted to me, too,
in his protective way. I could certainly tolerate his lec-
tures if he were the one I fancied most."*

*"Are you blind to the way David feels? You have
led him on—encouraged him. No one feels for you the
way he does." It was a lie. Walter felt more for her
than any living creature ever could. But his tongue
would shrivel in his head before he could say such
a thing.*

*"What he feels is but a childish crush. He will get
over it soon enough when I tell him to go on his way."
She shrugged again. "If I had to chose one of the three
Pennington men, Lyon would be my preferred choice."*

"Lyon? But you don't even know him. He has been gone from Baronsford more than he has been here. He is ten years older than you!"

"But Lyon is the next Earl of Aytoun." The smile returned. "And I shall be the Countess of Aytoun. Baronsford will be mine. I shall never need to worry again about income or inheritances or the ill blood between my parents. If I decide never to see either of them again, that shall be my right."

A thousand objections arose in him. Hurt for himself, for his cousins, for everyone who cared for Emma but was blinded by her, burned within his brain. But he forced back the pain that was ripping through him. He could not think straight. The pulsing in his ears was blocking out all sound. And then she spoke again, her words cutting through it all.

"But I am faced with a dilemma," she said quietly. "Why must I decide on one of those three . . . when you are the one I want."

He looked up in surprise. His heart was hammering in his chest. She walked toward him.

"But I cannot have you, can I?" She brushed her lips against his. She kissed him until the wall of resistance crumbled away—until Walter was kissing her back with wild abandon. Suddenly, she broke away, pulling back from his embrace.

He watched her back toward the door. Her gaze was fixed to his face. Her eyes clear.

"But you will not do. You know me like no one else . . . but you cannot give me what I truly want."

And then she was gone.

Chapter 9

Three days of being jounced around together in the carriage. Three nights of adjoining rooms in Stoke-on-Trent, Lancaster, and Penrith. David was impressed at how the little imp continued to carry on her pretence of indifference flawlessly. She was polite, but distant. She was civil in her responses and refused to be provoked by any of his antics or be drawn into any arguments. She also appeared content to go along on the trip without another attempt at running away or tricking him. And that was not for the lack of opportunity. David asked the driver to make frequent stops and each day made sure he wasted at least part of the morning before getting on the road.

Initially, Gwyneth's restrained disposition had been a reprieve. He had finally caught up with his sleep. He had actually been able to relax and do a little thinking about what awaited him once he arrived unannounced at Baronsford, and how he was going to deal with seeing his family again. But the boredom of the journey was setting in fast. He had too much time on his hands watching her scribble away in her notebook. He thought back on Gwyneth's drastic change of mood after he'd read part of her tale. He guessed she had been offended by the comments he'd made about her writing and how she spent too many hours daydreaming.

Of course, in spending every waking moment scratching away on the paper as they jounced northward, she was proving him right. At the same time though, she was silently reprimanding him, teaching him a lesson, showing him that her passion for writing ran far deeper than any attraction she still carried for him. As far as David could see, Gwyneth had convinced herself that he was no longer even worthy of notice, and she was flaunting it splendidly.

As they rolled along, David was determined to prove her wrong, and he could think of no more romantic place to do it than in the very village that hundreds of couples ran away to every year to exchange their marriage vows. He would win her over in the very same place that Gwyneth had been trying to reach with her beau.

The sun was descending fast on the western sky. The Scottish border was drawing near. He guessed they would arrive at Gretna Green shortly after dusk. And this suited his sinful plans perfectly.

Despite her act of indifference, he had not been immune to her these past three days. No, David corrected himself, he had not been impervious to her charms from the moment they'd met in London. Every day, he watched her deep crimson locks arrange themselves on her ivory neck and shoulders. Gwyneth's lack of attention to her clothes and her increasingly rumpled condition only evoked more erotic images in his mind. He remembered the silky texture of her skin and how it had felt when his fingers were trailing a path under her layers of skirt. He could still recall the heat. She'd wanted him, too. He felt no guilt in wanting to make love to Gwyneth. He had no problem with the knowledge of it being known, either, since he intended to marry her. But he needed to have her consent. He wanted her to be as caught up in that moment of desire as he. Just as it had been during their first couple of days of travel, David wanted the feeling to draw them together like lightning to the rod.

He gazed at the sunlight streaming through the carriage window, setting her red ringlets on fire. He stared at the freckles on the bridge of her nose, at the full lips. His gaze fell down on her strong fingers gripping the pencil as it moved smoothly across the page of her notebook.

"Two witnesses and a quick stop at the blacksmith shop, and we could become legally united."

Gwyneth obviously considered the comment to be facetious, for she didn't even bother to look up. The pencil did not pause. He wondered for a moment if she'd even heard him.

"Then you and I can have the blacksmith lock us away in his back room. I believe the custom is for him to have all of our clothes taken away, as well."

The pencil faltered. A blush colored her cheeks. After a moment, though, she went back to her writing.

"I hear the man keeps a bed back there . . . for the situations involving angry fathers in close pursuit. When the irate parent demands that the door be opened, he finds himself witnessing firsthand the marital bliss of the newlyweds. There is no question of consent after that."

"I have no father, but that matters not, for there is not one chance in a thousand that I would get into a bed with you."

A reaction. David was extremely pleased. He watched Gwyneth try to focus on the page before her, but the pencil was slow to move. She was obviously distracted.

"One in a thousand. That sounds like odds for a wager. Are you issuing a challenge?"

Gwyneth sat back. Her green eyes sparkled. "Now that I think about it, I believe you have just suggested a method for how I could successfully achieve being married, as I had intended."

"Well, if marrying just anyone is your goal, why not take me up on my offer?"

" 'Tis absurd of you to think that I would marry just anyone. There is only one man I would consider taking as my husband."

"A man whom you do not love, nor have ever been intimate with. A penniless coward who is only after your fortune. A nameless rogue who is afraid of his own shadow."

"What makes you say that?"

"If he were not a coward, he would have come to your rescue by now. A dog knows no honor."

"You know nothing of what he has done or has planned," she said, venting her temper and frustration. "And he has a name. A very good name, indeed."

"Of course! How could I forget? I believe the name Adams was the one he was hiding behind last week. I wonder what name he is going by this week."

Gwyneth crossed her arms over her chest. " 'Tis so easy to attack someone in their absence, but I assure you after he and I are wed, your opinion of him will be very different."

"Indeed, since I shall be remembering him as your late fiancé, who died tragically on the way to the altar . . . or rather, the anvil."

Her mouth opened but then she clamped it so tight that he heard her teeth click.

" 'Twill be safer for your beau and far more pleasant for you just to accept my offer." He bumped his knee against hers. "What do you say, Gwyneth?"

"No!" she shouted. " 'Tis unthinkable. And even in the event that the world itself should somehow turn upside down, you, Captain Pennington, would be the least likely candidate for me to choose as a husband."

"Unthinkable, you say?" He felt his spirits lift. Now they were getting back to their normal way of communicating. "And would you care to say what you have against me?"

"I would not."

"You do not believe I would make a good husband?"

"I do not."

"And why is that?"

"You are too arrogant, too stubborn, too proud." She waved a frustrated hand before her. "You are too wounded. And not I, nor any woman, can help you heal scars you carry from the past."

David sat back, trying to formulate a response. She'd caught him off his guard. She was referring to something David didn't care to look back on. He didn't want to think of Emma now. He had healed. He just didn't care to reopen the wound.

"I can be more agreeable," he said.

She shook her head and tucked her notebook away.

"Do you at least think that I would make a good lover?"

She turned her gaze out the window. They had passed the border and were approaching the village of Gretna Green. David moved next to her and pretended to look out, too. Her silky ringlets brushed against his cheek. He looked down at the stretch of smooth skin on her neck and fought the urge to press his lips to it. Several of the buttons on the back of the dress had been left undone, and he wondered what she would do if he were to undo the rest of them.

"But of course, you cannot answer since you haven't had the opportunity to test my skills as a lover. But how about it, Gwyneth?" he whispered against her delicate ear. "Would you care to test the sheets with me first and then decide if I would make a good husband?"

"Not in a hundred years, Captain," she croaked.

The carriage stopped at Headless Cross, where five old coaching roads came together in the center of Gretna Green. Gwyneth scrambled to get out of the coach ahead of him. The carriage lurched, though, sending her stumbling out onto the street and up to the very door of the blacksmith's shop.

She had to find a way to marry Sir Allan before David drove her insane. She had to accomplish what she had planned before he jeopardized the only way she knew of solving her problems. Gwyneth had told him what she thought of him. What she hadn't dared mention, though, was that he would never understand her need to write. But even if her writing was not an issue, her answer would still have been the same. He could never be a good husband to any woman, for he had been in love with Emma, and his heart would burn for her forever. One man, one woman, one love . . . forever.

Gwyneth knew all about that. The feelings that smoldered in her own heart would never change. And she knew she could not cool the way her body responded to his touch. Her only salvation lay in finding her baronet.

Pacing her room, Gwyneth assured herself that Ardmore could very well be waiting for her here in the village. He possibly could be staying at any one of the inns or taverns within a stone's throw of Headless Cross. There was no way she could go in search of him, though—not in the dark, and not while she was still unfamiliar with the village.

She was given a reprieve for tonight. No adjoining rooms, no connecting doors that David required to be left open. Tonight, at least, she would not have to endure watching David parade about his room, shirtless and with his breeches half unbuttoned. No suffering, as she had the night at Stoke-on-Trent when she'd caught a glimpse of his naked backside as he'd lowered himself in a tub of hot water that had been brought up to his room. The devil take him, the villain had even taunted her that night, calling to her to join him in the tub.

Gwyneth touched her burning cheeks. The air in the room was hot to the point of suffocating her. She walked to the windows and pushed the shutters wide open, but there was no breeze. The dirt and sweat from days of travel made her clothes stick uncomfortably to her skin. She glanced at her small trunk of clothing, but she wasn't ready to waste a clean dress yet.

Arriving at the inn, David had offered to have a tub of water sent up to her, but she'd refused. In keeping with his stubborn character though, he'd ordered one for her anyway. And now Gwyneth was glad that he'd done so. In fact, she found herself growing impatient for it, for an hour had passed and still nothing had been sent up.

She considered going down and asking for one herself. She even contemplated walking downstairs and right out of the inn. David appeared to be taking his victory over her for granted. Indeed, perhaps just asking at the nearest tavern for Sir Allan . . .

The soft knock wiped away that idea. Gwyneth opened the door for a young maidservant carrying clean towels, and two boys carrying a wooden tub. She went to her trunk and chose a clean dress and undergarments as the lads ran for buckets of steaming hot water to fill the tub. She longed to wash her hair and her body. The thought of just sitting in the tub and allowing the weariness of travel to work its way out of her limbs was heavenly.

Their work done, the boys closed the door on the way out. The maidservant offered to stay behind and help her with the bath. Gwyneth considered refusing the offer, but the luxury of having a bath and actually having someone help her with it convinced her otherwise. Also, she realized that befriending someone who lived in the village might be her best chance at finding Sir Allan if he had indeed beaten them to Gretna Green.

The maid's name was Ann, and she was hardly shy about conversing. In fact, Gwyneth was unable to lead the conversation where she wanted as Ann obviously had her heart set on sharing stories of her favorite elopements and the notable weddings that had taken place in their village. One, in particular, had taken hold of Ann's fancy and she started with that one.

"The entire thing started at this house party in one of the grand manor houses near Carlisle, not a day's walk down the road and over the border. The good minister John Wesley was a member of the party, no doubt with a mind to do the Lord's work while he was visiting. While he was there, his brother Charles Wesley joined him, as well, bringing along an artist friend of theirs."

Ann started closing the shutters as she talked, and then came to help Gwyneth get out of her dress.

"The wealthy gentleman who was giving the party had a daughter nearly of marrying age. A bonnie wee thing, the lass was. Among the other guests was a well-to-do nobleman, come all the way from Germany as the travel companion to another German gentleman. Now, the young traveler fell head over heels in love with the lassie as soon as he laid eyes on her."

Being a storyteller and a romantic at heart, Gwyneth found herself caught up in the story. With Ann assisting her, she quickly stepped out of her dress but decided to keep her shift on as she stepped into the tub. The water felt heavenly and her undergarment billowed out around her legs as she sat down. Once in the water, she peeled off the wet garment and draped it on the edge of the tub.

"Being a fine gentleman and all, the German asked the blessing of the girl's father to marry the lass, but the old man had it in his head that he would marry his daughter to an English earl, at the very least . . . and to no foreigner, to be sure. So, stubborn as a mule, the old gentleman refused." Ann poured water over Gwyneth's head and worked on untangling the curls. "The story goes that the two Wesley brothers felt downhearted for the two lovers and told the German about us over here in Gretna Green and how the two could be wed without the old bull's consent. That same night, with the great John Wesley himself helping, the couple eloped."

Gwyneth stopped washing her arms and looked up at the maid. "That should have been easy, they being so close."

" 'Twas, indeed, miss. They say the girl's father rode hard after the couple, but he arrived too late to stop the wedding."

"So they lived happily ever after," Gwyneth concluded.

"Aye, miss. That they did, but that is only part of the story." Ann fetched a comb to work on the curls. "Now the artist I told ye about, the one who had come to the party with Charles Wesley . . . why, he painted four pictures about the whole event when he got back to London."

Gwyneth's imagination ran wild. A picture of the lovers when they first met. Another of them running through the fields with the father and his men on horseback in close pursuit. Another of the hasty wedding. The fourth one had to be of the father's blessing, or maybe it would be of the couple back in Germany.

"In one of the paintings there stands a wee village lass, barefoot and dressed in rags, staring in awe at the entire proceeding." Ann's voice brought Gwyneth back to the present. "Well, when the new bride sees the pictures, she asks her husband to bring her back here to Gretna Green to find the child."

"Was the child real? The painter didn't invent her?" Gwyneth pushed the wet hair out of her face to look up at Ann.

"Nay, miss. The wee lass was real as you and me."

"Did they find her?"

"Aye." The young woman beamed and nodded.

"The ragged lassie's name was Effie, and she was from a verra poor family that lived just outside the village. With six wee ones and a seventh on the way, the parents were quick to agree to sell Effie to the new bride."

"They sold their daughter?" Gwyneth asked in disbelief.

"Aye, miss."

"But they knew nothing about this couple. What happened if they intended to harm the child?"

"When ye are poor, miss, ye dunna worry about such things." Ann pushed Gwyneth's head forward and lathered up her hair. "But ye can rest your mind, for our Effie went to Germany with her new parents and was schooled and brought up as a gentlewoman. In fact, when she grew up, she married a count, they say, and ne'er looked back at her humble beginnings in that tumbledown cottage near Gretna Green."

"That is not a very happy tale," Gwyneth whispered. "Especially not for her family. The least she could have done was to come back, maybe to visit, or even help them financially in some way."

The maidservant started to rinse Gwyneth's hair, but some of the soap went into her eyes, burning them badly.

"I ne'er thought on it that way, miss," Ann said pensively.

A knock on the door startled them both. Gwyneth splashed her face with the water to wash away the soap, but the stinging only got worse.

"That'd be one of the lads with the pitcher of warmed rinse water," Ann explained, running to get the door.

Gwyneth sank down into the tub as far as she could.

There was some whispering at the door, and she was relieved when she heard it close quickly again.

"So are you by any chance any relation to this Effie?" Gwyneth asked when she felt the water begin to pour gently over her head and face to wash away the lather.

"I don't believe I know any Effie."

At the sound of his deep voice, Gwyneth almost leapt out of the tub. She sputtered and forced her eyes open despite the stinging.

"What are you doing here?" She grabbed her shift, covering her breasts and trying to stretch the length of it over her bare legs. She pushed the wet hair off her face.

"I have simply returned to my room," David said smugly as he crouched down beside the tub, the pitcher of water in his hand.

"What do you mean, *your* room? This is *my* room."

"Well, if you insist on being precise, our room." His gaze strayed from her face to her neck and to where she was holding the wet fabric tightly against her breasts. "Unfortunately for you, we haven't the luxury of separate rooms in this tavern. This appears to be the busy season for the marriage trade."

"There must be other taverns." She battled the end of her undergarment that was trying to float to the surface. She drew her knees tightly against her chest. "If not, you can just sleep in the stables."

"Indeed. But I'm quite sure I shall enjoy this far better. You still have soap in your hair." He poured more water over her head.

Gwyneth didn't have enough hands to battle him. "David Pennington. What you are trying to do is the most childish thing any man could pull. You are a rogue, a coward, and a villain. You are taking advantage . . ." She sputtered and stopped as he nearly drowned her, dumping the entire pitcher of water over her head.

"You have the prettiest array of freckles all over your shoulders. And you have the most beautiful back."

Gwyneth stiffened as she felt his fingers slide gently over her back. She had no success in fighting the heat pooling in her middle. As always, her body never listened to reason when it came to David. She pushed the hair off her face and turned to him. "David, I told you before that nothing can happen between us. That . . ."

His gaze was focused on her breasts. She looked down and realized that the wet shift she was holding against her body was nearly transparent. Her nipples were showing boldly through. She crossed her arms to cover them. "Why are you doing this to me?"

The intensity of his blue eyes burned her skin. "I am not doing it alone, Gwyneth. You started this when you were younger and chased me all over Baronsford."

"I was just a foolish child. I had painted a picture of you in my mind as a hero. There was nothing . . . well, there was nothing intimate about it."

"But that changed as you became older, did it not?" he teased. "Or was that all innocence when you would sit yourself in my lap not so long ago? And how about last year, at Baronsford, and when I came down to the cliffs to see you? You cannot deny that something passed between us that day. And I have not even begun on the way you have been behaving since starting together on this trip." His fingers slid from her back to the side of her throat.

Her face burned as her breasts strained upward, awaiting his touch. But he withdrew his hand.

"There is a history between us that we cannot deny, Gwyneth."

"Very well! I admit it, we *are* physically drawn to each other," she groaned, beaten. "But this should give us more reason to keep our distance. I have made up my mind to marry someone else, and you can have any other woman you want. There are surely a dozen beautiful girls at least, in this village alone, who would gladly climb into this tub with you. Go after *them*, not me."

He started pulling off his boots.

"What are you doing?" she asked in panic.

"You gave me an idea."

Gwyneth stared in shock when he pulled the shirt over his head. "David, I still have the semblance of a reputation left. You . . ."

"I am afraid I destroyed that by paying off that maid-servant when she let me in here. She does appear to be the gossipy kind." He stood up and started unbuttoning his breeches. "But I do indeed need to bathe."

Her mouth went dry. His chest was broad and mus-cled, narrowing at his waist. She closed her eyes as he pushed his breeches down, but not before catching a glimpse of the dark hair leading downward from his navel and then his hardening manhood. Hot flashes of panic swept through her.

"Give me my towel," she squeaked. "Turn your back. I should like to get out of here."

" 'Tis too far for me to reach."

She opened her eyes for a moment, only to shut them again at the sight of a muscled thigh right next to the tub. "You will not force me against my will. You are too much of a gentleman—"

"I was a rogue and a villain not a minute ago."

"I have changed my mind." Gwyneth reached out blindly toward the towel that she remembered lay at the foot of the bed. "Give me that thing and I shall be out of your way ...."

"I still need to wash your back."

"David, this is not funny. You are going far beyond any decent—"

His foot brushed against her buttocks as he stepped into the tub. In sheer panic, Gwyneth leapt to her feet. As David's arm encircled her waist, though, the thrill of her wet back against his warm chest froze her. His arousal pressed hard against her.

"Stay, Gwyneth," he whispered huskily into her ear. His mouth kissed the wet skin of her neck and shoulder. "I shall never do anything that you do not want me to do."

She was like a sheep being led to slaughter, and she was going willingly. There was no way on earth she could have moved from his embrace.

"Everything about you is so beautiful." His hands moved from her waist, caressing her arms, ever so slowly pushing her hands and the wet shift she was clutching away from her body. Her breasts spilled into view, wet and glistening. "You have been driving me crazy with desire."

There was no fear in her. That was gone, and only excitement filled her now. There was certainly no thought of decency. She watched one large hand gently rub the wet fabric across her stomach. The other hand cupped her breast, and his thumb and forefinger gently played and then squeezed her nipple. The sensation was maddening, and she felt her legs go weak.

He moved his other foot into the tub. His manhood nestled intimately against her. He tugged the chemise out of her hand and let it drop into the water. "Why don't you sit down here with me?"

"We shouldn't. 'Tis wrong," she whispered even as she leaned against him. She gasped with a mixture of shock and pleasure when his hand slid downward, stoking the heat that he had ignited in her. She said nothing as he lowered them both into the tub.

The water came up and splashed over the sides when he positioned her between his legs. There was no extra space in the tub, and he drew her tightly against his chest with his arms—leaning her back until the private parts of her body were completely exposed to his look and his touch.

"I like this," he growled. "We fit perfectly."

The contrast between their bodies alone was more exciting than she could bear. His arms and legs were long and muscled and covered with fine dark hair. She looked down at her pale skin, at her breasts floating in and out of the water with each breath she took. A new rush of liquid heat gathered in the center of her as his fingers started playing with the hardened tips of her nipples.

This was far more daring than any scene she'd ever written in any of her stories. It was more exciting than she could have ever imagined. When his other hand moved down her belly to the juncture of her legs, she knew David was set to make a liar out of her again.

"Open for me," he whispered, gently pushing her knees apart.

She grabbed his wrist. "I told you before. I have never done this."

"I know, my love." He bit on her earlobe, tasted her neck. "I shall be gentle. I shan't do anything you do not want me to do."

Gwyneth felt her breath go short as she watched

his hand dip into the water again, touching sensitive folds of her flesh. She tensed the moment he dipped a finger inside of her and felt the resistance.

"My innocent Gwyneth. I shall take care of you."

She looked over her shoulder at David to tell him she was frightened, and his mouth was there, capturing hers. And until their lips sealed, she hadn't realized how much she'd needed this. Gwyneth's tongue tangled with his, and she welcomed him deep into her mouth. This time it was she who heard his groan of pleasure.

He turned her in his arms, and more water splashed over the side. Their mouths continued to feast on each other as they moved together until she was straddling him. Her flesh ached for him, and she held his face, controlling the kiss, feeding on him and wanting to see him suffer as he was making her suffer.

He was breathless when he tore his mouth away. "This is . . . this is . . . I am losing control. I want you now."

She felt wicked and powerful in a way she had never felt. Instinctively, she slid her hips closer to him, her breasts rubbing against his chest. She locked her knees against his hips.

"I shan't let you be in charge." Gwyneth bit on his bottom lip before drawing it onto her mouth.

A deep laugh rumbled in his chest. "Then get ready to play, you pixie." Sliding his hands beneath her buttocks, he lifted her up.

Gwyneth gasped with pleasure when his mouth closed around her nipple. The sensation that shot through her was like lightning. The suction created by his lips as his tongue and teeth teased the sensitive bud made her hold David's head tight to her breast.

She never wanted the delicious torment to end. But the pressure inside her body continued to build. He moved from one breast to the other. His hand moved to the juncture of her thighs, and she arched her back and gasped as he slipped a finger inside of her, stroking the sensitive folds.

"David," she cried. "I feel like I am racing. I don't know how . . ." Her vision was a blur, her heart pounded. The need to move to some unknown finish made her move restlessly against him.

"Hold on to me," he growled.

Gwyneth's arms held him tight around the neck when he stood up in the tub. He stepped out, taking her with him. They were both completely naked, but she'd forgotten what shyness meant. Anticipation, hovering over the edge of an abyss and wanting to dive into it, was the only thing that ruled her mind.

David set her down next to the bed. Unsteady on her feet, she saw him fetch the towel and throw off the bed coverings. The muscled V of his back, his buttocks and legs—he could have been carved from marble, beautiful as he was. And his manhood! She stared at the size of it with disbelieving eyes. She knew how men and women mated. She shook her head.

"We shall never fit together," she whispered.

The sound of his laughter was strained. His eyes were smoldering with desire when he walked toward her, the towel in his hand. "I shan't hurt you, Gwyneth."

He gently rubbed at the wetness on her hair, dried her arms, her back. She watched the rippling play of the muscles in his chest and arms when he patted the water from her breast. She held her breath when he knelt beside her and dried her legs. Then, his hand moved between her legs, dipped into the wetness inside. Drawing her to him, he circled her nipple with his tongue. She let out a soft cry when he suckled hard on it.

"Let me dry you now." She tried to take the towel as he stood up, but he held it away from her.

"Not this time," he replied, hastily wiping himself off. "I won't make it."

"What do you mean, this time?" she asked in bewilderment.

"I asked them to leave the tub until morning." He brushed her lips with his own, a devilish smile lingering at the corner of his mouth. "I plan to ravish you at least a dozen times before morning, both in and out of that water."

Her sharp intake of breath made him laugh again. "I love your passion." He backed her toward the bed. She sat down when the backs of her legs brushed against the mattress. He leaned over, lifting her higher up the mattress. "I love your sense for adventure."

"You think I am bold," she whispered as he laid her down on the coverings.

"I think you are perfect." His blue gaze caressed her face and moved down her body.

Gwyneth couldn't lie still under his scrutiny. Her nakedness was complete. She'd wanted this for as long as she could remember. She wanted nothing more than to be David's. She wanted him to take her, to brand her as his own. She wanted back the dizziness she'd felt a moment earlier—that sense of floating on the edge. She was ready to go over that edge with him. She opened her arms to him, wanting to feel his weight on top of her body. He came to her.

"Make love to me, David." She kissed his jaw, the corner of his lips. She shifted on the mattress in anticipation when she felt the crown of his manhood nestle between her legs.

"I shall not share you with anyone, Gwyneth." He lay one large hand against her cheek, his blue eyes boring into hers. "Once I make you mine, 'tis forever."

Her reason cut through the cloud of passion. "We are joining our bodies. For as long as we are lovers, I shall be true to you."

He smiled down at her. "We shall be much more than lovers. I intend to marry you."

"You cannot. I already have another husband-to-be."

"And the cur can rot in hell. You are mine." His mouth hovered over hers, his thumb fondling her straining nipple.

Gwyneth couldn't stay still beneath his touch, but she forced out her words.

"I shall not marry you, David," she said, looking stubbornly into his blue eyes.

"Why?"

"I have already explained."

"Then I shall need to change your mind." He moved slowly down her body.

Gwyneth's hands clutched at the sheets as his mouth and hands busied themselves with her breasts. She looked up at the smoke-darkened ceiling, trying to fight the mounting waves.

"Only lovers. That's all I can promise."

The rogue laughed again, moving farther down her body. His hands pushing her knees apart, moving under her and cupping her bottom.

"You and I both know that you saved this for me, Gwyneth."

She was shocked by what he was doing. She burned

in sudden panic as he lifted her hip and his breath whispered against the very center of her. There was no fighting it, though—no wish for him to be doing anything other than exactly what he was doing. Her fingers fisted the sheets tighter.

"David!" she panted

"You are mine, Gwyneth."

She cried out aloud from the shock and the excitement when his mouth pressed into her. She shook and moved helplessly around him with no thought but amazement at the sensations of heat and cold as the colors of fire engulfed them. Suddenly, she felt herself being swept over the edge of rapture, her body convulsing as she curled around him.

An instant later, David pushed her back on the pillows. She was still riding waves of bliss when he positioned himself between her legs. She felt no pain as he entered and drove deep inside her. The instant they were joined, she felt herself close around him like a sheath. Awareness returned like a soft breeze slowly stirring a mist.

"We fit," she whispered, the only words she could utter.

He laughed again. This time, it was the laughter of the satisfied male, pleased with the fruits of his labor. It was a sound that made her insides go soft. Slowly at first, he withdrew a little and then slid back into her, even deeper than before. Again, and then again, he slid back and drove into her, and Gwyneth felt the pulsing thrill begin to build and she answered his thrusts as he gradually sped the tempo of the love dance.

"Think, lass, of forever," he breathed in her ear, "and what it shall be like to do this . . . for as long as we both shall live."

* * *

Frustrated and alone, he searched for solace in the arms of a number of willing lasses. Each time, he thought he might satisfy, in some way, the painful need that tore at him. He found, though, as winter gave way to spring, that he was only going through the motions. From Melrose to Peebles, a quick tumble was all that he sought. And he would bed each lass only once.

The women were young. Some might have been bonnie, he supposed. Strangely, he could not remember their faces. As he made love to them, though, each one looked like Emma. They had the same hair, the same eyes, the same slender frame. They resembled her in one way or another.

Not one of them meant a thing to him. No matter how hard he tried, he could not pry loose the hook that Emma had sunk into his flesh.

Each time, he tried to imagine that he was making love to her. He tried to see her face, her smile, but it was no use. None of them brought him the release that could satisfy him. They were not Emma, and he felt cursed to the pit of his very soul.

Chapter 10

⌒

Baronsford was a fairy-tale castle set in the midst of a grand deer park and with miles of footpaths weaving in and out along cliffs overlooking the river Tweed. A grand piece of architecture, well known throughout Britain, it had been painted many times by famous artists across the continent. The Pennington family seat was a safe haven where a tired traveler or a desperate vagrant could rely on the generosity of its owners.

There were many written and spoken accounts of the place; many glowing descriptions of it by those who had visited or even passed by the stone castle. But there were many faces to Baronsford, and over the years, Walter Truscott believed, the grand house became whatever its mistress wanted it to be.

As a child Walter had been brought here by his father—Sir William, a half brother to Lady Aytoun. Immediately drafted into the bands of the three older boys, he and his cousins had terrorized both house and countryside. From the very start Walter had known Baronsford as a welcoming and happy home.

Years later, after Emma's marriage to Lyon, as Baronsford had gone through excessively numerous reno-

vations of the rooms and gardens and furniture, he
had watched the castle become a grand showpiece. A
distant trophy with opulent looks but no usefulness.
During that time, Truscott had thought of the castle
as forbidding, hostile, cold. Those were the days that
he'd even considered leaving the place and the people
and everything he cared about.

This spring, though, since the new Countess of Aytoun, Millicent Gregory, had arrived at the Borders
with Lyon, Baronsford was changing again into that
safe haven of old. Once again, it was becoming a
home—warm and welcoming to all.

The land clearings of the Highlands were spreading
south to the Borders. Hundreds of vagrants were passing through Baronsford every month. Most of them
were hungry, desperate for work, or ill and wretched
like the young woman at Rita and Angus's cottage.

The travelers needed ways to feed their families.
The sick required care. Others just wanted to earn
enough to pay for a passage to the colonies. And Baronsford—the castle folk, the cotters, and the people
belonging to it—accepted and sheltered the vagrants.
The pattern was begun at the top. Millicent and Lyon
set the example, and everyone followed.

To Truscott, Baronsford had never been as beautiful
as it was now.

The sun had sunk halfway down the western sky
when he left his horse at the stables and walked
toward the house. The dowager and her friend Ohenewaa were sitting on a stone bench in the rose gardens,
and they ceased their conversation to wave at him as
he walked up the hill. Walter considered going to
them and asking Ohenewaa if she might know of
someone fitting the description of the mysterious lass

who might just be from Knebworth. Knowing his aunt's shrewdness, though, and her manner of asking a hundred questions before she allowed one to be answered, Truscott decided against asking now. If Millicent were not available to speak to him tonight, then he would just wait until he could catch Ohenewaa alone.

The newlyweds, Pierce and Portia, had decided to take a fortnight or two to see something of the western isles. Portia's mother, Helena, had gone south to visit the beautiful country around Windermere in Cumbria, where she had spent many years before being brought to the colonies. They were all due to arrive back any day, though. This renewed aspect of Baronsford—the sense of liveliness and a family together again—was another thing that added so much joy to the place.

If only they could hear from David, he thought.

Truscott found Millicent, Lyon, and little Josephine in the library. As was the laird's custom, whenever he was not engaged in the business of running Baronsford, they gathered as a family. Joining them there, Walter felt uneasy about mentioning anything distressing. He had no desire to spoil the peaceful mood that surrounded them.

"Oh, Walter, I am so glad that you are back," Millicent said brightly, greeting him from her seat on the sofa.

Truscott walked over and brushed a kiss on her cheek. The countess's advanced stage of pregnancy showed in her round belly and the swollen ankles that her husband insisted she keep raised on the sofa whenever she had the chance. For a split second, he imagined the young woman at the cotter's cottage must have been at the same time in her pregnancy when she'd lost her bairn as Millicent was now.

"You have not joined us for a single meal this week," the countess admonished him. "You have been working too hard, trying to do everything yourself."

A soft pat on his boots made Truscott look down. He smiled at the bairn who had separated herself from Lyon and was right now giving him a toothless grin. He reached down immediately and took Josephine in his arms. The baby began to babble immediately and kissed him sloppily on the chin.

"If you wish to avoid the scolding you're taking from these two bonnie lasses, I think we'd better see a wee bit more of you, Cousin."

Walter glanced at Lyon, who was grinning up at him from the floor near the sofa. He'd obviously been enjoying the attentions of the baby before Truscott had entered.

"Is the lass continuing to improve?" the earl asked, opening his arms as Walter lowered the baby onto his chest.

Truscott had kept his cousin apprised of what was happening at the cotter's place during the past days.

"Is someone ill?" Millicent asked.

Walter glanced at Lyon, seeking his permission. Earlier on, when he had first mentioned the pregnant traveler to the earl, they'd decided to keep the news away from Millicent. Then, when the woman had lost the baby, they were glad they had done so. Because of her own condition, and the tragedy surrounding the death of Josephine's mother, they did not want to cause Millicent further distress.

Lyon reached up and took his wife's hand. "Walter has been visiting a young vagrant who was left at the door of one of our cotters. The lass was with child and very ill. 'Twas a very similar situation to Jo's, I'm afraid."

Millicent's back immediately stiffened. Walter saw the look of worry that clouded her face. "Why did you not tell me? You should bring her here. Fetch a doctor and—"

"Everything that could have been done for her was done," Walter assured her. "We brought the doctor in from Melrose, and the midwife saw to her, as well. The first night after being left, she delivered her bairn, but the creature died."

"How sad." She sank back against the seat. "How is the girl doing now?"

"She survived and seems to be improving . . . physically, at least." Baby Josephine was crawling on her chest toward him again, so Walter took his cousin's example and sat down on the floor. "The fever is gone. She is moving around. Today, she was even helping the cotter's wife with some chores."

"Does she have any kin? Was there any husband?" Millicent asked quietly.

"She hasn't said anything to that effect. She appears to be all alone, and when her baby was buried outside the old kirkyard over the hill from the cottage, she said nothing."

"Has she started talking about where she came from? Has she told you her name, at least?" Lyon asked.

"She's said very little to Rita. Mostly, she just answers simple questions. Nothing of a personal nature, though. That is another reason why I continue to worry about her. She might appear to be improving, but she is still mourning her dead bairn. I fear there may be other things that we know nothing about, as well."

"Why don't you try to convince her to come to Baronsford with you?" Millicent said softly. "With everything else that is going on here, she might have less time to think."

"Thank you, milady. I shall try to talk her into coming here."

Seeing Walter as no challenge, the baby was crawling in a straight line toward the door, where she could be sure to get into more trouble. Knowing how Lyon still had some difficulty with his healing legs and knees, Truscott went after the impetuous imp. Handing her, complaining and squirming, back to her father, he sat on the sofa beside the countess.

Lyon turned Josephine on her back, and she started giggling and screeching happily as he tickled her neck. "You, my wee fairy, move around with more speed than I can possibly match."

It was fascinating watching them. The imposing earl, who had always been feared for his short temper and lethal skills, was now the very picture of the devoted father who would do anything to protect his child. Truscott knew he would be equally doting when Millicent gave birth to the bairn she was carrying. It was rewarding to see such happiness between these good people. So different from the disaster that would have occurred had Emma lived long enough to bear her child.

Truscott's mood immediately soured at the mere thought. Temper reddened his cheeks. He forced himself to push the image out of his head, but the one that replaced it was not too blissful, either.

In his mind's eye, he saw a woman's small frame

bent in desperate unhappiness over a wee grave, her raw, bleeding fingers making marks in the dirt.

"What is it, Walter?" Millicent asked softly, leaning over and placing her hand on his shoulder. "What is it that you haven't told us about her?"

He looked at her. " 'Tis something that she has been doing. She has written a circle of names around the grave of her bairn. At the same time, she's shared nothing of her own name or her history. I do not know why she does it, and it confuses me."

"What is it that she is writing? What are some of the names?" Lyon asked. "Perhaps we can identify her with one of the estates to the west."

"I stopped today to read them while she was busy with the cotter's wife. Very little of it remained after the rain last night, but . . . well, what I could read had nothing to do with any estates in the Borders." Walter looked at Millicent again. "There was something that appeared to be your name there. And the beginning of what I could only imagine to be Ohene-waa's. Then, there were names like Mary, Moses, Amina . . . and Holmes."

"Dear Lord!" Millicent shot to her feet abruptly, desperately grasping her husband's shoulder. "Lyon, could it possibly be Violet?"

Numbed by the chill of the approaching dawn, she stared at the name she had scratched into the dirt. Millicent. Tears dripped from Violet's cheeks and fell on her stained hands. It was so unjust that she herself still lived while her child lay dead beneath this pile of dirt and stone. A soft moan escaped her throat. It was wrong that she had sinned and her daughter had been buried in unhallowed ground.

Violet knew Mr. Truscott had seen the names. From hearing Angus and Rita talk, she knew who he was. He was kin to the earl himself, and he had become a good friend to the new Countess of Aytoun. He was kind and reliable, and she knew he would do the right thing. Lady Aytoun would see to it that the baby's body would be moved. The good mistress would understand and see to it.

And Violet herself would be gone.

It was the old earl's suggestion that Walter accompany Pierce on a grand tour of the Continent. The second brother had just finished his education at the university, and the old earl believed Walter should see and experience what was happening in the world before he settled down to run the affairs of Baronsford.

The trip could take as long as a year, and Walter was elated about the opportunity. It meant he would not need to see Emma.

And surely there was much a young man could forget in a year.

Chapter 11

⁓

The cool breeze of the summer morning brushed over David's naked shoulders and back. The noise from the bustling village outside the window pulled him slowly out of the enfolding arms of sleep. With his gradual wakefulness came desire—the need to once again join Gwyneth's body with his own, as they had made love repeatedly during the night.

Each time had been different, each act of lovemaking even more exciting than the last. Gwyneth's body was a temple. He could worship every part of it for eternity. And her passion was unbounded. She had been as eager as he when they'd made love in the cold water of the tub after their first time. And around dawn, when David had heard a distant cock crow, he had pulled her soft body beneath his, and she had eagerly guided him inside her.

Fully aroused now, he reached blindly for her across the bed, but she was not there. Opening his eyes, he stared at the empty bed. His gaze quickly took in the room. The tub sat by the foot of the bed. The towels had been folded neatly and placed on a chair. His clothing lay beside the towels. The sight of Gwyneth's small trunk lying open near the window eased his mind. She could not have gone too far.

David's stomach growled from hunger. He decided that she must have been hungry, as well. She was probably downstairs getting some food for them at this very minute. Still though, he pushed aside the covers and pulled on his breeches.

She could not have run off after the night they'd spent together, he reasoned. No, he had to learn to trust her, and before they married Gwyneth would need to know that he trusted her.

Still, the soft tap on the door was a relief. David cast aside the shirt he was about to pull over his head. A dozen things ran though his mind to say to Gwyneth as soon as he opened the door. But more than any words, there was one thing he planned to do. He intended to toss her back onto that bed and make love to her in the full light of day.

He yanked open the door, only to have the serving woman carrying a tray step back. Her gaze, though, immediately fell to the front of his breeches. It took him only a moment to recover from his surprise.

"Where is she?" he barked, not making any effort to hide his disappointment and annoyance. "Where is the bloody woman who was staying with me here last night?"

Without waiting for an answer, he pushed by her into the narrow corridor, looking up and down the empty passageway.

"The mistress came down a couple of hours ago, sir. She asked to have breakfast brought up to yer room now." The girl held the tray of food toward him like a peace offering.

He refused to take it. "Where is she now?"

"I believe she was on her way out, sir."

"On her way out *where*?"

His shout made her almost drop the tray, but she

was able to catch it at the last moment and nervously hold it on one arm. "I dunna ken more, sir, but what she told me. And this . . ." She searched in her pocket. "This note she left to be delivered to ye with yer meal." With trembling fingers, she held the sealed missive toward him.

David snatched it out of her hand and stalked back inside the room.

"If ye dunna want yer breakfast, sir, should I send the boys to take away the tub?"

Glaring at her, he slammed the door shut.

After last night, everything she believed about the relationship between a man and a woman went right out the window. Modesty and timidity might as well reside on the moon. Even Gwyneth's knowledge and understanding of the act of lovemaking had been proven completely inadequate. Within the first few minutes of David's arrival, she had been educated in ways unimaginable.

It hadn't taken long for her to feel so comfortable with him. In fact, being intimate with him felt as natural as eating food or taking a drink. The word *no* had been erased from her vocabulary, despite the acts that she would have previously described as wicked, to say the very least. And Gwyneth had learned there were more sensitive parts to her body than there were stars in the sky. She could feel that delicious warmth in her starting up again, just thinking of last night.

And this was only the beginning of why she'd fled this morning. One night had completely overthrown her, body and soul. If she stayed even one more day, her life and David's would be unalterably changed.

Her notebooks and her money purse were all that

Gwyneth took with her. Staying in Gretna Green and hoping to find Ardmore was out of the question. She could not risk being found by David. She would not be able to face him and defy him, not this soon.

The journey from Gretna Green to Greenbrae Hall would take a day and a half if she were to rent a carriage. She could cut that to under a day if she were to ride. The latter was her preference, so long as she did not have to ride sidesaddle. A woman riding unescorted through the countryside would be too conspicuous. For a few extra coins, a young groom at the nearby stables was more than willing to find some clothes for her to change into. Before the sun had completely risen above the eastern hills, Gwyneth was nudging a reasonably good mare into a canter along the road from Gretna Green to Edinburgh.

She was not so heartless as to disappear without letting him know where she was headed, of course. She did not want him to worry. At the same time, she didn't want to be chased through the countryside, either. That was why she had explained as much as she could in her letter. Still though, after a couple of hours on the road, Gwyneth had a strange feeling that she was being followed.

At the crest of a hill, Gwyneth slowed down enough to take a good look behind her. A solitary rider was traveling at a fairly good speed in the same easterly direction. She didn't think it was David, though.

She had no reason to be concerned, Gwyneth told herself. From a distance, a casual onlooker would think she was a young man. Her clothes hid her curves, and her wild red curls were tucked up into her large hat. Her horse and her attire did not indicate a gentleman of any substance, so even a highwayman might easily dismiss her. Still, though, she recalled the burly man with the smashed nose standing by the door of the tavern when she'd left early this morning. She'd seen him across the way from the stables when she'd come out dressed in the lad's clothing sometime later. She did not forget the suspicious look he had directed her way. Still, the two meetings could have been coincidental.

She spurred her horse over the crest of the hill. She was familiar with this part of the country, and she'd just stay ahead of the trailing rider. Nothing to worry about, she repeated silently to bolster her confidence.

Halfway down the hill, she glanced ahead at what was left of a stone cottage near the road. She thought she'd seen something move on the far side of it. Slowing down, Gwyneth recalled the many stories she'd heard of how highwaymen stopped and robbed unsuspecting travelers, blocking the road ahead while a gang member closed in from behind. She remembered the rider following her from Gretna Green. And hadn't someone else once told her how these rogues often chose their victims at a village or changing station?

Being unarmed put her at a disadvantage, and taking her money purse would be the least they would do to her once they discovered her gender. Gwyneth shuddered at the very thought of it. Yanking the mare's head to the left, she spurred the animal off the main road. A line of hills rose up beyond a grove of trees and she galloped madly toward it.

Catch her they might, but she was not going to be easy prey for them.

Violet did not know what had caused the desertion of the ancient abbey, but she had a good idea that the charred remains of a few village huts outside the broken walls were a clue. The battered ruins of the place still offered shelter from the wind and the weather, at least, and the well still provided refreshment to travelers passing through. Around her, she could see the telltale signs of cooking fires, and she sensed many folk had stopped here over the years.

She draped the old blanket around her shoulders and crawled into a corner formed by the wall and a stone building. From here, she could see the valley below. The sun still hung like a pale disk in the western sky, but she had walked as far as her legs could take her for one day. She hadn't gained back her strength completely. Being fed regularly by the kindly cotters had also spoiled her, as her stomach was already growling from hunger.

The thought of Rita and Angus sent a pang of regret through the young woman's heart. She had left directly from her baby's grave without a word of farewell. She had not gone back even to thank the good people for all they had done for her.

The loneliness she felt now was much worse than when she had been carrying her unborn child. As near as a fortnight ago, she had someone to talk to, a child to plan for, a vague future to dream about. Violet had been focused outside of herself for so many months now that she could think of no reason why she was even here. Why was she running away? Why shouldn't she just close her eyes and sit in this same place until she withered and died like a weed at the end of its season?

The movement in the distance caught her eye, disturbing her reverie. A solitary rider was galloping madly along the valley floor. Perhaps, she thought whimsically, it was the Angel of Death coming to claim her. Violet pulled the blanket over her hair and snuggled herself back between a pair of fallen stones. If it was her time to die, then she would be joining her daughter, at least. The grim thought actually cheered her.

It wouldn't matter what happened to her corpse. The worms and the wild animals could do their office. She wouldn't care. She would finally be at peace. She would no longer need to worry about her past sins or the shame she'd bring to anyone she might meet in the future.

The rider was now coming up the hill toward the abbey. He appeared to be a small man, though obviously very skilled in handling the animal he was riding. As Vi watched, though, she noticed that he seemed to be nervous or afraid of something. Several times, as he approached, the rider looked over his shoulder at the valley behind.

Violet looked back along the valley. It was empty of anyone else for as far as she could see. The rider disappeared behind a small grove of trees at the base of the hill beneath the burned village. Vi knew the man would be here in just a few minutes, and suddenly she wished she could crawl even deeper into her hole. He would be getting some water for himself and his horse and hopefully be on his way again, Violet told herself. Still, she didn't want to be seen. She thought about running for it, but before she could move, the horse and rider appeared at the abbey gate.

Clearly, he had been here before, for he spurred his mount directly across the rubble-strewn courtyard toward the well. This close, he was even smaller than she'd thought him to be. His clothes were worn and humble, which struck her as strange, considering how well he rode. A wide-brimmed hat was pulled low, keeping his eyes and most of his face in shadow.

Violet saw it too late to cry out in warning. The rider was getting down from his horse when a snake, warming itself on a smooth red rock by the well, darted across the dirt, startling the horse. As the animal reared up, the rider was thrown, one foot still in the stirrup. At the next instant, the steed was charging across the courtyard, dragging the rider behind. Luckily, the yard was small, and the horse stopped at the wall and stood wild-eyed, pawing the ground.

Violet immediately ran from her hiding place. The rider, one foot still stuck in the stirrup, was not moving. She stopped dead in her tracks, staring in shock at the unconscious person. It was a woman. The hat had fallen off her head, and long locks of red curls lay in the dirt.

The horse continued to paw the ground nervously, dragging its fallen rider a few more steps. Violet was no rider, but she had some experience with horses from watching the men at the stables of Melbury Hall. She approached cautiously, talking gently to the animal and finally reaching up to take the reins.

Violet held the reins with one hand and tried to release the woman's boot with the other. As soon as the foot came free, she pushed the horse out of the way and knelt beside the injured rider.

She was a young woman, probably of the same age as Vi herself. At closer inspection, the clothes were ill fitting on her. The boots looked to be far too big, probably an added reason for her foot getting caught. Violet had seen her on the horse. She certainly looked like an expert. She appeared to be breathing, so that was good news.

"Miss," Violet said gently, touching her face.

There was no movement. Her eyes remained shut. Violet reached to brush the hair out of woman's face, and that was when she saw the blood. The woman had banged her head hard when she had first fallen off, and probably bounced it on the rocky surface of the courtyard a number of times afterward.

"No," Vi said grimly. "You shan't die on me. If the Angel of Death is coming for anyone, 'tis only for me. No one else. Only me."

The surly group converged at the ruined stone cottage. Nightfall would soon be upon them. Separating and searching either side of the main road had turned up nothing. They had not been able to find even a trace of the woman.

"This'll teach ye a lesson about goin' places that we've no business goin'," the first of the outlaws to arrive back complained loudly. "What do we know about the 'idin' places in these cursed hills?"

"She was on the road ahead of me before going over the crest of the hill," the leader barked at the other two. " 'Twas up to ye two louts to watch her till she rode into the trap."

"The she-fox just bloody vanished," the third man argued.

"Just 'ow were we supposed to do that when we're tryin' to 'ide behind these bloody walls?" the first man added hotly. "If ye listened to us, we could've snuffed the chit as she was leavin' Gretna Green, instead of comin' so bloody far up the road. She would be lyin' in her own gore by now, and we'd be on our way to get our bloody money."

"Fightin' amongst ourselves'll do us no good," the third man put in wearily. "The fox is gone into the 'ills, and we've lost 'alf a day lookin' for 'er. Now, we've come too far to walk away not to see a tuppence fer our troubles. Let's think of what we should do *now*."

The leader scratched his chin. He looked up at the deserted road ahead. "She might've shaken us by going into the hills. But we know where the bloody wench is headed."

"Are ye sayin' we should try to catch up to her where she lives?" the first man asked, surprised.

"And why not?"

"We know less about this Greenbrae Hall than we do these bloody 'ills. And 'ow believable would it be that someone cut 'er throat or emptied a pistol into the chit in 'er own 'ouse. Ye said 'twas supposed to look like a robbery."

The leader shrugged. "We get paid when the wench is dead. I don't give a tinker's damn what our man believes. If we don't get the job done, they'll hire someone else to do it. So it might as well be us."

"Aye," the third man in the group agreed. "I'm with ye."

"We have to plan it right, though. We have to get onto the wench's estate, get ourselves hired on if that'll get us closer to her. We only strike when we can see we're free and clear." He paused for a moment. "Mind ye, now. Here's how we'll do it."

Millicent had finally agreed to Lyon's wishes, staying behind at Baronsford. He had promised to do everything humanly possible to bring Violet back. The young woman knew the earl. There was no reason why she would not trust him. He and Truscott had taken a carriage to make certain that they had the means of bringing her back to Baronsford. Millicent told them to use any excuse, to lie about Millicent's health if they need to. They must use any means at their disposal to convince Violet that she was needed here.

Even trusting their abilities, Millicent found the wait excruciating. They had gone off first thing in the morning, but there was still no news. Millicent could not settle down. She could not stop her worrying. She understood the magnitude of being given this second chance to do things right.

Violet had been fifteen when she'd left her mother's house to come and work at Melbury Hall. Despite her age, though, she had been hardworking, loyal, and very quick to learn. Millicent had spoken to the mother and grandmother. She'd accepted the responsibility of looking after their child, of caring and protecting her. It still crushed her that Violet's innocence and her beauty made her the prefect prey for a dishonest man. Millicent had not paid attention to what the needs of a young woman Vi's age might be. She'd failed to warn her of the lurking dangers. She'd been in the position of authority in the young woman's life, but she'd never offered any advice or direction.

Millicent had also failed to see the obvious. During the last weeks of Violet's stay at Melbury Hall, while all the distressing signs were, in retrospect, so apparent, Millicent had not seen them. She'd been so caught up in her own life and in Lyon's recovery that she had ignored the obvious. Violet was withdrawn. There were bruises on her face. For too many days, she appeared ill. And then she'd begged to be excused from coming to Baronsford. Millicent had let her, and it was a mistake that she hadn't been able to forgive herself for during these many months that the young woman had been missing.

Millicent went to the window again and looked out impatiently. A second chance, she told herself. They were all being given a second chance.

"I am becoming dizzy watching you pace back and forth between that chair and the window," the dowager scolded from the sofa.

Millicent looked over her shoulder at her mother-in-law and smiled. There was a hint of worry in the older woman's blue eyes as she peered over the spectacles perched on the bridge of her nose. She was considered a tyrant by many, but the dowager and Millicent had begun on equal terms from the day they met, and the fondness that now existed between them was solidly grounded in mutual respect.

"How is the book you are reading?" Millicent asked.

"What book?" Beatrice closed the book that she was holding on her lap and put it on the table beside her. She patted the space next to her on the sofa. "Come and sit with me."

"I cannot." She entwined her fingers over her swollen belly. "I am too anxious."

The dowager turned to Ohenewaa, who was sitting in a chair next to the sofa. Wearing a plain dress that she'd adorned with a colorful shawl that matched the scarf she had wrapped around her hair, Ohenewaa looked regal. The old black woman's eyes were half closed, but she was not sleeping. Everyone at Baronsford, starting with Millicent, was accustomed to the healer's habits. Meditating, praying, or perhaps just watching, Ohenewaa often sat quietly like this for hours.

"Are you awake?" Beatrice asked.

"Why does matter, old woman? You will intrude on my time, anyway."

"Sorry to bring you back from the ghost world," Beatrice grouched, ignoring the sharp glance from her friend. "But this is an urgent matter."

"What do you want now?"

"I want you to cast a spell on Millicent to calm her."

Ohenewaa shook her head. "How many times do I have to tell you, I have no knowledge of any spells."

"I asked you nicely, did I not?" Beatrice argued. "Still, you keep your secrets from me. When are you going to start being honest with your best friend?"

"Best friend?" The woman's eyes narrowed, and she looked down her nose at Beatrice. "We can barely tolerate each other's presence. But I would like a sip of whatever brew you have been drinking that makes you believe we are best friends."

"I will gladly make you some this afternoon . . . but that is only after you say or do something to put this poor young woman's mind at ease."

"I . . . I am truly . . ." Millicent tried to break into the argument, but stopped with a sigh. Beatrice and Ohenewaa were well into one of their daily contests of words.

It was amusing to watch and listen to them. They each complained and belittled each other and claimed they couldn't wait until one of them left Baronsford, but the reality of it was that the friendship between them continued to grow stronger and deeper with each passing day.

Despite their constant complaining, neither had spent a day apart from the other since the first time they met last spring at Melbury Hall. When the dowager had to leave Melbury Hall for a fortnight in London, Ohenewaa claimed that the old woman was too weak to travel alone and had volunteered to go and stay with her. The same was true for the rest of their travels, which had taken them to Baronsford, back to Herefordshire, to London, and back to Scotland again.

Last month, when Ohenewaa had come down with a fever and a cough, the dowager had refused to leave her friend's bedside for an entire week. And that was in spite of the doctor's insistence that Beatrice was too old and weak to endure that kind of hardship.

Both women had survived the illness healthier than before.

"You should sit rather than stand."

Millicent accepted the chair Ohenewaa moved beside the window for her and sat down. From this position, she had a clear view of the road while still being able to participate in the conversation of the two women, if she so dared.

"You see, she listens to you," the dowager said triumphantly. "Now order her to stop fretting."

"I do not order people." Ohenewaa placed a hand on Millicent's shoulder.

The dowager scoffed. "Now that is the most brazen lie I have ever heard. You order me around all the time."

Millicent felt the warmth from Ohenewaa's touch seep into her body. Even more so than the dowager, she was a believer in Ohenewaa's power, in her healing touch, in the way the old woman could look into one's soul and know the pain that resides there. Millicent had seen Ohenewaa's powers at work in her husband's healing. Lyon had come to them a broken man, crippled in mind and body, but the old healer had known the source of his pain. She had known what to do, how to draw him out of his stupor. What she had done for Lyon was something that no doctors had even imagined possible. Millicent's gratitude had no end when it came to Ohenewaa.

She also owed much of her happiness to the dowager. The old woman had arranged the marriage with her son, and had given Millicent a second chance at life.

A second chance. Her gaze moved to the road again.

"Hold in your mind my earlier words. Remember what I told you," Ohenewaa said quietly to her before withdrawing her hand and walking back to resume the argument with her friend.

Millicent watched the straight back of the black woman—the confident steps. She knew exactly the words Ohenewaa was alluding to. It was spring; they were at Melbury Hall. Guilt and worry over the disappearance of Violet was paralyzing Millicent, but Ohenewaa had told her not to mourn the loss of the young woman. Their paths will cross again, she'd told her. Millicent just had to be patient. They would have another chance at mending what had gone wrong.

Millicent looked over her shoulder at Ohenewaa's calm demeanor. She wondered if the healer knew if this was the time.

The sight of the carriage coming up the drive had Millicent out of the chair and running for the door. Mrs. MacAlister, the housekeeper, was beside her as she burst into the hallway. Baronsford's steward, Mr. Campbell, reached the front door before any of the other servants and opened it as Millicent reached it.

She knew Lyon had every person at Baronsford watching over her. She could not move without having a handful of people appear from nowhere to assist her. Millicent could not get used to this amount of attention. But as Lyon had warned her, it was for *his* peace of mind, and she would just have to resign herself to it.

And Millicent did. It took great restraint not to run down the drive to meet the carriage. A touch on her arm told her Ohenewaa had joined her outside, as well. She placed her other hand on the healer's—wanting to draw on the woman's strength.

"Finally," she whispered. "You were right. She is here."

"Not yet," she said quietly into her ear.

Millicent's heart sank. She looked at the oncoming carriage. She glanced over at Ohenewaa. "They did not bring her?"

The healer shook her head calmly. Her lined face showed no expression. "But she is coming, on her own, and in her own time. Be patient."

The carriage came to a stop, and the door opened. Millicent stepped forward as her husband alone stepped out of it. The disappointment was plainly etched in his handsome features. He took her into his arms.

"I am sorry, Millicent. Violet had already left before we arrived. But Truscott has gone on to look for her. He will find her, my love. I know he will."

Millicent laid her cheek against his strong chest, her hands clutching his back.

"I know he will, too," she whispered quietly. "Ohenewaa said that Violet is coming back. She is always right."

*   *   *

David started directly for Greenbrae Hall, as that was where Gwyneth had claimed in her letter that she was going.

He didn't bother with a carriage, but instead acquired a horse. Speed was his goal, and if she thought that he would arrange to have her trunk sent up after her, she was mistaken. David simply left everything with the innkeeper.

The ride from Gretna Green took longer than he wanted. But in his state of mind, growing wings and flying would not give him the speed he would have wished for.

Douglasses! Douglas *women*, he corrected. Here it was, happening to him for a second time. Emma . . . and now Gwyneth!

He immediately pushed Emma out of his mind. He had been a naive lad, he told himself.

Greenbrae Hall was located next to Baronsford. He had resolved to see his family very soon. Emma was a part of the distant past, and he did not intend to let that past disrupt his plans for the future. Both of his brothers had moved on with their lives. David was determined to do the same with Gwyneth.

Her letter said she did not regret what they had done last night. She filled an entire page with beautiful prose about how he had made her feel. Any other man's feelings would have been suitably mollified by such descriptions, but not David's. The last words of her letter were what mattered to him. They could not do this again. She could not stay. Their lives were leading in different directions. There could be no future for them.

Why in bloody hell not? was the question he in-

tended to ask Gwyneth as soon as he had his hands
on her. And her plea not to come after her—not to
make the situation more difficult than it already was—
didn't mean a thing to him.

David had done his share of running away from
what he wanted and from the conflict stemming from
it. He had been a fool, of course. Emma's eyes had
been solely on Lyon. She'd been entertaining herself
with him while waiting for her earl to arrive. David
had seen what was coming, though, and ignored the
signs. It had been only a matter of time.

With Gwyneth, though, he was confused as hell.
She'd always cared for him. He'd never thought there
was any competition when it came to her affection for
another. And their physical attraction was impossible
to ignore. The sparks between them had ignited the
moment they'd met in London. And last night, after
everything they'd done, the way they'd made love was
unlike anything either had experienced. Of that, he
was certain. They were compatible in every way, and
Gwyneth's running away made no sense at all.

There were still several hours of daylight left when
he arrived at Greenbrae Hall. The handsome country
house was still shut, though, and David was met by
only the caretaker and the meager crew of servants
who remained there when the family was away in London or Edinburgh.

"We were not told of Miss Gwyneth coming as yet,
sir," the old caretaker told him, obviously flustered.
"The housekeeper and the servants from the London
house always come up before any of the family arrive.
We've seen none of those folk. From what I was told,
her ladyship and Miss Gwyneth had no plans of being
here for another fortnight, at least."

"But Miss Gwyneth left a message for me that she was coming here. She came on horseback." This much he was able to find out before he'd left Gretna Green. "She should have been here by now."

Alone! Riding alone through the Borders country! She must have been out of her mind, David cursed silently.

"Miss Gwyneth was coming with no escort, sir?" The man wrung his hands nervously. "Well, she has not arrived, yet. But what should we do? I've only a couple of lads in the stables. We could go out looking for her. Do ye know which road she was traveling? We . . ."

"I shall take care of it," David told the man. "I shall get help from Baronsford. We'll find her."

And he *would* find her. Mounting up, David prayed that Gwyneth was still alive and unharmed, though he planned to strangle her as soon as he found her.

Walter left Baronsford frustrated, but he came back to it a different man.

He had a new appreciation for the place when he returned. His eyes had been opened by his travels abroad. He noticed things he'd never seen before. He appreciated what before he had taken for granted. The quiet countryside, the good, solid people he had known for so many years; all of them were more precious than he'd ever thought.

He now recognized the Borders . . . and Baronsford . . . as a corner of heaven, and he was tremendously grateful for the privilege the Pennington family had bestowed on him in asking him to manage their estate in the coming years.

No longer was Walter a young man being driven to

madness by thoughts of Emma, the one woman he could never have. Fourteen months away had given him a new view of women. The salons and ballrooms of Italy, France, and Germany had cured him of his youthful infatuation. Time and distance had taught him to separate dreams from reality. He knew who he was now. He knew what he wanted. Walter had matured into a man with a purpose, and he was determined to excel in that.

The old earl recognized Truscott's growth, too. That summer he was given charge of running Baronsford, and Walter told himself he could not be happier.

Chapter 12

⟿

Irregular patches of white, tinted with the faintest hints of pink and gold, puffed and scudded across the multicolored canvas. To one side, a halo emanated from the descending sun, the colors changing from deep reds and orange to violet and purple as the light bled across the darkening blue of the sky. A lone bird, her white wings spread wide, floated before the backdrop of colors. Gwyneth's first conscious thought was that she had never known how many different shades could be captured in a single sky. She thought to ask David if he'd ever seen anything quite so beautiful.

The realization that he wasn't with her came with the feel of the hard ground against her back. Her head rested on a soft padding. Gwyneth's body was stiff, as if she had been lying there forever, but she hardly felt rested. Snatches of what had happened pushed into her mind. The old abbey on the hilltop. Her decision to go up there to water and rest her mount. The horse startling and rearing up. The images became murky from that point. She did recall, though, a young woman bent over her, talking to her. Blue eyes, golden curls. For an instant she'd thought it was the ghost of Emma. But even in her faltering consciousness, she'd been able to recognize kindness and knew it could not have been her cousin, dead or alive.

Gwyneth's gaze wandered from the sky to the ruined walls of the abbey to the horse grazing on a patch of grass not too far away. She tried to lift her head to look for the woman, but her head began to spin and a sharp pain in her shoulder made her stay put.

"So you are awake."

The voice was soft and Gwyneth detected an English accent. She turned her head, trying to locate the voice and saw the woman as she approached. Framed by the light of the descending sun, her face was difficult to see. Her clothes were not just worn but threadbare, but the same familiar halo of golden curls encircled her face.

"You saved my life."

The woman shook her head shyly. "Your foot would have come out of that boot soon."

"Still . . . thank you." Gwyneth tried to lift her right arm, but the pain in her shoulder again stopped her. She tried the other and was relieved that the joint moved. In spite of the pain, nothing appeared broken.

"You have a good size cut on the back of your head." The stranger crouched next to her. "Watching you now, it seems that you have bruised your shoulder, too."

"I know I would have a lot *more* than a bruised shoulder and head to worry about if you hadn't helped." This close, she had a much better view of her face. They were about the same age. She was very pretty. But there was a sadness, too, in her expression. "My name is Gwyneth."

The blue eyes considered her for few seconds before she replied. "Violet. You were traveling alone?"

"I was." Gwyneth used her left hand to push the hair out of her eyes. She looked around as far as she could see. "A wee bit foolish, now that I think of it. What about you? Are you traveling alone, too?"

Violet nodded. "I was hoping to join the next group of vagrants passing through."

Her words went directly to Gwyneth's heart. Their situations were so different. This young woman had no place or family of her own. Gwyneth looked away, trying to hide her dismay.

"How long have you been waiting here?" she asked.

"I arrived just as you rode up the valley."

She looked back at the stranger. If one ignored her ragged clothing, there was little difference in their manner. She remembered the stableboy's clothing she was wearing herself. That made them similar in so many respects. She wondered if Violet was running away from someone or something, too.

"Are you traveling south, then?" Gwyneth asked, knowing that many of the displaced tenants were going that way.

Violet gave an indifferent shrug. "Or west. Where I go depends on the people with whom I cross paths."

"I was going north. A place named Greenbrae Hall, between here and Edinburgh."

"You are not too far from your destination. I believe I came by a place by that name not long ago. I think 'tis not a half day's walk."

"I believe you are correct."

The rough ground was digging into her back, and Gwyneth tried to roll onto her left side. A sharp pain shooting through her shoulder put a stop to that. Violet was immediately beside her, helping her to move a little. When she was settled a little more comfortably, the young woman pressed a wet cloth she was holding against the back of Gwyneth's head.

"The bleeding seems to have stopped. But I do not know much about your shoulder. Common sense tells me you should stay put, though."

Staying put sounded good at the moment. No one in Greenbrae Hall would be expecting her yet, anyway. She had lied to her aunt and promised to wait in Edinburgh at the home of one of Augusta's friends until she arrived from England.

The only one who would be going to Greenbrae Hall would be David. She knew that in spite of what she had done, he at least cared enough to stop there and make certain she had arrived safely. She thought about the highwaymen she'd eluded on the main road, deciding that David could take care of himself if they tried to take him. She could not warn him, anyway.

She tried to move her shoulder, which was stiffening up. This accident had knocked all of the bluster out of her. Her plan to show him how needless his interference was had become a lie. Still, she could not let David find her like this. Gwyneth looked up with hope at the woman beside her.

"Would it make a great difference in your plans if you were to travel with me to the north again?" she asked. "I know this is a great imposition, but a number of people will be greatly distressed if I do not arrive there. And to be honest, I do not know if I can manage it by myself at the moment."

Violet immediately withdrew her hands, and her back stiffened. "Others who can take you will surely pass this way."

"But what happens if no one comes tomorrow or the next day?"

Violet got up quickly and moved away. Gwyneth fought the pain and forced herself to sit up. It took a moment for her head to stop spinning, but she could make out the young woman by the well. Seeing her hunched shoulders, she thought for a moment that Violet was weeping.

Guilt quickly washed over her. Gwyneth's request had lacked judgment. She'd been abrupt and careless. She had no right to demand anything of someone she had just met. Moreover, she knew nothing of the circumstances that had driven the young woman out on the road where she was at the mercy of strangers. Her own insensitivity appalled her.

While there were similarities in their apparent situations, Gwyneth realized how different their lives truly were. Though she might lose her inheritance if her writing were exposed, little else was wrong with her life. She was not ill. She was not poor. Her life was not in any danger. She shook her head. David was right in saying she knew nothing about life's hardships. What did it really matter if David thought any less of her? Very little, really.

And yet, in contrast, here was Violet.

Gwyneth tried to push to her feet. She had to do something.

Because of Millicent's delicate condition, Lyon insisted that they retire to bed early every night while they were at Baronsford. Although he never immediately fell asleep himself, he found he enjoyed the feeling of lying in bed, holding his wife and making certain she got her rest. Tonight was no exception.

The clock on the mantel had not yet struck midnight, though, when Lyon heard the footsteps in the hallway outside their bedchamber. A moment later, he heard the soft tap on the door. He tried to roll gently away from Millicent's warm body without waking her up. Her hand, however, reached for his as soon as he moved.

"Something must be wrong," she whispered in alarm.

"No, my love. A soft tap only means that, since Walter Truscott is not here, Mr. Campbell is at a loss about some routine decision and needs to ask my opinion on it. Pounding on the door, accompanied by Mrs. MacAlister's shrill voice, would mean something is wrong."

A pretty smile broke on her lips, and her eyes looked up sleepily at him. "I had no idea there was such deep meaning to the various knocks at Baronsford or I would have developed one for the two of us."

He smiled. "You need a knock when there is a door. There shall never be a door between us." He brushed a kiss on her lips. "Now, go back to sleep, love. If there is any news, I shall awaken you."

"Hurry back," she whispered before laying her head back on the pillow.

Lyon tucked the bedclothes around her and pushed a curl behind her ear. As another knock sounded, he glared in the direction of the door. He hated to leave Millicent alone even for a minute. The doctor who came down from Edinburgh each fortnight to check on her, Ohenewaa, his own mother—they all continued to assure him that his wife was doing wonderful with her pregnancy. They all scolded him for fretting too much. But Lyon did as he wished. Millicent was more precious to him than anything in this world. He would go to any length to make certain she was well cared for.

Lyon pulled on his robe and went to the door. He

hoped that this was news from Truscott—specifically, that his cousin had found Violet. Pulling the door open, he was met with the steward's face and another servant, who was holding a candle. Campbell was obviously about to explode with some good news.

"Are they here?" Lyon asked, going out into the hallway and pulling the door closed behind him.

The steward actually rubbed his thin hands together. "*He* is here, milord."

"Who?"

"Begging yer pardon, milord, but I gave my word not to say anything, but only to ask ye to come down to yer study."

"Campbell," Lyon snarled. "Who is here?"

"This way, if ye please, milord."

"I am in no mood for games at this bloody hour of the night," Lyon growled fiercely, but the short, wiry steward did not appear bothered at all. Instead, he simply pushed the candle-bearing servant ahead of them down the hallway.

With the exception of the watchmen outside, the rest of the household had long ago retired to their beds. Coming down the grand staircase, Lyon could not—for the life of him—imagine who would be arriving so unexpectedly in the middle of the night.

It had to be someone that they knew, and, reaching the ground floor, Lyon saw Mrs. MacAlister, wrapped in a blanket, disappearing with several servants in tow in the direction of the kitchens. It was someone Campbell had been happy to see. Someone who felt comfortable arriving unannounced. As Lyon reached the door of his study, the only one he could think of was Gibbs, his manservant who was now the steward at Melbury Hall. But the Highlander would never have

left his new wife or his responsibilities in Hertfordshire to ride up here unless there was some trouble.
And Campbell did not look like a man bringing news
of trouble.

The servant with the candle opened the door, and
Lyon pushed past him into the study. The sight of the
tall young man turning to face him by the crackling
fireplace made Lyon's heart leap into his throat.

"David! By the devil, 'tis good to see you!"

He was standing, facing him. David looked with disbelief at the powerful shoulders, the straight back, at
the legs supporting his weight. The letters he'd received failed to prepare him for this. Although he'd
read them, he had not been convinced that Lyon had
truly healed. He was no longer the broken man who
lay indifferent to the world on a bed in a dark chamber. Incapable of seeing to his own most basic needs,
drugged to the point of being unable to recognize his
own kin, Lyon had not even been able to remember
the events that had put him in such a state.

David remembered how Lyon's inability to defend
his honor against the accusations had tortured all of
them. He also recalled the guilt he'd felt over this past
year about the way he and Pierce had deserted him
in the time when Lyon had needed them most.

David looked up into his brother's face and saw a
multitude of emotions pass over his features. Not one
of them might be construed as hostile, though.

"You are not in uniform."

"I've left my regiment."

It was difficult to remain rooted in one place, not
to move forward and pull him into an embrace. David
saw the slight graying of hair at Lyon's temples. There

were new lines around his intense blue eyes. He'd even gained a bit of weight. Lyon had aged somewhat. But with that, there was a sense of calm, too. The tension that had always charged the air during the time when Lyon had been married to Emma was gone.

"Have you?" the earl asked, obviously surprised. "Why now?"

"I've had enough of the military. 'Twas time for a change."

Lyon paused, his gaze searching David's face. "Was that the only reason?"

The younger brother returned the earl's gaze and then shook his head. "No, that was not the only reason. They were sending me to the American colonies to report to an Admiral Middleton. I've heard something of Pierce's involvement in Boston's affairs . . . and also learned recently of his new relations with the Admiral through marriage. I was not about to be used as a weapon against my own brother."

The earl's face was unreadable. "Putting your family above king and country?"

"For all my life, what I have known to be the truth has always had a way of separating itself from the dictates of king and country. That has become clearer to me lately. Perhaps 'tis the rebel Scottish blood that runs in my veins—or perhaps 'tis the perspective of the third son that makes it so—but I do not believe that wisdom and moral superiority necessarily come with a man's position in the world."

David waited anxiously as Lyon continued to study him for a few moments longer, realizing that, so far, there had been no warm welcome. He had not given too much thought to this moment before now. What if the hurt between them was beyond repair? Still, he thought, Lyon had welcomed Pierce back with open arms.

"I need to know what you believe about *me*."

For a few seconds, David stared uncomprehendingly. This was the last thing he had expected Lyon to say. His brother had never given a damn what anyone thought about him.

"I believe I am seeing a miracle. I am looking forward to meeting the new countess to thank her personally for what she has done for you."

A weary frown crept over Lyon's face. He walked toward his desk. For the first time, David noticed the slight limp. He had said something wrong. His answer had damaged whatever momentary pleasure Lyon must have had in seeing him.

David knew what his brother was asking. Watching Lyon crossing the room, he cursed his own inability to decide how much fault Lyon deserved to shoulder in Emma's death . . . if indeed he deserved any. David was also irritated, though, at his brother for pressing him for an answer. Even so, they were still brothers.

"Am I not welcome here?" he asked abruptly.

Lyon turned and rested a hip against his desk. "Baronsford is your home. It always will be. You are always welcome here."

"I am not talking about the place. I am talking about you."

Lyon crossed his arms over his chest. His blue eyes looked steadily into David's. "I cannot tell you how happy I am to see you. And I am tremendously relieved about the decision that you have made in not going to Boston."

"But you are troubled."

The earl nodded. "I am troubled, for I see the doubts still lingering in you."

"What doubts?"

"Do not deny it, David," he said wearily. "I am talking about Emma."

"Everyone is resolved to the fact that 'twas an accident."

"I care nothing for what *everyone* believes or is resolved to believe. I care about you, about your opinion, about what you think I did to ruin her happiness and possibly yours. I want nothing between us. I want no ill will based on doubts and suspicion."

Suddenly, David felt a wave of exhaustion descend upon him. True, he thought, he had spent the entire day in the saddle, frustrated at not finding Gwyneth, worrying where she was and not even knowing where to look. He could not even dismiss the possibility that, after everything they had shared, she may still have run off with her fortune-hunting beau. Nevertheless, that was not all that was weighing on him now. David felt as if his boots were filled with lead as he moved to the sofa and sat down.

"Lyon, I came back to Baronsford not to stir up the past, but to do what you and Pierce have been able to do—to leave it behind and move on into the future. I harbor no blame. No resentment for anything. I certainly make no accusations. I am perfectly content to move on and never look back."

"But that does not work," Lyon said gently. "I have tried to do that, David. I went through a period of rage as well as a period when I tried to deny that anything was wrong. I could not heal, though, until I was able to face the truth of the past—my mistakes, my flaws . . . and Emma's, as well. Wounds we carry from the past have a way of festering, infecting everything, and the pain can be unbearable."

"That is only if you allow them to fester. I do not.

I am already looking forward to future," David said with honesty. "I am looking forward to all the things that you and Pierce have each been doing this past year. Choosing a wife, putting down roots, starting a family."

Of course, he thought Gwyneth would jump at the opportunity of becoming his wife. But there was still time to convince her of it, David told himself. She might have taken a wrong road. He would find her.

The earl's arms unfolded, and a gentle smile tugged at the corner of his mouth as he walked from the desk and sat in a chair across from David. "I am in favor of all these things. But they might just complicate your life more if you have not come to terms with the past."

"Lyon, Emma chose you over me. That was the end of it. I put that behind me before your wedding. What else is there to come to terms with?" David was surprised at the note of bitterness in his own voice. His brother gave no sign that he had heard it, though.

" 'Twas not me, David. Emma chose Baronsford. I was only a means for her to get what she wanted."

"I do not disagree with you about that. But that's the end of it. I do not care to talk about Emma anymore. I do not want to go over what was and who did what or even how you and Pierce and I became strangers to each other because of one woman." David ran a tired hand over his face and leaned forward, his elbows on his knees. "I wanted to come back to Baronsford to see my family again, to bask a little in the warm feeling that I hear has made this place a home once again." He looked up into his brother's face. "I want to heal, too. Is that too much to ask?"

"No, David. That is not too much to ask. At least, not for the moment."

Lyon leaned forward in his chair and extended his hand. David took it. The grip was strong. The connection felt like a lifeline.

"Welcome home, brother."

Walter had no time to think of his tower house. His focus remained solely on Baronsford.

In the same way, he tried to forget that anything personal had ever passed between him and Emma. In the year since returning from the continent, he'd seen her many times but would not allow himself to think about her. He treated her respectfully, keeping his distance. At all costs, though, he avoided being alone with her.

Walter knew that, having turned eighteen this year, she would be presented at Court in London. Unlike the other young women of the ton, *her appearance in social circles would have nothing to do with finding a proper husband. Walter knew she was destined for Baronsford. The question was which of the Pennington men would be the unfortunate soul who would marry her.*

Walter was surprised when he heard rumors that spring that someone had been seen near the tower house. The vagueness of the talk was what made him ride over one wet afternoon to see for himself. The place still needed work, and there was nothing in it to steal, so if it were just a vagrant passing through, then no matter. If it were some potential troublemaker who might bring some harm to the people of Baronsford, though, that was another thing entirely.

Arriving at the tower house, he felt again the pride he had in the place. All the renovations were just as he had left them, but there were signs that someone had indeed been there. He walked through the empty chambers, but found no one.

Then, in the master's bedchamber, he sensed her presence. On the sill of a narrow window, he found a small bouquet of wild roses, not a few days old. It was Emma; he knew it. She was using the tower house as a refuge.

He was still holding the flowers in his hand when Emma glided into the bedchamber. Her smile of greeting was his crushing defeat.

"Walter, I knew you would come back here." She pulled the wet cloak off her shoulders and walked to him. "We both can try, but the invisible bond that connects us will always pull us together."

He wanted to deny her words, but he couldn't. As if in a dream, he stood there, rooted to the ancient timbers of the chamber floor. Unable to resist, he simply allowed her lips to find his. She tasted of the rain. Emma smelled of wild roses, and it was an intoxicating scent that seemed to belong only to her.

"I should not forgive you, though, for making me wait and suffer for so long."

The breath caught in his chest when he realized she was undressing.

"Emma," he said with alarm, stepping back.

"I told you before. You must be the first." She backed him against the wall. She kissed him again, her lips potent as any drug. "And I have decided to forgive you for not waiting for me."

She took his hand and placed it against her breast. The front of her dress was unbuttoned to the waist. Only the thin silk of her chemise separated her flesh from the hard calluses on his palm.

"I know you know what to do," she said thickly. "Your reputation amongst the women has spread. Even the servants at Greenbrae Hall know what magic you can perform. I want the same thing, Walter. You owe me at least the same pleasure."

"Emma, this is not right." He pulled his hand away.

"This is why you came here today," she responded, pushing her belly against his hardening manhood. "You cannot deny what you are feeling. I know what this means. You want me. And I have waited long enough, saved myself for as long as I could. Now I want you to take me."

He took hold of her shoulders and pushed her away. "Listen to yourself. You sound no better than a tavern wench."

"I care nothing about that if it means you give me what you have been giving all those others. Call me wench or whore, make love to me in a back alley tavern or against a rock in a pasture, it matters not. I will be anything you want me to be, so long as you are the first man I make love to."

"Listen to me, then." He shook her once and looked into her eyes. "You have a respectable future awaiting you. One that you've told me yourself cannot include me. Any one of my cousins could become your husband. They will expect virtue and dignity from you. Your husband is the man to whom you should be offering this."

She laughed and reached down, touching him through his breeches. "You shall be the first, Walter. You gave me my first kiss. You shall be the first man I make love to."

"You heard nothing I said."

She shook her head and shrugged off his touch. "This is our place. 'Tis the safest place for both of us." She pushed down the dress and let it pool around her feet. "If you do not make love to me here, then I shall have to come to your bedchamber at Baronsford. And if you reject me there, I shall simply corner you in one of the stalls at the stables."

Her gaze caressed the length of his body and focused on his bulging manhood again.

"I shan't even push you to make the first advances. You can just stand there and watch me." She pulled the thin chemise over her head and threw it aside.

Walter knew he should run from her, but he couldn't. His eyes drank their fill of her body. She was more perfect than he'd ever dreamed. As he watched, she pulled a handful of pins out of her hair, and the curls tumbled down over her shoulders.

"Do you know what other men would give for what I am offering you?" She came toward him again. "Do you know what David would do if I stood before him like this?"

Her lips touched the taut skin of his jaw. He pressed his head back against the wall. Her fingers moved down the length of his arm and she entwined their fingers. Raising his hand, she placed it on her breast again. This time she ran his palm back and forth against the hardened nipple.

"Last summer, I let David touch my breast. I did not even tell him to stop when he pulled down the neckline of my dress and suckled me." She started undoing his breeches. "The entire time, though, I imagined 'twas your mouth at my breast. I've even tried to think what 'twould be like to have your weight on top of me and you deep inside of me."

Walter let out an agonized groan when her fingers slid inside his breeches and grasped his throbbing member.

"Did you ever think about me while making love to the other women? Did you ever pretend 'twas me that you were touching? I have enough proof in my hand that you want me. What are you waiting for, Walter? Take me."

He put his hands around her and drew her fiercely against him. "I cannot fight you."

"I do not want to fight." She smiled against his lips and then kissed him hard, pushing her tongue into his mouth. She pulled back a moment later. "I want to feel you inside of me . . . here."

She guided his hand to her folds. She was wet. With no gentleness, he pressed a finger into her. She threw her head back and gave a satisfied cry, pushing herself against his hand. He could feel that she was a virgin. That was when Walter truly lost his mind.

Making love to Emma was unlike anything he'd experienced with any other woman. She was bold, demanding, wild. He was not even able to discard all of his clothes before she turned her back to the wall and put her legs around him, lifting herself onto him. She made him drive into her, taking her virginity. Eye-to-eye, equals linked in the most intimate way.

The satisfaction was unlike any Walter had ever experienced, either. But the guilt that immediately followed was overwhelming, and he doubted if it would ever be washed away.

Not for as long as he lived. Not for eternity.

Chapter 13

The night was cold and Gwyneth was glad for the small fire crackling inside the protective curtain of the abbey wall. Though she had tried to stand earlier, the world had gone spinning off, with flashes of yellow and orange blinding her. With the help of Violet, she had made it to one of the ruined walls. Sitting there as the sun went down, she'd had a perfect view of the valley below and the path she had taken. With the passage of time, she was feeling better, too.

In all the times Gwyneth had traveled through these sections before, she had never been aware of the extreme isolation of the abbey. The valley itself was now deserted. There was no cottage that was inhabited, not for as far as the eye could see. No travelers, even. Around dusk, she was aware of a small herd of deer on the far side of the valley. Staring at the scene was as intimidating as it was soothing. Gwyneth guessed that days could go by before anyone would pass. At least there was no sign of the highwaymen.

After Violet had taken care of the horse, the two women had shared some dry bread Gwyneth had in a saddlebag. It was not much of a dinner, but it had sufficed. She could hardly eat anything. Even as they broke the bread, their conversation had been scarce. Gwyneth did not want to press the young woman about her earlier request, but at the same time, she was eager to mend the breach between them.

As the hour grew late, she still had no desire to lie down or go to sleep. Moving at all aggravated the persistent throbbing in her shoulder.

Violet did not seem too keen on sleeping, either. She sat quietly, not too far away, feeding sticks she'd gathered earlier into the fire. She showed no sign of harboring any ill feelings but appeared to be simply lost in her own thoughts. The mystery of her background, though, continued to nag at Gwyneth.

She watched the other woman write something in the dirt with the end of a stick before feeding the wood into the fire. She remembered her own notebook in the saddlebag of her horse. Her mind was full of words she would have liked to put on paper. What she had experienced firsthand, riding through the countryside, dressed as a lad, trying to avoid what she was sure were highwaymen.

All that she'd written before was from her imagination, or from the bits and pieces of adventure and romance she'd read in other stories, reshaping it with different people in another setting and told in her own way. But now she had so much more to write about. The single act of falling off her horse with her foot becoming stuck in the stirrup was worth lines and lines. It didn't matter that she couldn't remember all of it. Her imagination was already filling the gaps.

Perhaps, in a story, Violet could be a wild child, raised by wolves but having a heart of gold. Her hero or heroine would be taken care of by this child in her moment of need, and later return the favor, raising her and caring for her. Still, Violet came alive for her now, in a completely new way, because of these moments. Gwyneth felt the excitement rush through her. Inspiration was surging within her, creative ideas flowing again.

Before writing about today, though, she needed to write about last night, about making love with David. Gwyneth blushed at the mere thought. She wasn't going to write down everything, she told herself, but she would try to capture the thrill of the moment, put words to the things that she'd felt. She wondered if she had the ability to describe the look in his eyes, the fit of their bodies, the soft warmth of his touches as they lay together afterward.

She flexed her right fingers. There was no pain. She glanced toward the horse tied loosely to a rock and wondered if it was worth going after her supplies. The saddle sat on the ground nearby.

"I can get them for you."

Gwyneth turned in surprise as Violet pushed to her feet and walked toward the saddle. She watched the young woman reach inside the bag and fetch her notebook and her Keswick pencil before coming back to her.

"Thank you . . . but how did you know what I wanted?"

"I saw you look that way." She placed the supplies on Gwyneth's lap and quickly moved to where she had been sitting before.

Violet had fetched the bread and the extra blanket for them before. Naturally, she would have seen what else was in the saddlebag, Gwyneth reasoned, opening her notebook to a blank page. She left the other story she was in the midst of alone for now. Picking up the pencil, she just let the words come.

The fire continued to crackle, but Gwyneth drifted

out of the present time and place. In her mind, she
was with him again. As her fingers raced to keep up
with her thoughts, her emotions struggled against
standing to the side. Gwyneth did not try for perfection, she just let the information flow onto the page.

David. The reality of having him look at her, caress
her, talk to her with such passion and need was still
almost impossible to believe. But it was not a dream.
She had felt his embrace, his touch, and she remembered all of it. And she also remembered what he had
said about not wanting to share her with anyone else.

Gwyneth had not admitted it to him, but after last
night, she didn't think she could ever give herself to
another man. The complication it presented—namely,
how to explain her change in feelings to Sir Allan—
was an entirely different matter. She didn't know if he
would still agree to marry her if she refused physical
intimacy as part of their union.

Her pencil stopped moving. She stared into the
darkness enveloping the abbey. She had run away
from David's bed, knowing that was not an end to it.
She could not even imagine how it would end. But
more important, how was she going to bring some
sense of order back to her life? He was constantly
working to confuse her, it seemed. His proposal of
marriage, as abrupt as it was, had thrown her completely. For all her life, she would have been thrilled
by the offer. But last night, faced with it at such a
moment, she simply could not accept it, no matter
how great a tear it caused in her heart.

Reality was so different from dreams. Even without
any of the complications of her writing and the letters
of ransom, Gwyneth's conscience would not allow her
to accept his proposal. David was still in love with

Emma. Passion, no matter how explosive and fulfilling, was not enough to substitute for the real love he would never have in his heart for her. Gwyneth did not wish to be forever second in his heart.

The sense of being watched made her look over her shoulder at Violet. The other woman quickly averted her gaze, staring into the fire. Gwyneth's jumbled thoughts, fears, dreams, the complications in her life, everything churned, forming a burning mass in her chest.

"You must wonder what I was doing dressed as I am—making a mad dash through the countryside. I was just thinking about the same thing myself, and I cannot come up with a logical answer. But the more I ponder it, I realize that I have unintentionally managed to make a terrible mess of my life." Hearing the truth blurt out was unexpected, but Gwyneth suddenly wondered if Violet's life might be on a parallel path. They both appeared to be in trouble.

"I . . . I took the liberty of reading some of your writing in that notebook," the young woman admitted guiltily. "You were unconscious. Since you were wearing lads' clothing, I was terribly curious. I thought if there was anything in there that said who you were . . ." She faltered and gathered her knees tightly to her chest.

"I would have done the same thing."

"Then you're not angry?"

Gwyneth smiled and shook her head. She had kept her identity a secret from everyone but her publisher. But in spite of her efforts, some vile and money-hungry rogue had learned of the truth and was blackmailing her. Gwyneth didn't think Violet's perusal of these pages was any threat compared with that.

"What made you think that was my writing, though?"

Violet shrugged. "I didn't, at first. But I thought the story you've started at the end is a wonder. When you were obviously excited to work on it again, I just thought . . ."

As Violet's voice trailed off, Gwyneth closed the book on her lap.

"I couldn't stop reading," the young woman said apologetically. "What you have in there is better than any tale I ever heard. I've never known someone who could write like that. I never heard of a woman doing such a thing."

Gwyneth became embarrassed by the compliment. She put the notebook beside her on the ground. "This thing . . . my tales . . . have been both my passion and the cause of all my troubles."

"You have more than what you've written there, miss?"

She gave a small nod. "Almost a trunkful."

"My lord!" The surprise was too evident in Violet's face. She inched closer. "What do you plan to do with all of them?"

She'd never told anyone about it. Now Gwyneth was tempted. She glanced at Violet. This was the most interest the young woman had shown. And what was the harm in sharing a little about herself? "If I tell you . . . will you promise to keep it as a secret? To tell absolutely no one?"

Violet nodded.

"I sell them. Actually, I have sold eight of them already."

"For money?" she whispered in awe.

Gwyneth nodded.

"And they print them?"

"That's exactly what they do with them."

"My lord!" she said again. "You must be so proud."

"It gives me immense pleasure to see them printed," Gwyneth admitted. "But in proper society, these stories are considered somewhat scandalous. And the fact that I—a woman—write them to be published and read by others is the most scandalous thing of all."

"And why should you care what they think?"

She did and she didn't. The answer was not so simple. Doing the respectable thing, though, was part of her upbringing, part of who she was. And then there was the matter of her inheritance. Gwyneth finally gave a halfhearted shrug. " 'Tis difficult to explain."

She'd come close to describing her passion for writing to David, and he'd clearly regarded it as a disaster. She could only imagine what he would think or say if she explained as much as she'd just told Violet.

"Can I ask you another question, miss?"

"You are my first confidante in this adventure, so ask what you will," Gwyneth told her.

"Would it be too bold to ask if the money you earn is enough to live on?"

"Right now at least, 'tis not even close to being enough to support myself in the way I was raised or have been accustomed to live. But the money would certainly be enough for someone to live modestly."

"Then you *do* care what society thinks."

"I suppose I do. But 'tis not all about money. At the same time, though, money is what has complicated everything. And now I find myself in so much trouble. Getting out of it should be simple, but 'tis not so easy. The whole thing is just so confusing," Gwyneth blurted out, frustrated. She leaned her head back against the stone wall. "How am I supposed to work my way out of trouble when I cannot even explain it clearly?"

A heavy silence settled over them for the next few minutes. Gwyneth stared at the sky and the thousands of stars that were now shining brightly overhead. Violet was the first to speak.

"I'm afraid I'd not be the one to offer guidance. The only accomplishment in my life has been to dishonor my family and ruin any future I might have had."

"That is exactly where I am headed . . . ruin," she admitted. "I write because that is what I love to do. And getting my tales published seemed to be such an innocent thing to do—completely harmless. In fact, it started as a game of chance that I played with myself, and I won. I never imagined the complications if anyone were to find out, or how it could strip me of my inheritance. I never considered any of the other difficulties that might arise."

"This is what happens when we make decisions with our heart instead of our head," Violet said quietly. "Or at least, that's where I think I have gone wrong."

"We make an interesting pair." Gwyneth smiled at her reflectively. "Do you think the stars above were at work when they caused our paths to cross today?"

"Do you believe in destiny?"

"I have an unruly imagination. To feed it, I always keep my eyes open. I do not believe we always know the reason that things happen. I think we need to keep our minds open to different ways of seeing things, as well."

A look of amusement actually flickered in Violet's

face. "You would have gotten along perfectly at the place where I used to live and work."

Gwyneth bit back the question of where that was. She wanted Violet to choose what she was going to reveal about herself and what she was going to keep secret.

"From the little you have said, though, there is a world of difference in where we come from," Violet added. "To be honest, I know I should not be speaking to you as I am. Though I come from a respectable family, I'm just a servant, a lady's maid. That is what I did since I was a girl."

"I lost both of my parents when I was nine years old," Gwyneth told her. "I was sent to live with my uncle's family, then. If 'twas not for their kindness and their generosity in taking me in, I would have been cast aside to the wolves. So you see, Violet, there is really very little difference between us."

"But there is, and you know it . . . though you're being very kind to say such things," Violet said seriously. "But in the end, you come from gentility and I'm just a poor girl who's come to no good."

"In that case, if it would make you feel better, I can make up some stories about how I was locked away in the attic and fed one meal a day and had to do the chores of a dozen servants, while my old and ugly cousin entertained the handsome prince."

The smile blooming on the young woman's face made her stop. She couldn't help but smile herself.

"I need no more servants," Gwyneth said, growing serious again. "But I should very much like a friend."

Lyon knew there was a great deal about Gwyneth Douglas that his brother was not telling him, but in

David's rather agitated condition, he let the questions wait.

At the same time, he couldn't help but worry about the young woman, too. Gwyneth had always been Lyon's only ally in the Douglas family, and this friendship had continued even after Emma's death. The young heiress had been no less of a supporter since he and Millicent had returned to Baronsford. Though much younger than her cousin, Gwyneth had always been mature beyond her years, in Lyon's view. She was certainly more responsible than Emma. And this was only one of their many differences.

During these past six months or so, Lyon had found himself increasingly concerned about Gwyneth, however. Augusta Douglas was certainly not a devoted guardian. She was a woman accustomed to living her own life. There was no supervision of Gwyneth, no one to keep track of who might be courting the young woman, now that she was of marrying age.

Still, he tried not to dwell on these matters. She was not his responsibility. With the strained relationship that existed between Augusta and Lyon after Emma's death, the earl knew he had no voice in any of these matters, anyway. But now, with David here and obviously involved in some way with Gwyneth's situation, he was happy to get involved, too.

"Take as many men as you wish," he said firmly, walking with David to the stables. His brother wanted to resume his search right away, instead of waiting until morning. They had already sent Mr. Campbell to awaken some of the servants and stable workers to prepare horses. Lyon had explained briefly about Truscott's search, too, and how their cousin was out searching the countryside, as well. "Perhaps your paths will cross."

"Greenbrae Hall has not yet been opened up for the family. After I find her, would you mind if I bring Gwyneth back to Baronsford?" David asked.

"I insist that you bring her here." Lyon stopped by the door of the stables, a hand on his brother's shoulder. "One thing, David. I want you to know that you need no permission for anything you do around here. What I tried to tell you in the house was not to create any further estrangement between us. I am truly happy that you are back. As I know Millicent will be. Of course, our mother shall never cease complaining once she finds out you were here and I let you walk out before making you visit with her first."

"I hope to be back soon enough."

Lyon gave a satisfied nod, but his hand remained on his brother's shoulder. "There was a reason for my reserve in there. If there is one thing that I have learned so far in my life, I will no longer allow any distrust to exist between me and those I love and care for."

The two brothers stood eye-to-eye. Seven years apart in age, but they were so similar in temperament.

"I expect no miracles," Lyon continued. "I do not demand that you put aside your prejudices and prior judgments or even pretend that nothing ever happened. I am not even saying that you should accept my innocence without question. But I *do* demand to be judged fairly. Now, after you find Gwyneth and come back, do you think you can do that for me?"

"I can," David replied, placing his hand on his brother's shoulder, as well. "And I will."

He had assisted her in a rite of passage, and now she was free of him.

Emma had never said as much, but Walter under-

*stood it, felt it, saw it in her every action. It was painful
to watch her. Her brazenness had increased at least
tenfold since the day they'd first made love. But he
was no longer the center of her attention. No one man
could be.*

*Walter often saw her ride out with some lecherous
fool panting after her, disappearing into the deer park
without a chaperon. She took her pick of the men who
came as guests of her father to Greenbrae Hall during
the summer and early fall. There were so many oppor-
tunities, so many parties, so many guests.*

*One look at these men's faces afterward, and Walter
knew what had transpired beneath those leafy boughs
and beside the loch or the river.*

*When David was back at Baronsford, though,
Emma's attention focused completely on him. She let
the youngest Pennington brother believe that there was
no life in the Borders while he was away, that she and
the world around them existed solely for him.*

*There were times when the guest rooms at Greenbrae
Hall were empty, though. There were times when David
was away. Those were the days when she cast her eye
on Walter again. But he rejected her. She would send
a message to him and go to the tower house. He would
not go, though. She would ride after him when she
knew he was making rounds of the estate, but he would
elude her.*

*He understood her better than anyone else. With
Emma, life was all about control. Her control. She
liked to set the rules, determine the time, and control
the play. Her obedient regiment of servants had been
well trained to respond to her whims.*

*Walter would not obey. He refused to stay in line.
In fact, as time passed, he found he took great pleasure*

in denying her and in watching her fury grow because of it.

He enjoyed punishing her, but he knew he was punishing himself, too.

Chapter 14

~~~

Violet did not know how it happened, but before the dawn had even begun to lighten the eastern sky, Gwyneth had revealed everything about her past.

She spoke of the early years of her childhood, of losing her parents. She described to Vi the refuge she'd discovered in reading and in writing stories, and later the reward she'd felt in publishing them. Gwyneth had gone on to tell her of the recent blackmail letters that had turned her life upside down. She'd even told Violet about her plans of elopement, ending her life's story with a brief account of having given herself to the one man she had loved all of her life.

Now it was Violet's turn to bare her soul. And she was ready.

"There was a time when I was a decent young woman," Violet said softly. "I lived with my mother, a respectable widow, and my grandmother in St. Albans. I was taught all the necessary skills of sewing, needlework, and cooking. I was educated in the village school, doing well in learning the reading and writing and arithmetic that would someday make me a useful wife to a tradesman, a shop owner, or even a minister.

"My mother's frequent illnesses, though, left me no

choice but to go to work to help support my family," she continued. "My employer was Lady Wentworth, who later became the Countess of Aytoun."

"You were at Melbury Hall?" Gwyneth asked in shock.

Violet nodded. "I started working for her when her first husband, Squire Wentworth, was still alive."

"The people and circumstances that connect our lives are stunning. I am a cousin to Lord Aytoun's first wife, Emma Douglas. I have met your former mistress several times since Millicent arrived at Baronsford," Gwyneth said excitedly. "But I want to hear about you, now. Tell me what happened after you went to work for her."

"I became her personal maid at Melbury Hall. She is a wonderful person. The kindest woman I have ever met in my life," Violet said earnestly.

Vi had remained true to her upbringing as she traveled back and forth from London to Melbury Hall with her new mistress. Unlike other young girls, she'd kept away from temptation. She had no time for casual flirting. She'd remained an innocent and kept her virtue.

"While at Melbury Hall, I developed friendships that were as dear to me as any I ever had. Some became like kin to me. People like Moses, Jonah, and Amina were like brothers and a sister to me. Have you been to Melbury Hall?"

Gwyneth shook her head.

"All of these good people were kept as slaves during the Squire's time. And later on, the old healer Ohenewaa became for me the very embodiment of courage and strength in a woman."

"I know Ohenewaa. I have met her. She spends

much of her time in the company of the dowager now," Gwyneth interrupted excitedly again. "But please continue."

"Once the Squire died, life improved so much at Melbury Hall. I had many friends. People liked me. I was able to send everything I earned to my family and still live a very comfortable life. My mistress appreciated me."

"You were happy." Gwyneth commented.

"Truly." Violet nodded. "But all good things come to an end. For me, the end came with the entrance of a certain man in my life. All my good sense dissolved like the morning dew the day I met Ned Cranch."

"Who was he?"

"Ned was a stonemason who came last fall to Knebworth Village to build the new grange. He was a very handsome man. And I met him outside of the village church one Sunday morning." She twisted a piece of rag around her fingers and remembered how every time she had gone to the village, the handsome green-eyed giant had been there, tipping his hat or making some sweet remark about how good she looked.

"Mrs. Page, the housekeeper at Melbury Hall, witnessed Ned sweet-talking me a couple of times, and she gave me an earful about being careful. But at the time I had just turned eighteen, and I thought I knew exactly what I was doing. I was getting myself a husband." Violet felt the embarrassment burn her cheeks.

Despite the frigid air, the frozen ground, the dark nights, and the threatening woods, Violet met the stonemason outside of the village at least twice a week for more than a month, listening to his sweet words and his promises.

"I . . . I went willingly to his bed." She managed to get out the words. "Right after it, though, Ned's treachery was quick to surface. He had other lovers in the village. About the same time, I also realized that Ned Cranch was a spy, paid by my mistress's enemy to keep abreast of the news at Melbury Hall."

"The vile dog!" Gwyneth muttered.

"To make matters even worse, I heard that he was married and had a brood of children."

Gwyneth reached across and put a hand on Violet's arm. "That is horrible. What did you do?"

"Despite my broken heart and crushed spirit, I hoped to walk away from my mistake, forget about Ned, pretend nothing had ever happened. But reality slapped me hard, for soon I knew I was carrying his child."

In a panic, Violet had gone to Ohenewaa, pleading with the woman to help her lose the baby before she started to show, but the black healer had refused, and helped Violet see what mattered in life. Thinking more clearly, Vi had realized what she had to do. She would keep her child, no matter the consequences.

"I had no choice but to come out with the truth and accept whatever came. But my mistress and Lord Aytoun were at Baronsford at the time, and fate had something different in store for me." Violet shuddered. "One morning, I was approached by Ned's new conquest in Knebworth Village. The girl told me of his plan to do something at Melbury Hall that night. I left immediately for St. Albans. I went to the tavern where he was staying, where I hoped I might be able to appeal to some shred of decency in him to stay away. If not, I hoped I could buy him off."

"Were you able to find him?"

She nodded. "At St. Albans, I heard and witnessed the full measure of his deceit. He was meeting with Jasper Hyde, the very enemy of Lady Wentworth. Overhearing snatches of his conversation, I also learned of their plans to burn Melbury Hall and steal Ohenewaa that night."

Violet recalled listening in a daze. She did not know how to stop them, and yet she knew somehow that she had to try.

"What did you do?"

The memory of what happened next still seemed like a dream to her. "I met him in a narrow hallway at the base of a stairwell. I tried to talk him out of what he planned to do, but Ned was deaf to any explanations. He accused me of trying to steal some of his share."

"What happened next?"

"I killed him." She had driven a knife into his chest and watched the father of the child growing inside of her die a death that no one deserved. "Wicked as 'twas, I had to do it. In killing the villain, I knew I was giving my friends at Melbury Hall a chance to live. But in burying my knife in his cold heart, I also knew I was cutting myself off from my past and all those people that I loved."

Gwyneth sat back and stared in wonder. "What happened then? You were with child. Alone."

Stepping out of that tavern in a haze, Vi had known her only path led away from there. "I had killed a man. I had to go somewhere far enough away that I wouldn't bring shame on my mother and grandmother. Or on Melbury Hall." She let out a weary breath. "I had ten shillings and a few pence in my pocket. My only escape was to take the daily mail coach north."

"But that wouldn't take you too far." Gwyneth whispered.

"It didn't." Violet stared at her callused hands. "When the money ran out, I wandered from village to town, estate to estate, anywhere that I could find work. I had no references, no place to stay, and I quickly found out that the few offers that came my way brought with them requirements other than washing floors or serving ale. Sometimes it was a matter of days, other times only a few hours before I would be back on the road again."

"How long did you go on like that?"

"Months," Violet said, knowing at some point she had lost track of time. "Somewhere in my travels, I found myself befriended by vagrants. They were good and charitable folk, for the most part, especially when their women discovered I was with child. But as most of them were heading for the great ports and for ships sailing to the American colonies, I drifted from one group to another, and then to another if they would have me."

"You didn't want to leave this country?"

She shook her head. "All along, in the back of my mind, I worried what would become of my babe if I were to die at childbirth."

Often in her travels, she had been uncertain where she was, though she knew that she was not traveling so far north as to be journeying into the Highlands. She never went south of the border into England, either. After she learned one day that she was near Baronsford, Vi never strayed more than a few days' travel from the place. She knew that Baronsford was the one place where she could leave her innocent child, knowing that the most compassionate person she had ever known would surely care for the infant.

Violet caught Gwyneth's solemn glance toward her belly, and immediately blurted out the rest of her story. The sadness, the guilt she felt over losing her bairn. Where she had been. Where her child was buried. The tears fell in abundance, and Gwyneth moved next to her. Her shared sorrow was real. Her words were comforting.

Time passed and they talked on and on until the sun appeared above the eastern hills.

Violet found herself actually considering Gwyneth's offer of a position at her estate. She'd asked Vi to return with her to Greenbrae Hall and resume life as if nothing untoward had ever happened to her. The temptation was enormous, but so were her doubts.

"There is no reason for you to keep running, Violet. Ned Cranch was an evil man intent on harming those you cared for. You did what you needed to do. You did nothing that was not completely justified and even valiant. You prevented a huge disaster in the making. I say you should consider yourself a hero."

"I am a woman. I shall hang for killing the stonemason." Violet knew the reality of what she would face. "I shan't bring more shame on those I've left behind."

"Nothing of the kind shall happen. Your life is your own, and you owe no one any explanations. Whoever knew and cared for you will be relieved to learn that no harm has come to you. You are back, but at the same time, you shall be no burden to them. You shall have your own means of supporting yourself."

"Things are not so simple. People knew of my connections with Ned . . . and there was the crime."

"As far as anyone knows, there was no crime that involved you," Gwyneth interrupted. "Who knows you killed Ned? Did anyone see you? Anyone who would recognize you today?"

"Probably not. But that is not the point. I know what I did."

"If you are so guilt ridden with what you did, then why have you not already returned to England and turned yourself in to the magistrates?"

"I was with child. I could not . . ." Violet's voice wavered and she paused. The emptiness inside her was vast, but she didn't want to think of her lost child at this moment. "Very well, perhaps I didn't want to be caught. Perhaps I do believe Ned got what he deserved. Still, I am not ready to chance the danger of discovery. I would just as soon go away from here . . . forever."

"But that is no easy road, either." Gwyneth touched Violet's hand gently. "You are young, beautiful, and sure to be considered fair game by all the Ned Cranches of the world. Worse than when you were at Melbury Hall, you are now alone. No one will help you unless they receive something in return. How many groups of travelers will allow you to travel with them as a beautiful unmarried woman? You might capture a son's or husband's attention. To make matters even worse, you are English, and that will inevitably raise their suspicion."

Violet knew Gwyneth was right about all of it. Before, she'd had no other options and no real future. But now . . .

"You are in so much trouble yourself." She looked into Gwyneth's face. "If the person who is blackmailing you succeeds, you'll be left with nothing."

"I shall have some income from my writing."

"You do not need another person dependent upon you."

"I haven't lost anything yet. And if I do, we shall take things as they come."

"I don't know."

"Think of it. We shall not starve. At first, I might

not be able to earn a great deal, but we can each support the other," Gwyneth said passionately. "I truly believe there was a reason for you and me to meet like this." She looked up at what was left of the abbey's walls, at the rolling hills around the ruined building. "Something brought us to this old abbey. Each of us is desperate in her own way. We have neither a place nor someone to turn to. We can help each other."

"You shall be doing more for me than I could ever do for you."

Gwyneth shook her head sadly. "I am alone, Violet. I have always been alone. I have no mother. No sister. There has been no one in my life in whom I could confide. I could use a friend. Someone to help me see things clearly, to make good decisions, to be my companion. I believe you were destined to be that friend."

Violet smiled nervously. "That is an enormous charge you are laying on someone who has not done one right thing in her life."

Gwyneth extended a hand toward her. "Will you accept my offer?"

She would be close to Baronsford. It would be inevitable that she would see Millicent again. She would need to have some kind of explanation for her actions so many months ago. There might even be hard feelings because she was accepting Gwyneth's offer and working at Greenbrae Hall, instead of resuming her old position. But then again, why would the new Countess of Aytoun want to have anything to do with her, anyway?

And then there was Gwyneth. The two of them had begun a friendship tonight such as Violet had never before experienced. There was a trust that each of them instinctively felt. For the first time in her life, Vi sensed that she had an opportunity to find a place that was truly secure. She also believed that they could help each other.

Everything was confusing, but for the first time since leaving Melbury Hall, doors were being opened to her. There was even a chance that she might someday see her mother and grandmother again. At least, she might be able to send them money she earned. She wondered how much hardship the two women had endured in the months she'd been gone.

"I am frightened," Violet admitted.

"I am, too. But running away will not solve our problems. We must face our fears."

Violet blinked once, making certain she was not dreaming. The sun was moving higher in the sky. The colors of the valley below were bright and clear. Gwyneth sat quietly before her, waiting for an answer.

"Do you think you are well enough to travel this morning?" Violet finally asked.

Robert, the caretaker at Greenbrae Hall, did not wait for a messenger from Lady Cavers to start readying the house for family and guests. Captain Pennington's visit last night had given him all the notice he needed.

The steward, the housekeeper, and a handful of servants customarily arrived from London and Edinburgh a few days ahead of the family. Lady Cavers's personal maids, of course, traveled with her wherever she went. Miss Gwyneth was not one who required much fuss, and usually accepted the help from any of the serving maids who were not busy with other chores. Men and women of the nearby villages and towns filled the rest of the staff for the household, the stables, and the grounds, as they were needed, and early the next morning, Robert sent one of the lads from the stables to take the news as far as Melrose. The skeleton crew already at the house was put to work opening windows, airing the rooms, and firing up the great ovens.

In the midst of all of this, Robert's concern over Miss Gwyneth's disappearance grew as the day grew later. She was a gentle soul, a kindhearted lass the serving folk were more than happy to serve. And unlike her guardian, who could barely tolerate to be at the country house—unless she had company—Miss Gwyneth would stay months at a time at Greenbrae Hall if she could. This was another thing in her favor. From Robert's way of thinking, it was good to have the house open and busy, and it provided steady work for everyone.

Robert and those he talked to couldn't wait until the young woman inherited the house and the estate, which made her present disappearance even more distressing. Already shorthanded, he told himself, he could do little, though. Captain Pennington was already looking for her, and twice today, grooms from Baronsford who were helping with the search had come over to see if there was any word from Miss Douglas. Robert wished he could give them some news, but he had none.

The two tired travelers riding the single horse arrived long after nightfall. The lad in the stables who had gone out to meet them told Robert later that the two were dressed so shabbily that he just assumed that they were vagrants . . . and maybe horse thieves. He'd been shocked when one of them turned out to be Miss Gwyneth.

Robert was fetched immediately and, despite Gwyneth's objections, everyone at Greenbrae Hall was awakened and put to work. The caretaker was no physician, but from the bloodstains in her hair and the stiff way she held one shoulder, it was obvious that the mistress was hurt. The young woman accompanying Miss Douglas knew exactly what ailed Gwyneth and appeared to be competent in caring for her.

"I have no need of a physician," Gwyneth said adamantly when Robert suggested it.

With the help of the companion and a serving maid, they managed to take Gwyneth upstairs to her room. Robert immediately went to the stables himself. He usually minded the young mistress, but he was not going to allow anything to happen to her while he was around. She was too precious. Finding the stable lad with the horse she'd ridden in on, the caretaker ordered him to ride to Baronsford with a message. Robert knew Captain Pennington would be out looking, but Lord Aytoun would know how to find him.

Her own room. Her own bed. She was clean and once again wearing her own clothing. Most important, though, Gwyneth was back in the house she loved—the only one she'd ever considered home.

"This must be the calm before the storm," Gwyneth told Violet once they had been left alone.

"They won't rest unless a doctor is brought in," Violet said quietly as she straightened and tucked the sheets around the bed. "And that is only right. You had a hard fall, and you cannot assume that the blow to your head will heal on its own."

Gwyneth's gaze wandered contentedly around the room before focusing on her friend. Once she herself had been settled, Violet had given in and cleaned up, changing into one of the dresses Gwyneth gave her.

"The color blue is becoming on you. It matches your eyes."

"You are avoiding what must be done." Violet said as she folded and tucked a blanket on the foot of the bed.

"Stop working and sit down with me. I do not want you to be my maid. You will not be a servant in this household. I want you to be a companion to me."

"I will do what needs to be done. I intend to be useful and earn my keep," Violet asserted.

"If anyone needs a doctor, 'tis you. I have only a few minor bruises. You, on the other hand, are not yet recovered from childbirth."

"I have recovered completely."

The quiet answer, followed by the young woman moving to the far side of the chamber to see to closing the curtains on the window, told Gwyneth she had broached the wrong subject. Violet was still grieving the loss of her baby. Any mention of it only scraped the scab off the wound.

"I shall agree to have a physician look at me only if you accept some of my conditions. The first is that you not look on yourself as a servant."

Violet stopped and looked in Gwyneth's direction. "We are born and raised to take our rightful place in the world. I cannot sit idle and pretend to be more than I am just because you wish it." Violet walked toward her. The dark circles under her eyes spoke of her weariness. "You gave me a new breath of life in bringing me back here. Now I must do what feels right for me to fit in. I am a woman of the serving class."

It was frustrating. There was so much she hoped to

do for Violet. Gwyneth had no choice, though. She didn't want to drive Violet away.

"Very well. But will you at least allow me to set some rules?"

"Perhaps. It depends on what they are."

Gwyneth motioned to the other woman to sit down on the bed beside her. She waited until Violet had done so. "Since you told me that you were a lady's maid before, then you should have no objection about accepting a position here."

Violet gave a nod of agreement.

"Then you shall be a companion to me here . . . with a salary. You will not be answerable to the housekeeper, and you shall do no manual labor in the household. Your duties are to attend only to me."

"Attending to you means addressing you properly, and dressing you, and arranging your hair, and using my needlework skills to sew or mend your dresses, and to see to—"

"None of that," Gwyneth said stubbornly. "I want a companion I can trust, someone I can talk to about my stories. I want to be able to read them to you, and ask your opinion. We can read together and I can teach you to ride, as well."

Violet sat pensively, obviously considering the conditions.

"You will find me far more demanding than Lady Aytoun. I shall fill all your time."

Violet looked at her doubtfully, and Gwyneth found the lack of argument encouraging.

"If I am not exposed and disinherited, your salary shall be twenty pounds a year. If you wish, you can have a half day off on Sunday, one evening out a week, and a day off each month. My other condition

would be that you will occupy a bedroom on this floor
where I can call you as needed."

Violet looked at her suspiciously. "You are getting
too liberal again, Miss Gwyneth."

"You shall call me Gwyneth."

"*Miss* Gwyneth."

"When 'tis just the two of us . . . Gwyneth," she
stressed. "And I shall take care of explaining the arrangements to my aunt and the housekeeper as soon
as they arrive."

Violet rose to her feet. "Then I shall go and ask
Robert to send for the doctor."

Gwyneth shook her head with a smile. "Do not
bother. Knowing him, he already has."

•

During their search, David had indeed crossed paths
with Walter Truscott and the two of them worked
together combing the area west of Baronsford. Thus
far, they'd had no success in locating the woman they
were looking for, but neither was ready to quit. They
were preparing to separate, however—David to
Gretna Green and Walter to cover the roads leading
to the ships at Greenock—when a groom sent from
Baronsford caught up with them and told them of
Gwyneth's arrival and of the second woman traveling
with her.

"This could very well be the one you are looking
for," David told Truscott as he turned his horse in the
direction of Greenbrae Hall.

"I doubt it, David. The coincidence is fairly unlikely, wouldn't you think?"

"Gwyneth left Gretna Green alone and on horseback," David argued. "We hear now that she arrived
at her house with another young woman of about the
same age."

"What did the other woman look like?" Truscott asked of the groom who had brought the news. "Do you at least have a name?"

The man shook his head. "I only know what I was told by his lordship. The lad from the Hall said naught to me, sir."

Walter shook his head. "Lyon and Millicent want Violet found even more than I do. They would have said something if they thought there were a possibility that this young woman could be her."

"Walter, I'm not going to argue the bloody point with you," David snapped. "I'm going to Greenbrae Hall. Gwyneth gave me the slip and I'm thinking she must have traveled through the hills to get there. Whoever 'tis at the Hall with her, she met on the way from Gretna Green. Now, how many bloody women do you think are wandering around out here?"

"I suppose there is only one way to find out."

"We should reach Greenbrae Hall by noon, if we ever start. If this woman is not the one you're looking for, you can get a fresh horse and still beat the lass to Greenock . . . if that's where she's going."

Riding back, David found himself growing more impatient. His inclination to strangle Gwyneth as soon as he got there did little to soothe his restlessness. She not only refused his offer of marriage, but by running away, she had rejected him, as well. The intimacy they'd shared and all of his assumptions of her attraction toward him meant nothing if she wasn't about to give their relationship a chance. He wondered how much of Gwyneth's objection to his proposal had to do with Emma.

He was trying to forget the past, but they were not letting him. Not Lyon. Not Gwyneth.

David glanced at his cousin riding beside him and

brooding in silence. Slightly younger in age, the two had been good friends for all their years growing up. He would have done anything for Walter, and he knew his cousin always felt the same way about him.

"I might need your help in a delicate matter over the next few days or so."

Truscott's expression cleared immediately. "Anything. What is it?"

"You are one person who was close to both Emma and Lyon from the start of their marriage to the very end. I need to dig into the past, find out what happened. You might be able to answer some of my questions or at least lead me in the right direction."

"I thought you came back to make peace, David. What do you think you can accomplish by churning up the past?" Walter asked, obviously annoyed.

"Nothing. I know I shall accomplish nothing," David retorted shortly. "But I am being given no choice in this. Lyon believes I am still consumed by my memory of Emma and her death. Gwyneth thinks the same. She wouldn't even consider my bloody offer."

"What offer?" Truscott interrupted.

David realized he had not mentioned anything about his marriage proposal to either Lyon or Walter. But how could he, when the intended had refused him and run away. "That's a long story."

"We've got a long ride ahead of us."

David shook his head. He was not ready to tell his cousin how complicated he'd made things for himself and Gwyneth. In making love to her, he'd left her no option but to marry him. Convincing Gwyneth of that, however, was obviously another challenge altogether.

"About Emma," he continued. "I know neither

Lyon nor Gwyneth will be happy until I bury the memory of Emma once and for all. So I plan to do exactly that."

"And it matters what Gwyneth thinks?"

"Yes. It matters."

Walter looked at him hard, but did not press him further on that.

"Well, David, your brother must not be thinking straight. In dredging up Emma's death, you'll only be stirring up scandal and hard feelings—I should think— for the new countess. The woman will be having a bairn soon, for God's sake. Why should either of you want to upset her?"

"I've not even met her, but I've no desire to do anything to insult or upset her. And I plan to be discreet," David explained. "I want only Lyon and Gwyneth, the two people who are pushing me to do this, to know what I'm doing."

Truscott rode a few moments in silence. His face was a mask when he finally turned to him. "Nothing about Emma shall ever be discreet. Do you remember the basket of snakes the Indian magician had in Edinburgh?"

"At Lord Eglinton's house. Of course I remember it."

"I believe opening a door to the memory of Emma is like lifting the cover of that basket. You shall find nothing but a twisting, writhing mass of poison and death. 'Tis an experience those at Baronsford could do without. We need not go through that again, David."

"I have no choice, Walter." David said, determined. "My words do not appear to be enough. My declaration that my interest is directed only toward the future is not enough. Lyon, for one, needs proof."

Truscott frowned and shot a glance at David. "I still think both of you are making a mistake."

"You may be right." David looked at his cousin. "But will you help me?"

"I have no other choice, do I?"

When Emma came looking for him in the village on market day, there were at least a dozen people standing nearby.

" 'Tis important that I talk to you."

"I cannot. I still have a great deal of work I need to do here."

"Please, Walter. I shall not take too much of your time." She placed a hand on his arm, despite the prying eyes. He paused, too long for her liking, for she snapped, "If not for my sake, then for your precious cousin's. I need to speak to you."

Walter knew she would make a scene if she had to. No price was too high for the control she seemed more and more to live for.

He knew he would be a fool to agree. More than a year had passed since they had made love in the tower house. It was almost that long since they'd exchanged a civil word with each other. He no longer dreamed of Emma, though. He did not fantasize about her when he was with other women. Making love to her that first time had opened his eyes. Her actions afterward and toward other men sealed his belief that she would never be happy. Never.

"I cannot get away now." He motioned with his head toward a grove of trees beside the small chapel. "But I shall talk to you there, if you insist."

She glared in the direction that he's gestured and strode off ahead of him.

Like an obedient dog, he was expected to follow. Walter was angry enough to let her wait, to ignore her, but for David's sake, he finally turned and walked after her. The trees would not hide them from passersby, but offered enough distance that no one would overhear them.

"He has asked me to marry him," she blurted as soon as he reached her. "He tells me he loves me. He wants to marry right away. He wants an answer from me today."

Walter had always known about David's intentions. A blind man could see how his cousin felt toward Emma. David never pursued any other women. Emma was the only one he ever saw— ever desired.

Walter pushed back the guilt he still carried about what he and Emma had done. It was like a fist in his chest. Anger flared within him. She acted as if it were a nuisance having the son of an earl ask for her hand.

"What business is this of mine?" he asked thickly. "You are going to marry him, are you not?"

She looked at him as if he'd grown two heads. "Why would I do such a foolish thing? Why would I tie myself in a marriage when I already know I should be unhappy?"

Walter had never had any expectations. He'd always known there was no future between them. But David's situation was different.

He stared at her, unable to comprehend what she was asking him.

"I shall never marry David."

Walter said the first thing that came into his head. "Then set him free. He can take a different road, given the chance. Tell him the truth. Send him on his way."

"I cannot!" She whirled to face him. "What happens

*if David's offer is the best one I am ever going to
receive? How can I say no to him when I am not certain my father will leave me enough to tempt someone
of more value?"*

*"And that is your only reason for not telling him the
truth?" he asked sharply, his head clearing. "You have
no regard for what he feels for you? For what he has
always felt for you?"*

*"I am still only nineteen years old. 'Tis not too late
for me to marry. He thinks that he needs to do something noble just because we've been . . . well, together."*

*David was so blinded by his love that he wouldn't
even think to ask who else Emma had been intimate
with before him. But it was so easy to be blinded by
her.*

*She paced before him on the grass. "What kind of
life is he offering me? A military life. I shall be locked
away in some horrible corner of the world. I shall be
away from Baronsford."*

*She continued to talk, but as she stormed and com-
plained, Walter realized that he was free. For the first
time in his life, he was free.*

*"Where are you going?" she said, a note of panic in
her voice.*

He said nothing, but continued to walk away.

Chapter 15

The bandages wrapped around her chest, added to the sling holding her arm still, might as well have been designed to torture her. She could not move, and Gwyneth felt trapped in her own bed.

"I suspect a fracture of the shoulder blade," the doctor from Melrose warned. "But of course, it could be only bruising. We'll know more when I come back in a week. By then, some of the swelling should get down. 'Twill be easier to tell."

"I am expected to lie here, trussed up like some holiday fowl, for an entire week?" Gwyneth shook her head. She looked at Violet and hoped for arguments from her on her behalf. The young woman appeared intent on receiving the doctor's instructions on some kind of medicinal tincture he was leaving behind.

When the doctor had arrived, it was clear the two had immediately recognized each other. Gwyneth guessed he must have been the one who had seen Violet before the childbirth. He appeared extremely pleased to find her there at Greenbrae Hall.

"The bandages should be changed frequently, should they not?" Gwyneth was determined to find a way out of this forced bondage.

"No," the doctor said sharply. " 'Tis important that they should remain as they are until I return. "Although 'tis recommended, I am not suggesting purging, as yet. But if ye do not remain in bed, young woman, there shall be no improvement. That I promise. Then, I shall have no choice but to proceed with more aggressive treatment."

She shivered. The threat was serious enough to shut Gwyneth's mouth. At least the cut on the back of her head was beginning to heal, and the lump had already subsided.

She had been well enough to ride most of a day with Violet to Greenbrae Hall. She should have refused this visit. Despite the continuous throbbing and the sharp pain whenever she moved her shoulder, she knew she had improved since her initial fall from the horse. Gwyneth chose to keep her complaints to herself, though. Over the years, she'd had a few visits from this same old physician, and she was well aware of his manner of dealing with disagreeable patients.

"Keep her on a bland diet. Ye may prop her up in bed, but that should be the extent of her moving about," the doctor directed Violet. The noise of arriving horses in the courtyard drifted in through the open window. "When is Lady Cavers to arrive?"

Violet looked at Gwyneth for an answer.

"My aunt should arrive within the next day or two," she lied, not wanting the man to think she might need more of his attention.

"Very well." He started gathering up his equipment, explaining again to Violet the medications he was leaving, and how and when they should be administered. After giving Gwyneth another lecture on the importance of staying in bed, he turned to Violet. "Ye look better, lassie, than when I saw ye last. How are ye feeling?"

Gwyneth listened intently. She was more concerned about Violet's condition. Her own injuries were nothing but a few bruises.

"I am very well, sir."

"Ye *are* getting plenty of liquid nourishment."

"Aye, sir," she said in a quiet voice.

Gwyneth considered objecting to the answer, but instead decided to wait and hear what else the young woman was supposed to do but was not.

"And do not forget what I told ye before about not spending too much time on yer feet during this first month."

"I do remember, sir. I am being careful."

Gwyneth cleared her throat and sent Violet a warning look when she looked in her direction. She didn't think walking all the way to the abbey where they'd first met could be considered staying off her feet.

"I'll walk you downstairs." Violet quickly took the man's arm, guiding him out the door.

Gwyneth watched them go. She was looking forward to talking to Violet later. Already, the young woman was doing more than they had agreed upon. This morning, while Gwyneth slept late, Violet had been helping with the work downstairs. They matched each other in temperament and stubbornness, which Gwyneth knew was another reason they had gotten along from the moment they met.

Violet was like so many of the heroines in the stories she wrote. She was down on her luck. She was forced to live beneath her station. In the same way that she weaved justice into her tales, Gwyneth felt responsible to change the young woman's life and help her find happiness.

She recalled what Violet had revealed about Walter Truscott's frequent visits to the cottage on Baronsford's land. She had not said it, but there was certainly a hint of trust and admiration.

Truscott came from gentry. Tall and ruggedly handsome in his own way, Walter would be a very good match for the young woman. Their different stations in life could be a problem, but only if Violet made it so. This was another good reason for not establishing her as a servant at the Hall, but rather as a companion to Gwyneth.

She snapped out of her reverie when the door of the room burst open and Violet rushed in. The young woman's expression was pale.

"They're here."

Gwyneth didn't have to ask. She knew it was only a matter of time before David would arrive.

"I heard Robert address one of them as Captain Pennington in the foyer as I was taking the doctor downstairs." She pushed the door closed and pressed her back to it. "Mr. Truscott is here, too."

"Did he see you?"

She nodded, her face totally flushed.

"What did you do with them?"

"Nothing. Captain Pennington practically pounced on the doctor, and I ran up the stairs to warn you."

Gwyneth tried to sit up in bed. She glanced in the direction of the window. "Do you think we can manage to climb out that way?"

"No!"

"Perhaps I can refuse to see him."

Violet gave a small shake of her head. "Captain

Pennington looked fairly determined, if you ask me. I think there is not much chance of refusing him anything."

Gwyneth tried to ignore the hard knot forming in her stomach. She was ashamed to admit that it was as much from excitement as fear. "Then at least do not leave me alone with him. With you here, there will be less chance of him taking my head off."

The knock was loud enough to break down the door. With her good hand, she pulled up the sheets to her chest. She was only half dressed. Her robe was draped over her shoulder. Gwyneth didn't even want to think how bad she must look. A second knock immediately followed.

"I think 'twould be best if I went and got Robert," Violet said in a small voice. "He would be much better suited to—"

"Do not leave me alone . . ." These were the only words she could get out before Violet opened the door and David was in the bedchamber.

Gwyneth sank lower in the bed. His hair was loose. He had not bothered to shave since she'd seen him last. His clothing was covered with mud from riding. His gaze was hostile when it turned to the direction of the bed. She'd never seen David looking this wild before . . . nor this dangerous. She fought her inclination to pull the sheets over her head.

He looked around the room until he saw Violet standing behind him by the door. Gwyneth thought the young woman looked more distressed than she herself felt.

"Who are you?" he growled.

"Violet Holmes, sir," she said in little more than a whisper, giving him a quick curtsy.

"Out." He jerked his head toward the door. "My cousin is waiting for you downstairs."

Violet shot a quick glance at her. She was bravely holding her ground, but her terror was obvious. She didn't know David. She didn't know he was not truly as fierce as he looked and sounded.

She gave a reassuring nod to her friend. "You can go. I shall be fine."

Violet's parting glance was apprehensive. Gwyneth imagined her running down the stairs and pleading with Robert to send up a dozen grooms to battle the madman.

The loud bang of the door behind the young woman made Gwyneth cringe and wish that was exactly what Violet was doing. She stared at David's large hands, fisting and unfisting at his sides. Her gaze shifted to his clenched jaw and the blue eyes. He was clearly angry. He started toward the bed.

"You should not be here, David." She straightened the sheets around her. "I am injured and in pain. Your presence here is not in any way conducive to the improvement of my health."

He gave a short laugh as he continued to approach. "I am delighted to hear you say that."

Walter Truscott had not recognized Violet at first, dressed as she was when she came down the stairs with the physician. The beautiful woman did not resemble in any way the dirty and frail creature lying on her bairn's grave. She was not the same helpless woman with no will to live. Once her blue eyes looked at him, though, he had no doubt about her identity. Before he could say anything, though, she'd fled back up the stairs.

He knew she would have to come back down. And just as he had expected, she did not come down the same stairs. Keeping watch through the large windows that looked out over the grounds and the pathway leading to the wing housing the stables, he saw her as soon as she stepped out of the house. She was walking and then running toward the stables. The fear that she might try to run away again made Truscott dash out the door after her. He caught up to her halfway down the path.

"Violet."

She immediately stopped and looked nervously over her shoulder. Her face was flushed. She gave a small curtsy when he reached her. Her eyes remained focused on the patch of gravel separating them.

"Good day, Mr. Truscott," she said softly.

"Walter . . . please call me Walter. I want you to know I've been—"

"Excuse me, sir, but do you know anything about Captain Pennington's temperament?"

"His temperament? I do."

She looked up hopefully. "Is he dangerous when he is angry?"

"On occasion, I've known him to be very dangerous."

"Are you able to handle him in such instances?"

"I've done so once or twice."

"Then you *must* come with me," she said, motioning toward the house, and starting back that way. "As a family relation, you may have a better chance of helping Miss Gwyneth. Please, we must hurry."

Truscott stood watching her, amused by her concern. She whirled around when she realized he wasn't following.

"Please sir! Captain Pennington was like an angry boar when he charged into the room. My mistress is too weak from her injury to defend herself. We cannot waste any time."

He started toward her slowly. "To put your mind at ease, I shall gladly come and stand guard by Gwyneth's door upstairs. But I shall not charge in there and be the cause of more trouble. What she did was foolish. She put her life in danger for no reason."

She opened her mouth but then closed it tightly.

"I believe she deserves whatever tongue-lashing Captain Pennington is going to give her. And I can assure you, that shall be the extent of his harshness with her."

She gave a curt nod. "I accept your offer of standing by their door. Just in case . . . if Captain Pennington's temper is not as contained as you imagined it to be, I would like to have you nearby."

Violet led the way and the two of them started toward the house. Truscott intentionally slowed their pace. "I shall look foolish standing there alone. Will you keep me company?"

A pretty blush darkened her fair cheeks. She looked away shyly. "Yes, sir. I shouldn't like to have you look foolish."

"Call me Walter."

This had not been the punishment David had in mind. Storming toward the bed earlier, he'd planned everything from giving her a long lecture about her foolishness to carrying her back to Baronsford. Something about those beautiful green eyes spitting fire at the same time as greeting him had undone him. He had pulled the sheets away only to kiss her. And she had answered his assault willingly.

"I am very angry," David was able to growl in the seconds that their mouths separated. He forced himself down on the edge of the bed. Before his temper could find voice again, Gwyneth looped her left arm around his neck and pulled his head down for another taste.

It was far too easy to be lost in the warmth of her mouth, especially when Gwyneth eagerly matched the erotic stroking of his tongue. David's body strained to be closer. His hand pulled the sheets lower. He drew open her robe and felt her breast through the thin layer of her chemise. She arched her back, her head dropped back onto the pillows, her eyes closed, and a soft moan of assent escaped her throat.

"The doctor put no restrictions on making love, did he?" he asked.

"No." Her eyes slowly opened and a half smile broke across her lips. "There must be no restrictions on it, for he was very specific."

David eyed the bandages covering her arm and shoulder. Worry again began to burn in his stomach. He looked into her eyes. "Why did you do it? Why did you run away?"

"Did you not read the letter I left for you?"

He placed a hand on either side of her head and looked into her eyes. "I read the blasted letter, but there were no answers in there. I want the truth, Gwyneth."

She looked away as a deep blush covered her face. "We shared a night of true passion, but that was all, David. That must be enough for us. 'Twas enough for me."

He leaned closer, forcing her to look into his eyes. "We both know that you are lying. You wanted me to make love to you only a moment ago, and I wanted

the same. The same thing will happen this afternoon . . .
and tonight . . . and tomorrow . . . and many days
after. We want each other, Gwyneth. There is no denying that."

"Only when we are together," she said fervently.
"That was why I had to run away. I cannot think
straight when I am near you. I am incapable of making
clear decisions at moments like this. You are too much
for me, David. Too much for my body and my mind.
We shouldn't have gone as far as we did. But I believe
'tis not too late to forget what happened."

He ran his thumb gently across her bottom lip. "Do
you think 'tis even *possible* to forget?"

Just as he'd thought, she had no answer to that.
She'd said it herself that she couldn't think straight
when he was around.

More than ever before David knew they were
meant for each other. He wanted Gwyneth as his wife,
as his lover, as his friend. But she was not one to be
told. He had to convince her of all of that. She was a
romantic at heart, and his approach had been nothing
like she deserved.

"There is no forgetting you, my love." He touched
her face before she could turn it away again. "And
you know that I wanted you the whole time you were
missing. I was lost when I arrived here and found out
you'd never arrived. I know I never formally wooed
you. I never talked to Augusta about my intentions,
nor have I made any formal proposal of marriage.
Because of the history between us, I made too many
assumptions. But I can change all of that. We can
start again."

Several tears escaped her eyes before she batted
them away with her one good hand. "Why me, David?

You can have anyone else you want. Why are you so determined to convince *me*?"

He put his answer in the kiss he gave her. Soft, tender, slowly building all the passion he could muster into it.

" 'Tis too quiet in there," Violet whispered, hesitantly putting her ear closer to the door. "You don't think he has already done something to her, do you?"

She frowned over her shoulder at Truscott when he cleared his throat. She noticed that he had a difficult time suppressing his smile. He shuffled from one foot to the other before leaning against the wall again.

"No, lass. I think Gwyneth is quite safe with David."

She felt foolish standing guard here. And Violet understood what Truscott's little smile was about. Perhaps he'd been told by Captain Pennington what had transpired between the two of them at Gretna Green, just as Gwyneth had confided in her. But there were no inappropriate noises coming from the room. There were no sounds of conversation, either.

The one thing that kept her from knocking on the door, though, was Gwyneth's declaration of how she truly felt about David Pennington. Violet had been looking for the right opportunity to bring this up again with her friend. If the two of them were as love-struck as they looked and sounded, she could see no reason why they could not talk through their troubles. Whatever prejudice toward women and writers Captain Pennington had, he needed to understand Gwyneth's interest was more than a mere hobby. If he loved her, then he would help her extricate herself from the blackmail plot against her.

"I think 'twill look quite foolish if one of them were to open that door and find us eavesdropping out here."

Violet looked over her shoulder at Truscott only to have the door swing open at that moment. She took an immediate step back as the doorway filled with the broad frame of the visitor.

"I did not hurt her too badly this time. But I am coming back this afternoon to mete out more punishment."

. All Violet could do was to nod like a fool. He appeared far more relaxed than before—far more approachable. The fury was clearly gone.

"I would appreciate it if you would ask one of the maids to prepare a room for me on this same floor. I plan to stay at Greenbrae Hall until Miss Douglas is well enough to be taken to Baronsford, or until her aunt arrives."

So much for Gwyneth's insistence that she never wanted to see him, Violet thought.

After a polite bow, the tall Scotsman closed the door to Gwyneth's room and started down the hall. Truscott fell in step with his cousin, but his departing glance told Violet that he would be back, too.

He was known for his intelligence as well as his kindness and compassion. He was stern yet tolerant. He had a temper, but no one ever called him unjust. He was proud but not vain. He treasured his family more than anything else in life. And Baronsford grieved fiercely when Charles Pennington, the Earl of Aytoun, died after a short illness.

Walter was as upset about the passing of the great man as Lyon, Pierce, and David. In many ways, Pen-

nington had been the only father he'd ever known. He certainly had treated the young lad who had been entrusted into his care no differently than his real sons. Walter had been given an education and an opportunity unmatched by anything he could have expected. Walter had been given a dream and a future.

Standing beside the other family members by the family vault in the old kirk, Walter looked around him at the other lives the Earl of Aytoun had so powerfully shaped. Though it had taken several months to gather at Baronsford, they were all here now for the memorial service. Lyon was back from India, Pierce from London, and David from Ireland.

Lady Aytoun had been a young widow when the earl had married her. The two of them had created three sons whom they were very proud of. Walter glanced at his cousins' solemn faces and wondered of the changes and challenges that faced the three men now that their father was gone. Of course, the greatest challenges would fall to Lyon. He was now Earl of Aytoun and as such would assume responsibility for Baronsford and its vast lands.

Uncontrollably, Walter's gaze was drawn to Emma. Without looking at either of the other brothers, Emma walked toward Lyon and put a hand on his arm.

Chapter 16

"So what do you think of her?"

David didn't need to pause to think of a response to his mother's question. He told her his true impression.

"On the first glance, she doesn't look like someone Lyon would have chosen as a wife."

"He didn't choose her, I did," the dowager interrupted proudly.

"Then you did very well, Mother."

David held the old woman's hand as they walked slowly down one of the garden paths. The dowager had given up her walking stick. She walked now with more energy than anyone had seen in years. David had spent yesterday afternoon being introduced to all the new faces, family and otherwise, around Baronsford, as well as visiting with the folk he'd known for years. He'd spent the night at Greenbrae Hall, but his mother had demanded a private audience with him this morning. So he was back.

"I must say that after just a few minutes in Millicent's company, I was won over. I know now why my brother is so enamored."

"I am happy to hear you say that . . . or you

wouldn't be my son," Beatrice said in a matter-of-fact voice. "She has the heart of an angel and a brain that matches Lyon in both intelligence and wit. Even her looks, though seemingly simple at first, grow on a person. There are many who consider her one of the most beautiful women in Britain. Of course, your brother is at the head of that group."

David would not argue that point. The warm greeting he'd received from Millicent had been a shock—especially after the air of reserve that had pervaded his first meeting with Lyon. And her feelings had come across as genuine. She was really very happy to see him, and that had made him feel truly welcome at Baronsford.

Regarding her looks, while she was not a great beauty, the light coming from within her had a way of brightening a room. The fact that she was with child added yet another special charm to her presence. The idea of another generation of Pennington children at Baronsford was very appealing, even to David, who had spent so many years away.

"I have not been around children in a long time," he said. " 'Tis amazing how that wee Josephine has a way of growing on you."

"She certainly does. Another great beauty, and one who has contributed a great deal to Lyon's recovery, too. To keep up with her, the earl has to push himself harder. He is becoming more agile with each passing day. At the rate he is going, he will be a young man by the time his bairn is born."

" 'Twill be in just a couple of months, I understand."

"Indeed. And to think I shall be here to witness it."

She stopped before a stone bench and glanced back

at the towering castle on the hill. The look of pride and happiness in the old woman's face was one David had not seen for many years. He wanted to comment that the dowager appeared younger, too. Since yesterday, not once had he heard his mother complain of any illness or remind him, as she once did with almost every breath, how she had so few days left to live.

"And I cannot wait until you meet Portia, as well. We expect her and Pierce back any day," the dowager continued, sitting down on the bench. She motioned David to follow suit.

"I know for a fact that you did not arrange *that* marriage," he joked, sitting beside her.

"I would have, if I were in Boston before those two met," she said breezily. "But she is a prize, too. Quite strong willed. Beautiful but unpretentious. A dreamer in many ways. In temperament, she is very much like her father"—her voice dropped to a whisper—"Bonnie Prince Charlie. You were told of her parentage, were you not?"

"Walter Truscott told me." David was also told that Portia's first meeting with her royal father had been at Baronsford, and that the Pretender had been proud to claim Portia as his daughter by Helena Middleton.

"She and Pierce are a perfect match. My only regret is that they are both determined to return to that godforsaken place in the American colonies." The dowager's blue eyes met David's. "You made an old woman very happy in giving up your commission. I could not endure more discord between my children."

David let his gaze sweep over the serene countryside. His resignation from the army would not make the life that awaited Pierce in Boston any easier. There was a great deal of danger awaiting him there.

A wave of unrest was building against British laws. The burning of the *Gaspee* this year was only the most recent event. Change was coming. It was only the question of when . . . and how violent the change would be.

David wanted to talk to Pierce before he and his new wife went back to America. His own loyalties were with his family now, and he would do anything to protect his brother against the dangers that awaited him on that faraway continent.

"We have spoken of your brothers and their wives, but not about you," the dowager said, breaking into David's thoughts and drawing his attention back to her.

"As you have already heard, I resigned my commission. Beyond that, what I am going to do with the rest of my life is a mystery that I have yet to solve."

"Your father's settlement was a handsome one, I know. Unless you've gambled it all away, I know I shall never need to worry about your financial situation. What interests me, David, is your personal life."

David stared into his mother's expressive eyes. "Don't be shy. Say what is on your mind."

The dowager gave a regal nod. "Your intentions had better be honorable. I like that young woman very much. And if 'twas not because of the problem that exists between Augusta and our family, I would have suggested a match between you and Gwyneth long before now."

"She only turned eighteen this year," he reminded her.

"And you are only twenty-six. Eight years is not too much of a difference. But more important, you do intend to marry her, I hope."

He had to bite back his smile. It was amusing that everyone assumed the worst of him, when Gwyneth was the one who was fighting against the match. He had returned to Greenbrae Hall last night only to have Violet relay a message that her mistress was asleep. This morning, before he'd left, it had been the same story. Violet was not around, but one of the maids had told him that Miss Douglas, following the doctor's instructions, was sleeping late.

"You have not answered me."

"What makes you think there is anything between us?"

She snorted derisively. "Even strangers who have met Gwyneth know the esteem she feels for you. And what I hear of your actions this past week is proof enough that there is a strong interest on your part. Now, am I wrong?"

There was no point in holding anything back. Especially when there was a chance he could use the dowager's influence to his advantage. He recalled more than one occasion when Gwyneth had listened to Beatrice better than Lady Cavers.

"You are correct, as always," he admitted. "I am very interested."

"What is stopping you, then? Have you spoken with Augusta yet? Would you like me to speak to her on your behalf?" She shook her head in an answer to herself. "No, that would only damage your chances. 'Tis best if we get our lawyer involved. Sir Richard Maitland is still the finest negotiator in Britain." She stopped, realizing David was not participating in the conversation. "But perhaps I am being too impatient. Tell me that you already have everything under control."

"You *are* being too impatient," he chided. "Before we get Sir Richard or anyone else involved, I need to convince Gwyneth. And that is what I am working on right now."

She gave him a disbelieving look. " 'Tis all very simple, David. You ask. She says yes."

David decided to keep his mouth shut. There was no purpose in disclosing Gwyneth's plan of elopement. He also did not want to tell his mother that she'd refused to marry him.

"Your wisdom is timeless," he said lightly to the dowager. "How foolish of me not to think of that."

"Do not patronize me, you impudent whelp," she said sternly. "Well, Augusta is not back yet, so you still have time. You went away too soon after Emma's death to witness any of the unpleasantness. But that woman has made up her mind never to give up the accusations and lies surrounding her daughter's death. 'Tis a good thing that neither Lyon nor Millicent have any fondness for the *ton* in London, for Augusta has apparently spread venomous tales about them there. By all accounts, she was upset at news of the earl's second marriage, and has now extended her hostility to the rest of us. Although we made a point of inviting her, she refused to attend Pierce and Portia's wedding."

"Well, Gwyneth obviously does not share her aunt's sentiments. She sang Millicent's praises and told me that *she* attended Pierce's wedding."

"Indeed. She visits us here often." The dowager pressed David's hand. "And that is one of the many reasons why I like that girl. She does not allow anything or anyone to influence her. She has a mind of her own and insists on making her own decisions. She is nothing like Emma and her mother. Who knows, perhaps she is not a Douglas, after all. Or perhaps the rest of them were fakes, and she is the real thing. Either way . . ." The blue eyes focused on David's face again. "You need to make your intentions known and get Sir Richard started with the Douglas family lawyers before Augusta gets wind of what you're doing." Her voice turned confidential. "That woman is sure to pick any penniless villain over you as a husband for Gwyneth, if she thinks that would somehow sting this family. What Gwyneth wants matters naught. What you want would mean even less!"

David had been so preoccupied in winning Gwyneth over that he'd never given any thought to Lady Cavers.

As relieved as Millicent was to know that Violet was safe at Greenbrae Hall, she did not want the young woman to feel cornered, or even to think she must answer any questions about her disappearance. Tears of joy sprinkled her cheeks, though, when she asked David the same questions that she had asked Truscott. Lyon's suggestion was for Millicent to give her some time before going there for a visit. After the ordeal that Violet had been through, she certainly needed some time to adjust to her new surroundings. As much as Millicent wanted to rush to the Hall and gather Violet up in her arms, she forced herself to be patient, for the moment.

This morning, though, the news Walter Truscott brought made Millicent once again concerned. Violet, borrowing a horse, had left Greenbrae Hall around dawn, telling one of the grooms where she was going and promising to be back by noon.

"It only makes sense that she should want to go

visit the old cotters out by the ruined kirk," Truscott assured Millicent. "When she left before, she said nothing to them. I'm certain she wants to thank them for their kindness."

His tense expression contradicted his words.

"Or perhaps she needs to visit her baby's grave," Millicent said sadly.

The young man said nothing to contradict it.

"I cannot wait any longer, though. I shall visit Greenbrae Hall to call on Gwyneth . . . perhaps this afternoon. Do you think Violet would be upset, seeing me there?"

Walter shook his head. "I wish I had all the answers, Millicent, but I do not. She is still quite vulnerable, but you know her better than any of us. I think you should do what you think is right."

There was no place that she could run. There was no place to hide, either. In staying at Greenbrae Hall, David was complicating everything. Gwyneth knew it would be a matter of hours and not days before she would run out of excuses. She had to see him. And there would be no denying him or herself. She just had no control over herself when they were together. This was why she had to act now. She had to force both of them to face the reality—no matter how painful or difficult it was.

Violet had told her that she would be away during the morning, so Gwyneth sought the help of one of the maids and undid most of the contraptions around her arm and shoulder. She was feeling much better and there was no way she would allow herself to remain confined in bed. It placed her at a distinct disadvantage in facing David.

Dressed, she told the young woman in which room

she planned to spend the morning, in case Captain Pennington arrived and wanted to see her.

She only wondered what time he would be here.

The visit with Rita and Angus was warm but brief. The kindly cotter and his wife knew why Violet was there. And as she left, they watched her climb the hill to the ruined kirk. They knew that she would be back there often.

The wind was blowing hard when the young woman reached the top of the hill. Violet raised her face for a few seconds to the dreary sky and fought back the tears. Swallowing the knot that had formed in her throat, she glanced briefly at the grassy kirkyard before letting her gaze come to rest on the small grave beneath the pine tree, outside the low stone wall.

Everything was as she'd left it. The pain in her heart was as sharp as the first time she'd been here. Her legs shook a little as she moved to where her child lay . . . alone, separated from the rest, unprotected. The unfairness of placing the mother's sin on a child born dead pried loose the tears she had been trying to control. She crouched beside the grave. She touched the small stones and ran her fingers across the dirt to wipe away what was left of her marks.

"You were loved. I wanted you to live," she whispered. Rather than swallowing her guilt, she voiced it. Instead of wallowing in her misery and allowing grief to return with its numbing emptiness, she spoke of her mistakes, of her sins. She told her unborn daughter what she had planned for her. But those were promises that would never be fulfilled. Violet whispered the only thing that she could give her daughter now. "I shall come back. You shall not be alone."

Before leaving, she found a stick again and scratched in the dirt the names of people and places who were part of her daughter's past. She wrote the names of those who cared. This time, she added Gwyneth's name to the list.

"And Greenbrae Hall," Violet said softly, writing the words.

The country house was still mired in chaos. The newly arrived help and the existing servants were trying to organize Greenbrae Hall without the benefit of the housekeeper and steward taking charge, and it was no small task. David found the caretaker at the stables when he arrived, so he made his presence known to the old man before going to the house.

The door was wide open, and David stood aside as a village lass he recognized came out the door carrying furniture coverings that needed to be shaken out before being stored. Inside, floors were being scrubbed, and feather dusters were out in abundance.

This was exactly the opportunity he was looking for. Instead of giving Gwyneth the chance to come up with more excuses, he would simply surprise her.

Upstairs, there was no answer to his knock on Gwyneth's door. David pushed the door open. The bed was empty and made up. The curtains had been drawn back and the windows were open. A gentle breeze was wafting through the empty chamber.

He looked up and down the hallway, but there was no sign of Gwyneth, or anyone else for that matter. He thought of the enclosed garden beneath the bedroom windows on this side of the house and wondered if she'd been taken down there for some fresh air. He walked into the room to check.

Everything about the chamber was like her. The neatness, the bright colors, the orderly stacks of books on a number of tables, even the tablets of paper on the writing desk with the pens and bowls of ink beside them. Though it was one of the smallest bedrooms at Greenbrae Hall, a sense of peace and comfort permeated the air. Looking around, he knew that she spent many hours here, and was content in that.

David glanced at the bed. How tempting she'd looked there the last time he'd stepped into the room. He tore his gaze away to look out, but he saw no one in the garden beneath. Turning around, he had just started toward the door when a shelf full of books lining a narrow bookcase beside the fireplace arrested his attention. The books protruded slightly and he started to push them back onto the shelf. When they didn't move, he realized other books were hidden behind them.

Out of curiosity, he pulled a couple of the books from the front and laid them aside. The ones hidden behind were of the same size and binding. He reached for the first volume.

It was a novel, written by an anonymous author and published by Thomas Ruddiman of High Street Edinburgh.

"Captain Pennington!"

The surprised voice from the doorway made David close the book with a snap. The young maid dropped a quick curtsy.

"Sorry to disturb ye, sir, but if ye are looking for Miss Gwyneth, she is spending the morning in the end room of the east wing. She asked me to tell ye to meet her there if ye wish it."

David tucked the book under his arm and started

for the door. "I thought Lady Cavers was the only one who used that wing these days."

"Aye, sir. That's the truth. But we've kept the large sitting room at the end the same as 'twas before. Ye know the room—the one looking out at Baronsford. 'Twas the one Miss Emma liked to use. That's where Miss Gwyneth is waiting to see ye."

Gwyneth had not stepped into this room for over a year. She was surprised by what she found.

The room had not so much been kept as a shrine to Emma, as she had thought. It was more a place where Augusta had stored some of Emma's things— all of which had been sent back from Baronsford after her death. A life-sized portrait leaned against the wall. It had once hung in the grand staircase at Baronsford and now dominated this room. All around her, draped over the chairs and sofas and tables were some of Emma's ornate gowns, as well as jewelry and knick-knacks that she was so fond of. A half-dozen other portraits of Emma posing in different gardens or rooms of Baronsford lay stacked against each other on another wall.

Gwyneth remembered when the news had reached them that everything belonging to Emma was going back to Greenbrae Hall. It was this past winter. She had been in London with Lady Cavers. The news of the earl's second marriage had reached them only a fortnight before they learned of Lyon's desire to rid Baronsford of everything having anything to do with Emma. Augusta, still riled by the first news, had flown into a rage upon receiving the second. Distance had been the older woman's salvation, or to Gwyneth's thinking she might have done something rash.

Lyon's action was as understandable to Gwyneth then as it was now. How could one even dream of starting a new life with another woman when he or she was still haunted by someone from their past? The ghost of Emma still hung over all of them. Gwyneth knew that Augusta avoided coming to this room. In fact, since Emma's death, the older woman had stayed away from Greenbrae Hall as much as she could.

Gwyneth tried to fight the suffocation she felt being in this room so long. She had flung the windows open as soon as she'd come in. Since entering the room this morning, though, she'd arranged some of the pictures and moved the clothing off the tables. She had tried to make the room a little more the way it had been when Emma was alive. She just wished he would come. She had only enough courage to face David in here once.

Gwyneth darted toward the windows as soon as she heard the knock on the door. She called out for him to enter.

"What are you doing out of bed? What are you doing in this room?" he asked as soon as he'd pushed open the door.

Gwyneth stared at him a moment before remembering to answer. Clean shaven and impeccably dressed, he looked much different from the rogue she had been traveling with for so many days. Looking at him now, she was not sure which David she preferred more. It would be a difficult choice, she thought.

His eyes focused only on her, but she sensed his struggle against the distraction of everything else around them.

"If you are well enough to be out of bed," he said finally, "then I shall accompany you for a walk in the gardens."

Bringing David here had been the perfect slap of reality for both of them. Surrounded by Emma's portraits and her belongings had to awaken whatever delusion they'd allowed to cloud their thinking. He had loved Emma, always had. Perhaps he always would.

"I thought you might like to see some of this." She made a sweeping motion of the room with one hand.

"No, I do not," he said sharply, never taking a step into the room, never looking at anything but Gwyneth's face.

His denial hurt.

"I am too tired to walk with you." She tried to hide her disappointment and started for the door. "I think I would just as soon return to my bedchamber and rest for the remainder of the afternoon."

"Then I shall keep you company there," he said, stepping back into the hallway.

"I would prefer not. I intend to sleep."

He took out a book from under his arm. "I promise to sit quietly and read. I found this in your room. Knowing your taste in adventure, this promises to be a good read."

Gwyneth groaned inwardly as she realized he was holding her first book of published tales in his hand.

The announcement of their engagement the summer that she turned twenty-one came as no surprise to Walter. She had pursued the new Earl of Aytoun at Baronsford and there were rumors that she'd been as attentive in London. From the moment Lyon had taken over his late father's title, he'd become the focus of Emma's desire.

For most of that time, David had been away with his regiment. During the few times when the youngest brother was back home, though, Walter knew the young man was battling the same feelings that had nearly crushed him years before. David did not understand Emma's games. He did not recognize the web she was spinning. He could not know how quickly Lyon would fall into her trap.

Walter had always known he had no future with Emma. David, however, had been kept on a string. As far as the younger brother was concerned, he still hoped and believed that Emma would accept his offer of marriage. He still had the stars in his eyes. The dream of the future kept his head in the clouds, even when Emma convinced Lyon to plan a grand affair for the announcement of their engagement. David arrived at Baronsford not knowing what awaited him—that his future was about to change forever.

The truth never came from Emma, but Lyon. David didn't stay for the party and the grand announcement. Wounded, he went away, and Walter watched him ride off. David did not even know how fortunate he was.

Chapter 17

Gwyneth paced like a nervous cat by the window as David read aloud.

"In the light of the full moon, Kildalton Castle gleamed like a diamond over the Firth of Lorn. The wind was now whipping the western sea into a surging demon, and the waves crashed with a devil's rage against the rugged cliffs upon which the Campbell fortress perched.

"No one could have expected the small sailing vessel that was scudding across the glittering firth. But it was, without question, being handled by a master.

"At the small boat's helm, a huge man wearing light armor and a cloak shouted orders to the sailor who, crouching by the single mast, was busy shortening the sail. The third voyager, a warrior nearly the size of the helmsman, sat in the bow of the boat, holding his head in his hands. The sea spray on his armor glistened in the moonlight, but he was no sailor; that was apparent. Low groans escaped from his handsome, full lips, and he kept running his long fingers through his golden red hair.

David paused and took a breath.

"What happened to reading quietly?" Gwyneth protested as she stopped pacing.

David looked up from the page. "You didn't look too eager to get into bed. So I thought you'd enjoy hearing the story. It has an excellent start.

"Do you really think so?" she asked, her expression going soft.

"Absolutely. In fact, I thought the chapter before this one was brilliant. Would you like me to go back and read that one aloud, too?"

She twisted her hands together and shook her head. "I've read it before."

"You know, I have a feeling that I may have read this before, too." He looked down at the pages open before him. "There is something extremely familiar about this tale. 'Tis as if I know what is going to happen next. But listen to this . . . *'The giant's gaze swept from his seasick friend to the shining castle that was now directly above them, and he pushed the tiller over with an ease that three men could not have accomplished. The seagoing warrior's long black hair streamed in the wind behind his massive shoulders, and the weathered look of his face could not belie the strength and agility of his muscular body.'*"

David looked up and smiled into Gwyneth's face. "He certainly sounds like one of the pirates from the tales you used to tell me."

"You should go now. I need to rest," she said hurriedly, looking suddenly pale.

"I told you before. I am not going anywhere." He stretched his legs out, getting more comfortable in the chair. "Do what you have to do. I promise to be quiet."

"David, this is completely improper." She walked a

couple of steps toward him and lowered her voice. " 'Twas one thing for us to be in such close quarters on the road, but here at Greenbrae Hall, with so many people around . . . word of this shall reach my aunt in no time and . . . and . . ."

"She'll take my side and force you to marry me?" he asked good-naturedly.

"No! She'll put me out on the road and make certain my uncle's lawyers know of the scandal. I shall get disinherited, for sure."

"I don't give a damn about your fortune. I'd marry you if you were penniless. In fact, I'd prefer you that way, as there would be fewer complications. As it stands now, we need to get too many people involved." He closed the book. "What do you say, Gwyneth? An elopement would suit me perfectly. We could be married before Lady Cavers . . ."

"No!" She spun on her heel and headed toward the window. "I can never marry you, Captain Pennington. I've told you that a hundred times."

"Why in bloody hell not?" He dropped the book on the chair and went after her. "And no riddles this time. I want clear and intelligent answers, without all the trickery."

Gwyneth turned around and held a hand up motioning David to keep his distance. "Do not come closer. I need distance to think clearly."

He continued toward her. "I don't *want* you to think. I want to know the absolute truth, not some watered-down version of whatever 'tis you think I should know."

She took a step to the side and pulled a chair between them. "You are not ready for that."

"I am ready, Gwyneth." He tossed the chair aside

and grabbed her wrist. "We haven't much time left. Once Augusta arrives, I have a feeling I shan't be welcome here at Greenbrae Hall."

"You think you are welcome now?"

"Of course." He pulled her wrist, and she fell against him. She was weak, still injured, and couldn't fight him . . . so David took full advantage of that and kissed her before she protested.

Gwyneth's complaint was in the form of a soft moan as her lips opened to allow him to deepen the kiss. After a minute of this madness, though, her left hand pressed against his chest, and she pulled her mouth free. "I cannot do this, David. I cannot go through with it, not after what I saw in your eyes in Emma's room."

"What did you see?"

She took a step back. "You are still in love with her."

"How can you say that?" he said angrily. "I didn't even walk into the room for the fear of upsetting you. I looked at nothing but you, so that you would know I have no interest in anything but you."

"You did not walk in there because of me?" she asked incredulously. "But you were upset. You were surrounded by old memories of what was between you two. You could not face your past at the same time that you were facing me."

"You are the damndest . . ." He shook his head. "You enjoy letting your imagination get out of hand, I think. Well, you listen. We are talking of real life here . . . not some story. What I felt for Emma is dead. It died a long time ago."

"Why can you not admit it?" she said stubbornly. "I went there today intentionally. I wanted you to recognize that you are still in love with Emma. You can never have any room in your heart for anyone else. She won't allow it, and 'tis only fair to me . . .''

"I'll show you what's fair." David took her by the hand and started for the door.

"Where are you taking me?" She planted her feet, but one tug and she had no choice but to follow.

" 'Tis time, once and for all, that you understood how I felt about her before she died and how I feel now."

"David . . ."

He didn't give her a chance to argue. There was a knock on the bedroom door just as he yanked it open. Violet took a step back as David pulled Gwyneth behind him into the hallway.

"Miss Douglas and I have some unfinished business in the east wing. Would you make certain that no one disturbs us while I convince your thick-headed mistress that she is the only woman that I love? That she is the only woman I intend to marry?"

Violet's eyebrows shot up. She curtsied, obviously trying to hide a smile, and stepped out of their way.

"Violet, please do not let him take me," Gwyneth called over her shoulder. "I do not want to go. In fact, I suddenly feel quite ill." She tried again to plant her feet.

"You will walk there, or I will carry you there. 'Tis your choice." David said firmly. Several servants walking down the hallway gave them a wide berth as they passed.

"You are the one besotted by the past," she muttered under her breath, reluctantly resigning herself to going. "You might as well go alone."

"*You* are far more obsessed with Emma's memory

than I am. We will face it together. And by God, if we have to burn everything in that room to be free of her, then we shall do that together, too. Understood?"

She kept her chin high, her back straight. Her green eyes were looking into his, but David saw the touch of vulnerability there. "I still stand by my belief."

"And I plan to enlighten you."

Gwyneth's feet dragged. She was actually afraid. Whatever it was that David was trying to do terrified her, even as it gave her hope. His words and actions had set a dim light burning at the end of the dark passageway that she'd assumed was a dead end. It was too much even to dream.

They stood before Emma's door. He pushed it open and waited for her to go in first. Gwyneth went in and found the room just as they'd left it. Emma's presence was everywhere—in the pictures, in her clothes, in everything. Gwyneth heard the latch and turned around to find David had locked them in.

"I want no interruptions."

There was no escaping it. She had to let him do whatever it was that he had in mind. Gwyneth backed up to the open windows to give him room, to be out of his way. Unlike last time, David's gaze surveyed the room, taking in everything before his gaze focused on the life-sized portrait of Emma. It was the work of Sir Joshua Reynolds. The bright red of the roses covering an arbor formed the perfect frame for Emma's beautiful face and white dress. Gwyneth recalled the days when this very picture used to hang at Baronsford, among the portraits of past and present Pennington family members.

" 'Tis unsettling how much this painting resembles her. I can see why Lyon did not want to have it around Baronsford." David moved closer and stood before the portrait.

Gwyneth averted her gaze. She did not know how to deal with the jealousy that was already burning within her. Every second felt like an hour. She felt the knot of worry in her stomach grow while a tight fist squeezed her heart as David continued to study the painting. All the insecurities she carried grew tenfold. The difference between them was so immense. She didn't have a fraction of Emma's beauty, or her sense of style, or her charm when it came to men. She feared at this very moment David might be comparing them, seeing everything that she lacked. Gwyneth remembered a day not long ago when Emma had stood before her and told her exactly what her flaws were.

Emma was dead, but her spirit still had a tight grip over all of their lives.

"I think a great painter's responsibility is to capture not just the obvious beauty of his subject, but to try to portray the real person within. Looking at it this close, 'tis amazing to see what I never noticed before."

David's comment drew Gwyneth's attention to his face. She didn't see any of the torment that had been haunting him for the last couple of years before Emma's death. His gaze was still on the painting.

"Sir Joshua has captured her features perfectly, but look what he has done with her eyes. They are cold. Unreadable. And look at the roses. Some of them are wilted, perhaps even diseased. The arbor itself appears to have places where the paint is beginning to bubble and peel, as if the wood beneath is beginning to rot."

Gwyneth looked at the details he was pointing out. He was correct. Even the sky in the background looked unsettled to her, where she had once thought it was only sky.

"When I think back, I cannot recall a time, no matter how far back, that she shared with me what was truly in her mind. I saw a beautiful face, felt the untamed lifeblood pulsing in her veins, but I never knew which direction her heart would take her. I believe I never really knew Emma, but I think Sir Joshua saw through her completely."

Gwyneth leaned against the window seat, understanding David's feelings.

"I tried to be her shadow for many years," she said. "She hated that. She did not care for anyone to be that close. She did not want anyone to really know or understand her. I do not believe she ever had a close female companion. She was a very private person."

"You are being far too kind. I long ago came to think of her as scheming." David said sharply. "It took me a while to learn that she often lied when it suited her. Her promises were always empty if they failed to bring her what she wanted."

"You are still bitter she chose Lyon over you."

"No, I was hurt . . . and bitter for a long time that she used me as she did before choosing him." David walked past the painting. He gave a cursory glance at Emma's dresses lying on the bed, at the smaller paintings against the wall, at the furnishings of the room. "I was young, eager. She was the first woman I was ever attracted to. I had known her for almost my entire life. I thought of her as a friend. Why could I suspect falsehood? She seemed to return my affection, so I trusted her. I planned my life around her. I thought I was even in love with her. She knew me, and I thought I knew her. I wanted her, and she made me believe that she returned my affection."

This was exactly what Gwyneth remembered of those days. He *was* a man in love. "I remember Emma's engagement to Lyon. You arrived at Baronsford not knowing what was being planned."

"Lyon thinks I still blame him for that." He shook his head. "But he had been away for so long. He had no idea what my feelings for Emma were. He had no idea how far our relationship had developed. To this day, he still doesn't know that I made a proposal of marriage to Emma two summers earlier—a proposal that she never rejected but only put off. But none of that mattered, anyway. Emma wanted my brother—or at least his title and all that he was inheriting."

Gwyneth never knew that David had actually asked for Emma's hand in marriage, either.

"But I have no one to blame for what happened then but myself. I chose to ignore the signs. They were so obvious. Being young and in love makes you blind. In my case, I was blind and foolish." He knocked a collection of porcelain figures from a table with one sweep of his hand. They broke into hundreds of pieces against the wall, but he paid no heed to them. Neither did Gwyneth.

"I was not the first man who was intimate with Emma, but I chose not to ask any questions. I told myself that I preferred not to know. I did not care to face what would be embarrassing for both of us. I did not care to think that I might have a competitor when it came to her attentions. But that was only the start. When Emma put off giving me an answer about my offer of marriage, I should have known. She used pretty excuses, but I learned once and for all who she was when Lyon told me about his engagement to Emma."

It was too painful to watch him. Gwyneth pressed her back against the window and stared down at the colorful twist of flowers woven into the ornate rug on the floor. There had been so much more between Emma and David than she had even imagined. She felt sick to think how her cousin could go from one brother's bed to the other's, putting off rejecting one's offer of marriage until she could maneuver her way into a more profitable one.

"I have only begun to tell you about Emma and me, and I can already tell 'tis more than you wanted to hear."

Gwyneth shook her head and looked up. "I thought I knew everything that there was."

"What *was* between Emma and me was a childhood of friendship that developed into a physical affair managed by a manipulative young woman. It had to end sooner or later." He raised a hand to silence her when Gwyneth tried to object to the simplistic explanation. "When I cornered Emma after hearing of her engagement to Lyon, I demanded an explanation. Her answer was that she owed me nothing. She had made no commitment. *I had to learn to let go,* were her exact words. 'Twas time for both of us to move on."

"But you couldn't. That is not the way life is. You had been inseparable for years. I saw how you felt about her, how you treated her, even after she was married to Lyon."

"It takes two people to be in love." David rose to his feet. "That day I realized that Emma had never returned my affection. She never felt the same way that I felt about her. Listening to her, I knew that I had been used. But my eyes were opened that day. I could see her for who she was. Even so, my wounds needed time to heal. Of course, she was marrying my brother, becoming part of my family. I had to find a way to deal with it."

"You did not do a very good a job at that," Gwyneth said frankly. " 'Twas dreadful when you stopped coming to Baronsford."

David walked toward her. His gaze fixed on her face. "Dreadful for whom?"

"For everyone," she said quietly. "For your mother . . . and Pierce . . . and even Lyon."

"And for you?"

Gwyneth gave a small nod before looking away. They had made love. She had done things with this man that she wouldn't dare put on the pages of her notebook. Still, with just a tender look from him, she felt the fire ignite in her belly.

"I am glad that you are not like her. I am relieved that you don't try to be. I have always been impressed with the person you were and the woman you have become . . . despite the influences around you."

He gave her more credit than she deserved. He saw more in Gwyneth than she saw in herself.

"But if I had ever been given the choice growing up," she admitted, "I would have changed places with Emma in an instant."

"I do not understand that. You had your own beauty—your own distinctive talents and intelligence." He reached her side. "You even ended up with an inheritance anyone would envy. And you never needed Baronsford. What did you think she had that you didn't?"

He raised her chin when she hesitated to answer. "She had you."

His expression softened. His thumb brushed her lower lip and caressed her cheek. "Where did I go wrong, then? How is it that I am trying to give myself to you today, and you no longer want me?"

She let out a slow breath. Her hand pressed his against her cheek, and she leaned into his touch. "This is my undoing, though, for you know I want you."

"But there is a problem." He forced her to look into his eyes.

"I've loved you for as long as I can remember. And somewhere, I became accustomed to you not loving me back." She pressed her fingers against his lips when he started to speak. " 'Tis so much easier for me to marry without love, to form a union that has no emotional or physical expectations. Marriage is a simpler thing when each spouse goes their separate ways with only the business arrangement that binds them."

He took her hand and pressed a kiss onto her palm. "With the exception of going separate ways, we can pretend our marriage is whatever you want it to be. You marry me, and I shall do all I can to make it easy for you."

She shook her head. "It cannot work. When it comes to you, I cannot bear the thought of a competitor. Not in marriage. Not in forever. I cannot be near you and share my life with you, believing that I might only be second in your affections. I cannot bear to think that when you make love to me, you might be thinking of Emma. I cannot . . ."

"You do not need to think any of those things," he said gruffly, silencing her with a kiss. His mouth was demanding, and Gwyneth gave in to it the moment their lips touched. She clutched at him as he drew out the need she had been trying to hide.

"You are the only one in my heart. You are the only one in my mind."

She felt herself being backed toward the sofa. "What are you doing?"

"Do you see this room? Do you see all of Emma's belongings? Do you see her portrait looking at us?"

She followed the direction of his gaze and guessed what was going through his mind. She shivered. "Not here, David."

"Why not here? On this bed, with her looking on." He swept everything off the sofa to the floor. He took her mouth in another kiss. "I am going to make love to you right here, surrounded by the belongings of a woman long dead and gone . . . and I want you to know that we have nothing to fear."

Her palms pressed against his chest. She half-heartedly tried to push him away, but the rest of her body fought her own protest. She answered another one of his kisses.

"I want you, Gwyneth. I want *your* body. I want *your* heart." He took her hand and pressed it against the front of his breeches. " 'Tis you doing this to me. No one but you. I want to make you cry out in pleasure. I want to bury myself deep inside you and feel you close like a sheath around me. I want us to become one—here and now—with the sun shining in on us and with dreams of our future in our heads. She cannot touch us, Gwyneth, for she is gone. 'Tis only us now. You and me."

Gwyneth pressed her lips against his neck. "Take me, David."

*   *   *

*Lord Cavers died in the autumn of the same year
that his only daughter was wed to the Earl of Aytoun.
There were many friends, but very few close kin who
attended the burial service.*

*Walter Truscott went up to the funeral as a represen-
tative of the family. He found the service to be just the
empty spectacle he'd anticipated.*

*The earl's widow shed not even the obligatory tear,
as far as Walter could see. Augusta, obviously furious
about something, was barely contained during the ceremony. She left immediately after the burial. Emma and
Lyon, though still considered newlyweds, arrived stone-
faced and somewhat distracted. Walter knew Lyon well
enough to sense that a great storm was already brewing
in that relationship.*

*Neither Pierce nor David could come. Walter deliv-
ered a letter of condolences from the dowager Countess
Aytoun to Lady Cavers, since her ill health was keeping
the older woman confined to her London town house.*

*The only person who truly mourned Charles Doug-
las's passing was Gwyneth. One would have to be blind
not to realize that the fifteen-year-old's grief was genuine. From everything Walter had gathered over the
years, Lord Cavers was the only friend the lassie had
ever had in that household, and the rumors were already spreading about the sizable fortune that had been
left for her.*

*The rumors were confirmed immediately after the fu-
neral. Lyon asked Walter to take the countess back to
Baronsford while he tended to some other business,
and Walter had no choice. No one but the two of them,
alone in the old closed carriage.*

"From the moment she first stepped into Greenbrae

Hall, I guessed what her game was about. She was there to steal everything that belonged to me," Emma fumed the moment the carriage started. "Gwyneth and her bright green eyes and singsong voice and sickening righteousness. She and her perfect manners. Her obedient ways. Pretty little Gwyneth and the insipid smile she pasted onto her ugly face whenever his lordship came around. She did a fine job of fooling the old bastard."

"She was and is a bright light in that house. She made his lordship happy," Walter asserted. "There are more than a few things you might have learned from her over the years."

"What the devil for?" she snapped. "I wasn't his child anyway, and he knew it. And why pretend I liked him, when 'twas obvious he hated everything about me. The old pig showed it, too, in leaving what should be mine to Gwyneth. He even robbed his own wife, giving more than he should have to his precious niece, his pasty-faced angel, his do-gooder ice princess—the lying bitch."

Walter felt his hackles rise on behalf of Gwyneth. Hers was an innocence that Emma would never comprehend. He also felt angered for the dead earl, who could not defend himself.

"You have nothing to complain about. Lord Cavers always treated you fairly. You were never deprived of anything . . . to the day he died. He never hinted to anyone . . . as far as I know . . . that he might not have fathered you. He made certain that your worth as a marriage prospect was not marred in any way."

"How foolish that people place any weight on reputation!" A tense laugh escaped her throat. "How empty that all is."

Walter shot her a hostile glare. "You say so now that you are married. You have nothing to lose."

"Nothing to lose?" Her smile was as false as the mole on her powdered cheek. She pretended that she had not a care in the world. "My reputation since my marriage has a few marks against it, not that I can blame my father for that. Lord Aytoun, my honorable husband, was deeply troubled when he discovered that I was not a virgin when he carried me to the marriage bed."

Truscott felt his stomach churn. A sour taste climbed into his throat.

"You have suddenly gone quite pale, my love." Her gloved hand rested on his knee.

He brushed it off with no gentleness.

She laughed again and pulled the black veil from her hair and face. Pulling pins, she shook her head and a mass of golden curls cascaded down over her shoulders. "You haven't a thing to worry about. Lyon believes David and I were intimate before my marriage, and I refuse to say anything to contradict that. 'Tis amusing to watch, though. He is so focused on one man, one relationship, that I might have had, when I'm fairly certain I can match the number of times he has taken a different woman to his bed with affairs of my own. 'Tis almost comical how a man's mind works."

He turned his face away. He needed to get away from her poison.

She slid closer to him on the seat. Her shoulder brushed against his.

"Now you are to be angry with me, too. And why should that be, my love? Are you jealous? Would you like to know how our lovemaking compared with those other times? With Lyon? With David?"

"I'll not be trifled with, Emma. Let me be."

"But I cannot let you be. You must be able to see that." She touched his knee again, this time sliding her hand up the inside of his leg. " 'Tis been so long, Walter. But I still cannot forget how 'twas between us." Her lips touched his chin. "We can escape to the tower house for a few hours and you can take me. You can have me as often as you want. You can do to me whatever you want. No one needs to know."

He shoved her away so hard that she fell off the seat onto the carriage floor.

"I'll know," he snarled. "I am not treacherous to my family. You are married to my cousin, a man I highly respect. Hear this clearly, Emma. I have put behind me what we once had . . . and what we once did. Nothing more shall happen between us. Do you hear me? Nothing."

Banging on the wall of the carriage, he shouted for the driver to stop. Before the vehicle had lurched to a complete halt, though, Walter was out the door and striding toward the woods and the river . . . away from his nightmare.

Chapter 18

As little as she knew of Captain David Pennington, Violet was confident that all would be well between him and Gwyneth. It was obvious that he cared deeply. And, as little as Vi knew about love, she also sensed that the man's affection was genuine. Obviously a passionate man, he was not one to give up on what he wanted.

Images of Ned Cranch flickered in Violet's brain. Gwyneth had never had any experience with the lying and cheating type that Ned had been. She might not even know what a blessing it was to have someone who truly cared for you, who was truly committed to you, who wanted a future that included both of you. A man who respected you and treated you right. Violet shook her head and began straightening the books on the shelves. She wanted no thoughts of her own past with the dead stonemason to cloud her thinking.

Captain Pennington would take care of Gwyneth, and a small light had been lit in the recesses of Violet's mind that maybe then she could stay there, where she could visit her babe from time to time.

She had left the door to Gwyneth's bedchamber open, and she turned as the excited maid arrived, breathless from running.

"A visitor has arrived for Miss Gwyneth, miss. We put her in the Oak Room."

Violet remembered David's threat and promise. She straightened her dress and headed for the door, thinking that maybe she could buy her mistress some extra time. "Did she give a name?"

" 'Tis the first time she's been to Greenbrae Hall, Miss Violet, but we knew her right off." The maid lowered her voice. " 'Tis the Lady Aytoun herself downstairs waiting. From Baronsford. Good thing Lady Cavers is not here, for she'd have raised a fuss, to be sure."

The girl continued to chatter away, but Violet stopped dead, her feet rooted to the floor. Her heart was racing with panic and embarrassment. A hundred other feelings rushed through her mind. She didn't know what she would say to Millicent. She couldn't think of any way to explain. She had no idea where even to start.

"I shall go and get Miss Gwyneth," she whispered, trying to force her feet to move.

"Actually, her ladyship said she wanted to speak with ye first," the maid said, staring at Violet. "Are ye unwell, miss?"

"I'm perfectly well, thank you."

"Well, we were all verra impressed that she knew ye."

None of them would have been impressed if they knew the circumstances in which Violet had left Lady Aytoun's household, Vi thought. She took a deep breath and smoothed the invisible wrinkles in her skirt before starting down the stairs.

David had underestimated how much he'd needed Gwyneth, how much he'd wanted her, how much he'd missed her. As a result, they lay in a tangle of partially discarded clothing, their bodies still hot from their frenzied lovemaking, and he was in no hurry to move. He also knew it would take almost no persuasion to coax him into repeating the performance.

"I must tell you, David," Gwyneth whispered, "this was even more exciting than our first night in Gretna Green."

She smiled and stretched lazily next to him, one slender leg moving on top of the breeches that David had never completely rid himself of. She pressed a kiss on his neck.

They had managed to open her gown at the neckline, so he could see the bandages and glimpse her ivory breasts. The skirts were a rumpled mass of material, and both of them were lying on them. Her curls were a tangle and the silky skin of her neck carried the marks where his lips and rough face had rubbed against it. She was a delicious mess, and he gathered her closer against him.

"Do you believe me now when I say that when it comes to making love, for me you have no peer?"

Gwyneth looked around the room first, her gaze pausing on each of Emma's paintings. The magical green eyes were misty when they finally met his.

"I believe you."

"Will you also believe me when I say that long before Emma's death—in fact, from the time she accepted Lyon's marriage proposal—any infatuation I had for her ended?"

"I believe you now." She gave a small nod. "But your actions spoke differently then. You left immediately following her death. You showed no regard for the condition Lyon was left in. Many, myself included, could only assume that 'twas your love for her that drove you away, and the fact that you clearly blamed what had happened on him."

"What drove me away . . ." David paused, studying Emma's portrait for a moment first. The events surrounding their fall from the cliffs whirled in his brain. The voices of so many people, the anger that permeated the air during that time, came rushing back. There was no mood of celebration at Baronsford that day, only hostility. He finally looked back into Gwyncth's face. "I didn't believe Emma's death was an accident."

"It had rained all night. The cliffs must have been slippery. She could have simply fallen off the rocks."

"She knew those cliffs better than anyone. She'd been running up and down that path since we were children," David argued. "But why would she go there, anyway?"

"Who knew why Emma did so many things?"

"Certainly not I." He glanced at her. "At the same time, though, I knew I had to leave Baronsford. I was certain that someone had pushed her. And with that kind of thinking, I knew that my presence would be of no help to Lyon."

Gwyneth extricated herself from his embrace and sat up, pushing her skirts down. She looked at him. "And you believed Lyon pushed her."

"He had the greatest reason. Of everyone there that last day, he was one feeling the most wretched about her. He never had a great deal of patience. 'Twas clear that she had now driven him nearly out of his mind." David rolled back and stared at the ceiling. "The fact that he was incapable of speaking after his accident did not help me, either."

"He was severely injured," she said sharply. "And you are his brother. You should have had more faith in him."

"I know. I deserve your reprimand," he said, turning back to her. "I now realize that. But at that time, all I knew was that I had to get as far away as I could from Baronsford, and Emma, and any memory of her. I had severed my ties with her once before. I didn't want to grieve again. I didn't want to think about anything. I had no desire to lay blame, either. I only wanted to forget."

Gwyneth studied him in a moment of silence. David could feel the emotions that she was battling. He told himself this was another thing that he loved about her. She never really could hide what she was feeling. She was so different from Emma. He didn't have to guess the true meaning behind what she did or said.

"And did you forget?" she finally asked, putting a hand gently on his.

"Forget Emma? Yes." David entwined their fingers. "But forget Lyon and what was happening to my family?" He shook his head. "I found myself starved for any news of them. The worry of what was going to become of Lyon never left me, and then there was all this other news. Lyon was married and miraculously recovering. And then Pierce coming back, and he was being married. In the end, 'twas the same as when we were children. My two older brothers were always a step ahead of me, and I had to work so hard to keep up with them. They were all getting on with the future. I did not want to be left behind. I wanted to be part of them—part of their lives."

"You are back with your family now. But what do you believe now about Emma's death?"

He stared across the bed at Emma's portrait. "Lyon told me he didn't kill his wife, and I believe him. I have told him as much. But I already know that saying the words will not be enough for him. Not after leaving Baronsford a year ago the way I did."

"So what are you going to do?"

"I need to find out who really killed Emma."

She sat up straight. "What you are talking about is not the simplest of tasks."

"It might be, if we think it through." He touched her knee, rubbing the dress against her skin. "Emma left the castle a number of minutes ahead of Lyon. She went straight to the path along the cliffs. Now why would she go there at that early hour of the morning, and right after a heated argument with her husband?"

"To cool her temper?"

"She could have taken a walk in the gardens, or gone to the deer park, or taken a horse out for a ride. She could have done any number of things more suited to the weather that day. Why would she choose to go somewhere as secluded as the cliff walk?"

"Perhaps she had a prearranged rendezvous," Gwyneth whispered.

David frowned and looked into her face. "We know a great deal about Emma now that I did not know then. Do you think she was going there to meet her lover?"

There was absolute silence. Gwyneth gathered her knees to her chest and stared into space.

"We have to find some answers," he said firmly. "We know who the guests were at the house on the day that Emma died. And I believe most of the servants here then are still here. We shall just ask some questions, find out what was going on in her life, and who else was angry enough to push her off that cliff."

"I'm not sure I like your use of the word *we*."

David grabbed one of her slender ankles and pulled until her legs were stretched across his lap. "Well, I'm sure."

"You are not the only one who has been trying to forget. There will be too many people upset over this. I do not think 'tis such a good idea to—"

"I think 'twould be a wonderful idea if we do it together." He pushed up her skirt and looked down at her smooth legs. Her fingers closed around his wrist when he began to slide his fingers along the inside of one thigh.

"You should just explain everything to Lyon. He'll understand. You have convinced me . . . you could do the same to him."

"I cannot, my love," he laughed. "I have no interest in doing with him what you and I have done."

"You are incorrigible. I am not talking about—"

She stopped with a gasp when he touched the very center of her pleasure. David smiled at the blush that crept into her cheeks. He could hear her breath growing short.

She tried to reach for him, but he further opened the neckline of the dress roughly. Hungrily, he took in the perfect swell of her breasts before his mouth closed around a pink tip. He suckled hard as his finger delved inside her.

"David—"

Her cry of pleasure made him crazy for more. He tugged on the arms of the dress, impatient to be rid of anything that hampered his ability to touch and caress and love her. He felt her begin a battle of her own, pushing at his clothes with her one good arm.

"How do you bring this out in me?" Gwyneth's fingers took a fistful of his hair and her mouth ground against his in a fevered kiss. "How do you make me want you this badly?"

" 'Tis the two of us, my love." He lifted her up and in a moment she was straddling him. He felt her lower herself until he was fully embedded inside her. "We were made for each other. We were never meant to be apart."

She didn't argue, and he smiled as she instead gave herself up to their dance of love.

Everyone reminded her constantly that she should rest, but Millicent simply could not. The movements within her of her soon-to-be-born child; Lyon's continuing recovery; Josephine's endless energy. Life was too exciting to miss a moment of it. And now the knowledge that Violet was safe and happily situated. It was all so thrilling. She was hoping to see this wonder with her own two eyes.

This was the first time that Millicent had made a visit to Greenbrae Hall. Her view of it from outside was just as it had been described to her by Truscott. A handsome stone house standing a full three stories high, with wings extending out to either side of the main structure. The grounds stretched a great distance around the place, with a long oak-lined drive leading up to it. Beyond one of the wings, she had been able to make out the deer park along the Tweed. Baronsford had been visible, too, its massive walls glittering in the morning light.

The inside was just as striking. In the high-ceilinged entrance hall, an ancient clock ticked away at the top of a marble tower set into one wall. On either side, arched marble pillars formed corridors leading toward the back of the great house, creating open galleries that looked down on the tiled floor of the entry hall. The effect was tasteful but somewhat cold, and she had been surprised when the servant had led her to a sitting room that was paneled with dark oak. The sun was shining into the room, which was very comfortable and warm.

She paced about the heavily furnished room to calm herself. This visit was about Violet . . . and about Gwyneth's injury. It had nothing to do with Lyon's first wife, she told herself. She was not going to allow anything spoil her happiness at this moment.

Millicent paused before two large paintings above the fireplace and decided that they must be the portraits of Lord and Lady Cavers. She studied the latter. There was a resemblance in the shape of the face and the eyes to her daughter, but Lady Cavers appeared to be larger, more buxom, almost imperial in her bearing. It occurred to her that the countess had the look of a woman who was directing the artist as he painted.

There had been no occasion for Millicent to have met Emma's mother in person, and she knew that Augusta had not yet arrived in Scotland. And that was fine with Millicent. She had heard the rumors. Lady Cavers carried a grudge about Lyon's second marriage.

There was a painting on an adjoining wall of Emma as a young girl, seated on her mother's lap, and Millicent looked at it. She was relieved that she had never known Lyon when Emma was alive, though she never thought of Emma as an enemy. She was just happy that she came into his life after Emma was gone. Their life was something that they were building together. They were creating their own history as they lived it.

Gwyneth was a completely different matter. Though she was a part of the history that existed between Baronsford and Greenbrae Hall, Millicent had met the young woman on several occasions and liked her very much. In fact, Millicent guessed that if it were not for the hard feelings that obviously existed between Lady Cavers and the Pennington family, she would have seen more of Gwyneth than she had. The fact that she'd found Violet and was sheltering her was more proof that Millicent's instinct about her had been correct.

David's obvious interest in the young woman presented so many wonderful possibilities, as well. In visiting her today, she was hoping to invite Gwyneth to come and stay with them at Baronsford while her aunt was away. Lady Cavers's opinion actually mattered little to Millicent.

Millicent sensed someone was watching her, and she turned to the door. For a brief moment, she didn't recognize the young woman half hidden in the shadow of the doorway, but as she stepped forward, Millicent's heart leapt.

"Violet!" she cried, walking toward her and forgetting her own vow of not frightening the young woman. " 'Tis really you! I can hardly believe you are finally standing here with me, safe. I never thought I would be given another chance of seeing you, of speaking to you."

Millicent gathered Violet in her arms, tears splashing onto her face. Her heart and mind sent a prayer of thanks to God for bringing them together again.

"Let me see you," she whispered brokenly, pulling back and holding her at arm's length.

Violet's chin quivered, and her face was wet with

tears. Millicent could see that she had aged. The
months since she had left Melbury Hall had been very
rough on her. The lustrous shine in the golden curls
was gone. The flawless skin was now touched by the
abuses of the harsh northern weather. The spark of
innocence in her blue eyes had been doused, replaced
now by sorrow and experience.

"I am so sorry, milady."

"No, I am sorry. I am sorry for letting you down—
for not taking care of you the way I should have. I
made a promise to your mother and your grandmother, and I carelessly forgot my vow."

"You cannot blame yourself. You could not have
been better or kinder to me. You gave me everything
I could have dreamed of—a good job, respect, free-
dom, even friends who were close to me to be kin."
She was fighting back more tears. "I was so wretched.
A complete fool. I thought I knew. I trusted when . . .
I . . . I did wrong. I sinned and . . . and my child had
to pay. No one would ever forgive me for what I
did . . . no one will . . . not even God can ever forgive
what I've done."

A sob stopped her from continuing. She covered her
face with both hands and could not catch her breath in
her grief. Millicent pulled Violet into her embrace and
took her to a sofa, forcing her to sit beside her. She
caressed the young woman's arms and back as her
tears mingled with Violet's.

A few moments passed and then a young serving
girl carrying a tray of tea came to an abrupt halt in
the doorway. She looked worriedly from Violet's bent
head to Millicent's tearstained face.

Millicent rose quickly to her feet and took the tray
from the girl's hand, putting it on a nearby table.

"Would you be kind enough to leave us alone for a short while?"

The maid nodded quickly. "So I shouldn't go after Miss Gwyneth for ye?"

"Not yet. Violet will go after her when the time is right."

"As ye wish, milady." Darting worried glances at Violet, the girl curtsied and backed out of the room.

Millicent closed the door shut and went back to the sofa. The sobbing of the young woman had become silent tears, but their intensity had not decreased.

"I do not know where you went when you left Melbury Hall," she whispered gently. "But 'tis obvious that you have gone through a great deal of hardship these past months. The one thing I want you to know is that I shall never think badly of you for anything in the past. You have never done me wrong, Vi. That I know."

"I caused you to worry. That's wrong enough," Violet whispered, her gaze focusing on Millicent's swollen belly. "I didn't . . . I didn't know you were with child."

" 'Tis a wonder, is it not?" the countess smiled, wiping the tears from her face. "At my age . . . I never thought it could be possible."

"You are healthy and blessed with a fine home and caring husband. You and your baby shall do well." She dashed at her own tears. "And you shouldn't fuss over your age. My mother was older than you when she had me. And she used to say that if my father hadn't passed away, she would have had at least a half-dozen more before she was done."

Millicent was relieved to see Violet getting over the tears. "I visited your mother and grandmother in the spring, and again just before we came to Scotland. They are both doing very well."

The young woman's chin sank onto her chest again. Millicent reached out and lifted it until she could look into Vi's face. "Your grandmum knew that someday you would be back. They shall be thrilled to hear you are well."

"I've shamed them, milady. They'd have been better off if I'd never been found."

"Don't say that," Millicent scolded gently. "Too many people have been praying for you to come back to them. Your mother and grandmother. All your friends at Melbury Hall . . . including me. People who you knew in Knebworth Village."

"I am not worthy of that," Violet said brokenly. "I've done nothing to deserve of such kindness."

"But you have." Millicent took the young woman's hand. "There is not a time that I run into Moses at Melbury Hall that he doesn't ask me when you are coming back. Jonah has told me at least a dozen times that they've found the old man out on the road to St. Albans, waiting for the mail coach. Moses tells him each time that he doesn't want you to walk back alone in the dark to Melbury Hall. And you should see the beautiful baskets he's been weaving for you. He told me himself that you always carried the first one he ever made when you'd go to the village."

Millicent took a handkerchief from her sleeve and handed it to Violet.

"Milady, these past months, whenever I thought that I could not take another step, or take another breath, whenever I thought 'twould be better just to lie down and die—I've thought of Moses. I remembered the first time that I met him, his black skin scarred and raw from a lifetime of beating. I recalled the stories I'd heard about all he'd faced during his life . . . and I thought about the kindness that never left his heart. He is one of the reasons I am still alive." Violet's teary gaze met Millicent's. "And you are the other reason. You've shown me what it means to be strong. Watching you over the years, seeing how you survived the Squire, knowing how much good you've done for all your people. When I was out there on the moors with the wind and sleet cutting through me, you were the angel guiding my way."

"Violet," Millicent sighed, pulling the young woman into her arms again. Her own emotions were so raw that she could not control the tears. She was unable to calm the quaver in her voice. She silently thanked God for bringing Vi safely to them. She thanked Him for Ohenewaa's power, giving Millicent hope as she waited.

"I need to tell you the rest." Violet pulled back. "I cannot bear to hold back any of the truth."

Millicent knew what Violet was feeling. She too had never been able to put her mind at rest until Lyon had been told all the circumstances surrounding Squire Wentworth's death. She knew she had to give the young woman the chance to lay down her burden. Even as Vi started, though, Millicent knew that no crime Violet had committed would change the way she felt.

Millicent had been given a second chance at life and at happiness. Violet would get that same chance.

There was no justice in this world, of that Gwyneth was certain.

How could David possibly walk away from all they'd done to each other and look so composed? She, on the other hand, was a complete mess. Her hair and her dress were in complete disarray. Life with him would certainly offer no justice, whatsoever. Wearing a very satisfied look on his face, he stood by the window and pretended to look out at Baronsford as she tried to put herself into some semblance of order. Her throbbing shoulder and ribs were not helping. Curious how she'd barely noticed them a few minutes earlier.

"Being away for so long, I had to promise the dowager to take at least one meal with her each day. Will you come back and dine with us at Baronsford?"

"The doctor's instructions were for me to rest, remember? No leaving my room, no travel, no arduous activities of any kind."

"Of course not," he whispered as they left Emma's sitting room and stepped into the corridor. "Still, come back with me to Baronsford."

"I really cannot."

He was literally sweeping her off her feet with his attention. He was making her begin to think that they could work through all their troubles, no matter what they were. They had already discussed Emma, but Gwyneth still needed to find a way to tell him about her writing and the blackmailer that was hounding her. " 'Twould be better if I stayed here and pretended to be following the doctor's orders."

"Come and stay. Since Greenbrae Hall is not fully staffed, I know Millicent would insist."

She shook her head politely. "Being here will be more comfortable for me and Violet. I wouldn't want to leave her here alone, and I don't know how she would feel about going to Baronsford right now." She sensed David was ready to argue further. She lowered her voice and put an arm on his sleeve. "I know you will be coming back here tonight, anyway. With my aunt away . . . the accommodations at Greenbrae Hall will be more suitable for—"

Pulling her into an alcove, David took her in his arms and kissed her deeply. Gwyneth had to lean against him when he finally broke off the kiss. "I shall be back sooner than you think."

"While you're gone, I shall look through some of Emma's belongings for some idea of who might have been involved in her death." Gwyneth looked down the hall in the direction they had come. "It would have been so much easier if she were fond of writing and kept a diary. There is so much one can learn by reading what a person writes."

She looked back to David and noticed he was eyeing her curiously. The footsteps of one of the maids coming up the stairs ended the awkward moment, though. The girl appeared eager to speak to Gwyneth.

"I shall see you tonight," he said. The backs of their fingers brushed momentarily, and Gwyneth stood at the top of the stairs watching him go. When he glanced back at her, she wondered how much, if anything, she had just revealed about herself.

Violet's surprise at hearing what took place at Melbury Hall the night she killed Ned Cranch was as dramatic as Millicent's reaction to her tale.

"So Jasper Hyde and his men still managed to get there even without Ned?"

"They did," Millicent said. "But the damage was lessened since they had no one with them who was familiar with the estate or the house and people. Your courage in stopping the stonemason made all the difference."

" 'Twas no courage, milady," Violet admitted quietly. "Just anger and necessity pushed me to do it."

"I wish you hadn't run off."

"I had no choice. I had broken every rule my family had ever taught me. In many ways, I was as guilty as the dead man lying at my feet."

"You were not. You *are* not!" Millicent said with passion, taking Violet's hand. "Ned Cranch tricked and used you from the start, just as Squire Wentworth used *me* in our five years of marriage. There were many times that I wanted to do the same thing to the Squire that you did to Ned. There were so many times when I cursed at my own cowardice for not putting an end to all of it sooner. You had the strength to do what had to be done. I am only now learning that strength. But there is no doubt in my mind that if an occasion such as the one you faced presented itself to me now—if it came down to taking the life of an evil man to spare the lives of innocent people I care about, I know I would do the same thing."

"I don't know that the law would agree, milady."

"Then the law will never know what really happened," Millicent said adamantly. "At Melbury Hall, in Knebworth Village, in St. Albans, the news was the same. A loudmouthed, drunken stonemason had met his fate in that tavern, probably at the hand of another drunk. No one saw anything, Vi, and no one cared to look for the assailant."

A small flame of hope kindled inside her. Violet knew it wasn't for her own sake, but for her family. The ordeal of seeing her hanged for murder would surely crush them.

"I think sometimes about Ned's widow and children," Vi said.

"There is no widow," Millicent said. "We asked Mr. Trimble, the rector of the church in the village, to go and notify the family. There was no wife. 'Twas just another lie."

Violet shook her head.

" 'Tis time to put that chapter of your life behind you," Millicent continued. "The same way that I have gone on since the Squire's death, you must put Ned Cranch behind you. He no longer has any hold on you."

Violet stared at her callused fingers. She could still see the dirt from her daughter's grave beneath her fingernails.

"My child is dead, though. She did not need to pay for my sins."

"Nor did she," Millicent said with feeling. "At the best of times, under the most expert care, babies die during childbirth, as do their mothers. This happens every day. Your child's passing had nothing to do with any sin. Knowing you, I am certain she was carried lovingly in your womb. Hearing the stories about you Walter Truscott came home with, you continue to love and care for her spirit even now."

Violet thought she had no tears left in her, but a few managed to escape, rolling down her cheeks. She immediately rose to her feet when there was a knock on the door. Upon hearing Gwyneth's voice, she rushed to open it. Vi had already told Lady Aytoun that Gwyneth knew all about her past. She'd even told the countess of the friendship they had formed immediately upon their chance meeting at the ruined abbey.

"I am so sorry to intrude on you . . . looking like

this . . . but . . ." Gwyneth looked worriedly from the countess to Violet. She took in her friend's tearstained face and grasped both of her hands, lowering her voice. "How are you holding up?"

Violet nodded and squeezed Gwyneth's hand. "Lady Aytoun knows everything. And she feels the same as you . . . about everything . . . especially about the stonemason."

The relief was evident in the way Gwyneth turned and smiled at their guest. She walked over and the two women shared a silent embrace.

"Just before you walked in, Violet and I were speaking of her babe," the countess said.

" 'Tis very upsetting where she is buried," Gwyneth said to both of them.

"Then we shall correct the wrong of burying that innocent soul so far away . . . and outside of the kirk-yard cemetery." Millicent stretched a hand toward Violet, inviting her to join them. "Whether it be in the chapel in the village, in the churchyard at St. Albans, or at Reverend Trimble's church in Knebworth, we shall see that it happens. The three of us shall find a place where you feel confident that she can rest in peace."

Violet nodded, fighting the tears, looking at two women she loved like family—two women who'd become her champions. "This was the one dream that I hoped would come true."

" 'Twill come true as sure as we are standing here, my friend." Gwyneth took her hand. "We promise you that."

Walter was good at carrying out his responsibilities, and he loved his position. He enjoyed the people he

worked with, and over the years had gained their re-
spect. The Pennington family depended on him and
trusted him. So did the crofters and the farmers who
lived on and worked Baronsford's land. He was happy
with his life. This was the only place he had ever really
considered home. When he gave any thought to the
future, he'd always imagined himself living here happily
for the rest of his life. Despite all of the advantages,
though, for the first time since coming to Baronsford
as a child, he was contemplating leaving it forever.

The continuing hostility between Emma and Mrs.
MacAlister, the housekeeper, was barely hidden. Even
nervous little Mr. Campbell, the steward who worked
like a partner with Walter, was often the target of her
malevolence. Servants, cooks, gardeners, grooms, ten-
ants—anyone who lived on the lands of Baronsford
was fair game for her malice, and the pot was about
to boil over.

Her arrogant attitude had many times spilled over
into acts of cruelty. Stableboys had felt the lash when
her horses were not saddled quickly enough. Dressers
were seen sporting bruises when a new style did not
flatter her. She took advantage of people who had dedi-
cated their entire lives to this family, people whom she
had known since childhood. She had even tried, with
little success, to lay the responsibility for her actions on
Lyon, hoping to turn some of them against their laird.
She tried to divide and conquer, but the people of Bar-
onsford were not about to be defeated.

The time Emma spent at Baronsford was pure hell.
It was not long before Lyon refused to be there at the
same time as her. The dowager was noticeably absent
after the first month of the earl's marriage, and it was
rumored that it was because of some argument they'd

had. Before long, Walter was left to defend the castle and its people against the monster that Emma had become.

As a result, there was rarely a moment when some-one was not whispering some complaint in his ear. Rarely a day passed when he was not acting as a peacekeeper. Several times each month, it seemed, he found himself pleading with Emma not to discharge one person or the other.

She claimed Truscott was the only one who under-stood her, but Walter was at a loss over the change in her. Strangely enough, the more she tried to control everyone around her, the more she lost control. And more and more, Emma stood alone, hated by all.

Chapter 19

⟡

"Gwyneth and I have talked, and we are determined to find out what we can about Emma's
death," David said, looking at his brother as the earl
stood by the fireplace in Baronsford's vast library.
"We are each resolved, for the sake of our own future together."

Lyon's gaze fixed on the floor between them. He
had been the only person accused of pushing Emma
off that cliff.

"You are happily settled now with Millicent. So if
at all possible, I want you to remember that I am
trying to do the same with Gwyneth. What we learn
might free all of us of the past and bring our family
back together."

"I should like nothing better," Lyon said with a nod
of his head, settling into a chair.

"Then will you tell me about your marriage, to the
day that Emma died and you were injured?"

"So much of it you already know."

"Pretend that I don't know any of it. What you say
might shed new light on something that I saw differently as a younger man."

Lyon nodded again and paused, obviously gathering

his thoughts. David took the seat across from his brother. Walter Truscott had warned him that this might be painful for Lyon, but he knew it was too late to stop.

"Our troubles seemed to start on the very day of the wedding." Lyon crossed his arms over his broad chest. "And for the next two years of my marriage to Emma, we fought. From the very beginning, everything about us was wrong. We were ten years apart in age, but it may as well have been a hundred. We did not understand each other. We did not seem to speak the same language. It was soon apparent that we would have no love match, but we could not seem to make it a civil union either. We could not even comprehend the other's needs. This was no one's fault but mine. I always thought I knew what she wanted. I had watched her grow up, following you around Baronsford, but then I believed her when she told me that she wanted only me." He gave a bitter laugh. "Vanity leads us down a difficult road, David. She did not want me. She wanted Baronsford. And I was completely blind to it."

David had also been blind to the game Emma was playing. She had played to his vanity, as well. He kept the comment to himself, though.

"I suppose I should have been able to live with this, but I couldn't. Being the mistress of Baronsford was not enough for her, either. She wanted to rule the place, make it all her own. Her behavior to everyone became more and more deplorable. My patience grew thin, and as she became more vicious, I only became more disgusted. After one particularly nasty fight we had one day—she had taken a stick to one of the scullery maids, for God's sake—something in her changed. I saw it happen right in front of me. I could see it in her eyes. She began to withdraw from me. She went to England immediately after that incident. In the end, we spent much of our time apart. When she was in London or Bath or Bristol, I made sure I was at Baronsford. When she came here with her friends, I tried to spend the time in Edinburgh or in the Highlands. And as great a fool as I had been, despite all of our difficulties, I was determined that this mockery of a marriage would remain as it was . . . so long as Emma did not disgrace us publicly."

Lyon turned to David, and the younger brother could see the pain in his eyes.

"What I regret most of this cursed marriage, though, was the fact that you and Pierce started to hate me."

"That's not true, Lyon. I—"

The earl shook his head. "We grew apart, and that was exactly what she wanted. Together, the three of us were a family, strong and able to help each other through anything. Divided . . ." He ran a hand restlessly through his hair. "She wanted to isolate me and control our family. You were away with your regiment and that suited her. So she went to work on Pierce—constantly complaining to him, making him believe she was being neglected and abused. Tearing the family apart was not enough, though. She began to hint at affairs. I tried not to rise like a fish to the bait. But when I tried to ignore it, she began to grow openly scornful of me, calling into question my sense of honor, even my manhood. She expected me to act. She grew so open in her affairs that I had no choice but to confront her and her lovers."

"I heard talk of your duels. 'Tis a blessing you weren't hurt then."

"I was a fool. I know she hoped I would be killed. Instead, even greater fools than I had to die."

That was when the title *Lord of Scandal* had been attached to Lyon's name. Now, hearing his brother's account of it, David doubted he would have acted any differently were he in Lyon's situation.

"Before she died," the earl continued, "I should have known she was up to something."

"Did you believe that everyone had been invited here for our mother's birthday?"

He shook his head. "I had my doubts, but I let her go through with it. It had been so long since our family and friends had gathered at Baronsford."

"There were over two hundred guests," David said, remembering.

"I know now that the ruse of celebrating the dowager's birthday was just a ploy to get us here," Lyon said quietly. "She had an announcement that required a sympathetic audience."

"Do you know what her announcement was?"

Lyon's eyes were fierce when they turned to David. "She wanted a divorce."

David sat back in his chair, perplexed. He thought back on the conversation he'd had with Emma the night before the event. She'd complained endlessly about Lyon, seeking David's help to act on her behalf and even speak to the earl, but she had never once hinted at wanting a divorce from Lyon.

"The greatest scandal she could create and a public announcement of it to spread the news. Emma wanted to have everyone that she thought admired or loved her there that day."

"You arrived very late," David said, recalling that he'd been waiting for the opportunity to talk to his brother that night, but never had a chance.

"She told me her plans the morning that she went off toward the cliffs."

"What did you do?" David asked.

"I told her I would not allow it, though not in so calm a fashion. I had put up with too much already. Whatever was to become of our marriage, I was not about to allow her to drag it into such a public spectacle. We argued, and she told me she would do as she wished. She was going to make the announcement, and I could live with the humiliation of it. And then she ran away."

"And you went after her."

"Not at first. I told myself this was all just another game she was playing. That she was toying with me like one of her playthings. That she would never do such a thing, for 'twould ruin her in the fashionable watering holes she loved. And then I ran into Pierce."

David had visited with Pierce briefly on his first night of arrival. He'd found their middle brother tired of being caught up in Emma and Lyon's marital problems. "He talked you into going after her?"

"Not exactly. He was angry because he had seen Emma upset, running off in the direction of the cliffs. He began to lecture me once again on how I did not treat her well, and how undeserving I was of her love. He asked me how I could upset her so, considering her condition."

"Her condition?"

"After telling *me* she wanted a divorce, Emma told *Pierce* that she was with child. She told him that we were going to make an announcement of it that evening."

David leaned forward, trying to piece together all Lyon was telling him. Bits and pieces of the conversation he'd had with Gwyneth a year ago came back to him. She had hinted at it in anger, but he had not been paying close enough attention to notice it.

David shook his head. "Emma said nothing to me about either a divorce or a child."

"The child came as a shock to me when Pierce told me."

"What did you do?" David asked.

"I went after Emma, but as I reached the cliff walk, I heard her scream in the distance. By the time I got to her, she was lying on the rocks at the base of the cliffs." Lyon rubbed the back of his neck. "Bloody hell! When I started climbing down, I was not looking for answers. It did not matter if this latest revelation was another of her lies. I was not worrying whether she was with child, or even who the father of her child was, though I knew for a fact that 'twas not mine. I remember thinking that she could not be dead."

David stared at his brother and felt the guilt build up inside him. He had left Lyon. Despite all the injuries, he and Pierce had walked away from Lyon when he'd needed them most.

"Was she really with child, or was that another of her lies?"

Lyon appeared to notice the change in David's tone. "I think 'twas our mother's doing to keep it all a secret, but the doctor who came to Baronsford afterward had no doubt that she was carrying someone's child."

Guilt washed over David, cold and merciless. How could he adequately express his sorrow for his treachery? He would try—and soon—but for now, he forced himself to focus on what he'd set his mind to accomplish.

"Do you know who the father of her child was?"

Lyon shrugged. "It could have been any of a dozen

lovers. So many names were thrown at me. I fought so many men during that last year. Even now, I do not know which of them were truly her lovers and which ones were only used for the sake of scandal. I simply called them out like a man possessed by the devil."

"Lyon, do you know why she went to the cliffs that morning? I mean, why there, in all that fog and rain?"

"I never thought about it," Lyon admitted. He looked up abruptly. "I can tell you that I shall never believe she took her own life, that was not her way . . . and I do not believe she slipped, either."

"Nor do I." David paused. "Did you see anyone else out there when you were going after her?"

The earl thought about that for a moment. "No one, but there was thick fog swirling up in great banks from the river. And once I heard her scream, I only remember looking down the cliffs through the mists, for I was certain she had gone over the edge."

David leaned forward in his chair, his hands forming into a steeple before him. "Pierce was the one who found you. There is a possibility that he might have seen someone else on those cliffs. Has he ever mentioned anyone?"

"No."

"Has he ever mentioned any of the guests who might have arrived before the others, perhaps even to help?"

Lyon shook his head. "No, we never talked about any of it. But he and Portia should be back soon . . . perhaps as early as this week."

There was nothing more that David could ask for now. But he knew that there was a great deal more to be said. He remained on the edge of the seat.

"There is no appropriate way for me to begin what

I wish to say. Nothing I can say can excuse what I did to you a year ago in running off. If you cannot forgive me for my actions, I shall never hold that against you. But, at the same time, I shall never rest easy until I ask." David looked into his brother's eyes. "I want you to forgive me, Lyon. And I give you my word, I shall turn over every stone in Scotland, if I must, until I find a reasonable explanation for Emma's death."

Lyon began to speak, but David held up his hand.

"Let me finish. I am not doing this to prove to myself that you are innocent of her death; I already know the answer to that. I am doing this to shake from your name the scandal that has dogged you for too long. But most important, I hope that someday you might forgive me."

"There is no *might* in this, David, and no *someday*, either." Lyon pushed himself to his feet.

David stood also and stared for a moment at the hand his brother extended toward him. He took it.

"Welcome home, brother," Lyon said gruffly, pulling him into a warm embrace.

At that moment, David knew that he was truly home.

It was midafternoon when Lady Cavers's entourage of carriages and wagons and carts rolled unexpectedly into the courtyard of Greenbrae Hall. Utter chaos accompanied the arrival, which looked and sounded more like an invasion with the arriving staff battling for ascendancy over the small group of servants at the Hall. Dogs ran about barking, while drivers shouted to grooms and anyone who would listen. The noise continued to bring the remaining staff running, and the steward and housekeeper sailed about like generals, trying to align their troops for the proper greeting of the countess to the country home. Gwyneth stood at an upper-floor window, horrified as Sir Allan Ardmore stepped out of the carriage just ahead of her aunt.

Augusta and Sir Allan did not immediately make their way past the line of servants to the front door, instead watching as trunks of clothing, personal belongings, and favored furniture began to spill onto the crushed gravel. Within a minute, the courtyard had taken on the look and air of a debtor's sale.

Stepping back from the window, Gwyneth immediately sent a prayer of thanks heavenward that Millicent had already left for Baronsford. She had no doubt she would not be very patient with her aunt if Augusta were to show any rudeness toward her new friend, no matter how Augusta felt about Lord Aytoun and his new countess. She was not, however, quite ready to see Sir Allan, and she needed to buy herself some time.

Turning on her heel, Gwyneth ran toward her bedchamber, dragging Violet with her. En route, she stopped a passing upstairs maid, instructing her to go downstairs and tell Lady Cavers when she entered the house of the severe injury Gwyneth had sustained and to relay the physician's instructions to the older woman, as well. As soon as the two young women arrived safely at her room, Gwyneth turned to a wide-eyed Violet.

"This is the tale we shall tell my aunt. You and I were introduced in London by some mutual friends," Gwyneth instructed her, taking a blanket from a small chest. Climbing onto the bed, she spread the blanket over her, positioning her sling-held arm on top. "We shall tell her that you are the daughter of a country parson. I've asked you to be my companion."

"I shall not lie about—"

"You do not know my aunt," Gwyneth interrupted. "Please let me have my way in this. Otherwise, you shall be treated like any other servant, and be subjected to the most awful behavior. Also, I need this tale to protect my reputation with Augusta. If she were to find out about how I traveled with David, never mind my journey alone from Gretna Green, she shall fly into a rage. Please, Violet. Trust me in this."

The young woman's resigned nod gave Gwyneth hope. She glanced nervously toward the open window.

"Can you tell me what they are doing?"

Violet moved to the window and peeked out discreetly. "The heavyset woman—"

"That is Lady Cavers, my aunt."

"She is saying something to the thin gentleman, and they are both moving along the reception line toward the front door."

"That is Sir Allan Ardmore."

Violet directed her a questioning look. "The baronet you were to elope with?"

"He is also a friend of my aunt's. I do not know what he is doing with her here, though. I would have expected him to be looking for me at Gretna Green."

"He certainly would be no match for Captain Pennington," Violet said meaningfully, looking out again.

Gwyneth certainly knew *that*. After all that had developed between her and David, she knew there could be no future for her and Sir Allan. She needed to find a private moment very soon to explain this to the baronet.

"But why are you in bed? Why should you wish to meet your aunt at such a disadvantage?"

"She'll probably hear from the servants about the doctor's visit. You and I were traveling together and . . . and I fell off the horse. There is no reason to change any of that." Gwyneth looked at her friend. "Also, being confined to bed gives us a good excuse for you to remain at my side. The fewer questions you need to answer, the better."

Violet did not appear particularly pleased with the arrangements, but said nothing more. Gwyneth watched her friend as she went about smoothing the blankct before walking toward the bookcases.

Although only couple of hours had passed, Gwyneth could see a noticeable change in the young woman. Her back was straighter when she walked. The cloud of melancholy appeared to be lifting. There was a liveliness in Violet's features that made her look ten times younger and more beautiful. Gwyneth knew all of this was the result of Vi's talk with Millicent.

"I understand that before he left, Captain Pennington asked one of the servants to come and fetch the book he'd left behind this afternoon."

Gwyneth looked nervously at the place David had placed her book. It was gone.

"Why? He promised to be back later. Oh . . . but he cannot!" she interrupted herself. "I need to get a message to him about Augusta's arrival. She cannot know that he was staying here."

"I do not think there is anything wrong with Captain Pennington making his intentions known to Lady Cavers," Violet said wisely.

Gwyneth stared at the door, feeling uneasy. She had not agreed to anything. At least, she didn't think she'd agreed. She touched her forehead to make certain there was no fever. The confusion in her mind was getting worse.

After a sharp knock the door opened and, without being announced, Augusta charged in.

The smell of powder and perfume preceded her as the rustling layers of lace and silk suddenly dominated the bedchamber. Gwyneth had never met anyone in her life who, after days on the road, still looked as if she had just left some ball in London or Bath.

"Welcome, Aunt." Gwyneth made a meager attempt to raise her head off the pillows.

"My dear girl. What have you done to yourself this time?" Augusta exclaimed, ignoring Violet, who curtsied politely as she breezed past her to the bedside.

A movement outside the doorway caught Gwyneth's eye. Ardmore was there, awaiting permission to enter. Unlike Augusta, the baronet showed the fatigue of the journey on his face.

"You have wrung me out like a rag, Gwyneth. I have been in absolute tatters for a week." Augusta sank into a chair near the bed and immediately took out a handkerchief, patting at tears that Gwyneth could not see. "When I heard the news that you were back in London a day after you left, escorted by the youngest of the Pennington scoundrels . . ." She rolled her eyes, spitting out the name as if it were a curse. "I was appalled. Now you shall tell me right off what you were doing with the rogue. What was he doing escorting you anywhere? And you had better not tell me next that he traveled all the way to Scotland with you."

"Even though he is a respectable gentleman and an old family friend, I think 'twould hardly be appropriate, given my situation. Do you not agree, milady?" Ignoring the look of suspicion on Lady Cavers's face, she motioned to the silent young woman who had not moved since the whirlwind had swept into the room. "I arrived with my friend, Violet Holmes."

Violet made another curtsy, and Gwyneth quickly related her tale of meeting the young woman. Luckily, that was not where Augusta's interest lay, for she gave Violet only a cursory look and quickly changed the topic back again to what interested her most.

"David Pennington . . . What was he doing with you?"

Gwyneth cast a hesitant glance at Sir Allan. He had not moved. With the exception of a polite nod, he had not shown any sign of giving away their earlier plans. "We ran into each other by accident while I was waiting for . . . Miss Holmes . . . to join me. He offered to accompany us as far as the outskirts of the city."

"Is that all?" she asked, her skepticism obvious in her tone.

Gwyneth again darted a look at the baronet. He walked into the bedchamber and stood just inside the doorway. She noticed, though, that he was avoiding her gaze.

"As far as Hampstead Village, to be exact," she said. That was where she'd seen Sir Allan last.

"But they tell me the blackguard is spending his nights *here*," Augusta said in an increasingly shrill tone.

"Really, Aunt, David Pennington is no blackguard. And . . . well, with so few servants here . . . I . . ." Gwyneth paused, feeling Augusta's hard gaze on her. "Considering my injury and the shortage of staff here, Captain Pennington believed 'twas the gentlemanly thing to do. The other option would have been for me to go and stay at Baronsford until you arrived."

"Not in a hundred years," Lady Cavers scoffed,

twisting the kerchief in her meaty hands. "At least you had enough sense to do one thing right. *No one* in that family shall get their claws into you, Gwyneth. I shall make sure of that."

Augusta waved her handkerchief over one shoulder. "Leave us!"

Both Violet and Sir Allan looked at Lady Cavers, not knowing to whom the sharp command was intended.

"Both of you," Augusta ordered. "And close the door on your way out. I want no interruptions. Do you hear me?"

The baronet obediently went out. Violet, however, lingered a moment, looking genuinely concerned. Upon receiving a hard look from the older woman . . . and a nod from Gwyneth . . . she quietly started for the door.

"I do not like her," Augusta proclaimed loudly.

"But *I* do, Aunt. She is the first person whom I have ever chosen as a companion," Gwyneth responded, loud enough for Violet to hear. She watched her friend nod as she closed the door behind her.

Augusta shook her head. "She is horribly willful in her manner. Very likely, too opinionated, as well. I suppose she might be considered pretty . . . and that is not a quality one wants in a companion. She shall be a distraction for your husband. If she is truly a poor clergyman's daughter, give her a few pounds for the sake of charity and send her off. You shall be better rid of her."

"First of all, I have no problem with her disposition . . . which is perfectly amiable," Gwyneth said, not trying to hide her annoyance. "And regarding the wayward eye of any husband, since I have none, there is no problem."

"Not *yet*, but we shall soon change that." Augusta leaned forward and looked sternly into Gwyneth's face. "You, my dear, have become far too great a problem for me. Worrying about you and your future is aging me by the day. The thought of some fortune-hunting rogue trying to soil your reputation or trap you into agreeing to marry him has been keeping me awake at nights."

"I . . ." Just as Violet had warned, Gwyneth suddenly felt at a complete disadvantage, lying in bed. She pulled herself into a sitting position. "I do not know why you are suddenly concerned."

"Suddenly? This is the gratitude I get for sheltering you, caring for you, raising you like my own daughter?"

"I do thank you and my late uncle for giving me so much. But I have caused you no trouble in the past, and I do not see why you should be so attentive now—"

"Actually, 'tis my own guilt speaking." Augusta laid her hand on the bed, smoothing the blanket, and gentled her tone. "During the past fortnight, I have come to realize that I have not been spending enough time of late, guiding you and introducing you to the proper circles. I fear I missed a great opportunity this past spring in London. I haven't done enough in the way of bringing you to more balls and parties and dinners. I know we could have managed to match you up with a fine gentleman of means who—"

"You cannot *force* me to attend such events, Aunt. And I sincerely doubt that I would have agreed to a marriage with anyone under those circumstances."

A frown etched itself in Augusta's brow. "As much as I should like to argue against such stubbornness, after all these years I know you better than to waste my time. Which brings me back to my recent neglect of you . . . and where I might have done well by you, but failed. At the same time I find I am fortunate enough to have been given an opportunity to correct my mistake."

Gwyneth stared at her aunt. "Would you be kind enough to explain what mistake you are referring to?"

Augusta pulled the chair closer to Gwyneth. She leaned forward, lowering her voice. "Before we left London, you hinted at a possible match with Sir Allan. Without thinking the idea through, I scoffed at the suggestion."

"Indeed, but . . . well, I understood your objection to it."

"I was wrong," Augusta proclaimed with a flourish. "You shall be a very wealthy young woman very soon. You have known Sir Allan for a number of years. He has watched you blossom into the young woman you are, and he admires you for your beauty and your character. You are obviously fond of him, despite his unfortunate financial situation, and you approached me to ask my opinion. During our journey to Scotland, he told me that he is very fond of you, arguing his worthiness and his interest in your future. In short, Sir Allan has won me over."

Gwyneth did not like the sound of this at all. She needed to speak to Sir Allan. A great deal had changed since she left London. Before she could say anything, though, Augusta charged on.

"You don't need to worry about your future anymore. I give you both my blessing. And I know that the arrangement can be handled quickly by the family's lawyers. The only thing I ask is that we not have any extravagant wedding. Perhaps just a simple ceremony in the next fortnight or so. I shall notify the lawyers to draw up the necessary documents . . . and I shall also arrange for proper announcements to reach the papers. Then, if the two of you would like to go on a newlywed's tour of the Continent . . ." Lady Cavers tucked her handkerchief into a pocket and pushed herself to her feet. "I'm so glad that is all settled. If you are happy with the arrangements—"

"But I am not happy," Gwyneth replied.

"What did you say?" Augusta barked, glowering down at her.

The suddenness of everything was making her head spin. She knew that only a few days ago she'd thought such an arrangement would solve all of her problems. But she couldn't marry Ardmore now. David was the one she wanted, though she could never say that to her aunt.

"I . . . I need to speak to Sir Allan first," Gwyneth said finally. "Before anything so definite is decided, he and I need to discuss many things . . . sort out our feelings. There are too many—"

"I have no understanding for young people," she said tersely. "I care nothing about such discussions. There is no need for any period of courtship here, niece, nor romance either. I have only just arrived at this house, and I am already feeling suffocated. I shall proceed with our plans. You two can discuss anything you please."

"Really, Aunt! There are many things that anyone I would agree to marry needs to understand and agree to."

"I shall send in your baronet." Augusta started for the door. She stopped and looked back slyly. "Woman to woman, I should say that lying flat on your back in that bed should be enough of an enticement for him to agree to anything."

As her aunt left the room, Gwyneth jumped out of the bed and ran for the door, locking it and putting her back against it. All her troubles before were nothing compared to the mess that she was faced with now.

David had told Gwyneth that he needed her help in sorting out his life. Hearing footsteps in the corridor, Gwyneth now realized that she needed *his* help, as well.

The news of his father's death reached Walter Truscott in late winter. Leaving Baronsford immediately, Walter followed the Tweed eastward along the St. Boswell Road, skirting the Eildon Hills and reaching the burgh of Kelso long after darkness had descended. It was here, in this ancient abbey town, that the old man had been living in relative comfort, thanks to Lyon. Then, one miserable afternoon, with the sleet beating on the tavern windows, Sir William had simply pushed the dice cup away, put his head down on a table, and died.

As they lowered the wooden casket into the frosty ground, Walter stood beside his father's young wife— a woman he'd had no knowledge of—and two young brothers that he never knew existed. There was no getting the news to his older brother. He'd disappeared out of their lives from that first day that he'd left for the colonies.

A freezing rain began to fall in earnest as Walter accepted hurried words of condolence from hard-looking strangers smelling of ale.

That night, at a rather lively inn in Wester Kelso, Walter himself drank tankard after tankard of ale, hop-

ing to forget how little he'd known of the man who had fathered him. With each drink, he grieved at the thought of how insignificant had been the parts they'd played in each other's lives. How strange then, he thought, how painful the old man's passing struck him now.

Sometime after midnight, Walter was ready for other sport to take his mind off his father's death, so he'd made a financial offer to one of the serving wenches and stumbled upstairs to his room. The small fire he'd paid extra for had burned down to embers, but the room was still warm. Passing out on the bed, he was soon dreaming. Faces of the dozen or so townswomen who'd been mourning at the graveside leapt at him in his dreams. Walter knew they must have been paramours of his late father.

In his ale-drenched dreams, though, the faces soon gave way to action. Once again, he was standing witness to his father's liaisons. He watched now—as he'd watched years ago—Sir William in all his drunken glory, bringing his whores into their own house and taking them wherever and however he pleased, with no regard to Walter's presence.

In the midst of the dreams, Walter suddenly found himself in the place of his father. He could feel the woman's hands on him. The dream was so real. The wench was peeling off his clothes, and she weighed almost nothing when she slid on top of him.

"Take me." The voice was a familiar whisper, one that he had heard so many times in his dreams. Emma. How many times had she come to him like this?

The dream world and the real blended in the flickering darkness. The room, the best in the inn, was small and narrow, and he had no trouble seeing the breasts that moved before his face. He took a nipple into his mouth.

"Harder," the woman gasped, pulling his head against her.

He scraped his teeth against her flesh as he suckled hard, and his hand moved down along the curve of her buttocks. She'd shed her clothes and her legs were straddling his. His fingers found her wet mound, and he thrust two fingers inside her. Her hips rose off his stomach, and she pressed herself against his hand. His fingers twisted inside her, his mouth rough on her breast, but she wanted more. Yanking his hair, she pushed his head back down on the mattress and climbed up along his body, spreading her legs over his mouth.

He thrust his tongue deep inside. She shuddered and turned and danced on him, moaning and growling low like a she-wolf in heat. Rising above him, even in the blurring shadow, she was a sight—her head thrown back, her hands out to her sides, her breasts undulating with each fierce roll of her hips.

Suddenly, she was sliding down along his body again, and Walter let out a groan of satisfaction as she drew his manhood into her hot mouth. He took fistfuls of her silky hair and guided her lips and tongue along the length of him. Then, when he was on verge of exploding, she abruptly pushed his hand away and moved quickly on top of him, burying him in a single stroke deep inside her.

He had no chance. He poured his seed into her, and their loud cries rang out in the darkness before she finally sank down and lay still on top of him.

When his breathing slowed, he touched the soft ringlets that lay across his lips. It had been no dream. The scent of love hung in the air. A cold feeling washed

*through him, though, and the hackles on his neck stood
up. Never had he known a country wench to make love
like this.*

Her lips were touching his throat when he heard her
murmur something low.

"What'd you say?" he asked, hearing the words slur
off his tongue.

"I said . . . thank you, Walter."

*In his rush to get clear of her, they both rolled off
the bed and onto the hard floor. He tried to extricate
himself, and she laughed aloud at his clumsiness.*

"How . . . ?" He shoved her away hard, suddenly
feeling sick. "What . . . ?"

"I told you years ago that you shall always be the
first." *Emma stood up and stretched languidly.*

"First? Why, you bloody whore. You're married to
Lyon. I cannot . . . I don't understand!"

"You shall be the father of my first child," she said,
casually gathering the clothes she'd thrown on the floor.

"NO!" he shouted, pushing himself unsteadily to
his feet.

*His head was spinning. Walter managed to stagger
forward and grabbed her roughly by the shoulders,
forcing Emma to face him.*

"NO!" he shouted again into her face. "No, this cannot be. Do you hear me?"

She shrugged off his touch and backed away. "Whatever you wish."

He grabbed her arm again. "This did not happen.
You were not here."

"But I was."

"Emma," he pleaded. "No one can know about this.
You cannot tell Lyon. By the devil, you cannot pit the
two of us against each other. I'll kill you first."

She ran a hand softly down the side of his face. Her

touch was surprisingly soft, the look in her eyes impenetrable.

Walter felt like crying. "Why are you doing this? Why in bloody hell are you here?"

"I was at the kirkyard today. At Sir William's funeral. I kept my distance so that you would not see me."

He looked at her, his ale-muddled brain unable to comprehend her answer. She freed herself of his grasp and pulled the dress carelessly over her head. Walter silently watched her as the words sank in.

"Why would you care to come?"

She draped the rest of her clothing over one arm and picked up her shoes. The room tilted as she walked toward the door.

"Why, Emma?" Walter asked again as she pulled the door open.

She looked over her shoulder at him. The cold breeze from the hallway stirred the embers of the fire, casting a reddish glow on her face.

"I had to come. This was my last chance to meet him."

He tried to focus on a tear glistening on her cheek.

"Augusta let me in on the secret. I found her in her sitting room, drinking Madeira from the bottle." She turned her face a little. "She received word, too, that your father was dead. 'Twas about time that she finally revealed to me that Sir William Truscott was my father, do you not agree?"

Walter felt the room begin to whirl again, and he put his hand against the wall to steady himself.

"I am sorry, Walter. Everything makes sense to me now. I finally understand why 'twas that you have always mattered so much to me . . . why I always needed *you to be first in everything in my life. We are bound to each other . . . in more ways than one." She closed the door and left.*

Walter stared at the door for a long moment, then bent over and threw up.

Chapter 20

The family was in the middle of a late supper when Mr. Campbell, Baronsford's steward, came in and discreetly advised David that the caretaker from Greenbrae Hall was waiting in the courtyard. He was carrying an urgent message. David strode quickly to the courtyard, where Robert immediately assured him that Miss Gwyneth was in the same state of health as Captain Pennington had left her in the early afternoon.

"She sent me to ask ye not to come to the Hall tonight, though, sir," the man said quietly. "She wants ye to know that Lady Cavers and her friend Sir Allan Ardmore arrived this afternoon, and judging from her ladyship's mood, Miss Gwyneth thought 'twould be best if ye avoided meeting her until ye had a chance to speak to Miss Gwyneth first."

"When can I see her?"

"She thought early morning would be best, as Lady Cavers is not overall fond of getting up early, especially after traveling," Robert said. "If possible, Miss Gwyneth wishes to meet ye by the loch in the deer park. 'Tis an easy walk from the stables at Greenbrae Hall."

"Did she say what time?"

David listened to the rest of the specifics of what Gwyneth had told the caretaker to relay, all the while fighting his inclination to drive over there right away and make his intentions known to Augusta.

For the sake of Gwyneth's peace of mind, though, he needed to do things properly, David told himself. "Please tell Miss Gwyneth that I shall be waiting for her."

As David watched Robert disappear toward the stables, his mind was already racing with everything that needed to be done. Gwyneth had not said yes to his offer of marriage, but he was determined to answer whatever hesitation she might have left. At the same time, he'd already taken the dowager's suggestion and sent a letter to Sir Richard Maitland, their family lawyer, to make whatever arrangements were necessary with the attorneys of the late Lord Cavers.

Because of her ill will toward the Penningtons, Augusta was probably the greatest stumbling block to this marriage. But the good news was, according to what he understood from Lyon and from Gwyneth herself, Lady Cavers had no real say in the matter, as Lord Cavers had made sure that she was not named as guardian to Gwyneth, instead leaving decisions for the young woman's future in the hands of his lawyers.

"So Lady Cavers has returned."

David turned around as Truscott stepped out of the house and walked toward him.

"Unfortunately. And her arrival has apparently curtailed my visits at Greenbrae Hall."

"And the same goes for me," Truscott admitted quietly.

"We should have abducted both women and carried

them back here to Baronsford when we had the chance."

"It may not be too late. If you decide to go through with it, I'll be there with you."

"I believe Gwyneth would not be so agreeable, should we try," David said with a smile, remembering the time he'd caught her jumping out of the window of the inn on the journey north. "In fact, I believe my ability to produce offspring would be seriously endangered."

"I'm sure I do not know what Violet would do."

The look on Walter's face was unlike any David had ever seen in his cousin. Such open interest had never been evident with any other woman.

"You are quite fond of this Violet."

"I am," Walter admitted frankly. "She is unlike anyone I have ever known."

"You've not known her long." He said it not as an objection, but only as an observation.

Truscott gave an indifferent shrug. "Something about her spoke to me the first moment I laid eyes on her. And 'twas not only the way the lass looks. There was something much deeper. 'Twas as if I could feel her pain." He stared up at the red tentacles of sunset streaking across the sky. "Already I know when I am with her, I am a better man. 'Tis as if I am the only one who can slay her dragons. Help her . . . even as she helps me."

"She has a past that you know nothing about."

"And she knows nothing about me, either." Truscott nodded and started off toward the stables.

Gwyneth didn't light any candles in her room when darkness descended. The excuse she'd asked Violet to pass on to Sir Allan was that she was just too tired tonight for any more company and she was taking the doctor's suggestion and staying in bed. She would be happy to meet with him tomorrow, she'd said.

Still, as Gwyneth paced the darkened room, sleep was the farthest thing from her mind. Robert had been sent off to Baronsford with a message for David a couple of hours ago, and Gwyneth had already asked Violet to go down to the stables to await his return.

As possible as marriage to Sir Allan seemed to her before she'd run into David in London, it was detestable now. She would gladly face open scandal and forfeit her fortune rather than commit herself to a life with someone she felt nothing for.

And then there was David and *everything* that she felt for him. It was foolish that Gwyneth had waited to admit her feelings until such time that their relationship was seriously jeopardized. Well, better now than never, she told herself.

She loved him. He was the only man she had ever dreamed of spending the rest of her life with. And now, finally, her eyes and ears were open. He wanted her, and all she had to do was reach out and take his hand.

David would help her through this. Gwyneth knew he would. Before they would meet tomorrow, though, she needed to think of a way to tell him everything. She also needed to be prepared to face his disapproval of her writing, as such a profession could only be considered unacceptable and scandalous to someone of his station in life. He'd all but said so in the carriage from London.

Gwyneth thought of the approval that he was seeking from his own family, and his efforts to solve the mystery surrounding Emma's death. That was an area where she could possibly help him. They were a few secrets about Emma that Gwyneth had never revealed to him—the pregnancy, the lovers she kept. She also recalled the correspondences that Emma used to be so fond of. Gwyneth wondered if any of them were still in Emma's sitting room.

There was only one way to get that answer.

Gwyneth crossed her bedroom and pressed an ear to the door. From what she'd been told, the baronet had been placed in one of the guest bedrooms in this wing. Augusta's suite of rooms was in the same wing as Emma's. There were no sounds coming from the corridor outside. She peeked into the semidarkness of the hallway and slipped out.

She ran into no one and was already past her aunt's door when she heard the voices in the distance. Augusta's voice was pronounced. Gwyneth disappeared inside Emma's rooms, though, before anyone could see her.

Baronsford slept, but David was too caught up in the tale he was reading to pay any attention to the passage of time.

A woman wrapped in the cloak of mystery and given the charge of saving the future of a nation. A warrior bewildered by the secrecy surrounding the woman and yet still falling in love.

The action and adventure captured on the pages was thrilling; the romance between the two was explosive. As good as it was, David found that it was the voice in his head that was forcing him to turn the pages. There were moments when he thought he was losing his mind. It was if he were not reading the story, but as if he were being read to . . . by Gwyneth.

The expressions on the pages were hers. The speeches were, at times, exactly what he could imagine only her saying. The descriptions of various people were too similar to the faces that he had seen around Greenbrae Hall or in the village or at Baronsford itself. And the way the story unfolded was very much like the tales she used to tell him when she'd been much younger.

Still, it couldn't be. At least a dozen times, David had gone back and stared at the title pages. No author's name.

It couldn't be her, though. Gwyneth would have no need to do this—she would have no means of accomplishing it. David remembered the hours she spent writing in her journals, though. The time she spent on it still. The idea of someone stealing her work and making profit from it occurred to him, angering him momentarily. He dismissed the thought immediately, for he had found these books in her room. She had to know about it. And there had been other volumes there, too.

Bits and pieces of the conversation he and Gwyneth had during their journey north slipped into his mind. His mockery of the hours she spent in solitude writing in her journals came back to him. He recalled Gwyneth's claim that she would never be helpless.

She'd hinted to him then about publishing her work!

David looked up from the open page and stared into the dark shadows of the library. Despite her obvious talent, the volume in his hand would be considered scandalous to the Edinburgh lawyers left in charge of her future. David wondered if she had considered the extent of the disaster she could be inflicting on herself in publishing her work.

* * *

The countryside was hidden beneath a thick blanket of fog when Gwyneth escaped the house through one of the servants' entrances and ran toward the deer park. With the exception of a few grooms and stable lads beginning their work, the fog hid anyone else from view who might be out at such an early hour.

Gwyneth had taken a couple of boxes of letters and diaries from Emma's room back to her own bedroom. There, she had spent most of the night scanning through them. With the exception of some newspaper announcements and a large number of invitations by anyone who was of any note among London's *ton*, nothing useful had turned up. The letters had given her no information at all. What Gwyneth had gone through, however, was only a sampling of what she saw stored in Emma's chambers. Gwyneth had hoped that her discovery of the letters would prove significant in David's eyes. She wanted some good news to soften everything else that she was ready to reveal.

A misting rain began to fall as Gwyneth hurried down the hill and entered the deer park. The visibility was poor, but this was her home. She knew every rock, every tree, every turn on the path. She pulled the wrap she had around her shoulders up over her head and tried without success to avoid the puddles of mud as she hurried along.

She was not far from the loch when a rustling of the leaves to her left startled her. A large shadow passed in the fog beyond a stand of trees, and Gwyneth stopped dead, staring into the murkiness of the forest. The drenched silhouettes of low pines were the only things that she could see. She adjusted the scarf over her head and decided a doe moving toward the loch had been her companion.

A branch cracked on her right. She whirled, looking in that direction. Again, there was nothing. Only the falling drops of the rain and the thick fog. Gwyneth couldn't calm the mad beating of her heart. The familiar had become suddenly frightening. The safety she'd felt moments ago was now gone. Panic was nearly paralyzing her. There was no reasoning with what her senses were suddenly attuned to—danger seemed to be all around her. She turned in a circle, looking in every direction, trying to see through the mists.

"Is anyone out there?" she called out softly.

There was no answer. She could see nothing. The fog and the woods around her had cut her off from Greenbrae Hall and the stables. She turned around at the sound of another footstep to her left. Another to her right. Someone was moving closer. More than one.

She stood still, but there was no sound. Gwyneth felt the hairs stand up on the back of her neck as a chill swept through her.

"David?" she shouted out in panic.

From behind a tree, a stranger stepped out. He was wearing boots and a dark coat. She turned as another appeared behind her, and then another, on her right. Gwyneth glanced around quickly in panic. She didn't know where these men had come from—or what they wanted from her.

"*David!*" she cried out again. As she saw the men start for her, she started to run. There were low curses behind her. Following the path, she quickly realized she was still heading for the loch.

She heard her name an instant before running into a pair of strong arms.

"What is wrong?" David asked. "You are shivering."

"They are after me. Three men." She clutched his hand and turned around. The mist had enveloped them again, but the men had disappeared. The soft dripping of the rain from the trees was the only noise.

"Three men?" David asked, peering into the fog.

"Never mind them." She shook her head, tugging at his hand and pulling him toward the loch. "Take me away from here. We need to talk. Please . . . where is your horse?"

"I left him at the water's edge. Did you see who was following you?" he asked, following the direction of her gaze.

She felt his tenseness. There were three of them, and David was not armed.

"I'll explain later," she said quietly, tugging on his arm as the rain began to fall harder, drenching them in a moment.

He was reluctant, but after another look back, he allowed her to lead the way. "I shall take you to Baronsford."

"No, you cannot. 'Twill take us too long to go there and back," she whispered, still unable to overcome her uneasiness. She was relieved, though, when they reached David's horse at the edge of the woods by the loch. "My aunt will be looking for me as soon as she is up and about. I . . . we just need somewhere private and out of the rain."

"Well, Truscott's tower house is not far. I do not think he'll mind us going there. I think he's given up on his dream of living there someday. I do not know if anyone has even stepped inside the place in years."

Gwyneth nodded. David helped her onto the horse and climbed up behind her. She nestled against the warmth of his chest, keeping her gaze on the woods they'd just left.

"You are still shivering," he whispered against her ear, gathering Gwyneth more tightly against his chest as he spurred the horse along the shore of the loch. "What happened back there?"

"Nothing happened, thank heaven. But I saw three men. I don't know who they were. They just appeared out of the fog. It might have been my imagination."

"Did they say anything? Did they approach you?"

She shook her head again. "It may have been nothing. I feel safe now."

He pressed a kiss into her hair, and Gwyneth wished that she was brave enough to ask him to elope with her. Right now. This was what she wanted. This was the man. She would forfeit everything she had for him. Never go back. A future just with him.

It took just a few moments to reach the tower house. Gwyneth had many times passed by the old structure. In the days when she'd spent her time following Emma, she had often hid in the woods and watched her cousin go in. Never once though, had she herself been inside.

The wooden stairs leading up to the door were still there. Heather was blooming where it had encroached on the little-used path, and ivy was growing onto the door itself, partially obscuring it. David helped her down from the horse and cleared their way. The door's rusted hinges complained loudly when he pulled it open.

Inside, the rooms were damp and airless, but Gwyneth was surprised at the extent of the repairs that had been accomplished. She looked around as she shook off the rain. It looked as if someone had at one time spent a great deal of time there. She turned to David as he closed the door, shutting out the rain.

"We have very little time, but there is so much that I have to tell you."

Her clothes were wet, and she wrapped her shawl tightly around her shoulders.

"My aunt has returned to the Hall, and I must tell you I am frustrated and angry at the plans she so neatly has made for my future. But before I even get to those, there is something else that I have tell you. Something that I know you shall not approve of. But for me to ask what I want . . . for you to become even more involved in the mess that my life has become, 'tis crucial to get past the first step. We never might, as I'm not sure you'll be able to forgive me for what I have done."

She shook her head, frustrated and unable to look at him. She started pacing the length of the room.

"I don't know why I am apologizing, as I really do not mean to apologize. I have pursued my dreams in what I have always known was my destiny. And as shocking as you might think it, I have succeeded. And I am proud of what I have accomplished."

"Gwyneth—"

"But that is not the way society shall view it, I know. That is not the way you shall see it, either. So I know that I am truly destined to be unhappy. I must beg forgiveness and give up the pursuit of my dreams to gain your approval." She peeled the shawl from her shoulders and wrung it out. "But I shall do that. If that is what you want, then I shall change and be what you want me to be. I'll never put a pen to paper again . . . if you share what I feel in my heart for you."

"What do you feel in your heart for me?"

She hadn't realized he'd moved from the door, but when she shook out her shawl, David caught one end of it. Gwyneth looked up at him. His hair was gleaming from the rain, his deep blue eyes were looking into her soul. She looked away quickly, not wanting him to see how her heart swelled with love for him.

He pulled the shawl, drawing her closer. "What do you feel, Gwyneth?"

"I love you," she whispered, staring at his mouth.

"And do you love me enough to marry me?" he asked, bringing her even closer and wrapping his arms around her.

"I . . . I do. But I do not think you will feel the same way, once you learn the truth about my past . . . about what I do."

"About the tales you have published?"

"You know about them?" she asked, stunned.

"I am a bit slow, my love, " he said with a smile, "but not the village idiot. Still, I am ashamed to admit that I needed to read half of that first volume before the obvious hit me across the face."

"You are not angry?"

"Of course I am not angry. And no, I should never ask you to stop writing. In fact, I have nothing against you continuing to publish your tales, so long as it makes you happy, and that is what you want to do."

"You really mean that?" Gwyneth stared up at him in disbelief as he nodded. A look of suspicion creased her face. "Then why were you giving me such a difficult time about it in the carriage from London? Why the sarcastic comments about it and . . . and . . ."

"If 'twere not your writing, then I should have needed to find something else to tease you about," he admitted, wrapping his arms tighter around her. "Put yourself in my position. I'd caught you ready to elope with some blasted fortune hunter. And if you recall, there were moments during our journey that you were less than friendly." He stole a kiss from her lips, then another from her neck, making her smile. "I am warning you, though, that once we are married, you shall not have as much free time to pursue your writing as before. You know how demanding I can be."

She smiled and kissed his lips as his hands moved down her back.

"I have already set Sir Richard Maitland to work approaching your uncle's lawyers. You are not angry with me about that, now, are you?"

She shook her head and smiled as she placed a kiss on his jaw.

"We can marry as soon as you wish. My inclination, though, still is to elope to Gretna Green."

"Mine, too, considering all my other problems."

"I would wager there is nothing that we cannot solve together."

"You need to hear about them first," she said, uneasy that she had to burden him with the rest so soon. The morning was advancing quickly now, though, and she didn't know for how long Violet would be able to keep Lady Cavers from coming to Gwyneth's bedchamber to see her. "My first problem lies with someone who is determined to make his fortune from my secret."

"From your writing?"

Gwyneth nodded and went on to tell him about the blackmail letters and the demand for money. "That was the reason why I was eloping when you caught up to me in London. By marrying . . . a friend . . . I would come into my inheritance and be able to pay off the damnable villain."

"But there was no guarantee that such a scoundrel would not ask for more money again."

"I know. But I thought that even if he were so ignoble, after I was married, 'twould not matter so much." It was uncomfortable talking about it, but she had to. "The gentleman I was eloping with cares nothing of scandal."

"Who was he?" he asked gruffly.

Gwyneth could hear in his voice that there was still a risk that David might hurt Sir Allan. "He was not at fault. I approached *him* with my problem and this solution. He was kind enough to agree to my terms. He'd done nothing, David."

"His name," he said again, his patience clearly stretching thin.

"Sir Allan Ardmore. He has been a friend of my aunt for years. A decent man."

"Ardmore . . . Ardmore. Ah, yes . . . from Lanark."

"That's Sir Allan. But do you know him?" she asked with some confusion, knowing that David had not recognized him in Hampstead Village.

"I know of him. He's a penniless cad, infamous for having his debts paid by older women whose company he keeps."

"I don't know how you could have heard such horrid things."

"Men talk, too, my love." He tugged on one of her curls. "You shall be indebted to me for life for saving you from a man of such low character. By the devil, he must have thought he'd found Blackbeard's treasure when you approached him. Your fortune would have kept him afloat for a good many years."

There was no point in arguing on Sir Allan's behalf, especially since David did not seem too angry at the man. "Still, I expect you to act in a civilized fashion toward him, since he has done nothing wrong. He took no liberties with me, treating me with only the utmost respect, in spite of my difficulties."

"That was because he never had the chance. I was too quick for the blackguard."

"Vanity, vanity." She punched him jokingly in his chest. "Civility. That is all I ask."

"I shall more than likely never see the man, so you have nothing to worry about."

She let out a long sigh and met his gaze. "That's my next problem. My aunt has made up her mind that 'tis in my best interest that I marry Sir Allan immediately."

He stiffened. "Not if I have anything to say in the matter."

She nodded sadly. "Sir Allan has accompanied her to Greenbrae Hall. He is there even now. And if I know my aunt, they are planning the wedding as we speak."

"Wait." His face was flushed with anger. "She cannot force you do any such thing. Did you tell her that?"

"She broke this news to me last night. You see . . ." She drew a deep breath. "When I was upset about the blackmail letters, I approached my aunt in London about the possibility of a union between Sir Allan and me. She must still be going on that assumption."

"But you corrected that."

"I did. At least, I tried. I do not think she was listening to me, though. I did stress that nothing could be arranged until I had a chance to speak with Sir Allan . . . which I have not, as yet. I tried to avoid him last night, and this morning."

"I will speak to him for you," David said hotly. "And when I am done with him, Lady Cavers shan't be able to find the vermin in a month of searching."

Gwyneth tugged on his arm. "No, David. We can handle this much more peacefully. I will speak to him myself. He probably thinks he is still doing me a favor in accepting my aunt's suggestion. He is a gentle sort of a man. He will withdraw agreeably, and that shall be the end of those plans."

"I am going to come and talk to Augusta myself. I shall let her know of my intentions . . . of our plans. I cannot risk waiting for the lawyers, only to have your aunt devise another disaster in the meantime."

Gwyneth let the sudden thrill his words caused flow through her, warming her blood. It was possible, after all. Nothing would stand in their way. It was too much to believe, but they would be married. She hadn't even realized that tears were standing in her eyes until David pulled her tightly into his embrace.

"I love you, Gwyneth," he whispered in her ear. "Everything will work out, my love."

She nodded, her chin hitting his shoulder.

"And the blackmailer shall get what he has coming to him, too."

"How?"

"When he contacts you again, we shall pretend that you are ready to pay his demands. He must show his face to collect. That is when I make sure that he wishes he were never born."

She had no doubt that David meant every word he said, and Gwyneth didn't care. The scoundrel had this coming to him, but she wanted to know the person's identity, too, and how it was that he had discovered her.

"I shall come and talk to your aunt this afternoon. I would bring the dowager or Lyon, if I thought they might improve the situation."

She shook her head adamantly. "Bringing either of

them would be a mistake. She shall probably be hostile to you, too."

"I am not frightened off so easily." He kissed her lips. "I have found the one love of my life. I am not about to let you go."

Gwyneth had no desire to go back to Greenbrae Hall. She was perfectly happy here in David's arms. She knew the day was passing quickly, though, and she needed to go back. Considering the confrontation that still lay ahead of them, she didn't want to aggravate Augusta more than necessary.

"Would you take me back as far as the stables?"

"I will see you to the front door of Greenbrae Hall." He pushed the wet strands off her brow and ran his thumb across her lips. "And blast whoever sees us. They cannot stop us, Gwyneth. No one shall come between us."

A pang of worry was gnawing at her stomach, but she believed him. She picked up her scarf, which had fallen to the floor.

"It has been years since I was inside this place," David said, looking around. "Truscott put many hours into repairing it. This used to be his favorite place to come."

"This was Emma's favorite place, as well," she replied.

"Emma's?"

She nodded. "In my childish devotion of her, I followed her here many times. After she became quite angry the first time, I wouldn't let her see me."

David seemed to look at the place with new interest. "I never knew there was anything between Emma and Walter. Or at least, no friendship of any sort."

Gwyneth looked around, too. A silk wrap of some

value lay folded on a three legged stool in the corner of the room. It looked like something that might have belonged to Emma. A pot of dried flowers bespoke of a woman's presence, too. There were other feminine touches, as well.

"They would have been an unlikely pair. Walter always seemed to ignore her, and she would never give him a second glance."

"I need to get back, David." The two of them headed for the door. The rain was still coming down hard and steadily.

"Did you know Emma was carrying a child when she died?" he asked, helping Gwyneth up onto the horse.

"I did," she said quietly.

"Lyon told me that he was not the father of her child."

"I'm not surprised," Gwyneth admitted. "The two of them had spent almost no time together for months, that I could see."

"Do you know who the father might have been?"

She shook her head. David climbed up behind her.

"I suppose 'tis possible that whoever fathered that bairn might also have pushed Emma off that cliff."

Gwyneth said nothing as they started off in the rain. She knew what David was thinking, and she didn't like the thought that Walter Truscott might have been another of Emma's lovers.

More important, she didn't like to think that Walter could be capable of hurting anyone.

Emma had been married for almost two years. He knew she'd had many lovers. What were the chances that she would become pregnant after one night? He himself had fathered no children that he knew of. What were the chances?

Such logic didn't help him. Truscott was a man cursed with a sickness unlike any he'd ever known. He watched. He worried. The guilt was crushing, but he didn't know what to do about it. Approaching Lyon was unthinkable. Running away was out of the question, too. He knew there could be no escape.

In the midst of all this, Emma glided through life like nothing was wrong. She looked healthier than ever before, more vibrant than ever.

Then, one late summer evening, he encountered her by accident as he left the castle by way of one of the garden terraces. Flustered to find Emma sitting on a bench there alone, he froze in his tracks for a moment, not knowing whether to retreat or forge on past her. She rose to her feet immediately upon seeing him, and he turned to go back in.

"Truscott," she called out softly to him. "I have some good news."

He stopped dead in the doorway, feeling the hot bile rise into his throat. His gaze turned uncontrollably to her.

Emma's hand slowly caressed her belly.

"Thank you," she whispered.

Chapter 21

The sky opened, deluging them on their ride back to Greenbrae Hall, and by the time David dropped Gwyneth off by a side door, she was soaked through.

"I am coming with you. I want to be sure you get to your room and change immediately."

"Don't be silly," she chided him, giving him a quick kiss despite the presence of a footman who rushed out to help her, having seen them come up. "Go now, so you can come back soon. I shall be waiting."

She hurried inside before he would disagree and ran up one of the servants' staircases, hoping that she could get to her room before seeing either Augusta or Sir Allan.

She was not to be so lucky. Halfway to her bedchamber, she nearly bumped into Sir Allan as he emerged from one of the guest rooms. The baronet's initial look of delight was quickly replaced by alarm as he looked at her.

"Miss Gwyneth, what in God's name has happened to you?"

"I was out getting some morning air and got caught in the rain." She'd slowed her steps but never stopped backing toward her bedroom. A puddle was forming a trail as she walked. "Now, if you'll excuse me, Sir Allan."

As she turned away, he quickly fell in step beside her.

"Of course, of course. Before you disappear, however, I should tell you that I am absolutely thrilled with the way everything has been settled." He lowered his voice. "Your generous aunt's suggestion is so much more agreeable than eloping to that godforsaken Gretna Green and being wed by a drunken blacksmith. I—"

"I have changed my mind, Sir Allan," she interrupted gently. "I am sorry to have to tell you like this, but after a great deal of thought, I believe 'tis absolutely wrong for you and me to be married at all."

The baronet became suddenly pale. Gwyneth had reached the door of her bedchamber, but she didn't think it would be right to just disappear inside after making an announcement of such magnitude.

"What . . . what about your problems?" he managed to ask softly.

"I shall pursue another solution to it," she said vaguely. "The truth is, two lives should not be ruined because some villain has found an opportunity to earn some undeserved money."

"I never considered marriage to you anyone's ruin. In fact, I have been very much looking forward to it."

"That is very kind of you," she said. "But other than being . . . well, my friend and supporter, you have no deep affection for me, and I am honest enough to admit the same lack of feeling for you. So you see, we both deserve better than having our lives so inappropriately linked."

"But I am fond of you. That is a very favorable

place to start a marriage, I believe. And you trust me . . . or you would not have come to me with your troubles. I would argue that we have a very strong foundation for two people to build a marriage upon."

"Thank you, Sir Allan. But no." She shook her head. "I am a dreamer. I believe in romance, in love. I believe that I shall only be happy spending the rest of my life with someone I truly love. 'Twould not be fair to a prospective husband for me to enter into a marriage otherwise."

"Indeed, a lovely ideal. But perhaps such quaint romances only exist in the pages of your books. I am speaking of real life here, my dear."

"So am I," Gwyneth said more strongly than she intended. He was wrong for her. He'd always been wrong for her. "If you can forgive me, I plan to change and go downstairs and clear up this confusion with my aunt."

He opened his mouth to argue more, but Gwyneth shook her head and quickly slipped into her bedchamber, closing the door behind her.

She was relieved to find Violet waiting for her.

"I told him no," Gwyneth whispered, feeling almost giddy. "I can feel the weight lifting off my shoulders."

Violet shook her head and quickly latched the door. "This is far from being over, Gwyneth. I think you might be in genuine danger."

The events of the morning Emma died were once again sharp in David's memory. Pierce had seen the bodies first on the edge of the river. Walter was the person who had climbed down the rocks with him. The two men were responsible for bringing up Lyon's broken body . . . and then Emma's lifeless one.

Walter had been there on the cliffs about the same

time as Pierce—perhaps even before him. He may have seen Emma fall. He may have been responsible for it. David did not care about any reckoning, if Walter pushed her. What mattered most was knowing the truth. David knew that the only way was to confront Walter directly.

His cousin was not to be found at Baronsford. In the stables, David was told that Walter had gone to the village.

There should have been no urgency in talking to him—in settling what he suspected to be the truth—but David wanted to finish the matter. He wanted to clear a path to the future, a future with Gwyneth beside him. The spirit of Emma had to be put to rest. Her mystery needed to be solved, her ghost exorcised forever.

He rode toward the village like a man possessed. He finally found Truscott outside the rectory staring pensively at the small kirk.

The rain had finally stopped, and small wisps of mist were swirling around the stones in the old kirkyard. Truscott moved to the low stone pillars leading to the kirkyard, staring at the stone building. An adjoining crypt had been added to the ancient building for the masters of Baronsford and their families. Emma had been laid to rest there. David dismounted and was only a dozen paces from his cousin before Walter noticed him.

Though he was always one to keep his own counsel, Walter had been a friend to David for all their years of growing up. It was the kind of relationship forged in kinship and tempered in shared experience. He had been more than a cousin. Walter Truscott was as loyal to each brother as they had been to each other. He was solid as the stone walls of Baronsford itself. He was the only one of them who had remained by Lyon's side after Emma's death.

Emma!

Memories from so many years ago swam in his mind. He recalled a number of times Emma using Walter's name, or relating something that he had done to make David jealous. But he was the only one who didn't fall at her feet. Or did he?

" 'Tis a dismal place on a morning like this," David said, reaching him.

There was a bittersweet smile on Walter's lips when he glanced over his shoulder at him. "We shall see if we can find a bright, sunny day when she sees it."

"Who?"

"Violet," he replied quietly. "Her one wish is for her daughter to be buried in consecrated grounds. Not so much to ask for, I'd say. That and a bright day to say good-bye."

David recalled what he knew of Violet. Her bairn had been buried by one of the crofters without ceremony and without a blessing.

"I just spoke to the rector about it, and he's agreed." Truscott stared at the crypt beside the kirk again. "She'll be safe here. Looked after."

The sense of peace surrounding the other man knocked some of the wind out of David. What did it matter what happened that day on the cliffs? Why was it so important that they know who was responsible? Would Gwyneth love him less if they never knew for certain? David loved her, and he was loved in return. Nothing of this mattered in his relationship with his brothers. No, he could walk away and not look back.

Truscott turned and looked at him with a frown. "What brings you here?"

David let out a resigned breath. It mattered. It was important.

"Gwyneth and I took refuge in your tower house this morning. 'Twas raining hard, and we needed a private place where we could talk."

Truscott's gaze moved again to the crypt where Emma lay. "You went inside?"

"The heather and bracken are taking over the place," he said, once again undecided whether to confront him. "The work you've done on it over the years is holding up."

"I stopped going to the tower house when Emma began to spend time there."

A sense of relief flooded through David. Of course! Truscott would have nothing to do with her. There was no point in pressing this. He looked up at the sky, and it seemed to be brightening. A glance at his cousin, though, curtailed his sense of well-being. Walter's distress was impossible to ignore.

"You have no need to talk about any of it, Walter."

"I know, but 'tis crushing me. I have to talk about it." He looked at David, and there was pain in his expression. "And I want you to know the worst of it, rather than make a wrong assumption."

David understood what he meant. Making wrong assumptions had driven a wedge between Lyon and himself. Walter had to speak to free himself of whatever was eating at him. Running away or hiding his feelings only made things worse.

"She was not who you think she was," Walter said, his voice thick with emotion. "For years, Emma played you along. She never felt for you what you felt for her."

David's gaze met his cousin's solemn one. "I know."

"I don't know when it started . . . when she changed . . . but 'twas not your fault."

"I know that, too."

Truscott's hand fisted and gently struck the stone pillar beside him. "She was never happy, and that unhappiness grew with every passing year. She despised what she had. She quickly bored of what she achieved. She desired anything she thought she could not have."

"Only to grow tired of it once she had it," David put in. "I saw that in her. I saw in the way she tired of Lyon . . . and Baronsford."

Truscott nodded slowly, but none of the pain in his expression seemed to go away. "There was . . . there was a vicious game that she played with me all her life."

"You never seemed to fall for her the way the rest of us did." David commented. "Perhaps that made her more determined to chase after you."

" 'Twas more than that. She was drawn to me by something inside her—something that drove her, I think. She came after me from the time we were too young to understand it." His eyes were burning when they turned to him. "What I tell you now, I am telling as a friend, as blood kin, as someone who was used by Emma the same way as you were. If you wish to tell any of this to Lyon, I leave that decision to you. I will tell you, though, that he was the one who would have been hurt the most if she had lived."

The swirling now surrounded them, cutting them off from the village and the rest of the living world. David stood with Walter and looked at the crypt and the kirkyard. It was as if the world no longer existed.

There was only the two of them . . . and their memories . . . and the ghosts of those trapped between the two worlds.

"I do not really know where to start. How can a man explain an eternal damnation that begins during this life? Know this, David . . . I was truly damned when she was finished with me."

David said nothing, but nodded for him to continue.

"Until last year, I never knew it . . . but Emma and I shared the same father."

"Lord Cavers?"

"Lord Cavers was not her father. Sir William—your mother's half brother—fathered Emma and me both."

"But Augusta was married to Lord Cavers for several years before Emma was born."

"True. And his lordship knew Emma was not his. Emma knew that, too, long before she knew who her real father was. She told me herself that was Lord Cavers's reason for bringing Gwyneth to Greenbrae Hall. That was the reason why so much was left to her."

Suddenly, David understood why Gwyneth's inheritance was tied to the issue of remaining free of scandal. It was Lord Cavers's final slap at an unfaithful wife.

"There is more," Truscott said.

David had a hundred questions, but he wanted to let his cousin say his piece.

"Emma came to me after my . . . our father's death." He looked David steadily in the eye. "I was the father of the bairn that died with her when she went off the cliff that day."

Violet pulled her away from the door. Her voice was low and guarded as she explained.

"I heard a couple of the maids whispering in the kitchen this morning. One of them saw Sir Allan leaving Lady Cavers's bedchamber around dawn. The girl said that when he saw her in the hallway, Sir Allan gave her some money and told her to forget what she saw. He told her he could be a good friend to her."

A month ago, Gwyneth's immediate reaction would have been to try to find a reasonable and innocent explanation for the incident. Today, however, she found herself pausing and thinking hard about it. Violet was simply reporting what she had heard. There was no reason for any of the servants to make up such a tale.

"Do you think my aunt and Sir Allan are having an affair?"

Violet shrugged.

"She is a widow and he is unmarried."

"Gwyneth, I care not what they have between them. But if that is so, then why was your aunt trying to talk you into marrying the baronet last night? You told me yourself that she was against it in London." Violet took hold of Gwyneth's hand. "What will happen to Lady Cavers after you wed? What type of a financial arrangement is she left with?"

"Well, I am to inherit most of my uncle's estate, but everyone knows she has a fine settlement. Moreover, she knows I have no intention of stripping her of anything she has and enjoys now," Gwyneth reasoned. "She would not notice any difference in her situation after I am married . . . no matter whom I marry."

"These are your words of assurance for her. But put yourself in her position. Why should she leave the future to chance?"

Though she didn't even want to think it, never mind admit it to Violet, during the last year or so, Gwyneth

had heard her aunt complain a hundred times how
she would be ruined once Gwyneth was married—that
Lord Cavers would burn in hell for leaving his estate
to a *niece*. Still, to think that her aunt would attempt
anything so devious as to marry her off to a man who
was her own lover.

"My aunt is not so malicious. If anything she may
just want me to settle with someone whom she knows
and trusts." Even as she said it, Gwyneth realized how
foolish that sounded.

"Someone whom she knows and trusts . . . and is
carrying on an affair with?" Violet asked bluntly.
"Begging you pardon, Gwyneth, but—"

"No," she said gently to her friend. "This is exactly
what I need—to be slapped when my daydreaming
keeps me from seeing the obvious."

Gwyneth looked in the direction of the bed and the
dry clothing Violet had laid out for her. "I know how
to put an end to it, though. I have already spoken to
Sir Allan. I shall change into those dry clothes and go
and explain my plans to my aunt. That way, there is
no confusion and no hard feelings. I shall also make
my aunt understand that in marrying David Pennington, I shall do nothing to injure her in any way."
Gwyneth began stripping off her wet clothing. "Everything will be well once I have spoken to her."

David's head reeled with everything Truscott told
him as they walked through the kirkyard. A window
onto Emma's life was opened that David never saw
before. David knew his cousin was holding nothing
back. Some of it was so sordid and miserable that only
a desperate attempt to clear one's conscience would
motivate anyone to confess such things.

After hearing Walter, David realized that how Emma's treatment of him had been almost kind. Lyon and Walter had both suffered bitterly at her hands. They had both been driven almost to the edge of insanity because of her.

"She made certain that you knew that she carried your child, and she intended to hold that information over you. She could have ruined you . . . or worse," David said, shaking his head. "I don't know what I would have done were I in your situation. But then, you have always been so much more in control. I have to ask this question, Walter. Did you hate her enough to kill her?"

The muscles in his cousin's jaws flexed. They were standing by the crypt. Her body lay just on the other side of the ivy-covered stones.

"Did I hate her? Yes, I hated her. Did I think about killing her? Yes, more times than I can say. Would I have done it if she continued to push me? Perhaps! But did I kill her that day?" He closed his eyes and shook his head. "No, David, I did not kill her."

"Other than Pierce, you were the only one out on the cliffs that morning. You were the one who helped him bring Lyon and Emma up from the river."

"We were not the only ones on the path. Lady Cavers was there on the cliffs that morning, as well."

She shivered once.

The dry undergarments and dress were slow to warm Gwyneth's insides, but she ran her hands up and down her arms. As she left her room with Violet, Gwyneth knew the chill inside her was not because of the cold or the rain of the morning, but the dread of what lay ahead of her.

She had always been afraid of her aunt, from the time she had arrived at Greenbrae Hall as a mere child. Even now, years later, the discomfort still lingered.

"Are you certain you want to do this right now?" Violet asked quietly as they headed toward the back stairwell.

Lady Cavers had sent one of the servants up, informing Gwyneth that she was going out for a walk by the loch. It was a favorite walk for her aunt, with lovely views where the waters tumbled down to the river Tweed. On a good day, one could continue on from there to the cliff walk leading past Baronsford. Gwyneth was directed to join her, since the younger woman was well enough to have already left the Hall once this morning.

"You can always give some excuse and wait to speak to her when she comes back."

Gwyneth shook her head. "I need to resolve this. I need to tell her everything and make sure she is prepared for David's visit. I do not want any confusion when he arrives."

At the end of the hallway, one of the smaller windows looked out along a patch of grassy meadow between the house and the stables. Slowing to look out at the sky for rain, she stopped at seeing a group of four men standing and talking. Sir Allan stood at the center of them, speaking. Smaller than the others, he was wearing the same brocade coat he had on earlier. His lace-edged tricorn hat and his wig were bobbing vigorously as he made his point. Her brow furrowed as she stared at the three strangers.

"Who are those men with Sir Allan?" Violet asked, following the direction of Gwyneth's gaze.

"I don't know them. But I feel as if I have seen them before." Worry pitted in her stomach. They could be the three men she had seen in the fog that morning. She knew them from somewhere else. Gretna Green! When she'd gone to the livery stable to get a horse before she'd left—one of them had been watching her. The thought occurred to her that these might have been the same men who had been lying in wait along the road. The baronet turned to point at the manor house, and Gwyneth stepped back abruptly from the window.

"You look pale. Are you sure you are well enough to go out?"

"I shall be with my aunt. I shan't go far," she replied.

She needed to speak to Augusta. She could not bear the thought of David arriving and the older woman rejecting him out of hand. At the same time, looking at the men move toward the stables, a sense of foreboding began to gnaw at her stomach. She shivered again.

"Violet, I need to ask you a great favor."

"Of course. Anything."

"I want you to go after David. He was planning to come back this afternoon, but I think he should come now."

"I . . . I shall ask old Robert to send someone. Any one of them would be faster than I am."

"That would be fine." Gwyneth nodded and pressed her fist against her belly.

"I shall be right back," Violet said before disappearing down the steps.

They had been preparing for this party for days. Most of the guests had already arrived. Every corner of Baronsford was being inhabited and explored by the invading visitors. The hour was late, though, and even the most dedicated revelers had gone off to their beds.

Walter Truscott could not recall the last time that he'd felt so tired, in body and mind. The grand celebration dinner was still to take place tomorrow night. After making one last trip to the stables to make sure the visitors' carriages and horses were secure and settled, he started back to the house.

Following a garden path beneath a stone-railed terrace, he paused for a moment and looked up at the looming castle walls. How long had this place been his home? He wished there were a way that he could disappear—or just sleep and awaken to find that all of the events of these recent months were just a horrible dream.

"You have been avoiding me all day."

Emma's voice startled him, but he did not turn to her. There was no escape . . . no end . . . to this nightmare.

"I need to talk to you." She hurried out of the darkness.

"No." Walter turned, but did not look at her. "Lyon has arrived. He wants to see me in the library."

It was a lie. Lyon *had* arrived, but he was in as foul a mood as Walter had ever seen him. The earl wanted to see no one.

"Then you will meet me tomorrow morning . . . at the cliff walk."

"I cannot. I have much to do to prepare for—"

"You will come or I shall announce to everyone the news of our . . . our little secret. The entire family shall know about us."

"There is no *us*," he said gruffly, trying to step around her.

"*How dare you deny me—your own sister? Even more, how can you deny this child—your child—that is growing inside me?*"

Walter heard a gasp from the terrace above them. Looking up, he saw the dark form of Lady Cavers staring down at them. Without uttering another word, he turned and strode off into the darkness.

Chapter 22

"**Y**our recovery today is nothing short of miraculous, I should say," Augusta said coldly.

Gwyneth had found her aunt pacing in the gardens, and the older woman had immediately started for the path leading toward the deer park and the loch just above the river.

"Of course, there is always the possibility that your inability to greet me yesterday—injured as you were and confined to your sickbed—was nothing more than pretense. I notice you no longer are wearing your sling."

"My shoulder is much better today," Gwyneth said, defending herself halfheartedly. "But truly, I did fall off my horse, Aunt."

Gwyneth looked over her shoulder, wondering if Violet had found Robert to send the message.

"I was only following the doctor's direction to stay in bed yesterday."

Though Augusta was an energetic woman, she was setting an unusually brisk pace. "Well, Sir Allan was quite disappointed at not having an opportunity to speak to you last night. Injury or not, the least you could have done was to meet with your fiancé, especially after the long journey he endured in pursuit of you."

The long journey in the company of his lover, Gwyneth thought. She wondered if the affair between her aunt and Sir Allan had begun on the journey north . . . or before.

She should not care about any of this now, she told herself. They could do as they wished—behave in any way they desired. Gwyneth had her own life to live.

"I had the opportunity to speak to Sir Allan this morning," Gwyneth said, anxious to put any *fiancé* references behind them. "I am happy to tell you that all of the confusion has been settled. I shall not be marrying Sir Allan."

"Why *not*?" Augusta almost shrieked, stopping and facing her.

Gwyneth had to stop herself from backing away under the withering glare on her aunt's face. "I tried to explain to you last night. Although I have, in the past, held Sir Allan in the deepest regard, I am not in love with him."

Augusta snorted and started off again, with Gwyneth hurrying to keep up.

"Moreover, I have another suitor whom I very much wish to marry, a man I am certain will meet everyone's approval."

They entered the shadows of the deer park. It was here that Gwyneth had seen the three men that morning and she looked about her now. They were not far from the loch.

"Sir Allan is the husband I have chosen for you." A handkerchief appeared in Augusta's hand as she dashed away the perspiration forming on her brow. "I do not care to hear a word about any other suitors. I have made up my mind and you will obey my wishes."

"But I cannot," Gwyneth responded. "The suitor I spoke of is Captain Pennington. His family—"

"His family will *not* be mentioned in my presence," Augusta snapped. "No Douglas shall ever marry into that family again."

"You are being unreasonable, Aunt. The Pennington family has done nothing to deserve your anger. David in particular—"

"Nothing?" she spat out. "You call killing my only daughter *nothing*?"

"Lyon did not push her. And . . . frankly, Emma may have been in some ways responsible for her own death. 'Twas all part of the life she was leading. There was madness in her, Aunt. You saw it yourself. She had some need to break every rule, to make life miserable for everyone around her. She would hurt anyone if it brought her a moment's pleasure. And that included being unfaithful to her marriage vows."

Lady Cavers stopped dead. "Emma was so good to you. She took you under her wing and looked after you. How could you tell such lies about her?"

"Lies?" Gwyneth asked incredulously. "There are dozens of letters in Emma's room that tell—with very little subtlety—of her affairs while she was married."

"Flirtatious letters mean nothing."

"I witnessed with my own eyes—in *your* town house—a sexual liaison with a man who was not her husband."

Gwyneth was unprepared as the older woman whirled and slapped her hard across the face. Her ear rang from blow, and she tasted blood in her mouth.

"You ungrateful wretch. You shall never drag down Emma's memory, I will make sure of that."

She balked as her aunt started to pull her down the path toward the loch. Letting go of her arm, Augusta took a handful of her hair and started dragging Gwyneth. She took the first couple of steps in a daze. Then she saw the loch. A closed carriage sat waiting beside it. Two men sat on horseback and a third steed was tied to the back of the carriage. The third man that Sir Allan had been speaking to near the stables was in the driver's seat. The baronet himself was standing by the open door of the carriage.

"No!" She planted her feet. Augusta yanked hard, hauling her down the path.

"You shall go with them. You shall marry Sir Allan."

"I shan't. You cannot force me. And if you try, I shall tell everyone what you did. The marriage shall be annulled. You shall be exposed. You cannot get away with this."

"You are assuming you shall have the opportunity to expose me, my dear niece," she hissed. "I shall spread the word that you have eloped with your lover. The unfortunate accident after your wedding shall have enough witnesses that no one would dare question Sir Allan, especially not with me—brokenhearted at my error in not sanctioning the union—speaking on his behalf."

"People already know about you and Ardmore. Your own household is aware of your illicit relationship with him."

Gwyneth cried out in pain as Augusta again tugged viciously at her hair, propelling her down the path. The strength of the older woman was stunning.

"David is coming to the house. He shall be waiting at Greenbrae Hall when you get back. He shall never believe that I eloped with Sir Allan." She cried out again as Augusta—still holding a fistful of hair in her hand—shoved her between the shoulder blades. Gwyneth felt like the skin on her head was about to rip off.

"I should have ended this sooner. Ardmore's scheme was too complicated to work. All it took was that blackguard Pennington to ruin it. I was an idiot to wait."

Gwyneth swallowed her next retort, realizing it was too late. The two riders were coming toward them. Sir Allan and the driver were approaching, as well.

It could not end like this. Gwyneth would not allow herself to go down without a fight.

She had been capable of killing a man before. Violet wondered if she was capable of doing it again. Last time, she had used a knife. This time, she was armed with a weapon she had never used before.

Clutching the loaded pistol she had borrowed from the caretaker's quarters, she stared from the line of trees at Gwyneth's struggle with Augusta as the group of ruffians drew near them.

The caretaker, Robert, had been easy to convince, and the older man had gone off for Captain Pennington after the briefest of explanations from Violet. Once he was gone, though, getting any help from the rest of the servants proved futile. She had nothing to offer in the form of explanation—nothing to rouse them to action other than speculation.

The men were almost upon them. Though Violet had often seen one of the succession of stewards at Melbury Hall fire a pistol for sport, she herself had never fired one. She wasn't even sure how to aim. Gwyneth needed a distraction, however, and she needed it now. Cocking the hammer of the pistol, Vi pointed the muzzle into the air, looked away, and pulled hard on the trigger.

Robert had caught up with David and Truscott as they'd been returning to Baronsford. Gwyneth's message was vague enough to terrify David. She never asked for help. She was not one to overreact to anything. For her to send someone after him meant the sword of Damocles was hanging over her neck. And Robert's report only added to his worry.

Their visitor, Sir Allan Ardmore, had asked the grooms to ready one of the carriages this morning—a strange request considering the man had arrived with Lady Cavers only the previous night. Moreover, the caretaker found it entirely too coincidental that the baronet knew three of the new stable hands—and had ordered that those three bring the carriage around to him when it was ready. It was all good that Gwyneth had sent for him. Now if he could only get there fast enough.

The loud report coming from the deer park made the three men slow their horses and look at the direction of the loch.

"That was gunfire," David said. Truscott nodded.

"Nae hunters are on the premises, sir, so far as I know," the caretaker asserted, obviously unnerved by the gunshot.

David could see the house at the end of the long drive straight ahead. He saw a handful of workers pausing in their work near the stables and glancing in the same direction. He made up his mind and turned his horse toward the woods.

She knew she was no good to them dead. They would not shoot her in the back. Augusta's troubles would begin only if Gwyneth were to die here before having a husband. The next one in line to inherit the Douglas fortune was a distant cousin—a gentleman serving in Parliament—and that would take everything from her aunt's grasp.

None of these thoughts comforted her, though, as she ran and clawed her way through the brush in her flight from the group. The gunshot had startled Augusta enough to loosen her hold momentarily. From that point onward, it was pure survival that was pushing Gwyneth.

She saw Violet step out of the trees, the gun still in her hand.

"Run! Run!" Gwyneth called to her friend. She had taken a path going through a bank of low-hanging branches. The men on horseback had no chance to follow her. But Violet was a clear target. From the corner of her eye, Gwyneth saw one of the riders go in her friend's direction.

"Run!" she yelled again. "Toward the house."

Violet finally seemed to understand, for she turned and ran.

Running along a creek that fed the loch, Gwyneth soon found herself in a more thickly forested glen. She could hear the shouts and the sound of footsteps behind her. There were curses when she scrambled over a fallen tree and slid down a muddy slope. Whatever distance she thought each hurdle had bought for her, it all dissolved into thin air as her feet sank deep into the muck at the edge of a small pool at the bottom of the slope. As she struggled to free herself, two of the outlaws appeared on horseback at the far edge of the pool, reining in their mounts and drawing their knives. She looked up the slope and saw the other villain there, glaring down at her. A moment later, a breathless Sir Allan appeared at the top, as well, fury etched in his features.

"Sir Allan, you should have run when you had the chance," she called up to him, as a third figure appeared behind him.

The stout piece of wood in David's hand was all he needed to dispatch the outlaw, and the warning shouts of the two men across the way were too late. The blackguard came tumbling down the hill into the muck beside Gwyneth. An instant later, Walter Truscott and Robert materialized from the woods behind the mounted outlaws, with Robert cudgeling one from his saddle as Walter dragged the other to the ground.

Gwyneth's worry, however, was focused on what was happening at the top, and she finally dragged her feet out of the mud, losing one shoe in the process. Scrambling back up the wet slope, she slipped and fell backward twice before finding firm enough ground. Nearing the top, she heard the sound of Sir Allan shouting fiercely and the dull clang of steel on wood. Just as her face reached the level of the battle, a flash of metal flew by, missing her cheek by inches. Looking down, she saw the baronet's sword disappear into the muddy pool of water.

Crawling up onto solid ground, she could see Sir Allan on his knees, pleading for his life.

David stood before him. In his hand he held the stick, and he looked ready to crush the baronet's skull. She could see his upraised arm was bleeding from a slash in his forearm.

"Out with it, you dog," he growled, glancing over at her as she stood up. She could see the flash of relief in his face before it hardened again. "What were you and Lady Cavers planning?"

"I was only a pawn in her scheme, Captain. Only a pawn who was to marry Miss Gwyneth."

"For her money."

"Indeed, I think Augusta . . . Lady Cavers . . . may have planned to do away with the girl, but I would have nothing to do with any of that. I swear."

"Why do I think you'd say anything, Ardmore?"

"I swear."

"And you were in on the blackmail scheme," David said accusingly.

" 'Twas Lady Cavers's way of forcing Miss Gwyneth to act. She'd have never chosen me otherwise."

"To be sure, you cowardly dog."

"You are the blackmailer," Gwyneth spat out, moving toward the two men. "You and my aunt."

"I'd have never allowed anything evil to befall you."

"Such as a carriage accident that you and these rogues would have staged to look real—an accident that would have claimed my life? Or were you planning to cut my throat and make it look like some highwaymen had attacked us?"

"No, I'd never—"

"Hold your tongue," David snapped. He turned to Gwyneth when she reached his side. "Are you hurt?"

"I am very well. But your arm is bleeding."

"Hardly anything. My coat took most of the damage."

"Wait." She walked to the embankment and saw Robert binding the hands of the three prone outlaws while Walter stood over them. She turned back to David. "It appears we are all very well."

"Then we need to get back to the Hall," he responded. "We have one more member of this gang to apprehend."

After directing Captain Pennington and the other two men to where Gwyneth had run, Violet turned in time to see Lady Cavers hurrying off toward the far side of the loch. With no idea of where the older woman was running, she knew it was critical to follow her. As there was no doubt now that Lady Cavers was behind all of this, Gwyneth would never be safe until her aunt was stopped.

The path the older woman took into the woods wound upward from the loch. She never looked back, and Violet had to hurry to keep up and still follow unseen. For her part, though, the young woman glanced over her shoulder a number of times and, at one turn in the path, was relieved to see Captain Pennington and Gwyneth riding the same horse out to the edge of the loch.

"There she is," Gwyneth said, pointing to the path rising from the grassy area on the far side of the loch.

David nodded, seeing the flash of material before it disappeared among the rugged terrain of pine, bracken, and rock.

Walter Truscott and Robert had taken charge of conveying their prisoners to Greenbrae Hall, and a handful of stable workers who'd heard the shot soon appeared and were assisting the two men. When asked, they told David and Gwyneth that they had seen no sign of Lady Cavers heading at the direction of the house.

"Why is she going that way?" Gwyneth asked, looking after her aunt. "That path leads to the cliff walk."

"I don't know, but she is clearly not waiting to see if her people have succeeded or failed."

"Could she be going to Baronsford?"

"I doubt it. She could be trying to get across the river farther along. Whatever she is planning, she is probably inventing a tale right now that will clear her of any wrongdoing, whether you have survived or not."

"This end of the cliff walk is too dangerous to follow her on horseback, but if we take the path by the tower house," Gwyneth suggested, "we may be able to cut her off before she reaches Baronsford."

"You may be right."

She tightened her grip around David's middle as he spurred the horse in that direction. In a moment they were racing along the wooded trail and it was not long before they crossed onto Baronsford land. Passing the tower house, they cut back toward the river.

"Gwyneth," he said over his shoulder. "Walter and I talked. Most of the mystery of Emma's last days is now clear to me."

Gwyneth wished she could look at David's face. "I like Walter Truscott. Please do not tell me he killed Emma."

"Walter is like a brother to me. He was as much of a victim of Emma's viciousness as Lyon was. I will explain it all to you later, but what I tell you must remain our secret. Nothing of what he told me must ever get back to Lyon or Pierce or anyone in the family."

Gwyneth understood. Too many people had suffered already.

"Did he kill her?"

"No, he didn't."

"I'm glad . . . but that doesn't help in finding who did kill her."

"Walter told me that your aunt was on the cliffs that day. She could have been the one who pushed Emma."

Through a break in the thick brush ahead of them, Gwyneth caught a glimpse of her aunt hurrying along the cliffs. David had obviously seen her, too.

"But David, she had no reason to kill her own daughter."

" 'Tis a long and twisted story, but Augusta may have thought she had a very good reason."

The path narrowed, and suddenly Augusta was looking down at the roiling water battering the rocks of the riverbank far below. The water was running high. It would be impossible to cross until she traveled much farther upstream.

She would cross if she had to go all the way to Clovenfords. The jewels she was wearing would be more than enough to secure her a coach south. There, she could take refuge in any of her friends' houses.

She would deny all of it. It would be her word against Gwyneth's. She had been kind to the grasping wretch for all these years. No one would believe the spoiled brat . . . especially when she exposed her as the writer of those scandalous tales.

And hadn't the Pennington family caused her enough harm? Everyone knew it. She would accuse them of being in on it with Gwyneth. Yes, she would survive this.

Augusta paused on the path, looking down again at the rushing water. She had survived other difficult times. She had managed to carry on after greater disappointments. She had lived on after Emma's betrayal.

Life's treachery, though, had started years before. Her husband had been unable to give her children, but Augusta had always taken the blame for that on herself. It wasn't until after her affair with Sir William Truscott that she learned the truth. It was he that gave her Emma.

She had a weakness for impoverished knights. Sir William. Sir Allan. How many others? But Sir William was the finest of them all. Emma's father cut a dashing figure in those days. Bold and arrogant, he knew his charm. Many women in Augusta's circle would have been thrilled at the opportunity to bed him.

Augusta had found herself at the center of the gentleman's attentions during one of his visits to Baronsford to see his sister. She'd been flattered and overwhelmed, rushing into his arms and giving little thought to the consequences.

The affair had been short-lived, and Augusta had walked away knowing she carried his child. Unfortunately, she had not been with her husband for quite some time before that, and Lord Cavers had known immediately that the bairn was not his.

Her husband, though, was a man of discretion. He abhorred scandal and a divorce was unthinkable. A verbal settlement was agreed upon. The bairn would be raised as his own child, and the two would continue on with their separate lives.

Over the years, though, the arrangement had turned out to be disadvantageous for Augusta. Although Emma was never told of her true parentage, Augusta knew the child must have guessed. She would have had to be daft not to realize it, especially after Lord Cavers had betrayed them both, making Gwyneth his chosen heir.

She moved quickly but carefully along the narrow path. The rocky path was still slippery from the morning rain. At least the sun was starting to burn through the lingering mist.

It had been very difficult for Augusta to overcome the financial straits Charles had left her in. She had run up some serious debts, though her credit problems had eased considerably when Emma had become Countess of Aytoun. With a daughter married to a man as rich and powerful as the Lord Aytoun, Augusta was set for as long as she lived.

Emma, though, had contrived her own bit of treachery.

Augusta knew about her daughter's affairs with other men. She had done the same herself. It was the way of the world. Her own marriage had survived it even after she had found herself with child. Emma was in a secure position. She was the mistress of Baronsford. The Countess of Aytoun. There was no woman more envied in the Borders . . . perhaps in all of Scotland.

And then, she had ruined it all. She'd thrown it all away. And for what. For a man she *knew* was her brother. Even now, it sickened Augusta to think about it. Lying with her own brother. Carrying his child.

Augusta's vision blurred, and she reached out and grabbed a branch to steady her as she stumbled over a loose rock. A few pebbles rolled down the cliff face. After all these months, she still felt ill thinking about what Emma had done.

"Aunt!" The call came from ahead of her on the path. "Please. Stop there. The path is washed out just ahead of you. Stay where you are."

She looked at the path between her and Gwyneth. David Pennington stood beside her. The path had indeed been washed out. The wretch's hands were stretched out toward her.

As if she would believe her. As if she could believe any of them. Augusta turned around.

The ethereal figure was standing on the path that August had just traveled. The pale golden hair shone in the sunlight. She had materialized out of nowhere. The pale skin. The accusing eyes. She'd come back.

"Emma!" she cried out in shock.

With no thought but to escape the dead, Augusta whirled in panic and stepped over the edge.

She did not want the title. Baronsford could crumble into the pits of hell, for all she cared. She wanted nothing to do with her husband or the power that went along with being the Countess of Aytoun. She just wanted to be loved . . . and loved by one man alone. She wanted Walter Truscott's love.

What difference did it make that the blood of the same father flowed in their veins? They had different mothers. That was enough.

"What are you doing here?" Emma cried out in surprise as her mother stepped out of the heavy mist enshrouding the path.

"You cannot do this, Emma. You cannot ruin your future . . . and mine."

"Was I not clear enough, last night? How many times must I say it? You ruined your life in staying with a man for whom you felt not one shred of affection—by staying with a man who never loved you. Well, you chose your own life. Leave mine to me."

"But you know the truth! Walter Truscott has the same father as you. This child you carry shall be cursed. God can never forgive you for what you are trying to do."

"I do not need God's forgiveness, and I certainly do not need your blessing," she snapped. "I am finally seeing a clear path before me. Walter is the only one

who has ever understood me. We two are the same. We share the same destiny."

"No."

Emma heard Lyon calling in the distance. He was coming after her. She needed to get away. She stepped forward to pass her mother.

She was unprepared when Augusta's hand darted out, driving her to the edge of the path. Waving her arms desperately, Emma looked in horror at her mother's face as she tried to regain her balance.

"Then you can share your destiny with him in hell," Augusta said, shoving her again.

Chapter 23

⌁

Gwyneth and David decided to marry in September. Portia and Pierce were back. Helena, Portia's mother, also returned to Baronsford for the event. Millicent, on the verge of delivering a bairn herself, insisted on seeing to all the arrangements and preparing a celebration that would rival a royalty wedding.

No one outside of the family had been told of the events of the past summer, but whispers had soon spread from Edinburgh to London. The first wife of Lord Aytoun—the news went—had died by the hand of her own mother. Lady Cavers, finally driven mad with guilt at her crime, had jumped to her death from the same cliffs above the River Tweed.

As the day of the wedding approached, the Pennington family—Lyon and David especially—appeared to be finally at peace with the past. Walter Truscott had started a new journey of healing—one that involved Violet Holmes. He knew that the secret of his past with Emma was safe. No one else would be hurt by it. David and Gwyneth had assured him that it was a tale they would take to grave.

Walter and Violet still had a long road ahead of them. She was learning to trust again, but her heart was opening slowly. Each step was taken deliberately, and with great deal of hesitation. Truscott, though, was there, beside her at every step. Even as their commitment to each other became clear, there was no pushing them into anything. They put a quick end to Gwyneth's wish that they all be married in a double ceremony. There was little doubt in anyone's mind, however, that before the winter sun shone upon Baronsford, another wedding would be in the offing.

So on a brilliant September afternoon, the village kirk saw a radiant bride and a handsome groom. As pipers filled the Great Hall with music that night, the Dowager Countess Aytoun looked with so much pride at her sons and the wives they'd been lucky enough to woo and win. Of course, this was when she was not arguing with Ohenewaa about some secret potion that would make her live for at least another score of years.

The music and the dancing continued late into the night, when Gwyneth was carried to a wedding chamber filled with wines and fruit and delicacies to rival a sultan's table. After readying herself for the wedding night, she opened her notebook, picked up her Keswick pencil, and wrote the final lines of her current tale.

Standing in the gray mist on the rain soaked hill, she wrapped her arms tightly about the man she loved. Looking down into the villain's unseeing eyes, she knew she had found her liberty. Finally, she was free of the evil that lay in the mud at her feet. Finally, after so long, after so much, she was completely and truly free . . . to love . . . to live.

"Perfect timing," David whispered as she closed the notebook. Wrapping his arms around Gwyneth's waist, he drew her tightly against him.

"I didn't even hear you come in." She tossed the notebook onto the table beside the bed. She smiled over her shoulder at her husband.

"I was reading what you wrote. I have been more impatient to read your next tale of pirates and Highlanders than any of your devoted readers out there."

"Have you, now?" she turned in his arms and kissed his chin, his lips. She looked up into his blue eyes. "And why is that?"

"Because I am proud of you." He pressed his lips to her brow, to her cheeks. "Because I respect your wit and intelligence and because I find myself enthralled by a vastly entertaining talent."

"Is that all?"

"Oh yes . . . and because I love you and look forward to an eternity together."

She pushed his jacket down over his shoulders. Her fingers undid the ribbon holding his hair tied at the nape of his neck. "And is that all?"

David smiled. "And as your resident pirate, I also find myself eager to offer my services in the name of research." His hands gently opened the front of her robe. He gazed reverently at her breasts showing through the silk nightgown. "Do I have to say more?"

Putting her arms around his neck, Gwyneth kissed

her husband with all the passion in her soul. Drawing back from him, she looked lovingly into his eyes.

"Does that mean you'll show me how to handle a cutlass?"

Authors' Note

We hope you enjoyed our *Scottish Dreams Trilogy*.

In *Borrowed Dreams,* you met Lyon and Millicent and had a brief introduction to Emma's murder. In *Captured Dreams,* you met the second brother Pierce and his wife Portia. Violet—who showed up initially in *The Promise* and then disappeared from Melbury Hall at the end of *Borrowed Dreams*—had many of you writing and asking us to bring her back. We hope we did her justice in this book.

By the way, for the many readers who have been following our novels from our first book on, you might recognize the portions of Gwyneth's tales that you read in this book. They were taken from the first of our own Highland tales, *The Thistle and The Rose.*

Lastly, we could not close this novel without thanking the many readers of our Jan Coffey novels who discovered us through our tales of suspense set in the contemporary world. Thank you all for your goodwill . . . thank you for your loyalty . . . thank you for reading this far!

As always, we love to hear from our readers.

May McGoldrick
P.O. Box 665
Watertown, CT 06795

McGoldMay@aol.com
www.MayMcGoldrick.com